WAITING FOR THE ONE

WAITING FOR THE ONE

L.A. FIORE

Montlake
Romance

Published by Montlake Romance, Seattle
www.apub.com

Amazon, the Amazon logo, and Montlake Romance are trademarks of Amazon.com, Inc., or its affiliates.

ISBN-13: 9781477829295
ISBN-10: 1477829296

Cover design by Laura Klynstra

Library of Congress Control Number: 2014958170

Printed in the United States of America

To Jenni and Michelle, you've totally got this.
To Trish, my friend from Down Under, tough year but
all's well that ends well.

CHAPTER ONE

I'm going to hell. I'm resigned to my fate and have been ever since I was ten and siphoned the holy water from the fonts at church, bottled it, and sold it, after convincing most of my neighbors that a coven of vampires had moved into town. The thing is, I really thought that vampires had moved into town and truly believed I was protecting everyone. My ten-year-old logic posited that it wasn't technically stealing, since I did add extra money to the collection, but as an adult, I understand that my actions crossed a line and that my mortal soul now tap dances along that very fine edge. The church and I have gone our separate ways in the many years since, but I still do keep a bottle of holy water near my bed. You never know.

It is for this reason that I can sit on the beach as my best friend and her husband cuddle, the little green monster on my shoulder speaking words only I can hear. I'm not truly jealous of Gwen, but I am envious, since I haven't had a date since man first discovered fire.

In truth, I don't mind waiting, not if at the end of it I find the right person. Even if the wait is ridiculously, hopelessly long. He's out there, somewhere, maybe trapped under a truck or surrounded by feral wolves, which is what's taking him so long to get to me. I'm creeping up on thirty and not only haven't I found the one, I've only had a handful of boyfriends.

In my defense, I do live in Harrington, Maine, whose staggering population of 862 contains mostly people age sixty-plus. It isn't easy to find men my age to date—they are already married, or seriously dating, and the few remaining eligible bachelors are treated like the last piece of chocolate cake at a Chocoholics Anonymous meeting.

Leaving Harrington has never crossed my mind, because it's home, but I need to get a more active social life. Currently it revolves around my three best friends. Gwen Drake has been my best friend since the third grade. Her parents run the one really nice restaurant in town. When Mitch Drake applied for the position of head chef, he not only landed the job, but he also won Gwen's heart. Six years later they have two beautiful children: Michael James and Callie Saffron. I love Gwen but she has this whole other part of her life. That's why I'm here now, dropping off the little cherubs to Mommy and Daddy after having filled them up on sugar.

And then there is Josh Taylor, whom I dated once upon a time, and who decided to come out while we were dating. We still hang out, but he's getting rather involved with Derek Bennett, so sometimes being the third really is like that unwanted wheel. I tend bar in the evenings at Tucker's, my third best friend Tommy Tucker's bar. It wasn't my intention to make a career out of it, but I love my job, love connecting with my neighbors. Glancing at my watch, I realize that if I don't get a move on, I'll be late for my dinner with Frank. Mr. Frank Dupree is a lovely older man I visit in the nursing home several times a week. He's become family, in a sense, since my own family isn't really much of one. No hostility or disappointment on my end, just indifference on theirs. The emotional distance became quite literal when my parents moved to Florida several years back.

Frank and I met when I was eight. Standing on the front stoop of his bait-and-tackle shop, I demanded he release all the minnows, claiming it was cruel and unusual punishment to keep them captive only to serve them up on the end of a fishing line. My concern did not extend to the bloodworms, because they were gross. As it turned out, Frank didn't stock minnows. My intel was clearly not good. After that, I visited him every day. He listened to me, he cared about what I had to say, and he liked me being there. He gave me the love, support, and discipline that I didn't receive at home. Even at the age of ninety-four, he's still giving me all those things.

Leaving a happy Gwen, I climb into my car and head for home, a very small Cape situated near the banks of Harrington Bay. The cedar shakes have weathered to a dove gray, the shutters are dark green, and the one chimney sits centered on the roof. Inside, everything is very light and airy with hardwood floors and lots of natural fabrics in ivory and tans. I love my home.

Frank is expecting me at four for an early dinner. I am hoping to entice him afterward into the dancing that is held every week in one of the community rooms. Frank has lived most of his life in Harrington, though he never married or had children. In his golden years, he has only his friends at the home and me.

I slip on my little black jersey dress and step into my heeled sandals. Trying to tame the mass of unruly chestnut-brown curls can be daunting, but tonight I manage to whip it into a knot on the top of my head. Normally, I don't bother with makeup, because not only do you have to apply it but you have to remove it. Who needs that? But because dinner with Frank is special, I go to the trouble: darkening my eyelids to make my cyan-colored eyes really stand out and tinting my lips pink. A glance at the clock makes me reach for my handbag.

Harrington Commons is the only full-time nursing facility in Harrington. Since we don't have a large population—despite the average age of the population—there isn't really a concern about running out of space there. I wheel Frank to our table in the large dining room before getting in line for our meatloaf specials, complete with mashed potatoes and peas. We are even splurging tonight by enjoying a glass of red wine.

L.A. Fiore

"So what's new, Frank?"

"Bob broke his hip." Bob Cantor lives under the false belief that he is twenty years old. Not even I go mountain climbing and sky diving, and I'm twenty-nine.

"What was it this time?"

Frank looks up from his meatloaf and a grin cracks over his face. "He was doing the horizontal mambo with Claire Davis."

I nearly choke on my peas. I can't have heard him correctly. Perhaps the horizontal mambo means something else to his generation.

Leaning closer to Frank so no one else overhears, I ask, "Are you saying he was having sex and broke his hip?"

"Yup."

I can't help it, a visual of Bob and Claire pops into my head. Yep, there it is—the image forever burned on my brain.

"I don't think I want to know the details," I mutter.

"Makes you wonder what kind of force the man had to be exerting to break his hip."

"Frank!"

He isn't at all contrite as he laughs and scoops up some mashed potatoes. "I can't help it. I know you won't go there. Oh, and I took your suggestion and watched that show you recommended."

"And?"

"I liked it."

"Those Winchester boys are just about the coolest."

"What's new with you, Saffron?"

"I'm handling crowd control for the Swordfish Festival."

"You hate swordfish."

"I know, but Chastity asked, so how could I say no?"

Frank's dark gaze spears me from across the table. "Easy: no."

"Not easy. I've blown off every request in the last year and, as Chastity points out, we young folk have a responsibility to our community."

Frank snorts. "Chastity Forrester is pushing sixty, she is not young folk."

"Honestly, in this town, she pretty much is."

He thinks on this for a minute, then shrugs his shoulders. "Yeah, I guess so."

And then he sort of zones out, like he has a tendency to do, and I wonder what he's thinking about. I've asked him about these odd silent spells, but he just dismisses the question.

I'm pulled from my thoughts when Shalee Barnes comes strutting over. Shalee has somehow managed to find four men, all under the age of sixty, to marry, though Billy Bob just barely makes it into this category at fifty-nine. It's a mystery to me that she even attracts these men, since she looks down her nose at everyone. I know she does so because her parents are the richest folks in town. How they acquired their wealth, here in the land of swordfish, has always baffled me. Shalee is thirty-two and, outside of getting married and divorced all the time, she doesn't have a job. I realize I work at a bar, but at least I'm working. She went from living with her parents to living with her various husbands, and yet she feels that she is a person that the town should look up to.

"Saffron, who's your boyfriend?"

She stands there in her skin-tight red leather dress, her breasts practically spilling out of the indecently low neckline. This is dangerous, in a place like this, since the viewers of said dress could easily go into cardiac arrest. There is no getting out of the introductions, though.

"Frank Dupree, Shalee Barnes."

Frank's dark eyes rest on Shalee's. "Ms. Barnes."

I guess thinking he may be hard of hearing, she bends over and practically suffocates Frank with her bosoms.

"It's my pleasure, Frank."

I watch in disbelief. She's not concerned about his hearing; she's flirting with Frank—she who recently wed for the fourth time. Did she exhaust the dating pool in her preferred age bracket? Frank's eyes find mine. He knows it too.

"Shalee, you're barking up the wrong tree. Frank is penniless."

"Oh good, that would have been gross."

My face burns hot with my anger. Launching from my seat, I almost overturn my chair. "Apologize now, Shalee."

She seems clueless for a minute.

"Now!"

"I do apologize, Frank." And with that she saunters off.

"Bitch," I hiss under my breath before returning to my seat. I am more than a little surprised to see Frank laughing.

"Why are you laughing?"

"You, Saffron, coming to my defense."

"She was being insufferable and mean."

He reaches his frail, pale hand over to cover mine. "She is insufferable and mean. You can't change a leopard's spots."

"I suppose not."

"But I do appreciate you looking out for me. It's nice to know there is someone who cares."

"Of course I care, Frank."

We finish dinner without another incident, but when I try to get Frank interested in dancing, he declines. "I'm tired, but thank you very much for dining with me this evening."

"My pleasure."

Wheeling Frank to his room, I call for a nurse to help him prepare for bed. How tired he looks. The man is ninety-four, but I guess I never realized just how old he is.

Feeling the involuntary hitch in my heart, I force my unpleasant thoughts away. "Well, then I'll see you on Sunday."

"I look forward to it, Saffron."

After a quick trip home to change, I drive to Tucker's, Tommy's bar, to start my shift. It isn't much to look at, but it is the happening spot in town. That is, if a town consisting mostly of people rapidly approaching their midlife crisis has such a place. For me, though, Tucker's is about hearing the tales from the fishermen who frequent the bar. I know a fisherman's life is a hard one, but I still find it to be very romantic.

Tommy Tucker was a few years ahead of me in school. Like most people, his parents lived here forever and their parents before them. Mr. and Mrs. Tucker recently retired, turning the bar over to Tommy when they moved to Portland, Maine, and, according to Mrs. Tucker, back to civilization.

"Hey, Saffron, you're early tonight." Tommy's rich tenor greets me as soon as I enter. The familiar scent of his famous buffalo wings makes my stomach growl. Placing my coat in the back, I join Tommy behind the bar. I had a crush on him in high school. Who didn't, with his dark-blond hair and hazel-green eyes? Years later I learned that he had a crush on me too, but by then our relationship had evolved into that of siblings.

"Frank wasn't in the mood to dance."

"How's he doing?"

"Good. He looks tired, though."

"He's ninety-four, Saffron. When ninety-four you become, look as good you will not."

I stick my tongue out at the Yoda wannabe. He chuckles in response. "The specials today are the fish and chips and beef stew."

At this moment the door opens and in walks Jake Matthews. He moved into town last year, taking over the auto body garage after Mr. Dickinson died. Now, Jake is considered the most eligible bachelor in town. Practically a child at the age of thirty-four, he's hot—warm brown hair that looks as if a woman has run her fingers through it, and dark-blue eyes. He has that vulnerable-bad-boy thing down pat.

Personally, I find him a bit shallow and self-absorbed, but since I am in the minority he has a smorgasbord of ladies to choose from. Even Hattie and Hilde Fletcher, seventy-one-year-old twins, are vying for Jake's attention. Well, either that or they are finally losing their eyesight. Their car is in his shop all the time because they're driving into something every other day. I hear Tommy's voice just behind me.

"We'll be busy tonight."

He isn't wrong. Practically every woman in town makes a showing at Tucker's after a Jake sighting. I feel like I am watching the National Geographic Channel on mating rituals in the wild. I can hear the narrator in my head.

The female approaches, the sway of her hips a sign of her willingness to reproduce. Obviously in heat, her open blouse exposes her unnaturally large . . .

"Hey, Saffron, can you clear a few tables? Sarah's swamped."

"Sure." Grabbing a tray, I move around the bar to the small dining area, collecting empties and dirty dishes. Someone laughs across the bar, distracting me, and that's when I collide with a wall. In slow motion, the stacked glasses tilt over the edge of the tray. But they never fall, because a rather large hand wraps around them. A hand that my eyes follow up to the arm, shoulder, neck, until I land on the face. Logan MacGowan. I can feel my heart pounding in my throat, but whether that's because of the near disaster or the fact that I'm standing this close to Logan, I can't say. "Thanks. Nice reflexes, you're like a cat." Like a cat? What the hell is wrong with me? Yes, Logan, you're like a small, furry animal. Well, he was furry, but not small. Definitely not small.

He smiles, a rare treat, and waits to make sure I've got my balance back before he walks to the bar and takes a seat.

I place the tray on the counter in the kitchen and take a moment to berate myself over how cool I'm not. Logan MacGowan moved into town over six months ago. I assume he's a fisherman, since he's always dressed in flannel and jeans. Black whiskers cover his face completely;

his hair, long and unruly, brushes his shoulders; and he's tall, like several inches over six feet tall. He comes in several times a week for a drink. He's quiet, but he's not shy. He studies the bar scene with extraordinary focus. He fascinates me—he has from the first day he walked into Tucker's. Trouble is, he's never spoken to me, and it isn't as if he doesn't speak to people in general. He does and yet he has never said a word to me.

I don't know what it is about me that repels Harrington's seafaring yeti, but I am contrary enough to take his silence as a challenge. It has become a sort of unspoken battle of wills between us for him to remain silent and for me to attempt to break that silence. I have gotten grins and, on a rare occasion, an out-and-out smile, but so far his reign of silence is still intact.

Taking a few calming breaths, I return to my spot behind the bar, and Tommy calls to me. "Saffron, can you get Logan a Harp?"

"Sure."

Grabbing a longneck of Harp, I pop the top before strolling down to the end of the bar. Logan watches me as I approach, and I know he's waiting for the games to begin. I don't disappoint. "Hey, Logan, so I had my date with Frank," I say as soon as I place the frosty bottle before him. Frank knows of the battle of wills between Logan and me so he often helps me with ridiculous things to say to try to force Logan to break his silence.

"We went to The Harbor for dinner, but he forgot his teeth so I had to chew his food for him, you know, sort of mush it up so he could gum and swallow it like a baby bird. It was so romantic." Logan's eyes light with humor, but no smile.

"Frank and I are planning on robbing the First Bank and Trust. We just need to pimp out his wheelchair for our getaway."

He takes a pull from his beer.

"Tommy wants the place to go topless."

He almost spits out his beer. I grin because he knows that I know that he almost laughed out loud.

"I suppose I shall take that small victory and leave you be. As always, Logan, it has truly been a pleasure speaking with you." I raise my hand. "Please don't say anything, because I understand completely that you are secretly so in love with me that I leave you speechless. My supermodel looks are my cross to bear."

Turning from him, I head back to the other end of the bar, but I do chance a glance over my shoulder and, sure enough, Logan is watching me with a slight grin tugging at the corner of his mouth.

Harrington has a festival for pretty much everything including Mrs. Cantor's—daughter of Bob the daredevil—apple pie. I am not kidding. It won first place at the county fair, and so naturally a festival was born. The Swordfish Festival is coming up. When people attempt to create "fair-like" cuisine from swordfish . . . it makes my stomach ache just thinking about it.

I have been drafted into helping with this festival, but luckily for me I am handling crowd control. Crowd control seems unnecessary in a town of under a thousand. Even the hordes of visitors drawn to our town during festival time tops out at about a hundred. Regardless, I will walk the one main street through town and ensure that the wheelchair folks don't run over the ones with walkers. As I walk past the post office, I see Gwen and the children just leaving it.

"Hey, Saffron, how are you?"

"Hi, guys." I kneel down next to Michael and Callie. "Are you guys excited about the Swordfish Festival?"

Even they, both festival freaks, look less than enthusiastic. "No," Michael murmurs.

I lean even closer. "Yeah, me neither."

"Come to dinner on Friday, Saffron. Mitch is making cod in parchment pockets."

I love Mitch's cod.

"I'll be there. Where are you off to now?"

"The dentist."

"Ah, definitely won't be joining you for that."

"You sure? We could both lapse into a coma from the music that's pumped into the waiting room."

"Tempting, but no. I'm on my way home for my car. I need to go grocery shopping. I'll see you on Friday, though."

"Some friend you are: eat my food but let me slip into madness all alone listening to elevator music."

Flashing Gwen a smile, I hug her and kiss the little cherubs before I start back down the street in a near run.

My car—I use the term *car* loosely—is a 1981 Chrysler LeBaron, held together with duct tape, and it's a crapshoot if the thing will start. On grocery day, though, I take it into town because it definitely makes lugging my groceries home that much easier. Not even halfway into town, my lovely car decides to break down. Since it does this often, I know that Jake's response time for a tow is anywhere from ten minutes to three hours. I'm better off walking back home.

It's only six in the evening, and even now the road is deserted. As I come along a stretch of road that runs up against the bay, I notice the Harrington Lighthouse. It isn't a particularly big lighthouse, but it is very well cared for. There is a light on inside and I realize that someone lives here now. The spotlight itself is all done through computers, but the fact that the house part has actually been turned into a home is pretty cool.

The door opens after a moment and out walks none other than Logan. Logan MacGowan lives in the Harrington Lighthouse. Why didn't I know this? It's a small town; you'd think it'd be common knowledge. Maybe it is, probably it is, and it's just me in the dark. Not surprising, since I seem to be the only one the man doesn't speak to. I can certainly use this new information in my quest to break his silence. And then the robe he is wearing comes off to expose the James Bond–like swim trunks under it. My face turns red as heat creeps along my skin, but I don't take my eyes from his body. Hard muscle and sinew bunch and cord under smooth golden skin. His shoulders are huge—his impressive left bicep has a tattoo that wraps around it—his waist narrow, his thighs muscled, and his movements deliberate yet graceful. It's going to be hard to see him now and not think about the spectacular body he's hiding under his flannel and jeans. And I thought he was fascinating before.

I watch him for a few minutes before I realize I am standing in the bushes, in the dark, watching a nearly naked man swimming without his knowledge. Yeah, I believe that is the classic definition of stalking. On a sigh, I turn from the god in the water and continue to walk home.

CHAPTER TWO

Thursday night is packed at Tucker's, which is good since staying busy keeps me from obsessing over Logan MacGowan's body. And that is all I have been doing since I walked away from him last night. In my lifetime, I have never seen a more perfectly put-together body, and isn't it just my luck that the body belongs to the one man in town who makes avoiding me a full-time job? Life just isn't fair.

I need some air so I call, "Tommy, I'm taking a break." I walk from behind the bar and head outside. It's cooler tonight and the stars are unbelievably bright. I don't generally like to take stock of my life, but after my voyeuristic adventure last night, I am willing to admit that I'm in a rut. My three best friends are growing and maturing and here I am still doing the same thing since graduating from college. Do I want to get married and have kids? Yeah, I do, but I am not making any progress toward that when my only prospect is a man who, for whatever reason, has no wish to speak to me. As much as I dislike the idea of online dating, I think that I, Saffron Mills, am going to have to bite the bullet and sign up.

I'm only halfway back to the bar when Jake stops me. "Hi, Saffron."

"Hey, Jake. How are you doing tonight?"

"I'm good. Hey, would you like to have dinner with me?"

I didn't see this coming. Jake Matthews is asking me out? He's single, I'm single, and who knows, maybe I'm all wrong about him.

"Sure, Jake, I'd like that."

"How about tomorrow night?"

"Oh, I can't tomorrow, I'm having dinner with Gwen. Saturday works for me."

A smile spreads over his handsome face and his blue eyes sparkle. "I'll pick you up around seven?"

"Sounds great. I better get back to work."

"See you on Saturday, Saffron."

I'm grinning as I make my way behind the bar.

"What was that?" Tommy leans up against the counter next to me.

"I have a date with Jake."

One of his dark-blond eyebrows arches ever so slightly in response.

"Is that hard, Tommy, that thing you do with your eyebrow?"

"You're trying to get off-topic."

"I'm just trying to shake my life up a bit. I'm stagnating, if you haven't noticed. I don't have lofty goals like winning an Academy Award or being the Next Top Model, and my social life is lived vicariously through you, Gwen, and Josh, and my only prospect is a man who refuses to speak to me. I need to get a life."

"Saffron, it's not like Logan does all that much speaking to begin with."

My shoulders slump. They often do when I feel defeated. "Maybe my spinning his rejection into a game just makes me a loser."

Tommy stands straight and grabs my arms. "You are not a loser. I don't ever want to hear you say that again."

"Yes, sir. We know why I'm alone, the male-female ratio of this town does not work in my favor. But you, you must have to beat the women away. Why aren't you married, again?"

"Never met anyone I wanted to make that kind of commitment to."

"Do you want to get married?"

"Are you proposing?"

"You're a clown, but if I was, would you say yes?"

"No, and you wouldn't ask."

"That's true. You refuse to acknowledge that I am the master of the known universe and that you should do my bidding. We would never work."

He leans closer. "Now who's the clown?"

———

"So Logan lives in the lighthouse?" Gwen stands against the counter sipping from her glass of red wine as Mitch fillets the cod he purchased at the fishmonger earlier. I am telling them about my stalker adventure from the other night.

"And he was taking an evening swim?"

"Yeah, and I have to tell you, Gwen, the man is built . . ."

Mitch looks up from the cod. "Seriously, I'm standing right here."

"You're not interested in the details of Logan's very fine form?" I ask innocently.

He responds by pointing the knife in my general direction.

"I'll take that as a no."

Gwen reaches for a mushroom-stuffed puffed pastry that Mitch just happened to have whipped up for us. Man, how lucky is she?

"Do you guys eat like this every night? It seems only fair that if you get to make a habit of indulging your taste buds that you should both be at least two hundred pounds." Since I don't often get to feast on such magnificent fare, I have no problem with taking another shrimp and dipping it into Mitch's homemade cocktail sauce.

"We eat in moderation," Gwen says. I see the smile curving her lips before she adds, "Unless the dish is really good and then to hell with moderation."

"All of his dishes are really good, though."

Mitch eyes me through his lashes. "We have fast metabolisms."

"Lucky bastards," I mutter. At this moment Michael and Callie come running into the kitchen.

"Come play," Michael squeals as he reaches for my hand.

"Okay, I'll be in the living room." I see the look that passes between Gwen and Mitch. "I'll keep the little ones occupied."

Mitch reluctantly turns his attention on me. "That would be very much appreciated, Saffron."

And then his smoldering gaze is back on his wife. To be on the receiving end of a look like that . . .

When we reach the living room, I notice the toys everywhere, even though the room was immaculate when I arrived. Michael and Callie have been very busy.

"What are we playing, Michael?"

"Cowboys and Indians."

Cowboys and Indians, which makes me the horse. My back is going to protest this tomorrow.

"All right then, giddyup."

<hr>

After Mitch puts the kids to bed, the three of us sit at the table nursing our glasses of wine.

"I have a date with Jake tomorrow night."

Neither says it out loud, but I can hear it anyway: *no freaking way.*

"Really?" Gwen asks, eying me over the rim of her glass.

"Yeah, he asked me last night and since I haven't been on a date with someone my own age in . . ." I stop talking and try to think of my last date and am having a hard time bringing the memory into focus. "I can't remember the last time I was out on a date."

"It has been a while," Gwen says softly.

Mitch adds, "You haven't been on one, outside of Frank, since I've known you."

I just stare, openmouthed, at Mitch. It can't possibly be that long ago, can it? "Six years is a really long time."

"You graduated college and then your parents moved to Florida to retire. That was a bit of an adjustment for you. Six years isn't really all that long."

I smile at Gwen. She is trying, and I really love her for it, but there is no denying that six years without a date is pretty damn pathetic. But, chin up, little lady, because I am going on a date tomorrow night with a very handsome man. Life is good.

———•——

I want to kill myself. I want to take my butter knife and work on my wrists until I bleed out. My initial assessment of Jake Matthews was spot-on. The man can't stop looking at his own reflection. The first time he gazed longingly at himself was in the foyer of my house. As I attempted to get my coat on, no help on the Jake front with that, he stood admiring himself in my hall mirror. I felt as if I should give him and his reflection some alone time. The looks he was giving himself were rather steamy. For dinner, the place Jake selected for our date was none other than Tucker's.

Now, I work there every night of the week. On my occasional night off, especially on a date, don't you think the gentleman would offer to take me somewhere else? Anywhere else? Nope, doesn't even dawn on him. What is worse is that there are no available tables, so we have to sit at the bar. It's just a stroke of dumb luck that I am wearing wide-legged black pants and a silver silk tank or I'd be extremely uncomfortable on a barstool in a skirt.

This isn't even the worst part of the evening—no one seems to be able to tell that we are on a date and that includes my date himself. Every woman that comes up to flirt receives a welcoming smile, and when he isn't flirting he's looking at himself in his spoon.

Tucker's is really busy tonight and since Tommy has his hands full, I might as well help out since the date is a complete dud. To my surprise, Jake takes notice when I walk behind the bar. "What are you doing, Saffron?"

I just stand there a moment, because he can't be that stupid. "Really, Jake, you need to ask?"

"We haven't even had anything to eat." Or maybe he can.

"You know what? I'm not that hungry." After witnessing his actions all evening, his good looks pale before his vanity.

At this moment, a table of single ladies calls him over.

"Well, then I'm going to go hang with them."

"Please, go."

He stands, clearly confused by the turn of events, before he moves on to greener pastures. I walk over to the shelf and pull down the Jameson. I pour two fingers into a glass and kick it back.

"What happened?" Tommy's voice comes from just behind me. The whiskey burns its way to my belly.

"My last date preferred men, and while this one prefers women in general, he doesn't prefer me in particular."

"Well, he's a fool."

"I'll stay and lend you a hand."

"Are you sure?"

"Yup." Across the bar, Jake is chatting up the ladies, completely undisturbed by the fact that his date just dumped him. "Suddenly my evening is wide open."

Around half past nine, the door opens and in walks Logan. Immediately the image of him on the beach in the moonlight dressed in only a pair of swim shorts fills my head. You'd never know what he hides under those baggy clothes.

He starts for the bar, but seeing me, he stops. Those green gems take a leisurely journey down the length of me, but his expression doesn't give any clue as to whether he likes what he sees. It's silly, this attraction I have for him. For all I know, he hacks people up in his basement and eats them for dinner. He might prefer sleeping with goats, or be as dumb as a post, but it doesn't matter, because every time I see him, my body tingles.

The sound of Tommy's voice breaks the spell. "What will you have, Logan?"

"A Guinness," comes the response in a sexy deep baritone, and then it hits me that I have just heard Logan speak. He takes a spot at the bar and turns his head to engage in conversation with the man sitting next to him. His deep timbre cuts through the other noises in the bar. I get back to work, but a part of me is still focused on that voice, so I hear him laugh some time later: a sound that causes shivers along my nerve endings. In that moment, an unexpected pang of anger spikes my shivers. Why won't the man speak to me? What have I done to be so singled out? I'm already circling the seventh level of hell coming from the worst date of my life, so why not put myself out there and ask him?

Building him another Guinness, I walk to him and slam it down on the bar in front of him. "So what's your problem?" Logan's head jerks, first to the glass and then up at me.

Silence.

"Are you three? I mean, why do you give only me the silent treatment? Have I offended you in some way?"

Nothing, no reaction at all. Frustration causes my face to flush, but I'm not about to stand there and blush in front of him. I have some pride left, even after a humiliating evening.

"Fuck it." Turning, I grab my purse from under the bar. "I'm going home, Tommy."

I don't wait for his response before I walk from around the bar and out into the dark night. I'm so annoyed, but I'm also a little hurt. After being so completely ignored by Jake, and unable to rattle Logan out of his silence, I can't help but wonder if the problem is with me. The walk home soothes my nerves, but what's now abundantly clear to me is that I'm really going to have to resort to online dating.

CHAPTER THREE

I spend the next few days setting up my profile online. I can't deny it's a bit strange trying to market myself. Has my dating life come to this? Once I confirm my profile, I'm surprised at the number of responses, though many are so far away that they really aren't practical. However, within a sixty-mile radius, I have twelve interested men and so I set up a few meets.

The first man on my list is Daniel Caine. He works as a manager in a department store—strong features, dark hair, blue eyes. Based on his profile, I have the sense that he's the silent type. Since Harrington's only social outlets are The Harbor, where Mitch works, and Tucker's, I decide to meet Daniel in Bar Harbor, where he lives, which is an hour's drive away. I don't need the entire town knowing that I'm online dating.

The day of the date, I ask Gwen if I can borrow her car.

"Sure, but I want all the details. Spare nothing, Saffron, I even want to know what he wore."

"As long as you don't tell anyone, including your husband." Gwen is about to protest, but I stop her. "No deal otherwise."

"Fine, even though I don't keep anything from Mitch."

"Yes, well, this is my private life, so you really aren't."

"Fine. You look beautiful. The teal in your blouse matches your eyes."

I smile absently as I rub my sweaty palms over my black pants and reach for my purse. "I'm a bit nervous."

"It'll be fun and, if nothing else, you can spend the day in Bar Harbor shopping."

"True. All right, I'll see you when I get back."

"Good luck."

----·----

Luck is not on my side. I meet Daniel at Starbucks and it only takes me a moment to realize that the man is gay. Since I have already caused one man to change his sexual orientation by dating me, I am not up for another go. Keeping the conversation very light, after about half an hour, the date fizzles and Daniel and I part ways. Having most of the rest of the day ahead of me, I go shopping. When I pass the hair salon, I decide it's time to tend to my locks. Two hours and two hundred bucks later, my hair is several inches shorter, falling just past my shoulders, which makes the curls even wilder, and it's liberally laced with burgundy highlights. It feels fabulous and I know it looks it too—when I drop off Gwen's car, not only does Gwen do a double take, but so does Mitch. Knowing how smitten he is with his wife, that's saying a lot.

----·----

In the weeks that follow I keep expecting improvement in the meet and greets, but if I am being completely honest, the date with Daniel was the best of the lot. When I meet Shane and his mother, Josephine, I start to think maybe online dating isn't for me. Shane's mother came with him on the date. Yes, it was the three of us because he claimed she wanted to make sure I had the proper birthing hips.

During these same weeks I seem to run into Logan an awful lot: on Main Street, at the grocery store, in the cafe. He still doesn't speak to me, but he looks different. He's been to a barber. Though his features are still completely concealed under black fur, the mustache and beard have been trimmed, taking away the shaggy and unkempt look. Those eyes still unsettle my well-being, especially when they shine with such unabashed heat as I find them doing often in my direction. I like to believe I am a fairly insightful person, and it seems clear that Logan is interested in me, so why the continued vow of silence?

———·———

The day of the dreaded Swordfish Festival has finally come. I dress in faded jeans and my *Sons of Anarchy* T-shirt, and tie up my Doc Marten steel-tip black boots. Grabbing my car keys, I head for my car. Twenty minutes pass as I attempt to get the car started. With the last attempt, a terrible sound—like a death cry—comes from the engine. It's safe to say that the LeBaron is officially toast.

The five-mile hike into town does not brighten my spirits and when I finally arrive at the one festival of the year that I truly detest, I'm almost knocked out by the smell of swordfish: that oily fishy smell clings to everything like cheap perfume.

As I stand on my allotted corner—I can't decide what I find more comical, the fact that I have an allotted corner or that I am wearing an orange safety belt like the ones we had in grade school—I monitor the flow of pedestrian traffic to ensure that there are no mad dashes to the swordfish funnel cake stand. Yes, you heard me correctly.

The atmosphere of this festival is like that of a funeral. I understand this. Typically our festivals revolve around food—stand after stand of deliciousness based on the star of the day. But when the best offering is the swordfish funnel cake, things look bleak. It seems to me that this festival should be retired, but Chastity is quite adamant about keeping it.

Personally, I think the reason she's so determined is because she secretly adores the swordfish funnel cake and they're only available during this festival. Anyway, due to the empty stomachs of the festival visitors, tensions run high. Most of the visitors are older, but there are quite a few teenagers, and if anyone gets rowdy, how exactly am I supposed to bring them to order? By using harsh language?

It's while I ponder this perplexing dilemma that I notice Logan across the street with Chastity, the most uptight person I have ever met. But as I stand there I watch as she dances around Logan like a schoolgirl with a crush. She is flipping her hair, batting her eyelashes, and, even from my distance, it looks as if she is blushing. And Logan is just sucking it all up: laughing, grinning, and even talking. The fact that he can act so friendly around a woman who is herself usually about as friendly as a rattlesnake brings my inner juvenile to the fore. But it's the smell of the wretched swordfish funnel cakes—and really, talk about what the fuck—that is to blame for what happens next.

George Ward, creator of the aforementioned swordfish funnel cake, is a fisherman who is forever experimenting with food, but unfortunately most of his creative efforts are based on the fish he catches—swordfish. I know he has lost money, money he probably doesn't have, trying to turn the armpit of the sea into some kind of fun festival food. And it is this fact that seals my fate.

"How much for the entire lot, George?"

His eyes widen at that. "You hate swordfish, Saffron."

"I know, but I have a plan to get this party started."

He snorts at that. "I can't imagine what you can do to make this fun."

"Trust me."

After filling George in on my plan and paying him for half of his inventory, I grab a handful of funnel cakes and start toward the center of the festival activity. As I move through the crowd, I hand funnel cakes to those I know and tell them to wait for the signal.

When I reach my desired location, I, Miss Crowd Control, inhale and scream the words that will bring some life to this dying party. "Food Fight!"

And then I let one sail right out of my hand. Chastity doesn't seem to understand what is happening, since she makes not a single move to prevent the funnel cake from landing smack in the middle of her face. Logan laughs out loud, but his laugh is cut short by the next airborne funnel cake. When those green eyes find mine, I gulp, and I turn tail and run, losing myself in the very merry, and messy, ruckus I have started.

———

Who could have known how very hard it would be to clean up smashed swordfish funnel cake? The cake, when exposed to the elements, turned a consistency very similar to cement. I shiver at the thought of eating one. Maybe George should try selling his creations to the local stonemason to use as an organic alternative to mortar.

The silver lining: the festival was a raging success. The downside: the sheriff was called and, though I wasn't arrested for disturbing the peace, I was given community service, hence the washing down of Main Street. It's going to take me two or three years to clean this mess up, but it was worth it, most especially for Logan's expression when that funnel cake nailed him right on the side of his face. He never did find me in the crowd. When I saw the pieces of swordfish stuck in his beard, I couldn't help howling with laughter. Good times.

"I can't believe what a mess you created, Saffron. What were you thinking?"

Chastity is probably the only person who didn't find my antics funny. Hell, even Sheriff Dwight, while he was reprimanding me, was trying desperately to keep from laughing.

"The festival was dragging, Chastity. It needed something to kick-start it."

"And a food fight seemed to you to be an appropriate response?"

"Well, yeah. George needed to sell his cakes and the festival needed an infusion of fun. It was the perfect solution."

"Needless to say, you won't be asked to be in charge of crowd control again, or anything else for that matter," Chastity says with distaste as she walks away from me.

"So I guess you aren't going to help me clean this up?"

No answer. I'm not surprised, but I can't help my smile—I am now officially blackballed from all future festival responsibilities. The rewards just keep coming.

In the second hour of cleaning, reinforcements arrive. Gwen, Mitch, Josh, Derek, and Tommy come with buckets, mops, and sponges.

"Want some help?" Gwen asks as she settles next to me and starts scouring the bakery's front window.

"Thanks, guys. I really thought I was going to die of old age right here in the middle of decaying swordfish."

Mitch starts on the hardware store, dipping his mop into the sudsy water before pulling it across the brick front of the building. "The mess aside, it was a hell of a lot of fun."

I grin at Mitch, who winks before he continues wiping down the building.

"What did our esteemed Chastity have to say?" Josh asks as he and Derek clean the sidewalk in front of the grocery.

"I have been banned from all future festival activities."

"You lucky son of a bitch." Derek hates the guilt of neglecting his festival responsibilities almost as much as me.

"Maybe you should burn the Fourth of July float, Derek—that should get you banned as well." Tommy offers this as a joke, but when Derek seems to be taking the suggestion under advisement, we all start to laugh.

"Is there room for one more?"

Turning at the question, I'm greeted by the sight of Logan standing over me. There's a smile on his face, but I have the sense that retribution's burning in those green eyes. His T-shirt shows off the sinewy muscles of his arms. The visual shimmers to life of him practically naked on the beach. He can't possibly know what I am thinking, but I look away anyway, just in case he can read minds.

"Please, there's enough dead swordfish to go around," I say.

Four hours later we're done. We don't look so hot and we sure as hell smell awful, but Main Street looks great.

"Thank you for helping me. I would have been at this for days."

"Well, everyone should have helped. We all participated." Ah, Gwen, spoken like a true mother.

"I need to get home and shower. I can't stand the smell of myself." Josh grabs his bucket, air-kisses me, and starts down the street.

"See you later, Saffron," Derek calls as he runs to catch up to Josh.

"Yeah, we should go too, since we have to get the kids," Mitch says, but he's rubbing the inside of Gwen's wrist with his thumb, small little circles.

It must be some touch because Gwen starts to respond, "We aren't picking up the kids . . ." but never finishes her thought because her eyes glaze over. Suddenly in a hurry, she says, "Right, okay, see you later, Saffron."

Tommy chuckles. "She has no idea how easy she is to read, does she?"

"Nope."

"I have to get to the bar. I'll see you tomorrow." Tommy brushes a kiss on my cheek before turning to Logan and offering his hand. "See you later. Thanks for helping."

"No problem," Logan says. Tommy starts down the street.

"Thanks, Logan, it was really cool of you to help." And with that I gather up my things and start down the street, too. There is no point in standing there staring at him, though I could have, and happily, for many hours.

I don't get very far when I hear that deep voice speak my name. My feet just stop of their own accord before I slowly turn back around. Logan is right behind me.

For such a large man, he is remarkably quiet when he moves. He's standing so close our bodies are practically touching, and, as I try to get my head around that, his hands reach up to gently cup my face. Electricity sparks, snapping the air between us, and, as I struggle to keep my legs under me, he brushes his lips over mine. It's barely a kiss, but the effect is like being hit upside the head with a cast-iron frying pan. He steps back and, without another word, he turns and walks away.

Logan kissed me when I smell like *eau de* dead swordfish, of all times. I don't remember walking home, but I have a sense that at least for part of the journey, I actually floated.

———

I am having dinner with Frank. I had to bum a ride with Tommy since I am now carless. The tale of the "festival incident," as it is termed, is growing to near-epic proportions as with each retelling, the story is further embellished. Frank is so proud of me that he actually stands up in the middle of dinner and toasts me.

After dinner Frank asks me to go dancing. I didn't realize how worried I was about Frank this past week until now. My tense shoulders settle with the knowledge that Frank has the energy to go dancing this week. That has to be a good sign. As we make our way down the hall to the room where the dancing is held, he entertains me with stories of the Rat Pack, as he calls them: the seniors he hangs with during the week. Bob's hip is healing, much to Claire's joy, and he will be fully operational in a few short weeks. Ernie and Linda, two others in the Rat Pack, are actually talking marriage even though they are both only a decade shy of being a century old. We reach the dance hall and are greeted by the sound of "Begin the Beguine." For almost an hour, Frank and I dance to a variety of oldies, but it is during one swing number that I notice a change in Frank: he gets distant as if he's many miles away.

"Frank? Are you okay?"

"I remember this song from my youth. Amazing how fast time flies."

"Would you like to talk about it?"

He covers my hand, which is resting on the arm of his wheelchair. "Thank you, but no. Sometimes memories are not comforting, sometimes keeping the past in the past is for the best."

This I knew of Frank. As open and loving as he is, he rarely speaks of his time prior to coming to Harrington. I've wondered, but I never push since he has a right to his memories.

"I'm tired. Thank you, Saffron, for a lovely . . ."

"Evening."

My body gets all warm as I recognize that voice. Logan flashes me a smile when I turn to face him. To the best of my knowledge, which is decidedly limited about this man, he doesn't know anyone here. Why is he here?

"Hello, sir. I'm Logan MacGowan."

"Frank Dupree. Are you a friend of Saffron's?"

His gaze settles on me for a hot second before he responds. "I'd like to be."

"You visiting someone here?"

"Came to see Saffron. Heard she needed a ride home."

He heard I needed a ride home? Matchmaker Tommy. He was supposed to be my ride. Not sure if I should slug him or hug him the next time I see him.

"What happened to your car?" I forgot to tell Frank about the death of the LeBaron.

"It's in car heaven, well, maybe purgatory, with the amount of times it left me stranded."

Frank snorts; he actually snorts. "I'm surprised it lasted as long as it did. Duct tape has many applications, but holding a car together isn't really one of them."

"It looked pretty, though." And it did. I used all different colors and designs. I should have sent pictures to the manufacturer.

"I'm off to bed. Thanks for taking Saffron home. Nice to meet you, Logan."

"You too, sir."

"Good night, Frank." I watch him for a moment and feel the ache I always feel thinking about a time when Frank won't be here. There isn't a way to mentally prepare myself; his loss will be hard as hell.

"You okay?" The green of Logan's eyes pops against the black of his sweater and beard. I nod and he says, "Dance with me." Really more of an order than a question.

"I thought you were here to give me a ride?"

"Can't we do both?"

"Why?"

"Why not?"

Exactly, why not? Shut up, Saffron, and stop arguing with the man.

His large hands reach down to wrap around my much smaller ones. Lifting and placing them around his neck, his take a slow journey down my arms until he reaches my waist. He encircles me and pulls me up against him. Everywhere he touches burns, and my knees weaken. He's so much taller than me that my fingers have access to that marvelous inky-black hair brushing his shoulders. His focus never wavers from mine and, though no words are spoken, I'm surprised to realize that I don't need words because his eyes are speaking volumes. More surprising than that revelation is the simple fact that I want him to kiss me; I want that more than I want to take my next breath. As if he reads my thoughts, his mouth covers mine. Unlike the last kiss, it isn't a gentle brushing of lips. He kisses me as if his life depends on it and when his tongue brushes along my lower lip, I don't hesitate to open for him. Cradling my face with his hands, he deepens the kiss and I grip his sweater in my fists and pull him closer. I'm so lost in the feel of his incredible mouth that I don't realize the music has stopped. Honestly, I'm not aware of very much in my immediate surroundings—I'm totally focused on the man before me.

When he breaks the kiss, I have to consciously bite down on a whine of protest. He runs his thumb over my lower lip, but my gaze keeps returning to his mouth: that very skilled mouth that has the power to bring a woman to her knees. I'm so focused on his sexy lips that I almost miss his softly spoken words.

"Thank you."

My brain is in mild shock after that kiss. My next words are abrupt, but since it's the question I most want answered, I'm okay with that. "Are you seriously here to give me a ride?"

"Yes, but I won't lie, I wanted another kiss. Figured I'd work that in too."

He wants to kiss me and since I want to kiss him, we are so perfect for each other. And then it hits me that Logan is actually talking to me. "You're talking to me."

"Is that okay?"

"Yeah. Why haven't you before?"

"Words can be overrated. You can learn a great deal about someone just from watching them."

I had noticed his tendency to silently observe. The idea that he's been observing me makes me feel all warm inside.

"Makes sense, I guess. So what's changed? Why the switch from observing to talking?"

"You hit me in the face with a funnel cake."

"And?"

No answer. I say, "That's it? I hit you in the face with a funnel cake. So any fried-dough product would have brought this about, or was it specifically fried dough with swordfish?"

"Are you ready to go home?"

"You're not going to commit to your preference for swordfish funnel cakes over all the other funnel cakes in the land? Your prerogative. Yes, I am ready. And thank you for the ride."

His hand on the small of my back is setting off little electric bursts under my skin like static shock, but it doesn't hurt, it feels good, really, really good. He escorts me to the parking lot. A beauty of a motorcycle is sitting just near the door.

"Is that yours?"

"Yeah, you okay with that?"

Oh, the visuals of us on that bike. "Yep."

He climbs on and hands me his helmet. There's something awfully sexy about a man on a bike. Sexier still with my thighs cradling his ass. The bike roars to life, my arms finding their way around his hard, flat stomach. I never want to get off this bike, ever. It feels nice, the salty mist brushing over my skin as we drive along the bay. Maybe I should get a motorcycle, but I suspect I won't like the ride nearly as much solo.

We reach my house far too soon. Climbing off, I hand my helmet to Logan, who stores it. He follows me to the door; my stomach is in knots and my lips are still tingling from his kiss. I turn to him, the pad of his thumb rubs along my lower lip.

"Good night."

And before I can stay a word, he's strolling back to his bike.

Yup, I would definitely call it a good night.

———

The following morning I wake up with so much pent-up energy, no doubt a side effect of Logan's staggering kiss, that I decide to take a run. I love running these days, quite the opposite of my feelings toward the activity when I was younger, which was that it should only be done when being chased. I took laziness to a whole other level as a child. My usual route is along the bay, three miles down and three miles back. As much as my body loves the run, my mind is on Logan, more specifi-cally on his behavior.

I remember the first day I saw him. It was a Thursday night, and fairly late, when the door to Tucker's opened and in he walked. He was a bit less shaggy then, but as soon as I looked into those green eyes, something in me shifted. I can admit it to myself that I have, from the very beginning, been attracted to him. His arrival stirred interest in the town for a few days, mostly because he was a new face, but there wasn't the rapt interest of the ladies like with Jake's arrival six months earlier. As sad as it is to say, I know the lack of female interest in Logan is due solely to the fact that you can't see his face. As far as anyone knows, he's covering up some hideous deformity under all the facial hair, but I don't care. There is something about his quiet presence that really gets to me and so it came as a bit of a shock, and a little hurtful, that he chose to keep quiet around me and only me.

Last night he broke that silence.

Technically he still isn't speaking to me, that brief exchange last night hardly constitutes conversation, but now he's kissing me sense-less—a change I can wholeheartedly get behind—but why?

I suppose I could continue down the path we're on and allow the man to blow my head off with kisses despite the fact that we really don't know each other, but that seems a bit dysfunctional. Which means that I am going to have to suck it up and initiate the conver-sation that's the kiss of death in the guy/girl dynamic. I resign myself to the mature course of action. Logan and I are going to have to talk about our feelings.

When I return home from my run, there he is sitting on my front stoop as if I've conjured him with my thoughts.

"Logan, hi."

His head lifts, and the sight of him sets off lovely little fireworks under my skin.

"Hello, Saffron."

"So what brings you here?"

He stands up, and my head tilts back. "Continuing our game is growing too difficult for me."

"Game? You mean me trying to break your silence? Pretty sure I won that game."

He isn't touching me, but he's so close I can feel the heat from his body and can smell the spicy scent that is uniquely Logan. My mouth starts to water. If I take just one step, I'll be pressed up against him. Will his arms come around me? Will he pull me up against the length of him like he did at Harrington Commons? I'd sell my soul to Satan to make it so.

When his finger touches my jaw, I almost swoon as lust burns through me. "I am willing to declare you the winner."

And then he's kissing me, that wonderful hot mouth capturing mine. My hands reach for him and his powerful arms draw me closer. His breathing is as erratic as my own when we end the kiss, and my heart slams into my ribs at the lust burning hot in his dark green eyes. He takes a few deep breaths before stepping back.

"I should go," he whispers.

"Why?"

He doesn't answer, but then he doesn't have to because I know what will happen if he stays. So instead of stepping away, I step closer. "Come inside, Logan."

Desire, pure and simple, flashes across his face. "Are you sure?"

"Very."

In one smooth move, he lifts me into his arms and carries me into the house. The door has barely closed behind us before we're all over each other. His mouth is on my neck as my hands grab at his shirt to lift it over his head. The second I see the beauty of his chest, my mouth is on him, my tongue licking that golden skin. He yanks my sports bra up seconds before his mouth closes over my breast and I moan since it's been too long. I fumble with the snap and zipper of his jeans and then he's tugging my shorts and panties down my legs before he lifts me into his arms and presses me back against the wall. He touches me and finds me so ready before he shifts his hips and in one magnificent move, he's buried deep inside of me.

"Oh God."

We freeze, both of us, because we didn't use protection. He's about to pull out, but I tighten my legs around him. It's all the encouragement he needs and he starts to move. I frame his face with my hands and kiss him like I'll die if I don't have my mouth on his. As I feel the start of the orgasm, his fingers move between our bodies to stroke me in just the right spot. I fall over the edge, my body splintering apart from the pleasure. His hips don't stop and he keeps up the relentless pace until he follows after me. My head falls on his shoulder and his arms tighten around me. I wait for the awkward after, the moment that we realize we barely know each other and just had mind-blowing sex up against the wall.

So when I lift my head, I'm prepared for disappointment, but instead I see a smile that is sexy as hell. "I need more," he purrs.

Chills shoot down my body even as a naughty smile curves my lips. "Bedroom's down the hall."

CHAPTER FOUR

"You slept with him?" This bewildered question comes from Gwen as she, Josh, and I sit around her living room during our ladies' night. Snatching the pillow off the sofa, I cover my face with it to muffle my response.

"I know, I know." I try to feel repentant, I truly do, but I can't. All day, night, and into the very early morning, Logan and I enjoyed each other, and for someone who hasn't had a sexual encounter since the Bush administration, I feel no guilt. Just thinking about that body, the sexy Celtic knot tattoo that wraps his left bicep, his abs, his chest, his shoulders . . . I had my mouth on every delicious, muscular inch of him. It's a good thing I have the pillow to my face to block out my moan.

"He doesn't even speak to you," Josh says.

I lift my head. "We're speaking now."

This causes a bark of laughter from Josh. "I bet."

"No, seriously. He came to tell me he couldn't play our game anymore and I will note that he did agree to declare me the winner, since I was, after all." It's an important fact, me winning, that shouldn't be excluded in the telling of the tale.

Gwen's lips twitch. "Well, I suppose that's something."

Josh reaches for his glass of wine. "So have you exchanged words beyond *yes, please, don't stop, faster*?"

I throw the pillow I'm holding at his head, and his catlike reflexes keep the wine from spilling on the floor.

"There wasn't really an opportunity for a heart-to-heart."

"But you said he didn't leave until this morning, so what did you two do . . ." Gwen stops midthought as a smile curves her lips. "All night and this morning? The stamina. You are a naughty girl, Saffron."

"Yes, but a very satisfied one."

Josh chuckles. "So how did you leave it?"

I just glare at Josh. What is he? An investigative reporter for the *Boston Globe*? I'm not really mad at Josh. No, I don't want to answer his question—I still don't know quite how I feel with the way things were left. When I awoke, I found a small bouquet of flowers he had cut from my garden resting on his pillow, but no Logan. As romantic as it was, I can't determine if the gesture is just that, romantic, or if it's Logan's way of laying down some unspoken ground rules. As in—this is only sex, so don't get attached. Does he generally love a woman blind before disappearing without a trace? He probably has hundreds of broken hearts out there, hence the disguise of the beard. It's a thoroughly depressing thought.

"So?"

"It's new, Josh, for both of us."

He clearly doesn't like that answer, but he leaves it alone. "We've exhausted that topic. So what's next?"

I am only partly paying attention to my friends. My thoughts are still on Logan and the uncertainty I feel at seeing him again.

I bought a new car, an old VW bug that will probably not last out the year, but it only cost me five hundred bucks. Even if it lasts only a few months, it'll be worth the investment.

Added bonus, I get to punch my friends every time I show up in it.

After dinner with Frank on Wednesday, we retire to his room where he pulls out his chess set. He has been trying to teach me the art of chess for as long as I can remember. I'm a terrible student. Strategic thinking is not my forte.

As he does every time he takes it out, he places the pieces on the board with love, even taking a few moments to hold a few as if lost in thought.

"Do you believe it's possible that an object can hold a piece of someone's soul?"

To say I'm surprised by the question is an understatement. Clearly he's remembering someone, probably the same someone he never discusses. I won't pry, but I do wish he'd unload his burden because he has been my rock and I'd like to be that for him.

"If the object was significant in someone's life, yes, I believe it can hold a piece of their energy. Will you consider sharing with me whoever it is you're thinking about?"

"It isn't that I don't want to share, it's just reliving it is too difficult. But I want you to promise me something."

In his direct gaze, I see the intense young man he must have been. "Be happy. In your life, be happy, and if you aren't, make the changes that will allow for it. If you learn nothing else from me, learn that life is short. In a blink of an eye it can be over. Find your happiness, and then hold on to it with both hands. Will you do that for me?"

My heart aches knowing that his advice is based on personal experience. "I promise, Frank."

Nodding his head, he places the piece he's holding on the board. "Good. Now, do you remember what I told you about the Sicilian Defense?"

Knowing Frank as well as I do, I know the subject of his past is over. And as much as I'd like to push the topic, I respect him too much to do that. So following his lead, I switch gears to chess and answer his question. "Only that the Sicilian Defense has nothing to do with pizza."

———·———

Logan is in hiding. I try not to take it personally during the first few days after our sleepover. I just assume the man is busy. He does have a life, a secret life that no one seems to know anything about, like what he does for a living, where he came from. Key things like that. However, when it grows closer to a week with still no sighting, not even at Tucker's, which catches Tommy's notice, Logan's disappearing act definitely feels personal.

I don't regret our night together—hell, I'll probably never forget it—but there isn't going to be any repeat performance. I am mad, but more at myself than him. For Logan to be so callous and obvious about his intentions, or lack thereof, means that the man I thought he was— the man that I wanted to sleep with—really doesn't exist. It's never pleasant to realize that you've been played.

Lesson learned, but now that I have truly exhausted every available man in Harrington, I find myself back at square one.

Firing up my laptop, I check my profile; there are two requests to meet pending. What's the worst that can happen? I respond to both men, shut down my laptop, and get ready for work.

———·———

"That is so not true. That would never happen," I tell Tommy.

"Saffron, you don't see it because you are in denial, but I am telling you that an Alien will defeat a Predator every time."

"That is such bull, Tommy. Predators are complex beings that are born to hunt and Aliens are just extremely large cockroaches."

"I'm afraid we will have to agree to disagree."

Yanking the band from my wrist, I pull back my hair. This is an argument Tommy and I have often. The man is clearly mental, and deluded, but making him see reason is above my pay grade.

"I'm with Saffron, no contest." Doug Smithers is a lobsterman who stays pretty much to himself, but Tommy and I have discovered that he too has a love for a good science-fiction movie.

"Ha!" I point to Doug and grin. "Common sense from someone."

Tommy rolls his eyes at us. "Moving on. Who would win in a battle between Luke Skywalker and Dumbledore?"

Doug and I both groan, but Doug also says what I am thinking: "Not a fair question. They would never fight one another."

"Pretend they would," Tommy counters.

In the process of making a face behind Tommy's back, I see the door open. In steps a beautiful woman. With long pale-blond hair and big blue eyes, she's wearing Prada and Jimmy Choos and her bag is a Dolce & Gabbana. I may not be able to afford the latest fashions, but I sure as hell know what they are.

I am still admiring the cut of her coat when her lunch date steps up beside her. All the air leaves my lungs when my gaze collides with Logan's. I don't realize my hand has curled around the neck of a bottle of Cabernet until Tommy comes up beside me and covers my hand with his own.

"No bloodshed, Saffron," he whispers. Tommy knows about Logan, so he understands a bit how this move of Logan's is affecting me.

Logan actually has the nerve to smile before walking his lady friend to a table.

"Maybe that's his sister?" Tommy says weakly.

"I don't know much about biology, but I'm pretty damn sure it's close to impossible for those two to be related."

Tommy's arm comes around my shoulders. "You want to take a break?"

I'm really surprised by how strongly seeing Logan with another woman is affecting me. I barely know the man, so what's up with the stabbing pain centered in my chest? "I do, but I won't. I might as well get it over with."

When I start around the bar, Tommy stops me. "I'll wait on them."

I see the worry on his face, but I don't miss his anger. "I appreciate that, but I'm good."

He looks skeptical, but he doesn't say anything further. I check on a few other tables on my way to Logan and his lover, because I don't want to look too eager to be their server, but before long I am standing before them.

She has on a lovely fragrance. It's the kind that sort of only hints, so you want to get closer to get a better whiff. The visual of me burying my face in her neck makes me snort, which is met by a raised eyebrow from the lady and a small, endearing grin from Logan. Stop, he isn't endearing; he's a bastard of the first order.

"What can I get you?"

"Saffron, how are you?" Logan asks and he sounds genuinely interested. How am I? Small talk, right.

I rest my hip on the table and give my back to Logan as I look down at his date. "Would you think it odd for a man to come to a small town and proceed to not speak to you for six months?"

Her perfect lips form a grin. "Everyone or just me specifically?"

"You, specifically."

Her eyes light with humor. "Yes, that is odd."

"Odder still for that man to then take you to bed and blow your mind with sex for almost twenty-four hours before ditching you and then staying off the radar for a week?"

The humor has left her gaze now, but she answers anyway. "Indeed."

"So what would you think when that same man shows up at your place of employment with a beautiful woman and attempts to engage you in small talk?"

Her eyes leave mine for Logan's, but I don't miss the emotion in her gaze. She's mad.

"Exactly." I turn and give Logan my full attention. "So how am I, Logan?" I pull out the chair next to him and sit down. "I could pretend to be a cool, sophisticated woman and lie to you and say I'm fabulous, but that just isn't me. What I am is hurt and more than a little pissed, so the idea of making small talk with you is repugnant to me, unless that talk is centered on what I'd like to do to you. For example, I'd love to reach for that dull butter knife and stick it in your eye, giving it a hard turn just for good measure. The idea of strapping you to a man-size lobster trap and throwing you into the ocean holds a great deal of appeal, as does the thought of running your ass over with my car, repeatedly. I could sit here all day making small talk about that, or you could just shut up and order some goddamn lunch."

He isn't hiding his anger now. "Are you finished?"

"Oh yes, Logan, we are definitely finished. I'll send Tommy over to take your order."

I start to rise, but he stops me by grabbing my arm. He's gentle, but he applies enough force to keep me from moving.

"You'll hear me out, especially since you've already aired most of our dirty laundry to half of Harrington."

He has a point. At lunch hour, Tucker's is packed. I'm not about to agree with him, but I do sit down and attempt to give him my best belligerent glare.

"The morning I left I had an early flight to New York and I tried to wake you, but you sleep like a dead person. When I got to the airport, I realized I didn't have your phone number, so I called Tucker's for it. The young woman I spoke with gave me your cell number."

It could be a web of lies, but I know deep down that it isn't. My never-charged cell phone is a bone of contention with my friends. If he called my cell phone, I wouldn't have gotten the message.

"I left you three messages, Saffron. One that day, one when I landed in New York City, and one today with information on when I was returning to Harrington. As soon as we landed, we went to your house and when you weren't there, we came here. This is Maria St. John, my agent."

I feel about the size of an ant. If only the ground would open and swallow me. To add to the ridiculousness, the only question I can form after all of this is "Agent?"

"I'm an artist and had a showing at a gallery in Manhattan. Maria came back with me to see some of my new work. I wanted her to meet you."

At that moment, I feel like Ralphie from *A Christmas Story* after he dropped the f-bomb. There is just no way to pull that back. If I ever felt more ridiculous in my life, I can't recall it. Trying to navigate the minefield of my thoughts is impossible, so instead I rise and somehow manage to maintain eye contact with Logan even though I want to crawl into a very dark hole.

"Hope all went well in Manhattan." I turn to Maria. "Welcome to Harrington. I hope you enjoy your stay." And then I walk out of Tucker's and keep on walking until I end up on Josh's doorstep.

CHAPTER FIVE

For two days I hide at Josh's, unable to show my face around town. I lie on the bed in his guest bedroom as my mind replays the abysmal scene at Tucker's. I want to curl up into a ball and die. It isn't that I don't feel justified in my feelings. If he hadn't called, then I was spot-on. The fact that he did call makes me feel like pond scum, fungus on pond scum, lice on fungus on pond scum.

My cell phone was still in my purse. After Tommy dropped it off for me, I charged my phone, and sure enough there were three new voice mails. I saved them, since it is highly unlikely that Logan will ever again address me with the tenderness that his first message held. He mentioned the gallery showing, the trip, and then he told me how much he enjoyed our time together and how he wanted to see me again. The second message seemed a bit apprehensive and the third was almost curt, but I understand why. The man called and I never returned his calls, so the fact that he actually came to Tucker's to see me took a lot of courage. And how do I respond to that kind of chivalry? I tell him I want to jab him in the eye with a butter knife, want to feed him to the lobsters. I bury my face in the pillow and groan. Maybe it's time for me to grow facial hair and hermit myself somewhere. There are caves along the bay; maybe I can hole up there for a few years, decades, until the story of my profound stupidity is reduced to a mere urban legend. A slight knock on the door alerts me to Josh's presence.

"You can't stay in here forever, Saffron. He deserves an apology."

I sit up as Josh comes over to join me on the bed. "I know, but how exactly does one apologize after messing up so superbly? I mean if there was an Academy Award for shoving your foot into your mouth, I would win it, hands down."

"It was a misunderstanding. You didn't know he called. Explain that to him."

"I told him in detail how I planned to kill him."

Josh smiles as he takes my hand into his. "But that is a part of your personality. It's who you are. If he likes you then he'll not only understand what motivated your death threats, but will probably be charmed by them."

I am looking at Josh like he has just grown donkey ears and a tail. "Charmed by it?"

"Okay, maybe not charmed, but he'll understand."

Groaning, I drop my head on his shoulder. "And if he doesn't?"

"Then you accept that you messed up royally and you move on."

"He hates me."

"No, he doesn't, but you won't know that until you go see him."

"You're right, but when this crashes and burns, can I come back and cry on your shoulder?"

"You don't have to ask."

"You're the best."

The meaning of the expression *dead man walking* sinks in as I make my way to Logan's. How exactly am I supposed to start the upcoming conversation? Hey, Logan, got any butter knives? What must he think of me? It doesn't take me nearly as long as I'd like to get to Logan's, but when I arrive, it's very quiet. The emotion that washes over me is probably very similar to that of a death-row inmate when the governor calls just in the nick of time. And points for me on keeping with the prison analogy.

While I am patting myself on the back, Logan comes from around the side of his house. As soon as he sees me, he stops dead.

"Where have you been?" His greeting is far nicer than I was expecting. I had it in my head his first words to me after the scene I made would be something along the lines of "Get the hell away from me, you crazy bitch" or "I'm calling the police."

"Hiding," I say.

"From me?"

"No, Logan, from my outrageous behavior." My nerves twist my hands together. "Look, I never got your messages. Anyone who knows me knows I never use my cell phone. We had a fantastic time together and then you were gone and stayed gone for a week. When I see you again, you're with your outrageously beautiful agent. I was hurt and angry and I flipped out. I'm not proud of my behavior and I'm sorry I embarrassed you in front of your friend."

There is no reaction at all from him to my apology. I'm tempted to say the words again on the off chance the first time was only in my head, but it's more likely that we have just come full circle and are back to the silent treatment, not that I don't deserve it.

"I'm sorry, Logan, for all of it. I hope my freak-out doesn't keep you from Tucker's." And since there is nothing more to say, I feel much like a dog with his tail between his legs when I start to walk away from him.

"Stab me in the eye with a butter knife?"

My feet stop, but facing him is impossible.

"How long did you wait before you started plotting my death?"

"Not until you walked in with beautiful Maria."

"Are you still feeling homicidal around me?"

"No."

"Would you like to see some of my work?"

I do turn at that. "Shouldn't you be helping me off your property?"

"Do you want me to help you off my property?"

"No, but the last time we spoke I was plotting your death."

The grin on his lips turns into a full-out smile. "I think I'll take my chances."

Moving to stand just in front of me, he runs his hand down my arm in a delicate caress. "I'm sorry I didn't mention the trip while we were together, but my mind just wasn't on the trip; it had something infinitely more fascinating to contemplate."

"You're not mad?"

"No, I'm not mad." Linking our fingers, he starts toward his house.

If I hadn't liked Logan before, I would now at how he is handling all of this. He chuckles as we reach the door.

"Why are you chuckling?" I ask.

"You were jealous." He's definitely smug, though I can't blame him.

I am about to deny it, but what for? The whole town has either witnessed or heard about my jealous rage. Besides, with how decently he accepted my apology, it seems honesty is the only choice.

"Yes, I was."

His hand snakes around my neck to draw me to him. His mouth fuses to mine in a very thorough kiss as his tongue seeks and savors. He reaches again for my hand and leads me into the lighthouse.

It's charming—the rounded walls, portholes, and rustic furniture. Logan leads me up the spiral staircase until we reach a room that has canvases leaning up against the walls.

Logan starts from me. "This is my studio."

He grabs one of the two stools in the room and brings it over to me. Once I'm settled, he plants a hard kiss on my mouth before digging through the canvases and putting one after another on the easel for my viewing pleasure. He places before me a painting of Tucker's that is a little off-center, so George Ward's beat-up pickup can be seen—the owner walking around the trunk, heading to the bar still wearing his fishing garb. How beautifully he has captured the heart of Harrington. He's pulled a stool over and now sits right in front of me, watching me with those incredible eyes.

"That's my favorite," I whisper, my gaze moving from the painting to Logan. "You understand. That painting shows that you understand the magic of Harrington. Your work is breathtaking."

He leans a little closer to me so that our mouths are only inches apart and then, without saying a word, he closes the distance and proceeds to take my breath away again.

———————

Logan and I are taking things slowly since we had, for all intents and purposes, put the cart before the horse. We're at the lighthouse, sitting on Adirondack chairs while looking out at the sea.

"What a view. Is that what sold you on the place?" I ask.

"That and it's quiet."

Shifting in my chair to face him, I ask, "Quiet so you can paint?"

"Yes, and I'm not really a big fan of crowds."

"Me neither. I have a confession."

A slight raise of his eyebrow encourages me to continue.

"I watched you swimming a few weeks back."

His head tilts slightly and there's definitely the beginning of a smile. "Watched me? For how long?"

"Long enough to realize I was acting like a stalker."

"So do you often stare at nearly naked men in the moonlight?"

"How did you know there was moonlight?"

"That's when I like to swim. You didn't answer *my* question."

"Only when they've got a body like yours."

He stands so fast, I nearly get whiplash. In the next second, he's reaching for his shirt and pulling it over his head. Tingles sweep my entire body. "What are you doing?"

"It's a bit hot, don't you think? I've a need for a dip. You want to join?"

"I don't have a suit."

"How's that a problem?" He follows that comment with stepping out of his jeans so that his body is completely exposed except for the boxer briefs, which I have to say are my absolute favorite of the male undergarments. His six-pack—I want run my tongue over it.

The idea of stripping down to my bra and panties so I can get wet with Logan has me doing so in record time. "Race you," I holler, since I'm already running to the water. The man, despite his size, can move. He comes up behind me, sweeps me up into his arms, and carries me until the water reaches his waist.

"Hold your breath."

Thinking he's going to toss me, I'm delighted to find that he goes under with me instead. The water is too murky to see him, but I feel him, his strong arms holding me tight. Coming up for air, I wipe the water from my face and then his, but I don't stop at his face. My hands travel over his shoulders and arms, down his back, brushing over his ass. I want him and know he feels the same, since I can feel him grow-ing hard against my stomach. Since sex in the bay, however appealing, is likely illegal, I seek to temper our hormones.

"Did you live in Manhattan before you moved here?"

"Yes."

"Why did you move?"

"Not a fan of crowds."

Since that's the second time he's said that, I'm guessing his feelings about crowds is stronger than not being a fan. "But why here? It's not like we're a particularly well-known town."

"That's the appeal."

"Manhattan to Harrington has got to take some adjusting."

"About six months," he says with a wicked grin.

I can't tell if he's being a smartass or if he's serious. Either way, I like it. "I bet you left at least one broken heart in Manhattan."

His mouth closes over mine and his hands move to cradle my ass, rubbing me against the hard length of him. Conversation is apparently over and I am very okay with that.

———•———

For the past few days Logan has sequestered himself in his house while he works on a painting. Part of me would love to watch him work, but I know he likes his solitude. His focus is amazing, because though he's made it clear that he would prefer to spend time with me, our relationship being so new, he is dedicated enough to his craft that he can make himself stay away. I don't have nearly as much willpower, but I do find ways to stay busy and it is during my jog one morning that I meet my new neighbor.

The house, my only neighbor about a mile down the road, has been on the market for almost two years, so it's nice to see that it has finally sold. I would have stopped by later in the week with a housewarming gift, but my neighbor beats me to the punch. I find her waiting at my front door, a pretty brunette in fabulous clothes.

"I'm Elise. I just moved in down the street."

"Saffron. Hi."

"This is a great little town."

"It is. Where did you move from?"

"Boston."

"Really? Is this your first experience living in a small town?"

"Yes, it's going to be quite the change for me."

"I bet."

She leans a bit closer before she adds, "Is it me or is there a shortage of younger men in this town?"

"No, it isn't you."

"Are you one of the lucky ones who has a beau?"

On the surface Elise is quite friendly, but for some reason she puts me on edge. I have no plans to discuss Logan with her but my smile in reply wasn't enough of an answer.

"Maybe you wouldn't mind showing me around sometime? Are you free tonight? I could take you to dinner. Oh, or do you have plans with your boyfriend?"

My head is starting to hurt. Maybe it's because she's a Bostonian, but Elise seems awfully pushy. "Tonight doesn't work for me—I work at Tucker's in town—but maybe later in the week."

"I'm sorry. I know I'm like a charging bull. How about if you give me your cell number and I'll give you a call in a couple of days?"

"Sure." She doesn't need to know that my cell phone is more than likely already dead weight in my purse, as long as it gets her moving on and away from me. "It was nice to meet you, Elise."

"I'll call you."

"Welcome to Harrington." I wait until she realizes the conversation is over and starts back down the street. I walk inside, closing the door behind me and, as an afterthought, I flip the lock.

———•———

I'm beginning to grow tired of my own company by the middle of the day, so I decide to walk to the docks. I'm halfway out the door when the phone rings. My heart jumps—maybe it's Logan, but when I hear the voice on the other end, that hope is immediately dashed.

"Saffron, it's your mother."

"Mom, how are you? How's Dad?"

"Oh, we're great. Your father is having lunch with some friends, so it'll just be me today."

"Oh, okay." I can't deny I'm a little upset about this because I only speak to my parents exactly once a month, at a time convenient for them. I have tried calling them more often, but they never answer and they never return my calls. So the fact that my father can't make himself available for the ten-minute monthly call he allows me is a bit callous, in my opinion.

"How have you been, dear?"

"I'm good. And you?" I ask.

There is silence over the line because my mom is gearing herself up to start in on the lecture. According to her, I am wasting my life away because I am not married with children. She'll start in on the bartending shortly.

My friends were under the delusion, until recently when I filled them in, that my parents' move to Florida was tough on me, but I was thrilled that they left. All they ever seem to want to do is harass me about my lack of a husband and kids. I'm not really sure why they are so insistent on it. They don't have a maternal or paternal bone in their bodies. It isn't like they are waiting with bated breath for grandkids while knitting booties and receiving blankets.

I slump in my chair and attempt to listen to the lecture I now know by heart.

"Really, Saffron, you're turning thirty this year. You're running out of time to have children. Stop wasting your youth and get a real job: one that will attract a husband."

Oh, because that is what I want—a man who likes my bank account. "Maybe I don't want to get married or have children."

"Nonsense, of course you do, but you work at a bar, dear, so most men will assume you have very low morals."

My temper starts to simmer at the same old argument. I am nearly thirty, so isn't it time for my parents to back off and let me live my life? They have no problem with living theirs—moving to Florida without even telling me. My parents sold their home while I was still in college and made all the arrangements for their move. On my graduation day, they dropped the bomb and a week later, they were gone. So, I think they kind of gave up their right to a parental opinion when they walked out.

"Are you dating someone?"

I really don't want to share anything about Logan, but I can't lie either. "Yes, I am."

"Oh, how nice. What does he do?"

Here we go. "He's an artist."

"Honestly, Saffron, what are you thinking? You met at that bar, didn't you? He's only interested in you because you have a paycheck. Why can't you date someone with a real job, like a plumber or an electrician?"

There are just so many things wrong with her statement that I can't even begin to get into it, so instead I resort to sarcasm. "Because our plumber is seventy-three and the electrician is sixty-seven."

"Don't talk back to me. You know what I'm saying. Your friend Gwen had no trouble landing a man with a paying job. Why can't you?"

I start to bang my head on the counter. Why the hell do I answer the damn phone? Note to self, do not answer the phone ever again when they call. After a few months they'll stop trying, probably assume I died from my wild ways.

"Well, this has been really great. Thanks for calling, Mom."

"Oh yes, well, good-bye, Saffron."

I want to hurl the phone across the room, but instead I take a few deep breaths before settling it back in its cradle. Why do they even bother to call? Unless my mom gets off on lecturing me, which is a definite possibility. They don't care about me, never did. How many times was I told I was a responsibility and a burden? That's why my relationship with Frank means so much. He is someone who really cares. I will not let the conversation get to me. I leave my house and head to the docks as planned.

When I arrive, I notice George Ward's boat is on its way out to sea in search of the mighty swordfish. Doug is already out checking on his lobster traps. Now the lobster festival I do enjoy. The activity at the docks is fairly slow, though, so I walk the rest of the way into town.

Town seems a bit more active. There is no festival scheduled for quite a few weeks. What else could draw people to this little town? I grab a cup of coffee and take a seat along Main Street to people watch. I am not there long when Josh walks over to join me.

"What are you doing?" he asks.

"Just enjoying the day."

He studies my face for a minute. "What's wrong?"

"My mom called."

"You of the low morals. I bet she had a field day about Logan, the artist."

I'm not sure why it continually surprises me that Josh has grown into such an insightful man. Maybe because I still see him as the kid who ate dirt. "Better. Logan who is only interested in me for my paycheck."

Josh throws his head back and laughs. "At least they're consistent."

A piercing noise practically makes my ears bleed. There is only one thing in this town that can make such a horrendous sound. Josh and I both turn to see Hattie and Hilde Fletcher driving down the street in their huge old beat-up Buick.

We notice the parking spot at the curb at the same time. "You don't think they're going to attempt to parallel park that boat?" Josh asks.

"Considering they can't drive a straight line without hitting something, no. I couldn't even parallel park that thing."

But as we sit there and watch Hattie pulls up just past the spot and stops. I groan out loud. "Oh no. That is an extraordinarily bad idea."

"Whose car is that?" Josh points to the car in front of the spot Hattie is attempting to park in. It's a fancy car, one I haven't seen before, and it probably costs more than I make in three years.

"I don't know but it's about to become a hood ornament."

"We should stop them," Josh says as he starts to stand. I'm getting up after him, but then I spot my new neighbor. I immediately grab Josh's arm and pull him back down to the bench.

"What are you doing?"

"My new neighbor—hide me."

"What new neighbor? You don't have any neighbors."

"The old Keller place sold."

"The Keller place, when?"

"I don't know, but I noticed the moving van earlier on my jog. I planned on stopping by later in the week to say hello, but she was on my front step when I got home."

"She moves fast. So you didn't like her?"

"In the ten minutes of our conversation she asked me what I did, if I was dating, and would I take her around town. Abrasive and pushy puts it mildly."

Josh turns to look at the woman in question. "I won't like her either, then."

"No, you won't."

"She sure does dress nicely, though."

He isn't wrong. She's wearing Seven jeans and an Armani tweed jacket in Harrington, land of the swordfish.

"Why, Josh? Why would someone who dresses like that move here?"

"Good question. Looks like the car is hers."

Elise runs in her Manolos to get to her car before Hattie starts her parallel parking attempt.

"Shouldn't we help?" Josh asked.

"We're likely to only make it worse. If we startle Hattie, who knows what she'll do."

Josh turns fully around so he can glare at me. "You're hoping that Hattie hits your neighbor's car."

"No, Josh, that's an awful thing to say, but I do wish I'd thought to bring popcorn, because this is turning out to be one hell of a show."

Elise is now yelling at Hattie, Hilde is yelling at Elise, and all of that commotion is dangerous with Hattie's foot so close to the accelerator. On a good day Hattie gets the two confused, but with someone yelling at her, it's going to make her panic and then anything goes. I can hear the *Jaws* music playing in my head, Hattie's car being the shark.

"Oh no," Josh whispers as Hattie does hit the accelerator too hard and the car lurches backward. The movement startles her and she moves the wheel any which way. She comes inches from slamming into the car behind her before her car comes to a jerky stop.

"Let's go help." We're about to move from our spot when Jake appears.

As Jake handles the situation, my neighbor glares at him and even appears to glare into the car at Hattie and Hilde before she climbs into her own car and peels away.

"For a woman looking for a man, she didn't pay very much notice to our most eligible bachelor," I comment mostly to myself.

"Maybe he isn't her type."

I start down the street with Josh but I don't agree with his comment. For someone who specifically asked about eligible young men, her behavior wasn't just rude, it was odd.

CHAPTER SIX

Standing behind the bar at Tucker's, I study the few new faces that are becoming regulars. There are three women: two brunettes and a blonde. They stand out because their faces are so made up it has to take them at least an hour to apply their makeup. And the blonde's hair is beautifully highlighted. She definitely didn't get her color treatment here. So why all the glam to sit in a fisherman's watering hole? My curiosity, which is much like a cat's, finally gets the better of me and I saunter over to their table.

"Can I get you another round?"

"Yes, please," the blonde, maybe in her late thirties, replies as she stops her conversation to look at me.

I feel compelled to say something, since she's continuing to stare at me rather intently. "Are you enjoying your stay in Harrington?"

No answer except for a nonverbal one that passes between the ladies in reaction to my question.

"Actually, are you familiar with David Cambre?" she asks.

"He's that famous guy, an artist or something."

"A sculptor. We were just discussing him and his work. He's a genius."

I have to take their word for it, since I have never seen a David Cambre sculpture.

"He would feel at home here, all the inspiration and the solitude." The woman hesitates a moment before she takes out a black-and-white photo of a man. My God, he is the most beautiful man I have ever seen: short, spiky hair and a face that even Adonis would envy. But the eyes hold my attention—there's an arrogance about them that is both wickedly sexy and oddly familiar.

"Wait, isn't he the one who modeled that line for Armani a few years back?" How could I forget that face or body? Not only was he splashed over all the fashion magazines but every tabloid wanted a piece of him. A bit of a playboy, that one. I think I taped one of his spreads on my wall for a time.

"Yeah, have you seen him?"

"Here, in Harrington? No. Believe me, if that man was here, we would know."

The woman's shoulders slump, which I understand completely, before she slips the photo back in her bag. "That's what I thought. Oh well. We'll take the next round and then the check."

"Sure. Can I ask why you're looking for him?"

She regards me as if I've started to drool as I speak. "Well, he's gorgeous, single, and aloof, and the combination is too great a challenge for us."

I'm tempted to point out that they are acting very much like stalkers—having tested my feet in the waters as a stalker that night at Logan's house, I know what I'm talking about—but instead I smile despite my disgust. Poor David.

A few hours later the door opens, and in walks Logan. I haven't seen him in over a week and, I have to say, he is a sight for sore eyes. I've missed him, my Bigfoot. His facial hair is shaggy again, which means that while he paints, he clearly doesn't groom. He walks to his spot at the bar, catches my eye, and winks. Tommy is there to take his order and calls to me from down the bar, "Saffron, can you get Logan a Guinness?"

"Sure thing." I build the Guinness and bring it to him. He isn't chatting with anyone. His focus is solely on me. After I place his beer down, he reaches for my hand to press a kiss in my palm.

"I've missed you," he whispers. My hand tingles where his lips touched.

"I've missed you. How's the painting?"

"I finished it."

"That's exciting. Are you happy with it?"

"I am, but it's the opinion of the one I painted it for that matters to me."

"Oh. Like a special order?"

"Something like that. Have dinner with me tomorrow night?"

"Sure."

"I'll pick you up around half past six?"

"Okay." Before we can continue our conversation someone calls an order to me.

"I better get back to work. Enjoy your beer."

"I'll enjoy watching you more." In response, I nearly fumble over my own feet as I turn to walk down the bar, the sound of his chuckle following me.

As I fix the drink, my thoughts remain on Logan. I love his grin and how the subtle movement of his lips transforms his face and causes that sparkle to flash in his emerald eyes. I love how he can do something as casual as glance at me from over the rim of his glass and it causes my pulse to soar. I love how incredibly sexy he looks in his flannel and faded jeans and how my name rolls off his tongue with that deep intonation that is so Logan. Standing there thinking about the man that stirs these reflections has me realizing that I am dangerously close to falling in love with him. The bottle of gin I'm holding slips from my fingers and crashes to the floor.

"Ah hell."

"Saffron, are you all right?" Tommy's at my side in an instant. "You're as pale as a sheet."

It takes me a minute to find my voice because I'm still in mild shock. It's too soon, I know very little about Logan, but my heart doesn't seem to care. "I'm fine, I just think I need a bit of air."

Before he can object, I move from around the bar and step outside into the cool night. I'm not alone for long when Logan appears before me. "What happened in there?"

No way I am sharing. "Nothing."

"It didn't look like nothing." There's curiosity in his expression, but there's also tenderness. He touches a lock of my hair before his finger brushes lightly against my cheek. His voice is very soft when he asks, "Why are you looking at me like that?"

Oh, how easy it would be to fall completely for him. I answer almost without thought, "I've missed you."

Sitting on my front step the following night, I'm waiting for Logan. My thoughts are on Frank's request that I make myself happy. *He'll* be happy to learn that I am happy, happier than I've been in a long time. Logan makes me happy. I've a bit of regret that we wasted six months, but then our six months of observing is probably why we're so comfortable with each other now.

The sound of a motorcycle coming down the street catches my attention seconds before Logan appears. Logan straddling a motorcycle; that is a picture. He shuts off the engine and climbs off to greet me as I walk down the path.

His perusal is both thorough and arousing because I know exactly what's going on in his head. He likes the dress on me, would like it even more off me.

"Beautiful."

Hearing that word from him about me makes me feel beautiful.

Logan is taking me to dinner at The Harbor, which is where Mitch works. When we arrive, a quiet table in a corner has been reserved for us. Wine is served, meals are ordered, and then Logan's focus narrows to me.

"The chef here is married to your friend?"

I don't remember mentioning that. "Yeah, how did you know?"

"When I called to make the reservations, the receptionist turned very chatty."

"More so because it was you on the line, I'm sure."

His grin is his only response.

"Mitch is the chef and, yes, he's married to Gwen."

"You, Gwen, and Tommy have been friends a long time."

"And Josh, you can't forget Josh. We're all only children, and found what we didn't have from siblings with each other. What about you? Any longtime childhood friends you left when you moved here?"

"No, but I have two brothers who live in Manhattan."

"Are you close?"

"Very."

"Older or younger?"

"One of each."

"Are they like you?"

"Meaning?"

"Hot."

Speaking of hot, I'm nearly scorched from the heat of his pointed stare. "I'm hardly the judge as to whether my brothers are hot, but we all look very much alike."

"So that's a yes. Your poor parents. Do they live in Manhattan too?"

"No, they're in Scotland."

"Really? Moved there or are they from there originally?"

"Originally, lived here for a time, but they prefer home."

"And you, when did you come here?"

"A long time ago. What about you? You never mention your parents."

The change of subject isn't lost on me, but I move on. "We aren't close. That sounds so generic. The truth is my parents didn't want kids. I happened and they dealt, but not well. For the longest time I thought there was something wrong with me that kept them at a distance. It was Frank who finally got through to me that my parents' indifference stems from something missing in them.

"I'd watch my friends with their families, the closeness, the desire to be together and I can't lie, it hurt that I never had that until Frank. And even with Frank, there were just some things I didn't get to experience."

"Like what?"

"It's silly but I always wanted to go on a family vacation. I didn't need Europe or South America, but somewhere that wasn't home, where we could be tourists together. Even watching movies in our room, in a place that wasn't home, would have been fun."

"Did you ever tell them that?"

"I did, once. Halloween was coming up and as it was my favorite holiday, I had this wonderful idea that we could go to Salem. What better place to experience Halloween than Salem, Massachusetts? I even did some research, finding bed-and-breakfasts, attractions we could see. I had the whole trip planned."

"What happened?" The tenderness I had heard only minutes before had an edge to it, a hardness.

My gaze met his. "Nothing. They said Halloween was a school night and that we couldn't afford to take a vacation. And that was the last time I asked about taking a vacation."

"How old were you?"

"Seven."

The mood definitely takes a nosedive. The waiter arrives at that moment with our food, Mitch following behind him.

"Hi, Mitch. Logan, do you remember Mitch from our funtastic time cleaning up dead swordfish on Main?"

Logan stands to shake Mitch's hand. "Yes, nice to see you again."

"Likewise. I hope you enjoy your meal."

The crab imperial smells divine. "Always do."

Logan had ordered the surf and turf. The smell of his steak gives me a temporary case of ordering envy.

Mitch presses a kiss to my head. "Have fun."

"Thanks, Mitch." But my eyes stay on Logan's dinner, because, damn, that really looks good.

"Would you like some?" This question catches me by surprise.

"Seriously? You're okay with sharing? Most of my dates hate when I ask to taste their food."

"Saffron." His tone has grown rather severe.

"Yes?"

"First, I don't want to hear about your other dates, it'll only piss me off. You are here with me."

Possessive much? And yet that declaration has my tummy flip-flopping in pleasure.

"Fair. What's two?"

"If I don't share then I won't be getting any of that and I really want to try that."

"Oh, Logan, yes you do. This is like crack."

His smile comes in a flash. "Then hand me your bread plate."

It's Wednesday, so I'm getting ready for my date with Frank. Thinking about turning thirty next week has me questioning my life choices. I'm not suddenly agreeing with my parents regarding my choice of vocations, but after my dinner with Logan, I haven't been able to get it from my head that I have never traveled outside of Harrington, except for school. But even then I was still in Maine. That's crazy.

There's a great big world out there and it's time for me to get out there and see some of it. New York City isn't that far, and though I'd love nothing more than to see it with Logan, he seems to want to keep that part of his life separate from the life he's making in Maine. I say this because though he knows I'm now dying to see New York City, dying to travel, he has never offered to take me. I'm forced to accept that for whatever reason, he doesn't want his two worlds colliding. Josh and Gwen would go to New York with me. We could take Josh's car so Derek and Mitch could join us. Gwen's parents would be thrilled to have the kids for a few days. I'll have to ask them if we can swing it.

After getting dressed, I hurry out the door. I'm about to climb into my car when I notice the one tire is flat. Hunching down, I see it isn't just flat. It looks like I tore it up on something. I don't have a spare. My cell is once again dead, so I head back inside and call Logan's cell.

"Saffron, hey. I thought you had dinner with Frank tonight."

"I do, but I've got a flat. Any chance you could give me a lift?"

"I'll be there in ten."

I'm waiting on my porch, looking at my pretty flowers, when the sexiest black car pulls up in front of my house. It's a Porsche; I know this only because I see the unmistakable emblem on the front. The driver's side door opens and Logan unfolds himself from it. Starving artist, he is not. I thought I'd be riding on his motorcycle, but I have to say, getting a chance to ride in a Porsche is sweet.

"Nice car."

He grins. "This old thing."

"Cute."

He starts up the path to me, but takes a moment to look at my car. He hunches down, and my eyes move over him as he studies my tire. I'm about to say something provocative, but when he stands, the strange expression on his face stops me.

"What's wrong?"

"Are you going to call Jake?"

"I have to, I don't have a spare yet."

That earns me a look. "You need a spare tire in your car, Saffron."

"I know. I just haven't gotten around to it."

"I'll have one delivered."

"Sweet, but not necessary."

"I'm going to do it anyway, so just say thank you."

"Pushy."

"You ready?" He grins.

"Yeah, and thanks for the ride."

He opens the car door for me. "Anytime."

I'm told that Frank isn't quite ready for me when I arrive and I'm asked to wait in the community room where the dancing is usually held. I make my way down the hall hoping that whatever is keeping Frank isn't anything serious. The room I'm instructed to wait in is dark, but as soon as I open the door, the lights glow to life followed by, "Surprise!"

It takes a moment for my eyes to adjust and for my brain to catch up. And then I see everyone, most of my friends wearing silly hats and carrying noise makers, grinning at me like lunatics. A surprise birthday party—I never had one. Josh, Tommy, and Gwen come immediately to my side, but I take a moment to look around the room filled with most of the residents of Harrington.

"You didn't know, did you?" Josh asks as he draws me into a hug.

"I didn't. I had no idea."

Gwen is laughing when she hugs me. "I thought that you might be suspecting something, but Josh and Tommy were certain that you were clueless."

"How long have you three been planning this?" I ask.

"Three months," Tommy says.

Three months, that's a long time. I look into the faces of the crowd that have come to celebrate my birth, finding two noticeably absent.

"We invited them, but they declined," Josh offers, knowing I am wondering why my parents are not in attendance.

"Yes, well, I'm sure they had better things to do than come to their only child's thirtieth birthday."

Gwen reaches for my hand and squeezes it. "I'm sorry."

I smile back at her. "Please. This is wonderful. Thank you so much."

Frank comes up to me then and, leaning over, I kiss his pale cheek. "Happy birthday, Saffron."

"I was a little curious when I arrived for our dinner and you weren't ready. When has that ever happened?"

He chuckles as his frail hand touches my arm. "Save me a dance."

"I will."

Making my way through the crowd, I'm showered with kisses and hugs and wished countless birthday greetings. The feeling of belonging that moves through me as I greet each and every person in the room renders me something akin to drunk. Finally, I stop in front of the tall, silent man in the corner. He draws me near and brushes his lips over my ear. "Happy birthday."

It's all a bit overwhelming, the outpouring from my friends, that it has the back of my eyes burning. "You knew?"

"Yes."

"You'll stay, right?"

"All night if you'll have me."

"I wouldn't want you anywhere else."

I swear I see my emotions reflected back at me, but then the toasts begin and we are pulled into the center of joyous chaos.

Later in the night I sit with Frank. "How are you feeling, Frank?" He looks really tired.

"I'm good. How do you like your party?"

"I love having all of my friends together in one place."

"You are a wonderful young woman, and I know there is a part of you that is sad that those sorry excuses for parents didn't come, but look around you. You are loved; remember that. Remember that you know what is best for you. Promise me you will always listen to your heart."

He's scaring me with how intense he's being, but I can see that it's very important to him, so I make the promise and mean it. "I will."

"I think of you as a daughter. Family is more than blood, and sometimes blood relations can be nothing at all like you, as proven by your parents. Family is the ones who you love and who love you and based on this turnout, I would say you have a pretty big, loving family."

Love for this man swells in me as I hold his hand to my cheek. "Thank you for that. I've always thought of *you* as my family."

"You've brought great joy to an old man's heart and gave me family when I had none."

"Likewise, Frank."

"I love you."

"Ah, Frank, I love you too."

Hugging him, I feel just how very thin he is, but before long he's pulling back and smiling at me. "Happy birthday. I think it's time for me to go to bed."

"I'll take you."

"No, you stay and celebrate."

"Okay, good night, Frank."

"Good night."

Frank is wheeled from the room and my heart hurts as I watch. He was so sentimental, and while I know part of it is because of the party, I worry that there is another reason. Almost as if he knows it will be the last time we will have the chance to see each other.

Much later that night Logan takes me back to his house so he can give me my birthday gift. We walk upstairs to his studio, and there resting on the easel is a small portrait of Frank and me. We are in the dining room at Harrington Commons laughing about something. You can feel the energy of the piece.

"I don't usually paint portraits, but when I saw you both that day I couldn't get it out of my head. It's beautiful to watch the two of you."

I haven't any words; it is hands down the best gift I've ever received and then I open my mouth and say just that.

He brings me to him and as his mouth fuses to mine, he lifts me into his arms and carries me to his bed. Gently he lowers me onto it. The loss of his lips is countered by nimble fingers working my sandals off my feet. His hands slide up my leg, over my calf and knee, up my thigh, and I inhale sharply because it feels *so* good.

Fisting my dress into his hands, he pulls it up and over my head before he kisses me, right over my heart. Licking the swells of my breasts, he pops one of those aching peaks out from under my bra and sucks it into his mouth. His clever fingers dance along my stomach, his mouth following the path, until he reaches the edge of my panties. Slowly he works the silk down my legs. Grabbing the back of his shirt, he yanks it forward over his head before he steps out of his trousers. He's magnificent and when he moves toward the bed, it's with the sleek movements of a predator. The bed dips from his weight seconds before his warm hands are on my knees pushing me open wider. My body is almost overstimulated because I'm so eager to feel his mouth on me. He tastes me, lapping at me like I'm his favorite flavor, teasing me as he works my overly sensitive flesh with his tongue. Watching him, seeing his dark head between my legs and feeling what his tongue is doing to me turns me wanton as my hips move against his mouth. He brings me right to the brink of orgasm and then his mouth is gone.

"Look at me, Saffron." My eyes lift to his as he slowly pushes into me. My legs spread wider and my hips lift and take him deeper. We freeze for a moment because it feels so goddamn good, and then he starts to move. Slowly at first, until he feels me coming apart, then his mouth finds mine and he moves harder and faster, and when I come, he does too.

The following afternoon I'm in the midst of pouring a glass of Cabernet when the bar phone rings. Before I can reach it, Tommy's there. He isn't on the phone for long, but when he walks up to me with sorrow in his expression, I know something is very wrong.

"What is it?"

"It's Frank. He's had a heart attack."

The bottle I'm holding slips right out of my hand, but Tommy's quick reflexes catch it before it falls to the floor.

"Jimmy, I'm taking Saffron to Harrington Commons. You and Sarah need to cover things until I get back."

"Sure thing, boss."

Tommy pulls me from the bar and gets me in his car and clicks my seat belt, since I'm fairly useless from the shock, before climbing in and driving the five miles to the nursing home. When we arrive one of the nurses, Sandra, is waiting for me. I know from the look on her face that he's gone.

"I'm so sorry, but he didn't suffer. It was very fast."

I'm completely and totally numb. I dread asking but I have to know: "Was he alone?"

"Some of his friends were with him."

That's good, that's something. Frank must have known or sensed what was coming. I knew he wasn't going to live forever, but now that he's gone there is a rather large hole in my heart.

"I need to make arrangements. Um, I should go. I have a lot to do. You'll let me know when I can . . . when he's ready."

"Yes, of course."

"Thank you, Sandra. Frank was very fond of you." And he had been. He'd often said the staff made the place feel like a home. They loved their work and it showed in everything they did.

I move with purpose out of the building and down the street.

"Saffron, I'll drive you home," Tommy calls as he comes up beside me.

"No, I think I'll walk." But I stop and turn to him to hug him hard. "Thank you, but I need to be alone."

"Call me if you need anything."

I pull away from him and my throat burns. "I will."

And then I'm walking and with each step that takes me away from Frank, the more the reality of my loss sinks in. I pass the lighthouse and see the lights on inside, remembering the night Logan and I shared, but not even Logan can heal the wound caused by Frank's passing. I keep on walking. As soon as I reach home, I see the answering machine light blinking. I know it'll be Gwen or Josh calling, but I can't deal with that right now.

Curling up on my bed, I stare at the portrait Logan painted. It was a spectacular gift when it was given to me last night, but now it's that much more. The man Frank was to me. I don't know how much time passes before the knocking at the door starts, but after a while whoever is there gives up and the blessed silence returns. Lying there dry-eyed, I stare into the darkness at the portrait I can no longer see until exhaustion claims me.

The following morning I make arrangements with the funeral home, the florist, Tucker's, and manage to avoid everyone else. Two days later I sit at the memorial and listen as the priest speaks the words while I stare at Logan's beautiful portrait.

So lost in my sorrow, I don't realize the priest has finished and, once I do notice, I can't get myself to move. I hear the soft hum of voices around me and realize that someone is talking to me. It's Hilde Fletcher.

"I'm sorry for your lost. Frank was a good man. He will be missed."

She doesn't wait for an answer and I'm grateful for that, since I don't think I have one in me.

"He was like a father to her. I can't believe he's gone," Claire murmurs to Bob, who looks to me. I try for a small smile, but it's weak. He understands, since he lost a friend too. Around me I hear people sharing stories about Frank, remembering the man and friend he had been and every one of those stories is in the past tense. The idea that Frank is gone, that any reference to him won't be in the here and now but as a memory, a recollection of the man he had been, tightens my throat. There's anger too, a bitterness because I feel cheated. Frank was everything to me, *knew* everything about me, and yet he held a piece of himself back. And now, it's too late to know that part of him. I'll never know what it was that put that lost look in his eyes or made the absent-minded smile appear on his mouth. He was gone—my friend, my family, was gone. The weight of my grief overwhelms me, the heaviness in my chest making it difficult to breathe.

"Saffron."

Tommy. Silently I move into him, borrowing some of his strength to help me make it through the day. He says nothing, offers no words of condolence, he just holds me close.

"We need to start over to Tucker's," Gwen says and thank God for her, keeping us on track, since I'm failing miserably at keeping anything on track.

"I'll drive her over," Tommy says and I allow him to lead me to the car, need him to, since my legs refuse to work. Tucker's is packed, the whole town of Harrington is present. Frank told me that he didn't want people to mourn for him, that he disliked funerals because the atmosphere was always so somber when the celebrating of a life should be joyous. Death wasn't the end, it was another beginning, and he wanted us to celebrate that. So in keeping with his wishes, I tap my glass to get everyone's attention.

"Frank didn't want a funeral. He wanted everyone to have a drink to him, wanted us to remember his life and not mourn his death. I had planned to share some of my own memories of Frank but"—blinking to keep the tears from falling, I struggle for control—"it's too painful and far too soon for me to remember and not mourn. So I will say, simply, he was for me all a person could be for another, and I hope that I was that for him too. He was truly the finest person I have ever had the pleasure of knowing."

I lift my Scotch toward his urn in a place of pride on the bar. "To his life and the great joy he brought to mine."

Returning my glass, my eyes collide with a pair of green ones. Logan is across the room, but he has made no move to approach me. In his expression lurks tenderness and understanding, offering me silent comfort while respecting that I may need space.

I can't stay any longer because the tears are too close. I want to be in my house when I fall apart, so I slip from the celebration of Frank's life and walk home with Frank cradled in my arms. There's a knock at my door just as I finish changing, and I know who it is even before I open it. Logan walks in and embraces me. And just like that, the tears I've successfully held back for days come pouring out of me as I mourn my friend.

CHAPTER SEVEN

I can't count how many times in the weeks that follow Frank's funeral I see something that I want to share with him and reach for the phone only to remember he won't be on the other end. I haven't been back to his room at the nursing home, can't get myself to do it. Seeing his bed, stripped of sheets, the walls bare, his belongings boxed . . . I'm not ready for that.

On the flip side, Frank's death has brought our town even closer. Most of the town make their way to Tucker's in the weeks since his death, neighbors sitting with neighbors, sharing their stories about Frank. It's touching to know how many people Frank affected.

One day I receive a call from his lawyer asking me to come to his office for the reading of Frank's will. I'm surprised by the call because Frank had very little. His possessions only filled a few boxes. The lawyer's office is in Bar Harbor, in a nice brick town house with an elegant but understated sign hanging over the door. Dean Finley, Esquire, seems a bit swanky for Frank, from his gray-laced blond hair to his perfectly tailored charcoal-gray suit, but then there are no lawyers in Harrington, so perhaps it's just his location that appealed to Frank. I have to give Finley points for greeting me personally.

"Ms. Mills?"

"Yes."

"Hello. I'm Dean Finley. Please, right this way."

I am led into a very masculine office with dark-chocolate-brown leather furniture, a walnut desk, and floor-to-ceiling bookcases. The rug that rests under the antique desk is done in deep jewel tones that complement the dark tan of the walls.

"Please have a seat. Can I bring you some coffee or water?"

"No, thank you, I'm fine."

He settles behind his desk before lifting open the file in front of him.

"First, I am really very saddened by the loss of Mr. Dupree. He was a friend even more than a client."

"I'm sorry, I didn't know or I would have called you about his memorial."

He reaches across the table and rests his hand on mine. "Please don't. I know this has been very hard for you. Frank often spoke of you and how much you meant to him."

My tears start again.

"I won't keep you any longer than necessary. Frank's will is pretty cut and dried. Since you were his only family, he has left everything to you."

A smile touches my lips thinking about the few possessions that Frank had at the home—the ancient chess set and his nice collection of baseball cards that, though I don't know much about baseball, I'll treasure always.

"His total estate, including the house in the Hudson River Valley, is worth just over six million dollars."

My mouth drops open and I just stare at the man. I'm sure my expression makes me look like a half-wit, but I can't have just heard what I think I heard. "Could you repeat that?"

"He invested well and almost tripled his net worth, which is now about six million dollars, as I said."

"And he left that to me?"

"Yes."

Standing, since I'm too worked up to sit, I start to pace. "What the hell was the man thinking leaving me all that money?"

"He knew you would know what to do with it."

Stopping my pacing, I turn and glare at him. "I haven't a clue what to do with all that money."

"I realize this is a lot to take in. The money is there whenever you are ready to claim it. Until that time, it will continue to be invested as Frank stipulated."

I am so not ready for this. "I can leave it as is for now?"

"Yes, for as long as you wish."

"I just can't think about it right now."

"Understood."

"He really had no one? You can't find any third cousins four times removed?"

"No."

"Doesn't seem right that someone so wonderful really had no other family."

Mr. Finley comes from around his desk to stand just in front of me. "He had you."

Yes, he did, and that thought brings a smile.

"Here's my card. If you need anything, please don't hesitate to call."

"Thank you, Mr. Finley."

"Please call me Dean, Ms. Mills."

"Saffron. Thank you for everything, Dean. I'll be in touch when I'm ready to accept Frank's gift."

Several weeks pass since my meeting with the lawyer and, though I know I need to address the issue of the six million dollars, I'm currently riding on the train of denial. I miss Frank to the point that I catch myself wallowing in sorrow, but Frank would not be pleased to see me behaving in such a way. He wanted me to be happy, wanted me to do what I needed to do to be happy. Luckily for me my quest to be happy is made a bit easier because another festival approaches—the God of the Sea Festival—dedicated completely to the sea and the fruits of her bounty. And she is bountiful—the food for this festival, unlike the Swordfish Festival, is amazing. Lobster rolls, fish and chips, shrimp scampi . . . it goes on and on. As part of the festival, because we're a dramatic group in Harrington, we've included an offering to the sea this year. I was selected as that offering, and so I'll be dressed in white and draped in flowers. I will ride a float down Main Street before being taken out into the harbor and dropped into the water. Yes, I am going to be tossed into the sea and since the temperatures are turning cooler, it isn't going to be pleasant.

Another thought that continues to plague me is that Chastity's blackball didn't include this activity. Even she will enjoy watching me being chucked into the ocean. In honor of my sacrifice in three days, my friends are taking me dancing. Bar Harbor has a very cool dance club that is geared to people in their thirties—the liquor is top shelf and the crowd is made up of young professionals.

While in the bathroom getting ready, a favorite song starts pumping from my iPod, so I grab my brush and start singing along. It happens to be good practice, since there will be karaoke tonight and Josh and I have an ongoing dare—a coin toss and the loser has to perform. It's nerve-racking when I lose the toss. My knees knock so hard people can hear them, but I love getting up on that stage.

Logan is joining us tonight, which both surprises and thrills me, because he really doesn't seem the type for dancing. He even offered to drive and I can't deny that if we are taking his bike, I am going to seriously enjoy the ride.

A knock at my door signals Logan's arrival and when I pull it open, I immediately forget how to breathe. He's dressed in all black: flat-front trousers and an Oxford shirt with the top few buttons undone to expose the golden skin of his neck and throat. He looks elegant but there is no denying the powerfully built body hidden under the tailored clothes.

His beard is trimmed and his hair is pulled back into a ponytail. He's absolutely gorgeous and before I realize it, I open my mouth and say as much. A grin tugs at the corner of his mouth before he leans in and kisses me.

"Are you ready?"

"Yes." I close the door behind me and take his hand. He leads me toward the street just in front of my house where his Porsche is parked. I run my finger over the top of the car. Even the paint job is sexy. "You think I could drive her sometime?"

"You can drive a manual transmission?"

"Yep."

He seems to consider this for a minute. "I'm sure you can find ways to persuade me to let you drive my baby."

The image of me, flat on my back, legs spread, and Logan between them flashes in my head. Suddenly I'm totally turned on. "Oh yeah, I think I can find a few ways."

He grabs me. "You look wicked. What are you thinking?"

"And spoil the fun?"

"Saffron."

"Well, let's just say it involves you, me, this car, and no clothes."

I'm pressed up against him, so I know he likes this idea, a lot.

"I shouldn't have asked," he grumbles.

"Why?" I ask in all sweetness.

"You know exactly why, brat."

"Maybe you'll have to spank me later." Where the hell did that come from? And yet the idea is not unappealing.

"Get in the car," comes out in a growl. He holds the passenger door open for me and I climb in. The seat envelops me with soft leather.

When Logan climbs in next to me, his large frame fits so comfortably, though I suspect there are parts of him that are presently not so comfortable. Reaching over his lap, I rub him. Oh yeah, definitely not comfortable.

His eyes close on a moan. Fueled by his reaction and the fact that my closest neighbor is a mile away, I unzip his trousers and pull him free.

"What are you doing?" he groans and yet he sounds hopeful.

Instead of answering with words, I lean over and take him into my mouth.

"Oh fuck."

I wish. He pushes his seat back so I have more room and then I just go to town. I love the feel of him in my mouth, so thick and big, the tip touching the back of my throat. Steel wrapped in silk. Grabbing the base, I squeeze while working him until I feel his body tense, moments before his saltiness fills my mouth. Swallowing, I give him a minute before I tuck him back in his trousers.

Our gazes lock and then he's kissing me, sweeping my mouth with his tongue, tasting himself and me.

I no longer want to go dancing.

The engine purrs to life like a large, feral cat. Logan turns to me with a wickedness about him, which I'm guessing is because he's feeling rather good at the moment. "You can totally drive my car."

I hold his gaze for a beat or two before I bust out laughing.

We reach the club and for the first few minutes, my friends drool over Logan's car. After, we make our way inside and grab a table and our waitress wastes no time coming over and taking our drink orders.

"You ready, Saffron?" Josh calls from across the table.

Logan looks from Josh to me. "Ready for what?"

Josh answers before I can. "We have a tradition. One coin toss and the loser has to sing"—Josh points to the stage where a nervous woman is butchering an Annie Lennox song—"up there."

Logan whispers in my ear, "I hope you lose the toss."

My body clenches from his nearness, especially after the fabulous way we started the evening. "Well, considering I seem to lose the toss all the time, the odds are very much in your favor."

Josh pulls out the coin and gives it to Mitch, who tosses it up and catches it. I call tails, but it's heads. Like always. At some point it has got to come up tails. Josh grins.

"I'll go with you to put your name in with the DJ."

"Thanks, Josh, you're so helpful."

We sit around chatting and then I'm called to the stage. I'm not sure what to sing, but the DJ is full of suggestions, so I settle on Pink. As the music pumps from the speakers, and my voice blends with it, I lose myself to the song and the moment. Before long the song comes to an end and I slowly come back to reality, my five minutes of stardom over. I'm met at the bottom by a friendly face.

"Hey, Saffron."

It takes me a moment to realize that the man standing before me in faded jeans and a black sweater is Dean Finley, Esquire.

"Mr. Finley, Dean, hi."

"You don't get nervous going up there?"

"A little, but it's so much fun. Have you ever tried it?"

"No chance."

"You don't know what you're missing." I take a minute to study him because he looks casual and comfortable, nothing like the professional I met a few weeks back. "It's nice to see you again, how are you?"

"Good, better now that I'm seeing you. Are you here with friends?"

Didn't pick up on the vibe the last time we met, but there's definitely more than a passing interest coming from Dean. A dry spell for years and now that I'm with someone: feast or famine.

"Yeah, they're around somewhere." Turning in a circle, I see Logan and wave him over. As soon as he's in reaching distance, I take his hand. "This is Dean. He was Frank's lawyer. Dean, my boyfriend, Logan."

The men shake hands and exchange pleasantries. Dean's not looking as excited as he had before Logan appeared, but now he knows. At our table, I make the introductions and, while Dean gets acquainted with my friends, Logan leads me out onto the dance floor.

He holds me close as we sway to the music. He studies me in that way of his. I'm about to ask what he's thinking, but my lips are soon occupied as he kisses me in a drugging, all-consuming melding of our mouths right there on the dance floor. I would never have thought that Logan would be one for public displays of affection. Of course after our semi-public display earlier, I could be a little off base, but with the way his kiss sizzles every nerve in my body, I am all for them. When the song ends, Logan leads me back to our table. He stands just behind me after I've taken my seat, so I don't hesitate to rest my back against his hard, muscled frame.

I'm enjoying the warmth radiating off Logan's powerful body when Josh says, "As usual, you kicked it big on that stage, doll."

"Thank you, but next time it's your turn. Don't you agree, Derek?"

"Oh yes."

Mitch and Gwen are both grinning at me. "What? What are you smiling about?"

"You haven't figured it out yet," says Gwen.

"Figured out what?"

Gwen urges Josh. "Show her the coin."

And then I know. "A two-headed coin, are you kidding me?"

Josh's smile is completely unrepentant. "One must make one's own luck, as I am forever saying."

"You never say that," Derek and I say in unison.

"Yes, I've been cheating, but I do so enjoy listening to you sing and, since you enjoy doing it, I didn't see the harm."

"Seriously, next time you have to get up there."

His hands go up in defeat. "Fine."

"Maybe we should have karaoke night at Tucker's."

"I think that's a great idea, Tommy, and Josh can be the first one to try out the equipment," I say.

Tommy points his beer at me. "You'll help me figure it out?"

"Absolutely."

"Deal." Josh groans and Tommy hides his grin with his beer.

"I'm really not getting out of this, am I?" Josh almost looks ill, but I feel no sympathy.

"Nope," I say with relish.

We stay for a few hours longer before we decide to call it a night. Outside, Dean says good-bye to my friends before he turns to me. "I really enjoyed this. Thanks for including me."

"It was our pleasure."

"You look happier than the last time I saw you, so I'm hoping that means you're finding your way through this."

"I am. Every day it gets a bit easier."

He reaches for my hand to brush his lips over my knuckles. "I hope the next time you're in my neck of the woods you'll look me up."

"I'd like that."

"Good night," he says before he turns and strolls away.

"Good night," I call after him before I turn around and notice that everyone has already gone to their cars. Only Logan stands there. Though he looks casual, with his hands in the front pockets of his pants, I can tell something lurks just under the surface. But he says nothing. I move to him and his arms immediately come around me to hold me close. I feel his words rumbling in his chest. "Are you ready?"

"One more minute."

He chuckles, but gives me my minute to hold him before escorting me to his car. We drive in silence and when we reach my house, Logan shuts off the engine and climbs from the car to walk around and open the door for me. As soon as I am standing next to him on the curb, he pulls me to him for a kiss—one that is almost painful at first until it softens and thoroughly melts my bones.

"What was that for?" I ask when he takes a step away.

Fire blazes in his eyes, but what or whom it's directed at, I don't know. A few tense moments later he rubs his hand over the back of his neck like he's rubbing the bad mood away. "I'm sorry."

"For what?"

The pause is so pregnant, I think he isn't going to answer, but when he does I'm baffled and overjoyed at the same time.

"I didn't like watching you with Dean. I know it's unfair of me, but I can't help it."

Was he jealous? If he's looking for a way to render me speechless, he has found it, but before I can even attempt to get my brain around his statement, he continues.

"I haven't told you much about my life because there isn't much worth sharing." His fingers lace through my hair. "My life before led me here and that's all that matters."

The beauty of that statement leaves me speechless and is all it takes for me to fall the rest of the way for him.

———

The next morning I wake early and head to the kitchen to start the coffee. Logan is still sleeping when I come back to bed. *My life before led me here and that's all that matters.* I haven't been able to get those words out of my head. Not only are the words the most incredible I've ever been on the receiving end of, but there was no denying he meant every word. As he lies on his stomach, the hard contours of his back are visible since the sheet has slipped to rest at the base of his spine. His face is turned to me and I can't help but wonder what he would look like if he shaved.

What I fear is that, underneath my yeti, there is a staggeringly beautiful man. Why would said man have any interest in me?

He speaks without bothering to open his eyes. "You're thinking too loud." When his eyes do open, they reflect the cloudiness of sleep. And then he moves so quickly, pinning me beneath his hard body. For a long moment we just look at one another.

"Shave it," I whisper. "I want to see your face."

He tenses, and I feel his muscles quicken against mine before he lowers his head and silences me with a soul-searing kiss.

CHAPTER EIGHT

Nervousness fills me as my float moves down Main Street. To my surprise there are lots of people along the parade route cheering me on, but I can't help wonder if they're cheering so boisterously because they won't be catapulted into the cold and turbulent sea. The weather isn't looking particularly pleasant.

My dress is a lovely confection of satin and lace. Gwen is the one responsible for my curling tresses laced with flowers and my perfectly applied makeup, but in under ten minutes I'm going to look like a drowned rat.

As I wave and paste a smile on my face, I think back to Logan. After I asked him to shave, he said not one word, but proceeded to swallow me up with the most intense loving I have ever experienced. He blew my mind with passion and then he left. I haven't seen or spoken to him since and that was two days ago. Our first time making love, he takes off for a week, and now this. Who would have thought the request for him to shave would have elicited that response? Maybe he's just hiding, but from what or who I don't know.

My breath freezes in my lungs at the sight of the sky as we reach the harbor. It's ominous but I'm not the only one to notice. Sheriff Dwight walks over to me as I climb from the float to stand near the bulkhead, his focus on the whitecaps.

"We're going to cancel. It's too rough out there."

My exhale turns into a sigh. "Thank you. I was really getting nervous."

"I can understand why. I'll let everyone know."

He walks away, but I stay where I am, watching as the blackest clouds come rolling in. The temperature has dropped too, and the spray from the sea is bitterly cold.

"Can I interview you for the paper?"

Glancing over, I see Elise. "Paper?"

"The *Harrington Times*."

What is there to interview about? The festival is canceled? I want to say this, but I decide it will be faster to just answer her questions.

"So, I imagine you are relieved?" A slight smile edges her face as she asks this.

"Yes."

"Can you tell me how this festival came to be?"

I imagine she already knows this, as does anyone who will read the paper, but I answer her anyway. She follows that question with another and another. Half an hour later she's wrapping up the interview. As she puts her notebook away, I wonder if maybe I misjudged her. She's abrasive, but she is not unkind, and she seems very sincere.

"Are you enjoying Harrington, Elise?"

She looks up at me and something is clearly on her mind but her expression puzzles me—expectant, or maybe eager is a better word— "I need to tell you something. I should have from the beginning, but I didn't want to blow my cover. You seem like a really nice person, though, and it's not fair to keep you in the dark."

My confusion must be etched in my forehead as Elise forges on.

"I'm not really moving to Harrington. I'm a reporter for the *New York Times* and I came here for a story. Do you know David Cambre?"

I remember the women in Tucker's a few weeks back who were also looking for David. Remember the black-and-white photo of the gorgeous man they showed me.

"I know of him."

"He's here in Harrington."

Another artist in Harrington? Not likely. Apprehension fills me. "And why is that a story?"

"He's famous, so that automatically makes him a story, but when the same man debuts a collection that leaves the art world in a frenzy to grab up his pieces and then disappears from sight, that's definitely a story." She studies me for a moment before she adds, "And when that same man gets engaged to a debutante, that too is a story."

Elise reaches into her briefcase and retrieves a sheet of paper. It's a photo, similar to the one the woman showed me in Tucker's. And though it's in color, I don't need it to be to see what I hadn't before. Logan looking back at me. The gorgeous man in the photo—the most beautiful man I've ever seen—is Logan without his disguise.

"Logan is David?" Stupid question, but shock is setting in.

She almost looks jubilant at the pain that is no doubt covering my expression. "Yes, and I'm sorry to have to be the one to tell you, but I think you have a right to know."

"Logan's engaged to someone?"

"Yes."

"Even though he's been living here alone for over half a year?"

She grips my hands almost painfully. "Saffron, they got engaged before he moved here, but she knows he likes his solitude when he's working, which is why she doesn't visit. He goes to her in Manhattan."

His words to me from the other night about his life leading him to me no longer incite joy but a pain that slices through me. My reply is barely audible. "Thank you for telling me."

She nods but says nothing else. After dropping that bomb, she just walks away. I stand there numb and sick as I replay her words in my head.

I don't want to believe her, but Logan's own actions are pretty damning: his refusal to take me to New York City and his odd reaction to my request that he shave. No wonder he keeps his face hidden. With a face like his, he'd constantly be drawing attention to himself. Turning from her retreating form, I see Logan coming down the street toward me. Clearly he sees me too, since he's moving with determined strides through the crowd to reach my side.

"You dodged that bullet." He reaches for a lock of my hair, but I take a step away from him. "Where have you been, Logan?"

He pushes his hands into the front pockets of his jeans. "I had business in Manhattan."

Manhattan. I feel my heart cracking and that turns my anger into something darker. "Really, why?"

He stands immobile for a minute and the only way I know he's even heard my question is the subtle clenching of his jaw.

"A sale."

Hurt turns to rage. "So what exactly is going on between us? Are we dating or are we just fucking?"

His eyes flash with anger before he lowers his head and hisses at me. "What's gotten into you?"

"How's the fiancée, David?"

He goes completely still and I can tell by the look on his face that Elise has told me the truth. A numbness spreads over me and my cracked heart shatters. I turn to walk away because I want to hurt him and don't trust myself not to. His hand wraps around my upper arm.

"Let me explain."

I refuse to look at him. "Are you David Cambre?" I ask, but my voice comes out no louder than a whisper.

"Yes."

"Are you engaged?"

"It's not what you think."

Despite my anger, I feel the sob burning its way up my throat.

"Give me a chance to explain."

And that is all it takes to unleash my temper. Spinning to face him, I snarl, "A chance, now, really? Because you had plenty of chances, but had no desire to share anything with me. So now that your secret is out, you're feeling chatty?"

"It isn't like that."

"Go back to Manhattan and to your fiancée because we're done." I try to pull from his hold, but he won't release me.

"Please," he whispers.

Looking into those green eyes, I know that I'm completely in love with him and, even so, everything between us was a lie. This realization makes me snap and before I know my intention, I'm curling my hand into a fist a second before I plow it right into his jaw. He releases me in shame, but with my balance off from throwing the punch, I pitch over the side of the bulkhead. The water is so cold. I'm struggling to keep my head up; I can hear the muffled voices of people screaming for help, the sound of footsteps pounding down the dock to get to me. My lungs burn and my arms grow tired. The weight of my dress proves too much as the sea pulls me under.

When I come to, I'm in the local clinic and it feels as if there's a hundred-pound cat on my chest between the pain in my lungs and the heating blankets they've piled on me. Recollection takes a moment and with it comes a sharp pain that spears the area near my heart, but I'm no longer in shock; I'm thinking more clearly. And that's why I doubt Elise's claim about Logan being engaged. Why she would lie? I have no idea, but I know Logan. I don't know Elise.

I trust Logan. But I can't deny that he, like Frank, has kept a big part of himself from me because I already knew there's a part of his world I'm not welcome in. Having that reality thrown in my face hurts like hell.

Gwen, Tommy, and Josh, seeing me awake, immediately hurry over.

"Oh my God, Saffron, you scared the hell out of us." Tommy brushes my hair back from my forehead, which gives me a good view of his face—he's so pale. My throat burns. Though I want to speak, no words come out. Gwen pours me a cup of water before helping me take a sip.

"Logan's outside and he really wants to see you."

I shake my head at that request.

"He saved your life. Not only did he jump into that icy water to pull you out, but he also revived you. You weren't breathing."

I died and Logan brought me back. I find that almost comical. He saved me, but he's also the one who broke me.

"He hasn't left all night and he looks like hell. You two had a fight, didn't you?" Josh can't hide his concern—it practically drips from his words.

I try to speak again and this time a sound comes out—soft but clear. "Elise told me he was engaged."

"What?" Tommy demands.

"And he's really David Cambre."

"The playboy?" Gwen asks, but I see the confusion on her face.

I can only nod in reply.

"I don't understand," Josh says, and I know it's what Gwen and Tommy are also thinking.

"When I asked Logan, he didn't deny it. I punched him and lost my balance and fell into the water."

A slight grin curves Josh's mouth. "So that's how you fell in."

I don't want to see Logan. I don't want to look into the eyes of the man I love, the same man who's been giving me only a piece of himself when I've given it all to him, but he saved my life so I don't really have a choice. "I'll see him."

"Are you sure?" Gwen asks.

"I owe him that."

A few minutes later Logan walks into the room. He's wearing sweats; clearly someone gave him something dry to wear, but there are purple smudges under his eyes and his complexion is pale. But it's his bereft look that softens my hardened heart.

"Saffron, how are you feeling?"

"I'll be fine. Thank you for saving me."

"I need to talk to you, but I know now is not the time."

"What is there to say, Logan, I mean, David?"

He reaches for my hand and lowers himself into the chair at my bedside.

"My name is Logan David MacGowan. I used David Cambre because I wanted some anonymity."

"And your fiancée?"

"That's a long story."

I don't realize a tear has escaped my full eyes until Logan brushes it from my cheek.

"I know you're upset and I have a lot I need to explain to you, but I hope you'll let me, because what I feel for you is something I have never felt before."

I want it all to just go away. It's too damn painful, but I give him more of a glimpse into me than he has ever given me of him. "In my heart I know you can't be engaged to someone else. In my heart I know there's no way you could have given all that you've given me and be committed to someone else. It isn't who you are. I know that. But it's my head that I'm having a problem with. You're an artist but you've never shown me that world, you've never brought me into the part of your life that makes you you. I'm sure you have your reasons, and maybe in time I'd have come to understand why you kept me at arm's length, but I want and need more. My parents keep me away. Even Frank, who loved me like a daughter, kept things from me. Maybe there's something about me that keeps people at a distance, but I think I deserve to find someone who draws me close instead of pushing me away."

"Saffron."

"I can't do this right now. Please, I need some time, and so do you. If you're not willing or able to be that person for me, then there's no point in continuing whatever it is that's between us."

Pain clouds his expression and I want to reach for him, but I don't. Because if it's going to end, it's better that we do it now. If I fall any deeper for him, I'll be wishing he hadn't saved me. He stands and when I see the one tear roll down his cheek, I close my eyes. It's just all too much. When I open them again, I'm all alone.

———

I've been home for three days and I've spent much of that time thinking, and the more I do the more I know Logan is worth taking a chance on. We work, Logan and I. He gets my quirkiness and I understand his need to be quiet and in the background. We've not just found common ground, we're better together than apart: he grounds me and I make him a little less serious. I'm not willing to toss that away. Yes, he has some explaining to do, but I think he's worth it. What I don't know is if he thinks the same about me or, more to the point, sees what we have as something lasting. Doubt wiggles into my resolve despite my effort against it. I hadn't felt insecure about us before, but that was before I knew that Logan is David Cambre. He's not just a famous artist, he's just plain famous. His face appearing often in magazines and on those entertainment news shows. He lives the jet-set life. How does a bartender from Harrington possibly compete with that? Sure, he's feeling overwhelmed now and wants a change, but will he always want this quiet lifestyle or will he eventually grow restless? There's a part of me that can't believe I didn't realize who he was, though his disguise was pretty damn good. But in fairness, what famous person hermits himself away in a lighthouse in a small fishing town?

I stand on my back patio and look out at the bay. It's so calm, the water particularly green today. Seagulls fly overhead, the sound of a child screaming in glee floats over the water. A breeze kicks up, flying my hair into my face. As I tuck it behind my ear, a movement to my right catches my attention. Logan is walking down the beach toward me. His face is turned to the water, his focus on some point on the horizon. My heart hiccups at the sight of him.

Stopping just in front of me, he doesn't reach for me, doesn't even offer a greeting. He's hurting; I know this because I see that same expression in the mirror every morning. "I'd like to tell you about Darla."

"Your fiancée."

"Ex-fiancée."

"Okay."

We move inside to the living room. Logan takes the chair opposite me on the sofa. "I met her family when I was touring. They were new money and were eager to make a reputation for themselves. I was just beginning my career, but even at an early stage, my agent knew I was going to be a huge success. Darla's family was interested in backing me, and so we entered into a business agreement. They helped fund my art tours and in exchange they were given a percentage of works sold until such a time as I could pay them off. After about two years, I was making so much money that I was able to pay off their initial investment and then some. Our business together ended at that point.

"I hadn't realized that part of their willingness to help me was because they hoped that I would marry their daughter, but at the time Darla was only nineteen—five years younger than me. Almost a decade later we met up again and she seemed to have matured into a beautiful, smart woman. So we started to see each other. It wasn't long into the relationship that her parents started to apply pressure for a wedding. Looking back on it, I realize that Darla was also pushing, but she was much more subtle in her campaign. A few months into our dating, I relented and asked her to marry me."

Logan leans up in the chair so his elbows rest on his knees. "I have always been very private, but I was beginning to become a recluse: reacting to the politics of the art world by trying to avoid it and everyone associated with it. It was because of this I asked Darla to marry me. She's a very spirited woman and I thought that maybe being with her would help me to acclimate to that world. We were engaged for all of five weeks when I knew I couldn't possibly marry her. Underneath the spirited woman was a vain, selfish, and spoiled child who was only interested in what people could do for her. I didn't love her, but I thought I could like her, but even that was impossible. I broke off the engagement and she refused to accept it.

"Not only was my personal life circling the toilet, but professionally I was being pulled in a direction I didn't want to go. I am extremely humbled to have become as successful as I have with my sculpting work, but with that success I found myself pigeonholed. Any attempt I made to move into a different medium was thwarted by my so-called patrons. I was being smothered, so I moved here and became Logan MacGowan again. Here I can create what I want and not what the public wants."

"And Darla?"

"The last I heard she was working the media circuit drumming up sympathy for herself."

I can't lie, having heard his story, I'm giddy knowing I wasn't wrong to trust him. Which brings up the question of why Elise twisted the facts, especially as someone who works with presenting facts for a living. What was her end game? I move on from that. "David Cambre has had more than his fair share of media coverage with the fashion magazines and tabloids."

He looks uncomfortable, but he answers, "I was rather wild in my youth."

"What made you get into modeling?"

"Thought I had to."

"Why did you stop?"

"Took too much time away from my art."

"I taped one of your spreads to my wall. Sexy." He looks embarrassed so I graciously change the subject. "Your secret is out—there have been women coming here in search of you. Did you know that?" I ask.

"No, but then, my attention has been on you."

"So what was with the silent treatment?"

"Being able to stay in the shadows has been very appealing. When you took my silence as a challenge and started in with your attempts to get me to speak, I really enjoyed being able to just sit and observe."

"So what did you get?" I ask.

"When you're telling a lie, you pull on your ear."

"I do not."

"You do. And when you're frustrated, you have a habit of chewing on the inside of your mouth."

I narrowed my eyes at him. "What else?"

"You tap your foot when you are uncomfortable, and when you're aroused, your eyes turn a deep, sapphire blue."

"Okay, I've heard enough." I try to keep a straight face, but I can't help my chuckle. "You've observed quite a bit about me."

"I am guilty of that. I enjoy watching you; you're more than what you seem, but at the same time, what you see is what you get. There's no ulterior agenda with you. I can be myself."

"When I mentioned the shaving, you knew people would know who you were if you did."

"Yes, I needed to tell you about the drama I left behind before we opened that can of worms."

"Did you really go to New York for a sale?"

"No, I gave a phone interview to the *New York Times* that they've been pestering me about."

"To Elise?"

"No, she's friends with Darla."

"She failed to mention that." So she lied because she was looking out for her friend. Misguided but understandable.

"I also paid a visit to my lawyers and filed a defamation of character suit against Darla, her family, and the papers she's pulled into her game. Once the papers hear about the suit, they'll write retractions."

"Why, Logan?"

"Because I want to show you New York City, so I need to clear up the drama I left behind."

He walks over and hunches down in front of me. "I wanted to take you to my showings, but it would have been like leading a lamb to slaughter. I couldn't do that to you."

I was feeling overwhelmed with his honesty and found myself sharing some of my own secrets, though I hadn't meant to blurt it out as I did. "Frank left me six million dollars."

Logan's only reaction is a slight arching of his eyebrow.

"What the hell am I going to do with six million dollars? And a house in the Hudson River Valley?"

"Something will come to you."

"That's what Frank told Dean."

"Dean, the lawyer?"

"Yes."

Logan traces the curve of my cheek. "I was jealous when I saw you talking with Dean that night in Bar Harbor."

It's my turn to attempt to raise my eyebrow. He alluded to that then, but now he's actually stating it out loud. "Seriously?"

"Big time," he adds.

I'm elated when I see the dark expression that crosses Logan's face, but then I sober. Reaching for his hand, I press it to my heart. "You were already going to tell me this before Elise interfered?"

"Yes."

"Thank you."

"I'm sorry I hurt you."

"I think it was more Elise who hurt me, but with her being a friend of Darla's, I guess I get it. She gets points for having her friend's back, even though I don't like how she went about it."

"Does this mean I'm forgiven?"

"I suppose you could find ways to persuade me to forgive you." I'm totally teasing, mostly teasing, sort of teasing, partially teasing.

He doesn't miss a beat. "Gladly."

———•———

Waking slowly, I feel something warm and solid pressing against my back. Logan. I turn to face him. His long, black lashes fan out on his cheeks and in rest, his face looks almost boyish. What was he like as a kid? There's so much I know about him and yet I find I'm thirsty to know more.

He obviously knows I'm staring, since his lips curve into the sweetest of smiles. I've only just brushed my mouth across his when his arm comes around me, drawing me up against him as he takes over the kiss: kissing me so deeply that my body goes boneless. He rolls and pins me under him while his mouth moves to my neck, nibbling his way down to my collarbone. I'm brain-dead by the time his gaze comes back on me.

"Good morning." The words are barely past his lips before they're working their magic again, sliding over my skin, causing chills to run down my arms. My legs spread to cradle him and then I move, rubbing myself shamelessly against him, but he is a man on a mission as that mouth moves from my neck to my shoulders before settling on my breasts, where he spends a good long time until I'm practically begging him to make me come. He slides lower down my body, but he's had long enough to feast; it's my turn. Rolling over, I straddle him, pressing my lips to his before trailing kisses over his pecs and abs. His skin is so smooth but hard, as his muscles flex in response to my touch. Looking at him through my lashes, I reach the part of him that's standing at attention. He shuts his eyes on a moan when my mouth closes over him. His hips jerk up, pushing him deeper, and everything below my waist throbs. I'm just finding a rhythm, my tongue running under his shaft while my hands fondle the heavy sac between his legs, when he flips me onto my back. I'm so turned on, aching to be claimed. He kneels between my legs, his eyes watching his finger moving through the curls between my thighs. Slowly, he moves over that aching bud, teasing it, making it throb more. My hips jerk, wanting him inside me, but his focus stays on that nub. He pinches and pulls, squeezing it until I moan, my body desperate for him. One finger moves through my folds, tracing and pressing but not entering. I want to weep from the exquisite torture. He's so hard, so fucking hard, and I want that in me. Spreading my legs wider, I touch myself. Logan's hands fall away. His gaze locks on my fingers stroking my aching flesh. Pushing one finger in, my back arches, my breathing turns shallow and all the while my eyes are on the part of him I want where my fingers are. Shifting, he settles himself over me, the hard length of him running over my swollen, wet flesh, lubing himself. Sliding his hands under me, he squeezes my ass and spreads me even wider, then lifts my hips and drives into me.

I cry out as my orgasm crashes over me. It feels incredible to be taken, and taking me is exactly what's he's doing, and I love every freaking second of it. He continues to move in and out so hard and so fast that my overly aroused body can't help but come apart again and when I do this time, Logan comes too as my name rips from his throat with his climax.

Minutes pass. Logan's still on me and in me. My breathing evens out, making speech possible again. "I totally forgive you."

His chuckle in reply tickles my neck.

In the kitchen later I'm grinning like a fool thinking I wouldn't mind starting every day like we did this one. As I whip up some scrambled eggs, I hear Logan coming down the hall. I turn just as he enters and I am thankful that I'm not holding anything because I would have dropped it. He shaved and now his truly magnificent face is completely visible.

"Wow."

His cheekbones flush a lovely shade of pink and the sight is both unexpected and endearing. I pull the pan from the stove and flick off the burner before walking to stand just in front of him. My fingers have a mind of their own as I trace his jaw, his cheek, his nose, his beautiful lips.

"I like you as my yeti too."

His eyebrow raises slightly in response before he asks, "Yeti?"

"That was how I thought of you: my seafaring yeti. You aren't a fisherman, though, so I guess that description really isn't accurate at all anymore."

"I'm not sure if I should be offended by that," Logan says, and I laugh.

"You have to admit you were really very hairy for a while and with you so tall, I think it was a fair description." I stop talking because I remember the wave of women who had come to Harrington looking for the man standing before me. To be so sought after only because of your outer beauty, what a drag.

"Thank you for shaving, but I'll understand if you want to grow your facial hair back."

Surprise covers his face. "Why do you say that?"

"I personally witnessed your fan club: women actually hunting you down solely because you have a face like that. If any of them realize that your outer beauty pales in comparison to your inner beauty, they'll never give you a moment's peace. That must really suck." He quickly pulls me into his arms, his chuckle rumbling up his throat. "Is it any wonder that I am completely taken with you?"

"Taken with me?"

"Mmm." His lips brush over my neck. "Totally captivated."

"Captivated, that's even better," I mutter. His lips are working down my throat to my shoulder.

"Dazzled," he purrs just before he presses wet kisses over my shoulder and along my collarbone. "Bewitched. I'd like to take you to New York City. Would you do me the honor?"

"Yes." My knees go weak, so it's a good thing he's wrapped his arms around me as he speaks.

"I have a showing next Saturday, so we can leave on Thursday and come home Sunday."

"Sounds perfect."

A smile spreads over his face before his eyes glance behind me to the eggs, which are now cold and congealed. "I'll take you out to breakfast."

"Okay."

"But after," he says.

"After what?"

He doesn't answer with words, but turns me and bends me over the table. His hands move up my legs, over my ass, moving my nightie up and out of the way. And then his fingers are past the barrier of my panties, rubbing me and instantly I'm wet. He teases the nub before moving lower. My back arches when he slips one finger inside, in and out in a gentle glide. I moan when he adds another finger, pushing deeper as he grinds his erection against my ass. I'm panting when he adds a third at the same time he presses hard on that pleasure point.

My hands are gripping the edge of the table, my hips pumping against his hand, my stomach tightening with my coming orgasm and then his fingers are gone. I hear his zipper seconds before his hands return to my hips; moving his feet to the inside of mine, he pushes my legs wider. I feel the tip of him right where I ache for him. A second later, he's buried deep inside of me.

I want to touch him but I can't, my body is pinned under his and completely at his mercy.

He presses my chest flat against the table, his hand splays over the small of my back as he pounds into me. His pace is hard and fast until I come in the most stunning orgasm. Having just had a mind-blowing one, that's saying something. He continues to move hard and deep until the last of my orgasm ripples through me. Only when my orgasm subsides does he give in to his own, his powerful body going still as his release moves through him. He bends over me, his chest pressing into my back just as his lips touch my ear. "Can't get enough of you."

CHAPTER NINE

Logan and I drive the more than five hundred miles from Harrington to Manhattan at a single clip. When we arrive at The Pierre, my mouth drops. I may not travel, but I know a luxury five-star hotel when I see one. The fact that we're staying here only adds to the magic of the trip.

Logan helps me from the car as a doorman walks over and greets him by name.

"Good afternoon, Mr. MacGowan, everything has been opened and aired." He must stay here every time he comes into the city.

"Thank you, Anton." Logan reaches for my hand as Anton unloads the bags from the Porsche.

"I'll bring these right up."

"Thank you," Logan says before he escorts me into the hotel. It's like something out of a fairy tale. The black-and-white marble tiles are so clean it almost hurts to look at the reflection of the chandeliers off them. Logan walks right past the concierge desk and continues to an elevator landing that is separate from the others. It also doesn't escape my notice that everyone we pass knows and greets him.

"Frequent visitor?" I mutter. Logan glances at me and grins, but he doesn't say a word. He hits the button and there's no wait as the doors slide open to reveal a stunning gilded elevator.

"Decadent, isn't it?" I whisper and this observation earns me a chuckle. As soon as the doors close, his mouth is on mine, the kiss so consuming that I'm surprised when the elevator doors slide open again. My surprise turns into confusion at the sight before me and not just because I'm a little brain-fried from that kiss. The place we've entered isn't a hotel hallway. There is a large black marble double staircase with wrought-iron baluster just before us and hallways and rooms on either side.

"What is this?"

"The penthouse," Logan says.

I look at him like he's lost his mind. "I realize that, but why are we here?"

"I own it."

I'm convinced I haven't heard him correctly. "Excuse me?"

He starts walking me around the staircase toward the hall on the right. "I own it."

I dig in my feet, forcing him to stop walking and turn to me. "You own this and yet you live in a small lighthouse in Harrington, Maine?"

"Yes."

It's only then that I realize just how much he hated the life he was living. "Why don't you sell it?"

"I won't get what I paid for it, not in this market, so I rent it out to friends when I'm not using it."

"It's beautiful."

"I'll give you the tour."

Lots of dark woods and rich fabrics fill his home but the double height ballroom at the top of the staircase steals the show. I can imagine an old Hollywood-type–party being thrown there with women in beautiful gowns, gentlemen in tuxes, and the champagne flowing.

"This is amazing."

"Yes, but I want to show you what sold me on the place," he offers cryptically as he leads me to the stone terrace. On second thought, the view of Central Park leaves me breathless.

"Oh my."

"Yeah, that's pretty much what I said." He comes up behind me and wraps his arms around my waist. "We've had a long day, so how about we check out the room service menu."

"Sounds perfect. I want to get changed and maybe we can watch a movie. You probably get movies still in the theaters here, don't you?"

His lips touch my ear as his warm breath brushes across my skin. "I do."

Dinner is delicious, prime rib, duck-fat potatoes, and watercress and smoked blue cheese salad, and for dessert we share my chocolate cake with saffron brittle and his Meyer lemon cheesecake with a berry salad. I'm glad I changed into my very loose-fitting cotton pajamas, since I've eaten my body weight in food.

We take our wine glasses and the bottle of wine to the bed where we settle among the pillows as we scan the movie lists and I convince Logan to watch *Woman in Black 2*. I spend most of the scary movie under the blanket tucked so close to Logan I'm practically sitting in his lap, but he doesn't seem to have a problem with that. When the movie is done, we're both so tired from our long day that as soon as we settle back, we're sound asleep.

The following morning Logan takes me to the Statue of Liberty. You really don't get the impact of her until you're looking up at her from the ferry. We take the steps up to the pedestal and then he surprises me with tickets that allow us to walk up to her torch. After our tour we go to the gift shop where he buys me a mug, a T-shirt, a mini statue, a puzzle, and a key chain. He's being a total tourist for me and I love him more for it.

Next we walk along Fifth Avenue where we duck into the Empire State Building and go all the way to the observation deck to see the marvelous view of the city. We resume our walk and pass the American Girl store, which is packed. The door constantly revolves as little girls leave the place with bright-red shopping bags and big smiles. We get a delicious slice of pizza, which we eat while strolling through Central Park and then we end the day touring through the Metropolitan Museum of Art. By the time we make our way back to The Pierre, I am exhausted. Logan needs to make a call regarding the showing tomorrow night, so I head into our room and though I only intend to lie down for a moment, I fall asleep, because the next thing I know I'm stirring awake at the sound of a pop.

"Hello, sleepyhead," Logan says with a bottle of champagne in one hand and the cork in the other.

Sitting up, I feel a cool breeze that chills my skin, looking down to see that I'm only wearing my bra and panties. This discovery earns Logan a questioning stare.

"You didn't look comfortable." If he feels contrite, I can't tell from his expression. "Are you hungry?"

"Starving." I start to rise and he's there with a soft, white robe that he wraps around me before leading me to the table and pulling out my chair.

"I ordered the fish and chips. They're amazing here."

"Sounds delicious."

"The showing tomorrow is at a little gallery in SoHo. I need to be there at half past six, so you can either come with me or I can have a car drive you there for the eight o'clock opening."

"I don't want to be in your way."

He doesn't let me finish as he reaches across the table and takes my hand. "You could never be in the way."

The next night I'm just finishing getting dressed and though I'm probably overdressed for the showing, I can't deny that I love my new gown. I felt like Julia Roberts in *Pretty Woman*, minus the whole prostitute thing, earlier in the day when Logan took me to Bergdorf's. People stood up and took notice when the owner of the penthouse in The Pierre was in the room.

The saleswoman picked out several gowns and showed me to the dressing room. Logan sat in one of the chairs with his long, denim-clad legs stretched out in front of him and his head resting on his hand. He didn't offer an opinion because he wanted me to pick the dress I liked, but when I tried on the gown I eventually picked I saw heat flare to life in his eyes. It was my favorite dress as well, so I was sold.

I look at myself in the mirror; the Theia petal ombre gown starts as sea green at the camisole top, but gradually turns to royal blue as the dress hugs my figure to my hips and flares to a bias pleat at the knee before falling to the floor. On my feet I'm wearing royal-blue suede Jimmy Choos. My hair is pulled up into a knot and I found silver hair coils with stones the color of my dress, which I have artistically arranged in my updo. But what I love the most, what Logan surprised me with on our way back to his penthouse, is a Judith Leiber dolphin handbag. It doesn't seem real how thoroughly Logan is spoiling me. There aren't words to describe seeing firsthand how the rich and famous live. And thinking this, I know I can't avoid dealing with the money Frank left for me forever. As much as I would love to go on a spending spree, I think his legacy should be more than new shoes and handbags.

I turn at a noise behind me to see Logan standing in the doorway, dressed entirely in black—an Armani suit, black silk shirt and tie, dressy black boots and with his inky black hair down around his clean-shaven face, highlighting those wondrous emerald-green eyes. The question is out before I can stop it.

"Do you get a lifetime supply of Armani clothes? I just bet their sales went way the hell up having their clothes on your body."

He chuckles and gives me the look he sometimes does, the meaning very clear to read: I'm adorable and crazy.

"You look edible, Saffron. When I saw this dress on you earlier"— he walks toward me, desire blazing in his eyes—"all I could think about was helping you out of it."

Brushing his hands down my arms, he promises, "Later, I'm going to peel this off you and kiss every single inch of your beautiful body."

My brain stops working.

He kisses me hard on the mouth and mutters, "Damn show."

Touching his cheek, I flash him a saucy smile. "After the show, we have all night."

He growls in frustration as he leads me from the room.

The show has just opened, but in the hour or so before it did, I had the opportunity to view Logan's work privately. There are no paintings here; every piece is a sculpture, either done in stone or metal. This is all David Cambre's work and it's stunning.

Not long after the doors open, a woman comes breezing in. The way she moves around, as if she belongs or owns the scene, makes it clear that she's someone important. She's tall, about five feet ten, and she's willow-thin with gorgeous red hair and cornflower-blue eyes. Her dress amplifies her beauty—an emerald-green sheath that she's paired with high-heeled jeweled sandals.

She has a posse with her—three women and two men—all of them dressed to the nines. Part of me wonders if she's famous. I notice the posse drops back while she continues on in the direction of Logan. And it is then that I realize this must be Darla. Sex just drips from her every move. She drapes those long, delicate arms around Logan's neck and presses her lips to his. Even knowing he feels nothing for her, watching that is hard.

Logan doesn't miss a beat as he reaches up and removes her hands from around his neck before he takes a step back from her. I see the huge rock glistening on her finger: Logan's engagement ring. Darla is still wearing it. She flips her hair back and then she pouts, a sexy little pout. A part of me wants to walk straight on over there and punch her in her pretty face, but instead I turn and head for the door. I simply cannot watch it anymore.

I don't make it to the door before a strong hand wraps around my arm. Logan's lips brush over my ear. "Please don't leave. She wasn't supposed to be here."

My breath catches in my throat at the desperation in his tone, but I manage to whisper, "I was just getting some air."

"I'll take you."

I turn to him but, before I can say anything, Darla appears and she wastes no time putting her arm around Logan's waist.

"Who's this, darling?"

Logan brushes her arm off and takes my hand, kissing my fingers. "This is Saffron, my girlfriend. Saffron, Darla, my ex."

Darla's expression is not pleasant. Clearly she is not happy about being called his ex.

"David, you and I have unfinished business. We need to talk. Let"—she eyes me from head to toe and back again and clearly finds me lacking—"your friend get a cab."

Logan's gaze never wavers from hers and his voice is so soft you almost have to lean forward to hear him. "There is nothing unfinished. I'm done with this. The next time you approach me you'll have to deal with my lawyers." He leans closer to her but in intimidation not intimacy.

"Move on, because I have."

Her face flushes with temper. Logan had said she was a spoiled child, and here comes the temper tantrum. Before she can make a fool of herself, her posse comes to the rescue and pulls her from the gallery. A chill goes through me at the look she throws me from over her shoulder seconds before she disappears out the door.

"She does not like me." I don't realize I've said this out loud until Logan speaks. I've never heard or seen him looking so fierce.

"She's a spoiled, selfish child, but she won't harm you."

I squeeze his hand and his gaze fills with tenderness as he turns back to me. "Your work is beautiful, Logan, or should I say David."

"I'm David to them." He gestures to the crowd. "To the people I care about, my family and you, I'm Logan." Though I'm still reeling from that marvelous edict, he asks, "Would you like to step outside for some air?"

"No, I'm okay now. You have lots of people wanting to chat with you. Go, I'll be fine."

"All right, another glass of wine?"

"Okay."

He signals the waiter for a drink. "I should only be another hour."

"I'm really enjoying watching you in your element."

He presses a kiss on my forehead. His mouth lingers a moment before he turns from me to mingle.

By the time Logan helps me from the cab in front of the penthouse, it's late. Taking my hand, we walk through the lobby to the elevators.

"I knew you could paint, but the sculptures tonight were just incredible."

A slight smile touches his lips, but it seems almost absentminded. He's distracted. "Are you okay?"

"She wasn't supposed to be there. My lawyers made that very clear to hers. If I had known there was a chance of her showing, I would have warned you."

"It was a surprise, I will admit. She's beautiful."

"When you get to know her, you can't see past the vanity."

"So you felt nothing seeing her in that dress? It was a pretty sexy dress."

The elevator doors open and Logan steps out. He hasn't answered me, which I take to mean he was stirred, but he's too polite to comment.

He is only human, as much as that stings. I head to the bedroom as Logan locks up for the night. I'm in the bathroom removing my hair coils when Logan's hands come to rest on my shoulders. My heart does one loud thump before speeding up so much it almost hurts. He holds my gaze in the mirror.

"The only woman in that room who stirred my blood is you. I've thought of nothing all night but getting you out of this dress."

He slowly pulls the straps of my gown down my arms. Kissing my neck, he lowers the zipper and kisses each inch of skin he exposes. Once my gown is draped over the towel rack, his hands move to my breasts. I can't help but watch him in the mirror as he cups me and gently squeezes. Turning into him, I press my mouth to his as his hands splay over my back. The sensation of my bare breasts against the silky texture of his shirt is erotic. He lifts me up onto the sink as I work his zipper to free him, palming his growing erection and running my hand up the hard length of him. There's a wildness about him when his mouth rips from mine and then he's shifting his hips and sliding into me.

There's something incredibly hot about being completely naked while Logan is fully dressed. His hands move under my ass, lifting me up and farther onto him as his hips rock back and forth. Instinctively my legs wrap around his waist, my calves pressing against his ass to pull him even deeper. Just at that precipice when my orgasm tightens my belly, Logan moves harder and faster, and euphoria washes over me, claiming him too as we both come.

His breathing matches my own as our hearts pound in unison. When he speaks, his breath tickles my neck as his lips brush across the skin of my throat. "So fucking beautiful." And then he lifts me into his arms and carries me to the bedroom.

CHAPTER TEN

After seeing Logan's art, I'm inspired to try my hand at painting. A week after our trip, I've set myself up on the beach with an easel before me. I look out at the vast untamed charm of Harrington Bay and try to capture it on canvas, but painting is not as easy as it looks. My rendering of the beauty before me looks more like a scene from *SpongeBob SquarePants*. I finish it, even though it's dreadful, and decide to give it to Logan. If nothing else, he'll get a good laugh out of it.

I find myself thinking a great deal about Logan, specifically how he amassed such a fortune. I didn't realize artists were so wealthy, but when you reach the level that Logan has, perhaps it's not surprising. I saw what some of his work was going for at the gallery and the sight of all those digits had my eyes nearly rolling into the back of my head.

Another topic I find myself pondering is Frank and that huge sum of money sitting in a bank waiting for me. Why did he choose to live so frugally? Frank wasn't the flashy type, but he didn't seem to spend any of his money. His suits were from the eighties, his room had been sparsely decorated, and he never went anywhere. He hadn't even booked himself in the nicest room the facility had.

As far as I knew, he never left Harrington. His emergency contact at the home had been me, so it wasn't like there was someone more important outside of Harrington. The fact that I was left his bounty makes me all the more intrigued about how he earned it. Was it linked to the part of his life he didn't share with me?

Checking my watch, I see I've an hour before the town meeting. Another festival is on the calendar, and though I am now banned from all festival events, I like to sneak into the room and listen as the wild ideas are tossed around. As I'm packing up my supplies, I hear my name being called and turn to see Elise approaching. Great.

"Saffron, hi."

I offer her no smile or greeting, and when she says, "Sorry about before," I know she understands my rudeness.

What's strange is that though she is apologizing, she looks angry. I'm angry myself. "What, for entirely misrepresenting the facts? For trying to make me believe a lie, which happened to result in me falling into the water where I drowned. Oh, but wait, I was resuscitated by the man you accused of being a two-timing ass? Is that what you're sorry about?"

She has the sense to look down, but something in her expression seems off. She whispers, "Yes."

"You also failed to mention that you're friends with Darla, so that makes your interest in the manner biased," I add. "It's over between them, Elise. Even if he wasn't with me, he doesn't want to be with her. She's not getting that message, not from the lawsuit or from the advice of her lawyers. Maybe as her friend, you can penetrate her hard head. It's over between them."

"I'll try. Is David going back to Manhattan?"

"No, he is staying here with me."

She didn't like that answer. I can see that clearly in her expression, before she walks away.

I've had an hour to cool off after my run-in with Elise. I'm sitting in the back of the town meeting listening as Chastity tries to pitch the idea for a seaweed festival. I realize that seaweed is used in sushi, something that I am not fond of, but I can't help but think that this festival is going to be much like the Swordfish Festival. The thought of having to scrape stuck-on dry seaweed off the storefronts in town doesn't make me happy. Luckily, I am not the only one to object. Tommy voices exactly my concerns. His objection is met with a moue of disappointment from Chastity. A woman approaching her sixties definitely should not be doing that.

Slipping from the meeting, I start along Main Street, but I'm feeling restless and it's still early so I head to Tucker's. The music from the live band pumps out into the night. Grabbing the last stool at the bar, I signal Sarah for a glass of wine. I recognize most of the patrons, but there are a few tourists crowding around the tables, more than the steady flow we've been having lately, and they are all female. And then it dawns on me that they are most likely here because of Logan. It's not really Logan, it's David. I realize he's still a famous artist, but these women aren't interested in his sculptures, they're interested in the model/playboy he used to be. Even though he hasn't been either for quite a while. Talk about a crush. It's only after I make that connection that I realize many of them are eying me. I guess they know of my relationship with him. Is Logan really painting or is he hiding?

As the drinks flow, voices grow louder. I start hearing tidbits about Logan's life. I'm angry that his life is so exposed, but as I listen my anger turns to hurt. I know his parents live in Scotland and that he has two brothers, but I didn't know that he moved to New York City alone when he was younger. Why didn't his family come with him? And then I hear a tidbit that has the green-eyed monster rearing his ugly head. His preference was for slightly older and wealthy women.

Jealousy morphs into insecurity—I'm neither wealthy nor older, so what's his interest in me? I hate to admit it, but sitting in that bar,

I'm nearly crippled with self-doubt. Blinding in its intensity, the glaring reality is that there is no real-world scenario in which a man like Logan would want a woman like me. The longer I sit, the more I convince myself that what I think is happening between Logan and me really isn't. Yes, he cares about me, but where I see this going and where he sees it going are not in the same direction. It just can't be. The mature course of action is to seek out Logan and talk to him. Clear the air, put my concerns on the table, and let him tell me I'm freaking out for nothing. I don't do that, though. Going home and stewing over it is out, staying here and being forced to face my doubts in the flesh is out, and my friends are all busy. I need to get away. I always loved clearing my head by driving, so I handle the situation by running, well, driving away.

A day or two to get my head on straight sounds perfect. A while ago Gwen and Mitch bought a cabin in Vermont. It isn't much to look at, but it's quaint, clean, quiet, and empty. I can't take my car since it's a fairly long trip, so Gwen offers me hers. It's late by the time I'm heading west on Route 2.

I leave Logan an e-mail about my impromptu trip. Not that I'm expecting him to read it, since he hermits himself away when he's working, but I do bring my charged cell phone just in case. Reaching the cabin at just after three in the morning, I lock myself in and go facedown for eight hours. I wake to the sound of my phone playing "Late at Night" by Buffalo Tom, and see it's eleven in the morning.

I reach for it. "Hello."

"Good morning."

Warmth fills me just at the sound of Logan's voice, but fear crowds it out, along with the worry that everything I hope is happening between us isn't. "How's the painting going?"

He's silent for a moment. "Why did you leave town without me?"

"You were working." This is a lie and beneath me, but I don't have the courage to answer him honestly.

"If you asked me to join you, I would have."

Despite my doubts, lingering warmth spreads throughout my body. "I didn't want to disrupt your work." That isn't entirely a lie.

"Why do I have the sense it's more than that?"

"You're right, it is, but having a heart-to-heart while you're in the middle of a project isn't the right time."

He's silent for a minute and I can sense his hesitancy before he asks, "A heart-to-heart about what?"

It isn't the true reason for my fleeing into the night, but I am curious, if we're being open and all, why he never shared his childhood with me. So I ask, "Is it true you came to the US as a child? Why didn't your family come with you?"

"Where did you hear this?" he asks with a terse tone.

"At Tommy's last night."

"You shouldn't believe everything you hear."

"So you didn't come here as a child?"

"I did, but that's not the point."

"I'm sorry, what is the point?"

"You shouldn't listen to idle gossip."

His tone fuels my own temper. "True, but when the gossip is regarding the man I'm in a relationship with, it's a bit hard to ignore."

Silence. It's so tense that I just know his jaw is clenching. My temper goes up a notch and I don't realize until after I've said it that the next words are part of what's causing my doubt. "Our weekend together was the best weekend of my life, so it's a bit unsettling to realize that I'm falling in love with you when strangers seem to know more about you than me."

"You know all about me that matters."

He pricks my temper, so the next words tumble out without my wanting them to. "Is it true you had a preference for older women when you were younger?"

I'm taken aback at the venom I hear in his voice. "Son of a bitch."

I don't understand why he's reacting the way he is unless I'm right and he doesn't see me as a keeper, just an enjoyable but temporary companion. One who is now asking too many personal questions. All the doubts I've been holding on to for the past twelve hours nearly suffocate me, but I force myself to ask because now I need to know, "Can we talk? I do have something on my mind."

"You're right. Now is not the time. Have a good weekend." And then the line goes dead. I stand there staring at my phone and as much as I would like it to be temper that's burning through me, it's not. Maybe after a day or two, once we both cool off, we can sit down and figure out where we go from here.

———

Walking from the little cabin, tucked in the woods of Stowe, Vermont, I take in the charm of the little paradise considered quintessential New England, but the beauty is lost on me because my thoughts turn to Logan. The bakery boasts that it makes the best apple cider and maple syrup donuts so I purchase one of each and a cup of coffee before I sit outside at one of the tables. My heart aches—Logan and I just had our first fight and I don't even know why. Yes, I ran away like a child, but his reaction to my questions about his past was overblown. Why would he react that way? Either he doesn't want to share it with me, or he's embarrassed by it. Regardless, I need to know, we both do, if we are on the same page. Leaving the way I did, stupid girl that I am, has now thrown that question right there in the middle of everything. Instead of going on as we were, blissfully happy, though maybe not truly committed, now we're really going to have to talk about our feelings. I may just lose the best thing in my life because I pushed for more than he's willing to give. And even as I'm berating myself I know that I'm not falling in love with him, I already am in love with him and if he's not on the same page, best to learn that now. I work to put Logan out of my head and finish my donuts.

The main street in town is quaint, storefronts painted in pastels running along the street on both sides. I duck into a few of the shops, enjoying the window-shopping, and that's when I see the sign in one of the store windows advertising puppies for sale. Always a sucker for puppies, I follow the directions from the ad to a farm that sits just off the main street. A long walk down a drive surrounded by maple trees leads to a white farmhouse. And just in front of that house is a penned-off area with six puppies. As I approach, one of the German shepherds comes right up to me. He licks my hand and I'm a goner.

"He likes you." I turn to see the old farmer walking toward me in overalls and a John Deere hat.

"He's beautiful."

"They're eight weeks old, neutered, and have their first round of shots."

"How much?"

"Forty dollars."

"I'll take him."

The farmer throws in a leash and twenty minutes later my new puppy and I are walking back into town. I stop to pick up the puppy food the farmer had been feeding him before we finish the trip to the cabin. He is a little fur ball and so goddamn cute I just can't stop looking at him. We play all day and that night, he sleeps in the bed with me. Sleep won't come for me, though, as thoughts of Logan fill my head. I wonder if he has had time to calm down. I try calling him, but get his voice mail. I'll see him tomorrow. That thought both delights and terrifies me.

Returning home in the early afternoon, I stop to see Tommy on my way to Logan's. When Tommy appears, a smile spreads over his face. He's a huge dog lover. He walks over and hunches down next to the puppy. "Who is this handsome man?"

"My new puppy, Reaper."

"Jax would be happy."

Yes, my puppy is named in honor of my favorite show, *Sons of Anarchy*.

"He's beautiful. How was Stowe?"

"Quiet, I needed the silence to pull myself from a self-induced panic attack."

He stands up again. "Are you okay?"

"It's a little intimidating, Logan being who he is. I guess I'm more insecure about it than I would like to be, but we'll work it out."

"First fight?"

"I wouldn't even call it a fight. I'm not really sure what it was, but we've both cooled down."

"Good. I'll see you tomorrow, right?"

"I'll be here."

"What are you going to do about Reaper?"

"I'll set up the kitchen, so if he has an accident it won't be too hard to clean up."

Tommy bends down and rubs my dog's head. "Welcome to Harrington, Reaper."

CHAPTER ELEVEN

After leaving Tommy, I call Logan, but am unable to get through to him. My assumption is that he's turned off his phone because he's working. I hate just popping over unannounced, but I don't want to leave things how they are. It's very quiet when I arrive, but then it usually is. I know it's probably what Logan likes best about the place.

The blinds are all closed. I knock, but I know he isn't here. I just stand there in shock as Reaper sniffs the ground around me. I guess asking a man to talk about his feelings really is the kiss of death.

I don't immediately panic, since there's a good chance he's off clearing his head like I had, but as the days turn into weeks, it becomes pretty clear that he has left Harrington. My anger eventually morphs into hurt before settling on fear. What if he was in an accident? After a great deal of deliberating, I call his agent.

"Hello, Maria St. John," she answers.

"Maria, hi, it's Saffron Mills. I'm a friend of Logan's."

"Yes, I remember. What can I do for you?"

"He's okay, right? Unharmed and not in a hospital somewhere?"

She hesitates before answering. "What? No. No hospital."

"He's there with you now, isn't he?"

"Yes."

My heart crumbles in my chest. "Sorry to have bothered you."

I start to hang up when she says, "It's not what you think."

A lump has formed in my throat so painful I can barely speak around it, but I do manage to say, "Well, it doesn't seem to matter what I think anymore."

———

A week later, I'm working on obedience training with Reaper outside when two strangers approach me from the direction of my house. As they grow nearer, I feel my heart start to pound. It's not Logan, but they look so much like him that I know immediately they are his brothers. They come to stop just in front of me and one rubs Reaper's head.

"Saffron?"

"Yes."

"I'm Broderick and this is Dante. We're Logan's brothers."

A small smile touches my lips. There is no mistaking the family resemblance, but then remembering how he just up and left me, my voice turns cold. "He isn't here; I haven't seen him for a few weeks."

"I know. He's an idiot, but don't hold that against him." Broderick offers this with a grin that looks so much like one of Logan's that my heart twists in my chest.

"May I ask who this fella is?" Dante asks.

"Reaper."

"He's adorable."

I study the two of them for a moment but then I just have to ask, "Why are you here?"

"We wanted to meet the woman who has finally sunk our brother," Broderick says with a mischievous look.

I am completely confused by his explanation. "I don't understand."

"He has spent the past few weeks moping around like a lovesick teenager and since he never was a lovesick teenager, we grew curious."

"Well, I guess I find that all very interesting considering we had our first argument and he runs for the hills. I'm sorry your brother is moping, but I assure you it isn't because of me."

Broderick noticeably tenses in response, but it's the look in his eyes that gives me pause: sincerity. "You don't really believe that, do you?"

I shrug, since I no longer know what I believe, but my voice when I answer sounds far more confident than I feel. "All I know is I had a relationship with a man, which culminated in the best weekend of my life and a week later, he runs. That doesn't sound like the actions of a man in love."

The reaction from the two is not at all what I'm expecting when they both howl with laughter.

"Oh man, so it is Logan that falls first. That's so awesome," Dante says.

"I'm sorry, but what are you talking about?"

Broderick turns smiling eyes on me. "Logan loves you, Saffron, it's obvious."

I can't deny I like, no, I love and adore, hearing those words, but I'm not really eager for Logan's brothers to know just how affected I am by them. Sweeping Reaper into my arms, I start for my house and call to them from over my shoulder. "You want to get a beer?"

They reply in unison and sound so much like Logan I can't help but smile. "Hell yes."

Sipping my wine, I listen to Broderick's story. Both are smart, sweet, and funny. It's obvious that the three of them are close so I ask, "Does Logan know you are here?"

"No," they both say in unison.

"Why?"

"He would kill us, but we were all too curious."

Narrowing my eyes at that comment I ask, "We?"

"Our parents are most eager to meet you."

Picking up my glass, I take a very large gulp before I ask weakly, "Your parents know about me?"

"Yes."

"How?"

"Logan talks incessantly about you."

I can't deny the flutter in my belly hearing that Logan talks about me to his family. "Where are you two staying?"

"The lighthouse."

"How long are you staying?"

"Long enough for word to get back to our idiot brother. No faster way to put a fire under Logan's butt than to make him jealous, and since his heart is engaged for the first time in his life, I'm guessing two, three days tops," Broderick says before he gestures to Sarah for another beer.

"Where is he?" I ask this very softly and it's Dante who answers me.

"He's home in Scotland."

"So I'm guessing by the 'Logan is the first to fall,' neither of you is married?"

"Nope."

"And may I ask what you do?"

"I'm a lawyer, but I work for the family business and Dante runs the security for it. We're MacGowan Enterprises."

"Why have I heard that name before?"

"Because we have our fingers in everything: entertainment, publishing, investments, real estate."

Broderick tilts his head and I suspect he's gauging my reaction to what he says next. "Logan's independently wealthy."

"So women aren't just chasing after the man because of his looks, but his money. And I suppose you were more than a little curious about the poor bartender from Harrington, Maine." I move closer. "Did you think I was using sex to lure him in?" My intention is to tease them but there's a part of me that wants to provoke them too.

They blush, which I find enormously funny. Broderick says, "We weren't sure, but his track record is not very good."

"Yes, well, I met Darla and she's just charming. I think I'm going to friend her on Facebook, but then I'd have to read every thought that enters her head." I stand up. "You can go back home and not concern yourselves with me. I fell for your brother when he looked like Bigfoot. I don't need his money. I have plenty." I hold their gazes and can't help the anger I know is burning in mine. "I don't chase after men."

I don't sweep from the room in outrage with my head held high only because I'm stopped mid-exit by a gentle touch on my arm.

"We've offended you. Sorry." The contrition in Broderick's eyes makes me relent.

"You were looking out for your brother. I admire that. I envy that you have siblings you're close to. We don't all have that."

"Can we take you to dinner tomorrow night?" Dante asks.

I am probably going to regret this, but I counter his offer with one of my own. "How do you feel about dancing?"

Broderick is clearly taken by surprise with my suggestion when he says, "Dancing?"

"There's a great club in Bar Harbor."

Broderick glances at Dante. "Sounds great."

"We'll come for you around seven," I reply.

The gang shows up at the lighthouse at seven the next evening. I hear the startled intake of breath from Gwen when Logan's brothers appear. They're hot.

I make the introductions before two pairs of green eyes look over at me. There is shock and a bit of wariness in their gazes. I'm dressed to party in clothes that are far too revealing and have lined my eyes in black, glossed my lips, and teased my hair so it's all wild and sexy. I look like a sex kitten on purpose and I'll more than likely act like one too. If Broderick and Dante are on recon, they'll pass that information back to their brother. Childish and immature, absolutely, but oh, so satisfying.

"You guys ready?" I ask but I don't wait for a response and start for Mitch's car.

———

The bar is packed, but we manage to find a table. After my second drink I'm feeling pretty damn happy, so I toss off my jacket and turn to the table. "Anyone want to dance?"

Broderick puts his beer down and offers me his hand. The bass thumps as he leads me onto the dance floor. He has got some moves—he's fluid and graceful when he dances. I can't help my laughter when he reaches for my hand and draws me closer so he can sashay me around the dance floor. When our song is over, he leads me back to the table.

"You're a lot of fun," he says.

"I was just thinking the same about you."

He winks at me as he helps me to my seat before returning to his own, but I'm not there long when someone touches my shoulder. "Dean, hi."

"Hi, Saffron."

The table greets him, but I notice that Broderick and Dante are looking at Dean in much the same way that Logan had.

"Broderick and Dante MacGowan, Dean Finley."

They shake hands, but there's definitely a chill in the air as Dean asks me to dance. I jump down from my stool. Just when we reach the dance floor, the upbeat song changes to a slow one. No spark or sizzle steals my breath when Dean's arms come around me. It's sweet and comfortable. I rest my head on his chest and close my eyes, but my thoughts are not on him. Every goddamn day I miss Logan, but it's been weeks with no contact from him. I know that Broderick believes Logan loves me, but I don't think so. I'm convinced that Broderick and Dante are only here to make sure I'm not some money-grubbing whore—that I'm not another Darla. The song is coming to an end and I lift my head and Dean takes that as an invitation and his mouth lowers to capture mine.

Pulling back, I push at his chest and he immediately releases me, but I see the heat and passion in his expression. He wants me and he's here. He isn't hiding himself or running away, and though his kiss doesn't spark the passion in me that Logan can so easily create, I wonder if I'm not being a complete fool turning away from him. He may not be the one that makes my blood burn, but he could be someone with whom I could happily grow old.

"I'm sorry, Saffron."

"Don't worry about it. I'm not ready, but if I ever become ready, I'd like to try that again."

His face lights up. "Absolutely, anytime."

Back at the table he offers his good-byes before he disappears into the crowd. I feel the hot stares from across the table, but I ignore them and order another drink.

Two nights later, I have Broderick and Dante over for dinner. I'm preparing twice-baked potatoes and salad. Broderick is outside at the grill tending to the steaks and Dante is attempting to teach Reaper how to fetch. Seeing Dean brings Frank's gift front and center in my mind. I can't think what to do with it. That kind of money can make a real impact, but where should I focus? While I'm blending the cheese, milk, and scallions into the potatoes, the phone interrupts my thoughts. I lean over and hit the speaker button.

"Hello."

My greeting is answered with silence and I assume it's a hang-up. I'm about to hang up myself when I hear a female voice that makes my skin crawl. "Back off, bitch."

"Who is this?"

But I hear the click a second before the line goes dead. I just stand there looking at the phone, a chill working its way down my spine. It sounded like a woman, maybe my age or younger. Back off from what? I try to dismiss it and finish preparing dinner. I'm not able to as easily dismiss the call when later that same night, while I'm plating up dessert, the phone rings again. When I hit the speaker button I hear, "Walk away, bitch."

I don't realize that Broderick and Dante have come into the kitchen until Dante growls, "Who the hell is this?"

But again the line goes dead. When Dante turns to me, his expression scares me. "How often does that happen?"

"Just started tonight. That's the second call. The first one came early."

"And what did it say?"

"'Back off, bitch,' but I'm sure it's just some kids getting their rocks off." Even as I speak the words, I know they don't ring true. We have very little crime in Harrington. This kind of thing never happens. That knowledge settles like a rock in my gut.

"Maybe," Dante says, but I can tell he isn't convinced either.

It isn't until the next day, when I receive the package with the severed head of a bird in it, that I accept this is more than kids playing a prank. With the head is a warning: a single line scratched on a slip of paper.

Keep out of where you don't belong or else.

I call Sheriff Dwight, who comes immediately, since the last time we actually had crime was when Bobby and Rickie Curtis lit the town Christmas tree on fire in '94. When he sees the package, I watch his transformation from the man I've known all my life to the cop. He pulls on latex gloves.

"I'm going to need to print you and your mailman, Gary, so I can discount your prints. Has anything else strange happened?"

I tell him about the crank calls and he jots it down in his notepad.

"Can you think of anyone who may have a grudge against you?"

I immediately think of Darla, but not being able to prove that, I hesitate to offer her name. "No."

"I don't like that they know where you live and have your phone number. It may be better for you to stay with Gwen or Josh until we either apprehend this person or it blows over."

"No, I'm not running off, but I will be very careful to keep my doors locked."

At that moment, Reaper comes padding into the kitchen, so I scoop him up into my arms. Sheriff Dwight scratches Reaper's head. "I wouldn't let him out of your sight."

I pale at that thought, thinking of it being Reaper's head in the box, and work to swallow past the lump in my throat before I reply, "I won't."

"I'll take this with me," he says as he bags the package. "Come down to the office tomorrow and I'll print you. Meanwhile, I'll see if Gary has any more information on the package's origin."

"Thanks, Sheriff."

"Be safe."

"I will."

———·———

News of my gruesome mail spreads quickly and before long my house is filled with my friends. I'm touched by their concern, but their worrying is making me edgy. It isn't until Broderick and Dante arrive that I actually lose it, because they don't come alone. Logan is with them. As soon as I see him, I can't help soaking up the sight of him. God, he really is beautiful. But then sanity slowly returns and I remember that he left.

"No!" I say as I throw up my hands. "No."

Turning from him, I walk through the living room filled with my surprised friends and out the back door to the beach. I don't get far before Logan's hand is on my arm, but I jerk free of his hold and push him in the chest with both hands. "Go home, Logan."

"Saffron." I have missed that voice, missed my name on his lips, but that knowledge only fuels my anger.

"Go. I don't want you here."

"I want to talk."

"No, you don't get to talk." I push him again, but since his chest is like a damn brick wall, it's pointless. There's patience and what looks a hell of a lot like love in his expression and this only makes me angrier.

"You walked, Logan. You left. You don't get to just show up here now and play the knight in shining armor. I didn't ask for your help and I don't want it."

There's an odd cast to his face, as if he has no idea what I'm talking about, and then he says, "I know I have a lot of explaining to do, but please hear me out."

"I don't think I'm interested in hearing you out. It was just too damn easy for you to walk away."

His temper flares and his eyes burn hot and dark. "I know I haven't handled this well, but considering you were prepared to stab me in the eye over something I hadn't done, I think I've earned the courtesy of you hearing what I have to say. Not to mention you walked first."

He had me there and, even through my temper, I know I can't deny him that.

"Fine, talk."

"Not now. Can I come back tonight?"

It's on my lips to tell Mr. High-Handed no, but I bite my tongue and hiss through my teeth, "Fine."

I'm about to walk back to the house, but his softly spoken words stop me. "I've missed you."

My heart flips over in my chest, but my head isn't on the same page. "You left and you can spin that any way you want, but you can't change that fact. Yes, I ran away, but I told you I was leaving. I didn't just take off. And more importantly, I came back. Even called you while I was away. You left and didn't look back. Getting involved with someone who is as emotionally stunted as my parents is not something I'm going to do. I can't and won't live that way again. I'll listen to you, but you and me? That's over."

"I don't accept that." I almost laugh at his arrogance as he continues. "I have fallen in love with you: madly, wildly, and completely. I know you feel the same, so despite my idiotic behavior, I am not willing to lose you, not after I've finally found you."

My emotions are just all over the place in response to that heartfelt declaration. I find I can do nothing more than stand there mutely for a few minutes until I finally open my mouth and say, "I'll see you at seven." And then I turn and disappear inside.

Seven o'clock arrives entirely too soon and there's a knock at my door. I pull it open—Logan's as punctual as usual. Then I head into the living room, leaving him to shut the door and follow after me. I'm sitting on the sofa near the fireplace when he enters the room and it really isn't fair that I find him appealing in every imaginable way; just being in the same room with him makes my blood pressure rise.

"Thank you for agreeing to see me," he says.

"I owe you that."

A slight grin touches his lips before he settles on the chair opposite me.

"I'm sorry I left, but I never stopped thinking about you. I missed you so damn much."

"Apparently not enough to pick up the phone."

"It isn't like that," he whispers.

"You keep saying that, but from where I'm sitting, it's exactly like that."

"That's fair. I want to try to explain."

Settling back on the sofa, I pull my legs up under me. "I'm listening."

"I've never told all of this to anyone, not even my family, but I think it might help you understand why I reacted as I did."

"Okay."

"I've always loved painting and sculpting and I was always good at it. Close friends of my parents visited us in Scotland when I was twelve and when they saw my work, they were quite impressed. They knew I wanted to make a living from my art and offered to sponsor me. I could stay with them in the States while they helped to foster my talent. My parents were hesitant because I was young, but I wanted it so badly that they relented, especially since they were unable to bring me themselves with a business to run and other children to raise. I packed my bags and came to New York City. My parents' friends treated me like their own son—got me into art classes run by some of the finest artists of our time and even enrolled me in the New York Academy of Art.

"The dinners started when I was sixteen. They were constantly introducing me to their friends. Networking, they called it, so when they suggested dinner parties, I didn't think anything of it. The first few were rather nice, but then the guest list shortened and the dinners became more intimate. If the wife's hand lingered a little too long on my shoulder or lap, I didn't think much of it.

"It was when I turned seventeen that the solo dinners started—older woman taking me out to dinner wanting to discuss my art and offering to become patronesses of a sort. From the very beginning, I found these dinners uncomfortable, but the women were friends of the people who were acting as my guardians, so I didn't want to upset the apple cart. I just assumed I didn't understand the society I was now socializing in.

"Then I started getting propositioned. At first I thought that these mature women were interested in me and that we were two consenting adults. I can't lie, I was flattered, so I took them up on it. And then I began to realize that it wasn't young and foolish me that they were interested in, but what I was becoming. They started offering to sponsor shows for me in return for sex, and I knew we weren't coming from the same place."

I can see him too, a young, trusting, beautiful boy. The bastards that were supposed to be protecting him were pimping him out. "And so start the rumors of your preference for older and wealthy women. I'm sorry, Logan. What did you do about it?"

"I started modeling to make some extra money. I'd been approached by several agencies interested in representing me. Modeling hadn't been a thought for me, but when my art dreams seemed to be dependent on me becoming a person I wasn't, I needed something to fall back on. I'll admit I lost my way for a time.

"My parents have a very successful business in Scotland, but they used to maintain a residence in the States when they were expanding the business and that's how my brothers and I were born here, but we all moved back to Scotland when my brothers and I were toddlers. I know the decision my parents made to send me back here at twelve had weighed heavily on them—fear I'd lose my way without their daily guidance because I was so young. When their fears proved justified— my face popping up in magazines and gossip about me getting back to them from the States—they dropped everything and came to get me back on track. My brothers came with them, and before they returned, they helped get my brothers and me settled: buying us an apartment, getting Dante enrolled in school, and when they returned to Scotland, my brothers stayed with me."

"And what happened to the bastards you stayed with?"

"They owned an exclusive gallery, but when I finally became a success, my first purchase was buying their by-then-overextended gallery for far cheaper than it was worth, and then I closed it. All of their money was tied up in that gallery, so they were forced to declare bankruptcy. I believe they're living in New Jersey now."

He walked over and hunched down in front of me. "I hate thinking about that time in my life, hate knowing that I allowed myself to be manipulated, but in all honesty I'm also embarrassed by it. Discussing what I consider the worst part of my life with the person who's rapidly becoming the most important part of it, made me freak. What if it made you think less of me or turned you from me?" He looks down for a minute before he adds, "David Cambre has quite the following, and at times it can be annoying and at other times it can be downright suffocating. The reality that you would be pulled into all that shit was another reason to stay away from you."

Hearing that his avoidance really does stem from embarrassment softens me a bit toward him. "I'm so sorry. It wasn't just morally wrong, what they were doing to you had to be illegal. I've heard enough about David Cambre to know how much you are admired. I can't even begin to imagine how trying that must be for you."

"But?"

I've softened, yes, but the reality of the past few weeks and how he just walked away keeps me distant. I brought this on, I know that, but my insecurity over whether I'm good enough for him is one thing. Him cutting all connections and shutting me out, that's something else entirely. What's to keep him from doing that again? I lower my head, trying to avoid his question, but he touches my chin with his finger and lifts my gaze to his. "I absolve you. Is that what you want to hear?"

"No."

Moving from him, I stand and walk to the far side of the room. "Look, I hate what those people did to you, abusing their power over you. They don't deserve to live, but I don't know what you want from me. You left. You walked away. I pushed to know more about you and you fled. No calls, no explanation, you just left. Do you have any idea what it felt like to find that you were gone? And weeks later, when I buried my pride and called Maria, you were there in that room with her, and you still didn't pick up the phone. You're right, I do love you, and maybe you love me back, but it's not the same. One is a soul-searing, breath-stealing kind of love and the other is much like the love one feels for chocolate ice cream. I am sure there are many ladies out there who would love to be your chocolate ice cream, but I'm not that girl."

He is clenching his jaw so hard I'm afraid he's going to break something. He sounds almost dangerous. "What are you saying, Saffron?"

I hold his hard gaze, even though my heart is breaking. "I'm saying that you and me, I don't think it's going to work."

He doesn't say anything, but I can see the pain in his expression, and then he starts toward the door; all the while I'm screaming in my head, *Fight for me, damn it.*

Just when I think he's going to walk out of my life forever, his head turns and his gaze spears me from across the room. "Staying away from you was the hardest thing I've ever done. And what I feel for you isn't like a preference for chocolate ice cream. Every beat of my heart and every breath I breathe I do for you."

And then he leaves, but as far as exits go, his was pretty fucking terrific.

"Tell it again?" Josh asks as he sits across from me at Tucker's. I've already shared the story about my conversation with Logan at least five times, but Josh is addicted. I repeat Logan's parting words again and can't help the fluttering in my belly. Josh pretends to swoon as he holds his hand to his forehead. "Dear God, you are one lucky woman."

"He said the right words, but living them is another story."

"So what happens now?" Gwen asks.

"I don't know."

"What do you want to happen?" Josh prompts.

"I want it all: the husband, the house, the children, and the dogs. I want to wake up next to him every day; I want to watch our children grow; I want to sit on the front porch in rocking chairs when we're too old to move. I want what Gwen and Mitch have."

Josh drops his head on his hand and sighs. "Me too."

"It isn't all flowers and rainbows, you know?" Gwen offers as she picks up her glass of wine.

"Of course not, where would the fun be in that?" I say.

"Yeah, not to mention missing out on makeup sex."

I roll my eyes at Josh. "You are incorrigible."

Gwen holds my gaze. "So what are you going to do?"

"He claims that he wants me, so I'm going to sit back and see how he intends to win me."

"You realize there are thousands of women who would die to be in your shoes, who would actually seek him out, and you have *him* wooing *you*." Josh wiggles his brows at me.

"Those women like the package. I love the man. Logan's smart enough to see the difference."

"This is going to be fun to watch."

Gwen grins at Josh. "You can say that again."

CHAPTER TWELVE

I'm sitting on a bench in town watching the activity from across the street, though what exactly is going on over there, I haven't figured out yet. A crowd, which in this town is about ten people, has formed a semicircle on the sidewalk. Two men with a truck that has a hoist are parked half on and half off the curb and there's a cloth-covered something on a dolly. I'm assuming whatever is under the cloth will be hoisted up and placed where the people have gathered. What, I wonder, is under that cloth? Sheriff Dwight is guiding traffic around the truck. Reaper sniffs around me as I sip my coffee. Moments later a shadow moves over me and I look up to see Josh. He takes the seat next to me and reaches for my coffee to share a sip, but his attention is also across the street.

"What the hell is going on over there?" Reaper sidles over for a scratch behind the ears, and Josh complies.

"I haven't a clue. I've been watching now for the better part of an hour and I still haven't figured it out."

Josh hands me back my cup. "Anything new with Logan?"

"Nothing, absolutely nothing. I think he realized that he was smoking crack and has moved on to greener pastures. It's just as well. Being involved with a famous person is just too much work."

"Yeah, and if you keep telling yourself that you may actually believe it one of these days."

"I know. I'm pathetic, but at least I have my hair."

"What the hell does that mean?"

"I'm trying to bolster myself up. That's the best I can do."

"Well, hell, Saffron, that's just sad."

"I know." I shift to face him. "So, what's up with you and Derek? You seem to be like peanut butter and jelly."

He gets the look, the major one, that warms my heart. My friend is in love. "He's pretty damn terrific. I mean, like Gwen said, it isn't all rainbows and flowers, but I love him. He's the one."

"And he feels the same. I can see it when you two are together."

"Yeah, he does. We're talking about moving in together."

"I think that's fabulous," I say.

"Me too."

At a loud crash we both turn in the direction of the activity across the street. "What the hell?" I jump to my feet. Something seems to be taking shape over there.

"What's that thing under the tarp?"

"I've no idea." I squint, as if that's going to clarify what I'm currently looking at, just as Chastity appears among the people across the street. With her is none other than Logan.

"It looks like some kind of ceremony, but I didn't read about it in the paper," Josh says just before Gwen appears.

"Did you hear?"

We both turn to her. "Hear what?"

"Logan's donating a sculpture to the town. He didn't want to make a big deal about it—wanted it on the down low, so they're doing a small unveiling."

"Down low, Gwen?"

"I know, aren't I cool?"

We all turn back to the scene across the street. I ask, "What do you think it is?"

"I hope it's a self-portrait, a nude one." Josh sighs.

Gwen and I eye him, but he has that faraway dreamy look about him. Clearly he's envisioning Logan naked. I lean over and whisper, "Whatever you're thinking, it's better."

His eyes narrow at me. "You are a hateful woman."

Grinning like the Cheshire Cat, I turn back in time to see Chastity doing her thing, talking to the people gathered, while waving her arms as she has a tendency to do. Without much pomp and circumstance, the sheet is removed. At first I'm momentarily frozen at the sight and then I roar with laughter.

"Is that what I think it is?" Gwen asks.

"I don't understand," Josh says.

But I'm still staring across the street, staring at Logan, who is looking right back at me with a sexy little grin. Logan's sculpture, the one he's donating to the town, is a life-size swordfish.

"You hate swordfish, Saffron," Josh says, clearly confused.

"I do, but I love that one."

"Have you seen the papers today?" Josh asks as soon as I open my door to him a few days after the unveiling of Logan's gift to the town.

"Hi to you too."

He steps into my house and holds one of the gossip magazines up to my face, and staring back at me is me.

"Holy shit, that's me."

"You're famous."

The picture is of me behind the bar at Tucker's. There's another picture, this one of Logan, but he's younger, minus the Bigfoot disguise. The caption reads:

Is the art world's famous playboy finally settling down?

There's nothing of substance in the article, merely speculation, but there's definitely a negative spin. As in: Why is someone like David slumming with the likes of me? As much as I want to, I can't argue with the question. Why indeed.

"You look sick. Why do you look sick?"

"Logan is Logan to me. The idea that there's this whole other part of him, the famous part, is unnerving."

"Why?"

"I guess I just never really put it all together that being with Logan, or David, means that my life falls under scrutiny too."

"The curse of being famous."

Logan said it. David has quite the following. He works really hard at keeping Logan and David separate; those who come here are coming to see David. David is the one people are interested in, David is the one people want to see. And now David is the one who I am being linked to.

"Why, Josh? Why would Logan be interested in me when he comes from a world so far removed from our little part in it?"

"Don't sell yourself short."

"It's not that. It's just that there are countless women out there who come from the same background that he does. Why would he settle for me?"

"He's not settling with you, but to answer your question, maybe it's just as simple as he likes the peace of our small world better." He starts toward the kitchen. "Do you have any of those brownies left?"

I follow after him but I don't think I agree with him.

Later in the week my mom calls. Even as I'm reaching for the receiver, I know whatever is about to be said will not be good. I have a sixth sense for this.

"Mom, how are you?"

"Saffron. I've just been visiting some friends and they informed me that my daughter is dating some millionaire playboy. Is that true?"

Wow, so efficient, the gossip mill. Too bad we can't use that efficiency in more productive pursuits like solving world hunger and finding world peace. The image of me on stage accepting my Miss America trophy pops into my head. We must think of the children.

"Saffron!"

Right . . . "Well, yes, I am dating a very nice man who happens to be semifamous."

"I don't understand. You drag your feet about dating a steady guy and now you're dating someone who is anything but. What are you thinking?"

Oh, I have so many problems with that statement. How does she know anything about Logan except for the crap she reads in the rag mags? And a steady guy? Yeah, that's exactly how I want to describe any man I date. Steady and sturdy, like a tree. If I weren't so annoyed, I'd laugh. "He likes me. I like him. We're giving it a whirl."

"He likes you because he thinks you're easy."

I am easy, well, I am with him. He can mold me like clay anytime he wants. Despite the fact that I'm trying to find humor in this, she's stirring my temper. "Why do you say that?"

"You work at a bar."

"So everyone who works at a bar is easy? That's an awfully narrow-minded and, I have to say, stupid generalization."

"Do not speak to me that way."

"But you can call me a slut because of my choice of profession?"

"Tending bar is hardly a profession."

"And drinking and playing bridge is?" Ah, did I just say that out loud? I close my eyes and wait for it. Three, two . . .

"How dare you! This is what I'm talking about! You are out of control and now you're throwing yourself at some man who is so far above you. Do you really think his interest in you will lead to a white wedding? You've nothing to offer him that he can't find on any corner in any city in the world."

"Are you comparing me to a prostitute?"

"What? I was talking about bars. Women working in bars."

My pulse pounds in my throat. For a minute there I thought I was going to have to catch a plane just so I could punch my own mother in the face.

"He's going to hurt you."

And she's not?

"Whatever it is you think is going on, I assure you it isn't," she continues. "Be smarter than that, Saffron. Think about what I've said. I've got to run."

And then she clicks off. Is it any wonder why I have such self-doubt? And as much as I want to dismiss everything she said, I can't. Laced through her bullshit rhetoric, she actually voiced some of my own concerns.

Founder's Day. This is another day I simply don't get. Like a smaller-scale Civil War reenactment, it confuses everyone, because the town wasn't really founded, it was stumbled upon. This does not deter Chastity, and in fact she has taken the liberty of rewriting history to make the day more eventful. How, you wonder? Well, for one the costumes are not historically accurate. Most are far too fancy to be anything the early residents could have owned. And there's a ball. Where they would have held a ball in the middle of nowhere, I can't say, but Chastity thinks it's good for the town that we all believe there was a ball.

Let's face it, hundreds of years later and we still can't claim a thousand residents. When the town began, there would have only been a handful of people, most of them related to each other. I doubt they would have thought, "Oh, let's have a ball."

So here I am wearing a period gown, probably more accurate for Victorian-era London, watching in the mirror as Josh twists my hair up and thinking of Frank. This is one festival that I shared annually with him. We sat in the background like Statler and Waldorf from *The Muppets*. With him gone, it just isn't going to be the same. And like the smell of swordfish that never seems to fade away, I have got to make a decision on what to do with his money.

My thoughts have detoured back to that article and my phone conversation with my mom far more often in the past few days than I would like. I wonder if Logan saw the article. Has the reality of seeing us in black and white finally knocked some sense into him? He can do better than me and that's not me being pathetic or agreeing with my mother. It is just a simple truth.

It is entirely possible that Josh is right. Logan finds the quiet life of Harrington appealing, for now, and I'm part of his life here. Logan has said it himself, the undercurrents of the art world are suffocating. But he's an artist and, good or bad, there's a part of him that loves that world or he wouldn't still be part of it. And he is. Every other week he's in Manhattan, he's David. So it's not too hard to believe that he will eventually return to the world that is so enamored of him, especially if his hideaway is overrun by the press, destroying that quiet life. And if he does go, he'll be leaving some wreckage behind, namely my heart.

And as I sit there, seeing my ridiculous reflection in the mirror, wondering if the man I'm in love with really feels the same or is only smitten with the idea of me, I realize the last place I want to be right now is at some stupid event that's not even historically accurate.

"Let's blow off Founder's Day and get drunk."

"Seriously?" Josh stops working on my hair. A poker player he is not, because he clearly likes the idea.

"Yeah. You in, Gwen?"

"Hell yeah. I couldn't drink a beer in this corset."

So we do get drunk and it doesn't take long, since we're just pounding them back.

"I'm hungry," Gwen says.

"Yeah, me too, and there is all that catered food at Town Hall," Josh adds.

"You want to crash the party?" I ask.

"We'll be like shadows, no one will know we're there." Josh holds an elbow out to each of us.

Gwen and I don't have to be asked twice. "Okay."

———

The ball portion of the night has begun by the time we arrive and the dance floor is packed with swaying couples. Logan is easy to spot, since he stands so much taller than the others in the room. He has his head lowered slightly as he talks to Broderick. He looks good—*sexy* is a better word. And because I'm drunk, I have fully convinced myself that he'll be leaving me, breaking my heart in the process. In this moment, I wish I had laser beams for eyes and giggle at the visual of Logan disintegrating before me, turning into a smoldering pile of black ash. Mean and completely uncalled for, but oddly comforting. Josh disrupts me from my fantasy.

"Look, a whole plate of shrimp."

"Grab it; I'll get the cocktail sauce," I say.

Gwen comes up behind us carrying a tray loaded with lunchmeats. "I nicked this."

Slang coming from Gwen is so uncharacteristic that I can't help laughing.

"What?" she says.

"You, what's up with the slang lately?"

"*Sons of Anarchy*."

"You're watching it?"

"Yep. You're right, it's awesome and I love Jax."

"Already called him. Wait, the slang, you trying to be an old lady?"

"I could pull it off."

Taking in her pink cashmere sweater set, I bust out laughing. "I don't think so."

She flips me off. On second thought . . .

"We should get wine," Josh says as he tries to balance the plate of shrimp and another of olives. We're so busy raiding the food table that we don't notice anyone's approached until Tommy speaks up from behind us. Josh almost drops our goodies.

Feeling a bit like an old lady myself, I channel Jax's mom, Gemma, and get all up in Tommy's face. "Didn't anyone teach you not to sneak up on people?"

"Didn't anyone teach you not to steal?"

"Steal? We're not stealing, we're eating," I say in outrage.

"That food is for everyone," he insists.

At that moment, I just snap. I poke Tommy in the chest with my finger.

"Everyone, really? Where was everyone during the Swordfish Festival cleanup? And during the God of the Sea Festival where I drowned?"

He looks sullen now, but my vision is less than perfect at the moment, so I don't notice. What else I don't notice is how loud I'm getting as I poke Tommy in the chest with each of my points.

"I deserve this shrimp. Born to people who clearly shouldn't have reproduced, I date my best friend and turn him gay, date another man who doesn't know he's gay, almost have dinner with a third man who's more interested in his reflection than me, and land on a yeti who turns out to be a millionaire playboy.

"I lost the man I thought of as a father, had my thirtieth birthday party minus any family, and now I'm being dissed in the gossip rags. I am only human and I can take no more, so, yes, I have consumed my body weight in wine and I plan on eating this whole goddamn plate of shrimp."

It's then that I realize every eye in the room is on me, but I'm drunk enough that I just don't care. "Does anyone have a problem with that?"

Silence meets that question. I turn to Gwen and Josh, who are doubled over with laughter. "Shall we?" I look back over my shoulder at Tommy. "Grab a bottle of wine and join us."

Winking, I walk from the room with my head held high. "You are so going to hell," Tommy says as he steers me down the steps of Town Hall ahead of our friends.

"I've been living there for quite a while now."

He stops and Gwen and Josh continue to stagger forward. Instead of anger, I see love and understanding in his gaze. "Did that feel good?"

I sigh. "You have no idea."

"Come on, I'm hungry," Josh hollers. Tommy reaches for my hand again as we follow the others.

———————

While I'm working the following evening, many people have approached me to talk: people I haven't chatted with in years. I guess everyone's allowed a meltdown, even as big a one as I had. Maybe we all deserved the shrimp, after all. The door opens and Logan walks in. When he's close enough, he asks, "Can we talk?"

I should talk to him, but I'm feeling a bit cowardly. "I'm working."

"It won't take long."

That doesn't sound good. Suddenly my stomach is doing that weird thing it does when I'm watching a particularly suspenseful movie. "Okay. Tommy, I'm taking a break."

I follow Logan outside, and we walk beyond the parking lot to where it's more private.

"What was that last night?" he asks without preamble.

"I was drunk."

"Don't bullshit me, Saffron. You were drunk for a reason. What's that reason?"

141

"Frank and I loved Founder's Day, so I wasn't exactly dealing well." It's part of the truth.

A softness enters his expression. "Understandable, but I think there's more to it. Did you see the article about us?"

The urge to lower my head is strong. Here it comes—his wake-up call that he isn't where he wants to be or with the person he wants. "Yes."

"I can't control the gossip. David has always been a popular subject for the paparazzi."

"I know, but how do you stand it?"

"It's not easy having your every move observed and commented on, your relationships held under a microscope to be picked apart by people who know nothing about you. It's one of the reasons I have never allowed myself to get serious about anyone. Putting dates through that is unfair. I never meant to fall in love with you, Saffron. My intention in moving here was to get out of the rat race, to get my life back. Walking into Tucker's and seeing you behind the bar, listening to you laugh and joke with your customers, you mesmerized me. When you started your game, seeming to understand that I needed space and yet still offering a hand, you had me. That article is wrong. You are far above me. I'm the one who should be counting my lucky stars that a woman like you— with your smile and the way your eyes twinkle with genuine interest and affection for those around you—would even look twice at a man like me. As much as I would like for it to be different, David will always be in the mix and that means the public will always want a piece of him."

He moves closer to take my hands into his. "Tell me you can live with that. Tell me I have a chance with you, even knowing that your life will be different if you agree."

My words won't come. Every one of the fears I've been stewing over for weeks has been obliterated with one very well-done speech. I am an idiot. Lifting his hands, I press a kiss in his palm, a tear slipping from under my lid to drip in the place I just kissed.

"Saffron?"

"My real fear, the one that had me running away, was that you would realize you were making a mistake. I was waiting for you to come to your senses, and the thought of you walking away from me was too hard to deal with."

"I'm not walking."

"I want a life with you, and that includes everything that makes up you."

"Will you have dinner with me tomorrow night?"

"Yes."

"I'll come for you at seven."

"Okay."

He doesn't kiss me, doesn't pull me close, just lifts our joined hands and mirrors my act of kissing my palm. And then he walks away.

Watching him go, I place a hand over my rapidly beating heart. I *am* an idiot, but a blissfully happy one.

———

Exactly at seven the next evening, Logan knocks at the door. I open it, but before either of us speaks a word, Reaper comes barreling into the room. Seeing Logan, he attempts to stop and fails to, instead falling on his butt, sliding along the floor with all four paws out in front of him.

"He's adorable." Logan shifts his eyes from Reaper to me. "He can come."

"Really?"

Humor twinkles in his eyes. "Yes."

"Okay." I grab the leash from the table and clip it onto Reaper's collar. Moments later Logan settles Reaper on my lap in the car, closing the door before climbing in himself. When we arrive at the lighthouse, I'm a bit confused to see several familiar cars in the drive.

Logan parks and shuts off the engine. "I invited a few people over. I hope that's okay with you."

"Why did you?"

"Because I'm asking you to take all of me and I want all of you. Your friends are part of you."

God, he's amazing. As much as I would like to have him all to myself, I can't deny that I like the idea of him getting to know my friends better. "Good answer."

We step inside and are greeted by the sound of voices, my friends' and his brothers', coming from down the hall. When we reach the kitchen, all eyes turn to us.

"Finally. I'm getting hungry." No surprise it's Dante whining about food.

"Saffron, come on over here and help me peel these shrimp, considering how much you like them," Tommy calls, which sets off laughter.

Logan comes up behind me, his hand at the small of my back, and he offers me a glass of wine. Reaching for his own, he leads me out back to where the grill is set up.

"We're having swordfish," he says, cleaning the grill grates. He looks at me from over his shoulder and winks.

"Funny."

"Did you like my tribute to the town?"

"I did, but why a swordfish?"

"The day you pelted me in the face with a swordfish funnel cake, and by the way—what the fuck—was when my admiration for you turned into something more."

"You can't be serious."

He takes a sip from his wine, eying me from over the rim. "Oh, I am."

"Why?"

"Because that was the day you were jealous over my dalliance with Chastity."

I've just taken a sip of my own wine, and I almost choke on it. Once I'm able to breathe again, I ask, "Are you kidding me?"

He says nothing, just stares at me.

"Are you feeling all right, Logan?" I nod at the grill just behind him. "Are you sure there isn't a gas leak?"

A smile slowly spreads over his face. He reaches for my hand and guides me closer to the water. "Never better."

Under the moon, he wraps me in his arms and slowly sways with me to a tune only he can hear. Being up against his hard, warm body is like a fix to a junkie and I settle myself more snugly into his embrace.

His lips are near my temple and I can feel his soft breath on my skin when he speaks. "You took a terrible festival and made it fun. You saved George from taking a bath by buying up half of his stock and making it so others would buy the rest and, in the process, made the day enjoyable. Even now people still talk about it as one of the best festivals ever. I fell in love with you that day."

I pull back, convinced I am going to have to smack him for teasing me again, but I see the truth in his eyes.

"That sculpture is more for me than the town. Every time I pass it, I think of you."

I kiss him then. I couldn't stop myself even if I wanted to. Logan doesn't hesitate to wrap his hands around my face so he can take the kiss deeper. His lips are possessive as they touch, taste, and reclaim and, with the coaxing of his seductive mouth, he's making me feel it all again—the profound emotion that only he is able to stir in me. How could I have ever doubted this? I'm lost in my raging need for him, but somehow he finds the strength to pull away.

His lips brush lightly over mine. "I have missed you. But now I need to get the steaks and maybe climb into the freezer for a minute."

I fan myself before replying, "You and me both."

He winks before he disappears back into the house.

Tilting my head back, I sigh. It's beautiful tonight with the stars dotting the twilight sky and the soothing sound of the water lapping against the beach. But the real reason for my sigh is that I'm not waiting for the other shoe to drop. Finally. It's not all going to be smooth sailing, but Logan and I are in it together and *that* is beautiful. Voices carry out into the night and my friends come outside, Logan in the rear with a huge tray of marinated steaks. He looks so handsome in the moment. More so because he looks so natural. All those magazines that see him as the millionaire playboy wouldn't believe it's the same person laughing with his brothers and Mitch while flipping steaks.

Josh walks over to join me. "How are you doing?"

"I am doing just fine."

"I was surprised and pleased when he called the other day and invited us for a barbecue."

"When did he call you?"

"Two days ago."

"So before the ball and my lovely performance." That makes me smile. "Let's see if we can help with dinner."

Broderick is just setting the table when we join him inside. "Can we help?"

"Could you get the silverware? It's on the counter in the kitchen."

"Sure thing. I'll get it." I'm sidetracked in the living room by a painting that I don't recognize. As I approach, I recognize Tucker's. In the picture, I'm building a Guinness and talking to George. My face is in profile and I'm laughing. The detail is so exquisite it's hard to believe that it isn't a photo. I don't hear Logan until he's standing right next to me.

"When did you do this?"

"While I was in Scotland."

My gaze shifts to him but he's still fixed on the portrait. "Like I said, I missed you like hell." He kisses my cheek. "Dinner's ready."

———

After his brother's strip steaks, baked potatoes, and grilled vegetables, Broderick whipped up a chocolate mousse cake that was so good Mitch asked for the recipe. I'm sitting in a chair near the fire that Logan has lit, with Reaper in my lap. The warmth from the fire and Reaper's snuggly body, combined with the food and wine, sends me into a dozy state.

"Would you like me to take you home?" Logan hunches down next to me.

I don't really want to go, but I know I'm not going to be awake much longer. "Okay."

We say our good-byes and before long I'm settled in Logan's very comfortable car. We barely make it down the street before I fall asleep. Minutes later, Logan is brushing his fingers over my cheek. "You're home, Saffron."

My eyes flutter open and I stifle a yawn just as he lifts me and Reaper into his arms and carries us to the door. He takes my keys and somehow manages to unlock the door while still carrying me. Lust stirs to life as Logan carries me to my room. It's so powerful that when he lowers me onto the bed, I almost pull him down on top of me. Reaper defuses the sexually charged moment when he jumps from the bed and runs around before darting out of the bedroom.

"Good night, Saffron."

"Thank you for tonight, it was perfect."

He starts from the room, but I call him back. "Stay, Logan, I miss sleeping next to you."

He has just reached the door when he turns his face to me. I know that I'm not the only one fighting the need to make love. "As much as I would love to stay with you, I can't. I broke your trust. I need to earn it again."

He isn't wrong and the fact that he knows this makes my heart thump almost painfully in my chest.

A few minutes later, I hear the door close quietly in his retreat.

CHAPTER THIRTEEN

"Are you sure you want to do this?" Dean asks as I sit across from him in his office. Since Frank died, I have been pushing the idea around about changing my last name to his, since he was my family and I want to honor the man he had been to me. After that phone call from my mom, the decision became that much easier. Changing my name might be unorthodox, but then so are my relationships.

"Yes, Frank meant the world to me and I'd like his name."

"Okay, I'll have these drawn up in a few days. If you'd like, I can come to Harrington and take you to lunch and we can go over them."

On the ride over, I worried that he'd be awkward around me after our kiss, but he is both professional and sweet. Still, I don't want to give him the wrong idea by accepting a lunch invitation.

His brows are furrowed when he glances up from his notes at my silence. "Friends, Saffron. I'm not asking you on a date."

The sigh escapes before I can hold it back. "I would really like that. And I'm still trying to figure out what to do with Frank's money. I want to use it for good, just don't know yet what."

"Okay. No worries, but before you go, I've been meaning to give something to you."

He moves from around his desk to the closet at the far side of the room and takes out a cardboard box. "This is the last of Frank's stuff from the nursing home; it was delivered a few weeks ago and I just haven't gotten around to getting it to you. I'll take it out to your car."

There's a little hitch to my heart at the thought of seeing Frank's things again. Dean seems to understand I'm a little overwhelmed and follows silently to the car. He doesn't hide his healthy ogle of Logan's Porsche. Which I drove, solo.

I pop the trunk for Dean and head to the driver's side, but before I can reach for the door he's there opening it for me. "Drive carefully. I'll call you in a few days to schedule lunch."

"Thank you. You've really been wonderful through all of this."

"Like I said, he was a friend and I'd like to count you among them as well."

"I would like that too."

When the engine roars to life, Dean whistles in appreciation. "Nice."

"You have no idea."

———

Later that afternoon, I'm sitting in my living room going through Frank's box. Just remembering Frank's frail hands showing me how the pieces move on the chessboard makes my heart squeeze in my chest. It's gotten dusty, so I spend a good half an hour washing all the pieces before setting it up on my coffee table.

His baseball cards are in the box as well, stored in a special book, which I place proudly on my bookcase. There are photos that are mostly of Frank and me through the various stages of our relationship, and I spend a good long time studying them and remembering. At the bottom of the box are ten well-worn black leather journals. I flip the cover of one and see the inscription:

For Saffron.

Taking out all the journals, I find they're all for me. I locate what seems to be the first and start to read. He wrote about us—that first meeting on his front stoop, the time he took me fishing and my line got snagged, yanking me into the water. A smile touches my lips as I continue to read, because I now have my answer about how he acquired his wealth. A fishing lure, the same very lure he had framed in his shop, made him millions. A few entries are dedicated to how proud he was on the day I received my college diploma. Even though he shared these experiences with me, to read in his own hand how he felt on not just the big days, but the little ones too, is precious.

One journal has a different inscription.

Sometimes a memory can be so painful it is impossible to speak it or to relive it, but I want the best part of my present to know the very best part of my past.

I read the first entry.

Her name was Margaret Phillips. I remember the first time I saw her, blond hair tumbling down her back like gold. She was laughing, her brown eyes bright from it and her cheeks rosy. I fell in love at first sight.

I worked with her dad near the docks in Boston, mostly mechanical work, fixing boat engines, cranes. He brought me home one night after a particularly long day and there she was sitting on the front step of their small rundown row house.

We became friends first, and then on our first date, a walk along the street where she lived, she let me kiss her. A light brushing of the lips, and I was sunk. She filled a place in me I never knew I needed filled. She made colors seem brighter, the sound of birds sweeter, life happier.

I could talk about her for days, weeks, years. There are so many memories, so many moments that are permanently etched into my heart, but I'm going to be selfish and keep them just for me.

I asked her to marry me after seeking permission for her hand from her father. Felt it important to include her family, since I had none of my own. She threw herself into my arms in the living room of her home, her joy mingling with my own. The wedding date was planned, her sister and mother had made her dress, her father had arranged for a dinner right on the lane where they lived—a neighborhood wedding.

Remembering her death is too painful. Even nearly seventy years later, the wound is still too fresh. People say you eventually move on, you make peace and find other things to fill the void. I filled the void, or rather, was gifted with the precious company of a young girl who had such fire and spark, she reminded me very much of my Maggie. But I never got over it and I never moved on. How does one do that when the best part of them is gone? For just a time, I had walked in paradise, had found true heaven on earth. That's not something anyone can get over.

Life is short, my dearest, dearest Saffron, and can be taken so quickly. Live and have no regrets. And if you are ever lucky enough to find the kind of love I shared with Maggie, hold on to it, fight for it, never give it up.

I'm sorry I never shared this while I was alive, but maybe you'll understand now why I didn't. I love you, Saffron.

The last words blur through my tears. Shaking from them, I hold the journal to my heart, hoping that somehow Frank will know I understand. The torment in his words, the agony Frank carried because of those memories and the loss of his Maggie, breaks my heart. I reminded him of his Maggie. He saw something in me that reminded him of her. This isn't just the first entry, it's the only entry in the journal. Perhaps he wrote in this journal last, or it was intentional: leaving this journal only for Maggie and his beloved memories that were too painful to write down.

Feeling what I do for Logan, I think I understand Frank's love, at least in some measure. Despite the bumps in the road, Logan is it for me. We may get off track and even hurt one another, but what we have is what Frank had. The idea that he could one day be taken from me terrifies me, especially since we've wasted precious time lately for rather silly reasons.

Jumping from my sofa with the journal, I run out of the house, Reaper right behind me. I run nearly the entire two miles to the lighthouse, gasping for breath, but I don't stop moving, not until I see him. He's in his studio, his body framed by the window. I don't call to him; he already sees me, like he knew I was coming.

Maybe it's the tears or my flushed face, maybe it's because I arrived with no car and am now panting, forcibly pulling air into my lungs, or maybe it's just that he wants to hold me, but the door flies open and he comes running out. As he wraps me into his arms, I bury my face in his shoulder and let the tears fall.

He doesn't ask what's wrong, just holds me until I pull myself together. Still held tightly against him, I lift my head to his.

"He lost her."

"Who?"

"Frank. He had . . ." A sob gets caught in my throat. "He loved her and she died. It's here in his journal."

Tenderness fills his expression, his hands moving up my body to frame my face, his thumbs gently brushing over my temples. "May I read it?"

"I would really like that."

Silently he studies me, taking in my features as if he's etching them into his memory, and seeing the parallel to Frank brings the tears again. He reaches for my hand and leads me inside. Settling on his sofa, he takes the journal from me.

"He wrote it all down, all about me and him, our lives together. It's better than pictures or videos because it's his heart pressed on those pages. And then there's this journal."

Logan settles my head on his shoulder and kisses me, then he starts to read. His body tenses, his arm around me tightens, his chest moving hard with the emotion stirred by Frank's words. Suddenly the journal is on the floor and he's folding himself around me. Splaying his hand over the small of my back, his mouth comes down hard on mine.

Reaching around his neck, I draw him closer and kiss him deeper, running my tongue over his, overwhelmed with the need to melt into him on every level. He yanks his shirt forward over his head. The need to touch is powerful but I don't, caught in the smoldering yet infinitely more meaningful spell he's casting on me. His jeans follow his shirt, his hands find my hips and he draws me to him, our bodies molding perfectly together as if we're a set. His lips claim my shoulder, then my neck, his hands moving down my back to my thighs, lifting my skirt to pull my panties off. Hard muscle and smooth skin meets my touch as I run my hands over him.

Holding me close, he shifts, his body coming to rest on top of mine. Mouths meet, tongues touch and taste. Spreading my legs, seeking the connection to him, my entire body sighs when he slides into me. It's never been like this. It's more than sex, it's like the joining of two halves to make them whole again. Logan starts to move, slowly at first, moving deep only to retreat, practically leaving me before sinking back in, deeper. The tightening in my belly and the chills moving over my skin intensify. Grabbing his ass, I push up as he thrusts deeper. The orgasm starts slowly shooting tingles down my arms and legs before exploding, consuming me with its brilliance.

We lie tangled together, Logan's light touch over my arm as much arousing as it is soothing. Thoughts of Frank are right there, knowing he had this with someone and lost it. The fact that he could continue to function was a miracle, in my opinion.

"Are you thinking about Frank?"

"I'm thinking about you and how if Frank had what I have with you and lost it . . ."

He holds me closer.

"I want to do something. Something to honor the man Frank was. I've been thinking about the house he left me and I had an idea. I really thought of it after you told me about moving here as a child. Students, like you, who come here to study—leaving home and being on your own is hard enough, but being so far from home must be even harder. I would imagine there are even students who choose not to come here because of how much of an adjustment it is, teenagers who need more support than dormitories can offer, at least for the first year. So I was thinking . . . what if I created a different kind of dormitory, a place that was a stepping stone between home and the dorms for those who need that additional support. I could have counselors, trained therapists on staff, to help them through the adjustment period—with the proximity of the house to Manhattan, it's the perfect location for students studying at any of the NYC colleges and universities."

"I think Frank was right when he said you would know what to do with the legacy he left you."

"Could you help me? I haven't a clue where to start."

"Without question."

"Maybe we could start today." I try to move but Logan rolls and pins me under him. "Not today. I've got you in my bed, so to speak, in the middle of the day, and I don't intend to let you out of it again."

I see the wisdom in this statement. "That's a better plan."

The following morning, I wake but Logan isn't in bed. After quickly dressing, I search the house and find him on the beach, looking out at the water. Reaper is farther down the beach, chasing his tail.

Logan's wearing faded jeans and a beat-up sweatshirt, his feet are bare, and the breeze coming off the surf blows his inky hair about. His back is to me, but even from my distance, I can tell he's tense. His shoulders are rigid and he's clenching his hands into fists. I start toward him and his head whips around, those eyes spearing me from across the beach. He's pissed; he starts toward me, his long strides eating the distance between us. As he approaches, anger is just radiating off him.

"What's wrong?" I ask.

"Were you planning on telling me about the threats?"

"What?"

He lowers his head so our eyes are level and man, he is spitfire mad. "The calls, the severed bird's head?"

"I thought you knew. I thought that was why you came to my house that first day."

"No, I didn't know. Broderick mentioned it when he stopped by earlier to drop off some supplies for me, mentioned it as if I knew already. You should have told me."

Broderick had been here? Damn, I really do sleep like a dead person. "Why should it have been me? If you hadn't run away, you would have been here and known all about it."

That comment is a direct hit since his face pales. "You're right."

I don't want to fight with him. We've done enough of that lately. Touching him, since I need the contact and I suspect he does too, I attempt to soothe him. "Sheriff Dwight is doing his thing, and I am being very careful, but there has been nothing since the package."

"I don't like it."

"I don't either, but there isn't much I can do about it. So, changing the subject. Can I pick your brain about my idea?"

He doesn't move from the subject as quickly, but it's the dark look that accompanies his thinking that sends a lick of warning lighting through me. He links our fingers, squeezing my hand as if to make sure I'm really standing there, and says, "Yes, I'll make some coffee."

———

Coffee turns into lunch and dinner at my house, and boy, did Reaper score with the hamburger Logan grilled up for him, as Logan and I discuss in detail what I want to do. He left me with some websites of places doing similar things.

Throughout the day I find myself pausing my work and just watching him. He's an incredible artist, but today I saw the businessman, and he's equally incredible at that.

Logan agrees that we should check out the house, but unlike our New York adventure, this time we'll catch a plane into LaGuardia and rent a car. Before he leaves, we walk Reaper along the beach, make out like school kids under the stars, and then he waits for me to lock the door before he climbs onto his motorcycle and drives off. He only left five minutes ago and I already miss him.

Turning off the lights, I head into the bedroom where I shower and change into my pajamas. I try to watch some television, but I just can't get into it, so I shut it off and try for sleep, but it's only nine o'clock and I'm not having much luck.

I can't seem to stop my brain from working as my thoughts drift from Logan to Frank. Frank mentioned that Maggie's mom and sister made her wedding dress. Was it possible that her sister was still alive? I'm surprised at how much I want to have a chance to talk to the sister of the woman Frank had loved and lost. Which leads to another thought. I still have Frank's ashes. I haven't figured out where to lay him to rest, but if I could find out where Maggie was buried, I could seek permission to bury Frank with her. Googling Margaret Phillips ends up being fairly pointless, since she died well before the computer age. And if she had lived, she would have most likely felt as Frank did about computers. He didn't like them nor did he use them: no ads on the Internet, no website or social media page. He thought it was all nonsense. His cash register was ancient and his phone had a rotary dial. And without any of those online links, search engines don't have as much to draw from. There has to be a way to learn her sister's name. Even her death records would probably give me next of kin. I'm not savvy enough on computers to figure it out, but Josh is. Looking at the clock to make sure it isn't too late, I call him.

"Hey, Saffron, what's up?"

"Is it possible to search death records online?"

"Well, that's a bit morbid, isn't it?"

"Funny. I'm trying to find a woman that Frank knew. It's a long story and I'd rather you read it in Frank's words than me tell you, but for now I want to find her, more specifically her sister."

"Frank's journals?" His voice softens, laced with understanding and tenderness.

"Yes."

"Death records are a matter of public record, so you should be able to look them up online, but how long ago are we talking?"

Remembering Frank's words of missing her even seventy years later, I quickly do the math. "Around 1945, give or take a few years."

"That may be a problem. Most states are working to get their records online, but it's very likely that those records are still only hard copy. Where is this?"

"Boston."

"Um, there's a chance. Here, take down this URL."

After I hang up with Josh, I search for Margaret, but the death records only go back as far as 1962. I then search for another Phillips on the off chance her sister never married, but none of them list a Margaret as a sibling. There has got to be a way to find Margaret's sister, yet my eyes are growing heavy so I shut down my computer, grab a glass of water, and finally, at three in the morning, I fall asleep.

I am informed by Tommy that Logan is looking for me and he is in the community kitchen in Town Hall with George, and I have to say, that is not anywhere I'd ever expect him to be. My late night of amateur sleuthing slows me down getting there because I'm just dragging.

As soon as I enter, I perk up, and not in a good way, because I smell something that is not as bad a smell as the dreaded swordfish, but it's pretty damn close. While attempting to breathe only through my mouth, I finally take in the scene before me. And I almost laugh out loud.

Logan is standing next to George, both wearing bright-red aprons and looking at a cookbook with matching expressions of panic. On the counter in front of them is flour, sugar, eggs, and butter, so I can only assume they're preparing to bake a cake, but for what?

I'm about to walk over and ask, when George says to Logan, "I think this is the most ridiculous thing Chastity has ever asked me to do. How did you get roped into this?"

"I told her I planned on putting down roots here and I wanted to have a more active role in the community. I didn't realize at the time that would include creating a kelp cake. What exactly is a kelp cake?"

George rubs a hand over his head. "I've got to tell ya, I've no idea."

I bump a sheet pan on the counter as I walk toward them, earning the attention of both of them. "Are you kidding? Chastity has you baking a kelp cake? Who the hell is going to eat a kelp cake?"

"That's what I tried to tell her, but she was adamant," George says.

Narrowing my eyes at George, I say, "If there is kelp cake, then there must be a festival lurking in the very near future. Chastity wasn't serious in that meeting about an actual festival for seaweed, was she?"

"'Fraid so. In just under four weeks. She wants us to practice making the cake."

"So not only are you to make a kelp cake, but you are to perfect the kelp cake?"

George sighs. "Yeah."

My gaze moves to Logan. "And you are okay with this?"

He leans his hip on the counter and grins. "I'm just trying to do my duties as a citizen of Harrington."

"It's the most ridiculous thing I've ever heard," I mutter but walk around the counter and wedge myself between them to look at the cookbook.

"So what? You're thinking a basic vanilla cake batter and then adding the kelp?"

Logan leans slightly in my direction so I can feel the heat coming from his body. Okay, maybe standing this close to him is a bad idea, since thoughts of the other night are chasing every other thought from my head. He seems to know the impact he's having on me. His hand comes to rest on the small of my back, which immediately sends heat up and down my spine. I grip the counter to keep myself steady. He only says one word, but so deep and soft that my toes curl, "Yes."

"It's really rather warm in here, isn't it?" Did I just say that out loud?

"I'm actually cold," George points out innocently. He goes to the other counter to get the baking powder, and Logan uses that opportunity to lower his head so his lips brush against my ear. Clearly he's thinking about the other night too.

"I want to see you tonight."

My knees go weak. George returns with the baking powder, oblivious to the sexually charged air around him. "What do you think, Saffron?"

I think I'm going to weep. Logan leans back against the counter as cool as can be and mimics George when he asks, "Yeah, Saffron, what do you think?"

He isn't fooling me because, while his voice is even, his eyes are wild. Since I believe in paybacks, I reach across Logan for the vanilla extract, making sure I press as much of myself against his hard body as possible. The aroused grumble that comes from Logan makes me feel rather smug and one look at him confirms that he is far from feeling cool. Good.

"Oh, please excuse me," I tease.

I can't make out a curse, but he definitely hisses through his teeth. Satisfied that I have thrown him off balance, I return my attention to the cake.

"I think vanilla is too bland a flavor and will become completely overpowered by the godforsaken kelp. However, if you make a more intense-flavored cake, like a spiced cake—carrot cake—I think you may be able to pull it off. We'll need to puree the kelp and make sure we balance the wet and dry ingredients to compensate."

Logan drapes his arm around my shoulders and looks past me to George. "I think we just found our savior."

George exhales before he replies, "Amen."

The kelp cake, and I will deny helping if asked, turns out to be very tasty. Chastity arrives not long after we finish and can't stop raving about it. We write down the recipe for future reference before saying good-bye to George. As soon as Logan and I step out into the early night air, I think of Frank.

"Do you have any contacts in Boston?"

He responds first with a slight raising of his eyebrow and then he asks, "Why?"

"I would like to find if Margaret's sister is still alive or at the very least where Margaret is buried. Her death records aren't online. I've already looked."

He stops walking and turns to me. "You want to bury Frank with Margaret." He isn't asking.

"Yes."

His thumb brushes along my jaw in the sweetest caress. "He would have wanted that. I know a few people. We'll find her sister if she's still alive, and if not, we'll locate Margaret's grave."

"Thank you."

We continue on in silence, which is broken when Logan says, "I'm not always going to do or say the right thing. I may shut you out or close off, I may even try to push you away, but I need you to know, Saffron, that you are the point I will always come back to." His eyes find mine. "You are my home."

Choking on the emotions that intimate glimpse into him stirs, all I can offer in return is, "And you are mine."

Arriving at my house, I want nothing more than to make love to him. Leading him inside to my room, I guide him to the bed. When he's sitting, I reach for his hands and move them up my body, under my shirt until he's cupping my breasts. Stepping closer, he responds by squeezing me gently. When he yanks my shirt over my head and rips my bra from me, anticipation escapes on a moan. His focus is completely on his fingers that are twisting and tugging on my nipples. He squeezes them, his tongue touching the tip, teasing. Straddling his one leg, I start to rub myself against him to ease the ache between my thighs. Releasing my nipples, his tongue flicks one before he lightly bites me and then he sucks me deep into his mouth. Needing to possess every part of him, to brand him mine, I find the hard ridge pressing against his fly and rub him through the denim. Flipping the snap on my jeans, his hand slips into my pants, between my legs, so I'm riding his fingers. He pushes two into me as his thumb works that nub. I feel the orgasm but I don't want to come yet. Kneeling down between his legs, my fingers work his button and zipper to free him. Pulling his jeans down, I stare at the part of him I want to taste. Hard and thick and yet I know he'll feel as smooth as silk against my tongue. Lifting my eyes to his, I lean closer just as he shifts onto the edge of the bed and slides right into my mouth. His hands fist into my hair, a primal growl rumbles in the back of his throat. My grip on his thighs is so hard I'm probably leaving bruises, but I can't get enough of him. He's getting close, I can feel his body tightening with his orgasm and I know he wants to pull me up his body, but I can't stop. I want his taste in my mouth, want to feel him lose control. Reaching for the sac between his legs, I squeeze him and he comes.

He grabs me and tosses me on the bed. In what seems like a blink of an eye, he finishes undressing himself and me.

"Spread your legs wider," he orders, and I obey.

"So pretty. Where do you want me?"

My fingers move between my legs where I am so wet and ready.

Reaching for those fingers, he brings them to his mouth and licks off my taste. This sampling has clearly fueled the beast because in the next second, his face is buried between my legs.

"Oh God, yes." My hips jerk, lifting off the mattress because his tongue feels so fucking good. He flicks it across that sensitive nub as his fingers tease before slipping in. He works me until he feels the tremors and then he sucks hard on that pulsing point as three fingers impale me and I come on a cry. He doesn't wait for my orgasm to end before he moves up my body, settles himself between my thighs, and thrusts into me. He must feel the orgasm ripping through me because he speeds up his thrusts to prolong it. And then he bends my legs, opening me wider for him, as his hips move harder and faster until his own orgasm rips through him. He drops down, cradled by my body, and just breathes me in.

He starts to move but I whisper, "Don't pull out yet."

Wrapping my legs around him, he rolls so that I'm on top, my legs on either side of his hips, my head resting over his heart. He pulls the covers over us and in a few minutes, I am sound asleep.

Logan is sleeping. He's lying on his stomach so his back is exposed for my viewing pleasure. My fingers itch to touch him, so I do, running my fingertips over his smooth, warm skin. My lips replace my fingers as I press a kiss on his lower back, right on the deep groove of his spine, before working my way up. Just as I place a kiss on his neck, he moves fast and cages me with his body. I get only a second to see that beautiful face, tense with desire, before his mouth covers mine. By the time he ends the kiss and rolls over to sit up, I'm fairly brain-dead. He tugs on his jeans and stands, reaches for his T-shirt, and pulls it over his head. The play on his muscles with that simple act almost has me weeping when he's completely covered.

"Why did you get dressed?" Because frankly I'm not done with him yet, not even close.

"We should take Reaper for a walk."

Now? I'm a boneless bundle and he wants to stretch his legs? Fine. I climb from the bed and slip on a pair of sweats and a T-shirt, pull my hair into a ponytail, and start from the room, but Logan hasn't made any attempt to leave the room, even though he is so eager to walk Reaper.

"What is going on with you?" I ask.

"You are so beautiful," he whispers. Unbelievable, it appears that he's struck shy. He pushes his hands into his pockets and looks down a second before looking up at me through his lashes. "I want to walk Reaper because my instinct is to not let you out of this room, ever. Knowing Frank had this and lost it, the idea of losing you, of losing us . . . I want to keep you locked away with me, safe."

Not shy: vulnerable, and maybe a little scared, but why? I don't get the sense his concern is a general one, but something specific he wants to protect me from. It's on the tip of my tongue to ask, but I don't want to spoil the mood, so I express his heartfelt words in a different way. "I love you too."

———

Reaper loves to chase everything: the birds, the sand, the water, and even things that I can't see. This makes me wonder if he can see dead things. He is also fast—so fast I fear if he ever took off I'd never be able to catch him; but as much as he loves to run, he always comes back.

Logan's hand is wrapped around mine and he seems just as captivated by Reaper as me. We walk along while Reaper's sleek puppy body winds in and around us. It's quiet and so peaceful, but I won't lie, there's a part of me worrying now too. What brought on that moment in the bedroom? Not that it wasn't a beautiful moment, but it was definitely fueled by something.

Logan lightly tugs on my arm. "When would you like to go see your house? I thought we might go next weekend."

"I'd like that. My schedule is flexible, so I can leave whenever."

He stops and picks up a stick, tossing it into the air for Reaper, who takes off after it like a bullet. He is great at catching the sticks, but bringing them back is something we have to work on. At home when we play, once Reaper finds his treasure, he hoards it in his favorite spot under the kitchen table. And after Logan and I christened that table, yeah, it's my favorite spot now too.

Logan asks, "Can you swing taking the week following that off too?"

"Why?"

"It's a surprise."

"No hint?"

"No. Can you?"

"Yeah, I think Tommy will be fine with that, but you're not going to leave me in suspense, are you? It's going to kill me having to wait a week."

He's walking backward now, just in front of me, keeping an eye on Reaper, who went to retrieve the stick he just tossed. "A week in suspense never killed anyone."

"Nothing I can do will persuade you to tell me?"

Considering my last attempt at persuasion, I get the wicked look that flashes over his face. "I will certainly not discourage you from trying to persuade me. The more varied and inventive your methods, the better, but I won't break."

"Tease. What do you have to do today?"

"I've a few calls to make. What about you?" He's vague in answering. Could whatever it is he needs to do be related to his need to keep me safe?

"I don't have work tonight so I'm probably going to veg out and watch a movie. Want to stay? We can cuddle up on the sofa and watch something scary?"

"Veg out?"

"Stay in your pj's for the day. You've never done that?"

"No."

"I have, and often; especially when I'm watching movies, pj's are required."

"Is this a law or just a guideline?"

I love that he's teasing me. "Guideline, but I'm working on passing it into law."

He responds with more than a grin but not quite a chuckle. "I'll stay and watch a movie with you."

The urge to exhale in relief almost has me doing so. Can't deny I'm a bit on edge. Logan's not the type to worry, so the fact that he's a bit off probably means there's a good reason for it. Eventually I'm going to have to pry it out of him, but not today, so I switch gears. "Yay! And since you don't have pj's you can watch in the nude."

My feet are no longer on the ground and the air escapes my lungs in a rush since I'm now over Logan's shoulder. I'm laughing as Logan walks us back to my house. "If I'm going to be naked, so are you."

CHAPTER FOURTEEN

Frank's house in Upper Nyack, New York, looks very much like the house from the Julia Roberts movie *Stepmom* in its magnificence. The place is right on the Hudson River on a nice lot with about five or six acres. It's not hard to imagine kids sitting around the yard, maybe a barbecue going, even a softball game.

Logan is walking along the perimeter doing whatever it is men do when they're checking out property. I turn back to the house. Dean explained that Frank's house was bought as an investment—a rental property. Why this house? Was it the type of home he and Maggie dreamed of owning? I step up onto the porch just as Logan comes up beside me.

"Are you ready to go inside?"

I had gotten the keys from Dean after confirming that the house is currently unoccupied. I nod and Logan unlocks the door and holds it open for me. The place is completely empty, but still charming with walnut floors and walls that are painted in a mossy green with creamy-white trim work.

"It's been kept in really great shape, most of the bones have been updated lately." Logan makes this observation but I'm not really listening because I can see it, in my head—Dupree House. Teenagers sitting at the bar in the kitchen doing homework, relaxing in the living room between classes or at the end of the day, holing up in the library reading. But beyond seeing that, I can see Frank and Maggie, building a life here. Having all of their children brought home from the hospital to this house, having all the major moments in a life here, surrounded by heart and home.

"Saffron?"

"He missed out on so much."

"Frank?"

"Did he see himself in a home like this with Maggie? If he had, and knowing Frank, he had, he never heard the sound of his children's feet running down those stairs on Christmas morning. He didn't play hide-and-seek with them in that yard or celebrate birthdays in the kitchen. He chose to not live life after he lost her. He chose to exist, to survive, but not to live."

"He did, though, Saffron. He did all of that with you."

"But I wasn't his child."

"Family is more than blood. He chose to live for you. He loved you so much that he pulled himself from his heartache for you."

"I changed my last name to Dupree." I realize I've blurted that out when Logan lifts a brow at me. "Dean drew up the papers. It was made official a few days ago."

"Like I said, family is more than blood. Frank would have liked that, very much. When we get back, we can start on the plans for the Dupree House." There was a note of reverence in his tone.

"We?"

"Was there ever a question?"

Love wraps around me and squeezes. "No."

"Broderick and Dante are good resources, working the legal parts, and before you say anything, they will definitely want to help."

"Okay, once we get back we get the ball rolling."

We leave Frank's house in the rental car Logan arranged for us when we arrived earlier and head off to my big surprise. "Since the day has arrived, are you going to tell me?"

"And spoil the surprise now that it's so close? No way."

Turning my head to stare out the window, I mutter, "You sure know how to keep a secret."

"Hm? I didn't quite make that out."

Gloating, I am certain there's gloating in his tone, and despite myself my lips curve up. "Can I ask you something?"

"Sure."

"How have you managed to keep Logan and David separate?"

The tensing of his shoulders is a clear indication that the subject is not a pleasant one for him. "Never mind. We don't have to talk about it."

He takes my hand in his. "It's okay. I don't mind talking about it with you."

Staring at his face, I wonder if there will ever come a day when I get used to the fact that this man is mine. I kind of hope not. Though his attention is back on the road, I still feel his focus on me.

"It's a juggling act. The shows I attend are only for David's work. I don't make appearances as Logan so no one can place a face with a name. No one's interested in Logan, he's just another painter. He doesn't have David's checkered past, a sordid past that makes him news to those who hunger for gossip."

"David's fans are coming to Harrington. Eventually they're going to put two and two together, that it's not David living there but Logan."

"Maybe, but from my experience, the ones hungry for the story are really only interested in the pictures. The stories they make up are whatever will help those pictures sell papers. The person I am is of little consequence to them."

"Don't you hate it?"

"Yeah, but I've learned to deal. My sculptures are viewed around the world. I have pieces in museums, private collections, there's even a sculpture in the White House. To have reached that level of success in a field I love, I can endure the bad that comes with the good."

"I'm sensing a *but*."

He glances at me. "I like that you know me well enough to sense the *but*. But yes, sometimes that bad goes beyond what's tolerable."

"Meaning?" And then I answer my own question. "You've had crazy fans."

"A few."

"Like stalker-crazy fans?"

"Yes."

Can't help the tingle of fear that raises the hair on my arms. Could he be worried about a stalker-crazy fan? "How bad?"

"One broke into my house once, slashed some things, took some others. The police arrested her down the street attacking some poor tabloid grunt who got her picture leaving my house. She wasn't after the picture to save herself, she wanted the picture for her collection."

"Creepy."

"And dangerous. Any attention that seems even slightly off, I take very seriously."

I have the sense there's more he wants to say, but he decides against it and changes the subject and since the old subject was disturbing, I'm just fine with that. But a kernel of fear has rooted firmly in my gut.

We're just passing Boston. The leaves on the trees lining the road are all changing colors, a palette of gold, burgundy, and rust. A sign with mile markings for the upcoming towns comes into view and it is then that I know the surprise. I have never in my life had the need to cry because of intense happiness, but I am feeling the need now. Emotion tightens my throat. "You're taking me to Salem."

"A family vacation." He smiles at me with an almost uncharacteristic warmth. "I'm not your family, but I would like to be."

The words can't be stopped, rushing up my throat and out of my mouth because every cell of my being is screaming them. "I love you."

He touches my cheek, wiping the tear away with his thumb. He doesn't say it back, not with words, but I feel it all the same.

———

Logan got us a room in the Coach House Inn—a hand-carved mahogany bed, a little sitting area with wingback chairs, and a fireplace combine to send me into movie-quality fantasies. Logan sets our bags near the closet before reaching for a black duffel that he drops on the bed and opens.

I try to reach into his bag and he actually slaps my hand away.

"Patience, Saffron." This new boyishness about him absolutely charms me. He glances over and grins before he starts unloading the bag. "We have popcorn, I made sure that there was a microwave in the room, Junior Mints, Sour Patch Kids, M&M's, soda, and wine."

"Logan . . ."

"I'm not done. As I've been instructed, proper movie attire is pajamas. Unfortunately, I own none."

This I know because the man sleeps in the nude and I have only two words to say about that.

Hell. Yeah.

He then lifts out a pair of black flannel pajama pants from his bag. "It's the best I could do."

I've always heard guys say it's more of a turn-on to have a woman scantily clad than completely bare because the imagining makes all the difference. "That should do," I say with sudden hoarseness. Logan in those, knowing what I know is hiding under them . . . Hell. Yeah.

He puts the candy and drinks on the table in the sitting area before he folds his pajamas and lays them at the base of the bed; I feel a pang of sadness watching him. He turns to me and clearly realizes that something has distressed me, so he walks over and brushes his hand down my cheek.

"What's wrong?" he asks.

"It's not really fair, is it?"

"What's not fair?"

"When people see you they see this." My fingers brush along his jaw. "And don't get me wrong, this is exceptional, but there's so much more to you than a pretty face, but those groupies of David's that won't give you any peace, they only see this."

"That doesn't bother me. I actually prefer it. You see the man under the celebrity and you're the only one that matters."

<hr />

We decide to start our adventures in Salem by riding mopeds through town. There's a place that rents them right near our inn. Reaper is vacationing at Uncle Tommy's, who will no doubt spoil him, but I do miss him.

I can't believe Logan not only remembered my story about wishing for a family vacation, but he actually planned one. Walking through graveyards, ghost tours, and haunted houses is so not his thing and yet he's going to do them with me. I'm not really sure what I did in my life that my karma landed me a man like Logan, but I thank the stars every night for him.

Logan is filling out the paperwork for our mopeds and I'm scoping out the shops because I've found I'm a bit of a souvenir junkie. It's a beautiful autumn day, the air crisp and cool. The tranquility is interrupted when two little girls just down the street from me get their ice cream cones knocked out of their hands by a boy who is as frightening as Scut Farkus from *A Christmas Story*. The cones sail through the air and crash into a messy blob on the sidewalk. Even from my distance, I can see the tears filling the girls' eyes. Their parents appear, taking the girls by the hand, leading them away from the boy and to more ice cream.

A dog barks, which captures the demon's attention and he walks over to the husky, who's leashed to a bench, and starts antagonizing the poor animal. Thinking of someone doing that to Reaper infuriates me. We all know how this will end. The dog will eventually feel so threatened that he will attack to protect himself, and will end up being put down. That is exactly where the little drama before me is leading.

As I stand there, I'm wondering where his mother is and why the hell she isn't paying any attention to her kid. He's captured the attention of pretty much everyone on the street except his own damn mother. I scan the crowd and my eyes land on a woman with the same orange-red hair, flirting like a schoolgirl with Logan; more than likely she's a David groupie. He's being nice about it but the back-off vibe is definitely clear. She either doesn't notice or doesn't care.

A few people seem to have started searching out the owner of the dog. I notice bikers parked across the street. Looking at the leather-clad bodies, the chains, the tattoos, and the hair, I get the glimmer of a wickedly childish plan. To be a part of perhaps the only time in his life where a little jerk like this will have the shit scared out of him.

As I cross the street toward the bikers, their attentions shift from the boy to me. A few even give me a very blatant perusal. My momentum slows with that hard, mean-looking attention. I stop in front of the man who appears to be the leader of the group and, though he isn't ugly, or as old as I expected, he is scowling. And then I realize he's scowling at me, so I immediately extend my hand. "Hi. I'm Saffron."

"Dirk."

"This is kind of out of the blue, but I noticed you were watching that future felon across the street."

"Yeah, kid needs a good kick in the ass."

"I agree. I would hate to see any harm come to that dog because of that little monster, so I had a thought."

"I'm listening."

After I share my plan, he throws his blond mane back and howls with laughter. He climbs off his bike. "Sounds like fun, count us in."

I shouldn't be enjoying this as much as I am.

Dirk nods at the little bastard across the street. "Any idea where his mom is?"

"Yeah. She's in the shop trying to dry hump my boyfriend."

This gets more laughter from several of the other bikers. "So we good?" I ask.

"Absolutely."

Crossing the street, I head for the devil's spawn. I don't have siblings, but, as I've already noted, I have watched more than my fair share of movies and television. It seems like kids at his age react to being asked to stop something in one of only a few ways. I'm banking that he's going to go with the most obvious reply. Stopping just in front of him, I slip my hands into my pockets before I attempt my best John Wayne impersonation. "I think you best leave that dog alone, kid."

A chill goes through me at the coldness in his eyes. He curls his lips and practically spits his reply. "Make me."

Bingo. I take a step closer. "Okay."

Shock flashes across his face, which turns to fear at the sound of shit-kicking boots thundering behind me. A wall of leather and muscle is starting across the street toward us. Beelzebub's eyes have widened with fear and his jaw has dropped nearly to the ground.

"My friends are animal lovers. If I were you, I'd run."

And just like that the kid takes off down the street, leaving a blazing trail in his wake. Applause breaks out. All the clapping and cheering finally stirs the mother from her lascivious plans for Logan and she hurries down the street after her son. Logan joins me just as Dirk and his gang step up on the curb.

One of the old ladies behind Dirk purrs, "Very, very nice."

She's eying Logan even though she's standing with a man who looks very much like the mythical Thor: big and tall with piercing blue eyes that startle a "Likewise" right out of me.

This earns me a hiss from the old lady and a grin and a wink from Thor.

"Dirk, this is Logan."

"Nice to meet you," Logan offers as he shakes Dirk's hand. "I guess I missed all the fun."

"Yeah, man, but you were too busy with that woman trying to get you to impregnate her."

A visible shudder goes through Logan as he makes an *ick* face. "She had nails like talons."

"Nasty business that. We're having a clambake later right on the beach. Why don't you two come?"

Logan glances at me before he says, "We'd like that."

And we did. We sat around a bonfire, ate clams, drank beer, and then later the guitars came out and Logan drew me up from our spot on the rocks so we could dance under the moon, joined by several of the other couples. Before we left, we gave Dirk our address in Harrington and told him and his crew to stop by whenever they were in the area.

The following morning, Logan and I set off for the beach for the annual sand sculpture competition. I wonder why Chastity never thought to do a sand sculpture competition. Maybe I should put that in the suggestion box, anonymously, of course. When we arrive the contest is well under way and most of the competitors have a fairly discernible sculpture, all but one. The kid is by himself and, though he's working very hard, there's no way he's going to be able to pull it off on his own. He's young too, maybe eight or nine.

"I wonder where his parents are?" I say this to myself because Logan is no longer at my side, he's approaching the boy. He stops to chat with him for a few minutes and then he moves to the judges' table. After a moment, he's given a number to pin on his shirt before he returns to the boy. It's adorable watching as Logan listens to his directions before he starts sculpting.

It's completely an unfair advantage having a master sculptor competing, but watching Logan turn sand and water into a dragon is incredible. The detail is so fine that it looks as if at any moment the dragon will either stand up and fly off or open his mouth and scorch us all with his fire breath.

Logan is so focused, though, that he doesn't notice the crowd forming around him, but he does stop every now and again and ask the boy for direction to make sure that what he's creating is what the boy wants. At this point, the boy is so in awe that he can only watch with his little mouth hanging open. Two hours later, the most incredible dragon I've ever seen stands before the crowd, but there are just enough childlike components to show that it wasn't all done by Logan. The judges do their thing and some kids that made a car out of sand win first place, but the boy doesn't seem to care as he looks in wonder at his dragon.

When Logan starts back up the beach to me, he's stopped and asked for autographs and photos since people now recognize who he is. He handles the requests with quiet courtesy. Some time later he drops down on the sand next to me and yanks me down so I'm lying flat on my back before he rests his head on my stomach.

"I need a nap."

"I think you've earned one. I love your dragon."

He eyes me through his lashes. "It's pretty fucking cool, isn't it? The kid was okay that it wasn't going to get judged, he just wanted a wicked dragon. His words."

Before he settles in for his nap, a woman appears, her head blocking out the sun. Unlike the others who waited a bit of a distance from Logan, this chick moves right up into our personal space as if she has every right to be there.

"You're David Cambre."

Logan sits up, game to give her an autograph. In the next minute she's got her phone out taking our pictures. I feel like I'm in a modeling shoot. Logan jumps to his feet, the girl steps back but she's still clicking away. Grabbing my hand, he pulls me up against his side, turning me into his chest so the camera doesn't get my face and moves us away from her at a ground-eating pace.

"Wait until I post these. My friends aren't going to believe it. Is that your girlfriend? What's her name?" The chick screams down the beach as she follows after us. What the fuck? "C'mon, what's her name?"

I can feel every muscle in his body go hard. He's about to lay into the girl, but she's saved by one of her friends, who calls her back. At least someone in her company recognizes that she's acting like an ass.

Her parting words: "Thanks for the pictures, sexy."

It's my turn to lay into her, my body is halfway around, but Logan's hold on me turns to steel. "Let it go, Saffron."

"Sexy, I'll give her sexy when I shove my size seven up her ass." I scream the last part.

Logan's shoulders are shaking with his laughter.

"What's so funny?"

"I'd actually like to see that."

"I'd ruin my shoes." Now he's howling with laughter. The sight of him with his head tilted back is magnificent and I am not the only one to think so; there is definite envy in some of the ladies we pass.

"I'm sorry, Saffron."

"Annoying and rude, ignorant and infuriating, but not a big deal."

"It's a fucking invasion of privacy."

He's not wrong, but getting upset over some stupid bimbo who doesn't have the sense God gave a mule is pointless. My arms tighten around his waist. "Let's go back to the room and fool around."

"Good plan."

"So is that what a stalker fan is like?"

"No, she was just a stupid kid, ignorant but harmless."

That was harmless? Just how far would these stalker fans go to get to him? That question is so disturbing I immediately force it from my head. Now is not the time.

"I don't want your first vacation ruined by shit like that."

"Won't ruin it for me, so don't let it ruin it for you. Deal?"

It takes him a beat longer to agree but he does, holding me closer and pressing a kiss on my head to seal it. "Deal."

Yep, I am a very lucky lady.

———

Looking up at the ceiling, I search for guidance and patience before turning my attention back to the man currently lounging on the bed. I realize he doesn't know what he's saying, but he's being extremely difficult in accepting that he's wrong: totally and completely wrong.

"As I've explained, Logan, an Alien will never defeat a Predator in a fair fight."

"I disagree. We're talking acid for blood, Saffron, that's a pretty significant weapon against any foe. The Predators aren't immune to it."

"Yes, this is true, but the Predator is a species born and bred for battle much like the Spartans. The Aliens are just mutant serpents."

"I'm sorry, but I agree with Tommy on this. The Aliens are serious badasses."

"You don't even believe in aliens."

He shifts so he can rest his head on his hand as a grin turns up his mouth on the one side. "I do, now."

We've watched *Alien vs. Predator*, but I don't know how anyone can watch that movie and take from it that the Aliens are cooler than the Predators. I mean, there's no competition. It's like comparing Brad Pitt to one of the dudes from *The Big Bang Theory*. I give up. Trying to make Logan see the error in his thinking is just more than I can handle, especially when he's lying there with that truly spectacular chest exposed for my viewing pleasure.

Crawling over to him, I straddle his lap as I run my hands down his chest. He's no longer thinking about Aliens or Predators either.

"There's a Jacuzzi tub in the bathroom. I think we need to check that out."

He rolls to shift our positions and grins down at me. "We'll check it out after."

And then his mouth takes mine. My hands move down that chest, loving the way his muscles respond to my touch. I barely have breath to say, "Too many clothes."

He's off me and pulling that flannel down his legs in a flash and I don't waste any time yanking off my nightgown and slipping my panties off, tossing them on the floor. He grabs me and rolls so I'm straddling him again and I take him in my hand and center him right where he needs to be.

The frenzied rush turns to lazy deliberateness when I slowly sink down onto him. His hold on my thighs is painful as his hips move against mine. My hands come to rest on either side of his head as I move, finding that right spot that makes my toes curl. Logan's tongue touches my nipple before he pulls it into his mouth. Moving, I guide the neglected breast to his mouth and he sucks on it hard. I feel the orgasm start just as Logan slips his hand between our bodies and hits that spot that sends me over.

"Come with me," tumbles from my mouth and he does, seconds later.

Logan has a surprise for me and he is so excited that he's got me really excited, not that anything can top the night we shared. Note to self: get a Jacuzzi tub. And then we reach our destination and I look over at him like he has completely lost his mind.

"I'm not sure this is such a great idea," I say.

"It's fantastic, trust me."

"Trust isn't the issue here but that"—I point in front of me—"that is."

"You'll love it, it will give you a whole new outlook." He reaches for my hand and starts toward the docks.

"I like my current outlook," I mutter, but he doesn't hear me since he's too busy negotiating with the captain. Twenty minutes later we are heading out into the great wide open on a seventy-foot sport fisherman to game the almighty swordfish.

I glance over at Logan, who's chatting up the guy next to him: an old weathered-looking fella with gnarly hands and a bent back—kind of the quintessential old man of the sea. I can hear the stories from where I'm standing. I question the stated lengths of the fish he's claiming to have caught, but there is no mistaking his clear love of fishing. There is an upside: this particular charter will not be hauling in the fish we catch. I detest swordfish, but only when they've been cut into steaks and grilled. The actual fish I have no quarrel with, and so I am happy to know that we will not be harming them.

Once the boat gets out to where we'll be trolling, Logan walks me to the stern where fishing chairs are arranged in a line with huge rods and reels attached to each. A vision of *Jaws* plays in my head. That fishing trip did not end well. I look to the horizon, but there is nothing but ocean as far as the eyes can see. A wave of nervousness washes over me. What if we run into Jaws out here or Moby Dick or, worse yet, an enormous squid? Glancing around the deck, I study those around us because we are all walking and talking chum for any sea monster waiting to devour us. How are we preparing to do battle to save our very lives? We're strapping ourselves into chairs and serving ourselves up like a smorgasbord. Logan's watching me and not even attempting to hide his humor.

"You never saw *Jaws*, did you?"

He's laughing at me now so his answer is barely audible. "No."

I look at the old fisherman Logan was talking to earlier as he straps himself into his chair, but he's looking at me with merriment in his old eyes. I nod at him. "Have you seen *Jaws*?"

"Yes."

"And yet you're assuming the role of Quint with no obvious discomfort."

His laugh sounds more like a cackle before he reaches for his fishing rod.

I sit in my sacrificial chair and glance down at my faded jeans and sweater. "I really don't want to spend the ever after in this outfit, Logan."

"Saffron, what is going on in that head of yours?"

"You don't want to know. Allow me to worry about all of our mortal—key word being *mortal*—souls." I reach for his arm and squeeze. "Don't worry, if it comes to it I'll do us both."

"What?"

I wave his question off. "Never mind, your lack of movie knowledge is shocking," I say, though I pause to think that it's good for me since he doesn't realize that most of what I say comes directly from movies. "I'm ready, strap me in."

Well, at least if I find myself in the stomach of a sea monster today, it's comforting to know that Logan will be right there with me.

Logan hunches down in front of me with his hands resting on my thighs. "You really need to tell me everything that is going on in your head, because you have the oddest expression on your face."

Reaching for his hand, I try for a smile. "I was just thinking of you and me together for all eternity in the belly of a sea monster, who even now is slowly rising for the depths below."

His eyebrow raises and I reach out and touch it. "Is that hard?" I attempt to mimic his look, the arching of the brow that all men seem to master by the tender age of five, but when my one brow goes up, so does the other.

"I was going to offer to get you a beer, but I'm wondering if you didn't sneak some earlier in the room."

"Sober, stone-cold sober, I am. That is a condition needing some modification. Just keep the liquor coming, Logan."

He wraps my face in his hands and presses a hard kiss on my lips. "I love you, you crazy woman."

"Crazy like a fox," I call after him, but he's already disappeared inside the cabin. I turn my attention to the sea as the music from *Jaws* plays in my head.

———

Three beers later and no one has caught a blessed thing. And no tentacles have shot out of the water either, so on all fronts we are looking good. Logan and I are sitting on the boat's edge—no longer strapped in—and that's when Earl, the old fisherman dude, grabs his line. The water sheets off the struggling fish like glass, the distinct swordlike nose pointing straight up into the air before he twists and turns and dives back into the water.

"Oh my God, did you see that?" I holler.

"A beauty, ten-footer," Earl says.

"Eleven," I say. I can't help the *Jaws* reference, which isn't lost on Earl, who cackles again—deep and throaty from obvious years of heavy smoking—but it goes completely over Logan's head.

The magnificent swordfish jumps again. He is a little closer this time and with another graceful turn of his body, he dives again. To look at calm and collected Earl, you wouldn't think he had that incredible fish on the end of his line. He expertly reels that baby closer.

Half an hour passes and still man and fish battle for supremacy and then Earl looks up at me. "Want to bring him in?"

"Me?"

Earl hands the rod to Logan as he unstraps. "It's one thing to watch, another to do."

Oh, wise Yoda.

I sit down and Earl straps me in before Logan places the rod in the cup. Earl hands me his gloves.

"Don't try to reel it in. He'll lead you, just follow."

The pull on the line, the tension on the rod, and the sight of that magnificent beast gracefully fighting for its life is awesome. I wouldn't enjoy it nearly as much if we were killing what we caught. Honestly, after putting up such a fight, the fish deserves to live.

Twenty minutes into it my arms and shoulders are killing me, so I can't even begin to imagine how the fish is feeling what with all that wild jumping. We can't actually bring it up to the boat since that nose could do serious damage, so the plan is to cut the line. Right before the line's cut, the fish and I have a moment and I swear it's almost like two battle-worn fighters acknowledging the skill of the other. And then the line goes slack and he's free. As soon as he realizes it, he jumps one last time in victory before disappearing into the murky deep. I am awed, moved in a way I have never been before. Unstrapping myself from the chair, I launch myself into Logan's arms.

"Thank you. You were right. I have a whole new outlook."

His lips brush over my ear. "Life changing, isn't it?"

———

In the car heading home after the best week of my life, I notice we're not on I-95 as we should be. "Is something wrong?"

"No, but I do have one more surprise for you."

"Really? Do tell."

"We'll be there in about half an hour."

"Where?"

He spares me a glance. "You'll see."

A half an hour later we're passing a sign for a nursing home and pulling in to its parking lot. I notice the ambulances and wheelchairs by the doors.

"Where are we?"

"My guy located Margaret's sister. I contacted her, explained who we were, and she was very excited at the idea of meeting."

A chill, like a wave, moves from my shoulders clear down my body. "She lives here?"

"Yes. Are you mad I didn't tell you?"

I throw myself across the car, wrapping him into a tight hug. "No."

"I didn't tell you before because I didn't want you to be distracted during your first ever family vacation."

"God, I love you."

"Good, cause you're stuck with me." He kisses me, quick but thorough. "Let's go. She's waiting."

Madeline Ann Phillips is a resident of Briar Hall Nursing Home. She's ninety, but in very good health, according to the receptionist.

Logan and I are sitting in one of the common rooms: a tasteful room done in earth tones with little groupings of furniture conducive to conversation. A large wide-screen TV hangs from the wall in the distance, but far enough away that its noise won't take over. Potted ficus trees are scattered about the space, and bookcases, filled with all the current popular fiction from floor to ceiling, line one wall.

A petite woman is wheeled into the room by an orderly, who applies the brakes on her chair before taking his leave. Her hair is up in a bun and she's wearing light makeup. Is this her sister? Is this what Maggie looked like?

"Hello, I'm Saffron Mills"—my name is officially Dupree now, but I don't want to confuse her—"and this is Logan MacGowan."

"Madeline Phillips. I was surprised to receive your call. You knew Frank?"

"Yes."

"I haven't heard that name in so long. I was sorry to hear about his death. Your young man mentioned you had something to ask me."

"Yes. I was very close to Frank. He left me his journals. While reading through them, I learned about your sister, Maggie, and how very important she was to him. He seemed to have felt her loss for the rest of his life. Frank was cremated but I still have his ashes at home because I couldn't figure where I should lay him to rest, but after learning of your sister, I'd like to bury him with her."

Tears spring into Madeline's eyes. "I think that's a wonderful idea."

"Frank meant the world to me—I would love to know more about the woman that captivated his heart. He was something of a father figure to me. Please? I'd love anything you could give me."

Logan reaches for my hand and I know he's doing so because he realizes I'm close to tears and he's offering his silent support.

Madeline is watching us with a slight smile curving her lips, but it fades as she says, "Maggie was so young when she died. I guess I should start from the beginning. We were poor, really very poor, and our dad worked the docks with Frank. That's how Maggie and Frank met. Dad brought him home for dinner one night and boy did the sparks fly. They were inseparable and it wasn't just romance; it was like seeing a soul torn in two brought back together again.

"It really was a wonderful thing to watch and I was envious of them and what they had found in each other. Never found it myself. They could sit for hours and just talk, never seeming to run out of things to say. She taught Frank how to relax and laugh and he taught her how to find beauty even in the ugliest of situations.

"They wanted to marry right away, but my dad asked that they wait until she was at least eighteen. So they did, and every time they planned to marry, something would happen to push the date back. It became a little bit of a family joke! But almost four years after they met, the date was set, the rings purchased, and the dress sewn.

"One week before the wedding, Frank and Maggie were out at dinner. The problem with the two of them was that they tended to forget anyone else was around. Maggie wasn't paying attention to where she was going as they walked home. Frank had stopped, though, to purchase flowers for her at the corner stand. Neither of them saw the out-of-control truck barreling down the street. We lived near the docks and, though it wasn't a really congested lane, it did see its share of trucks making deliveries. By the time Frank realized what was happening, he was too far away and the truck was too fast.

"He held her broken, lifeless body in his arms for hours until the cops had to pry her away from him. He changed after that, but who could blame him. Then Pearl Harbor happened and he enlisted and just left everything behind. I never saw him again.

"Years later when I was going through Maggie's things, I realized he hadn't left everything behind. He had taken a reminder of her. They used to sit for hours in front of an old chess set that Maggie had picked up at the local pawnshop. Frank was always trying to teach her, but she was a terrible student. It made my heart happy to know that he took that piece of her with him."

Tears spill down my cheeks as Logan presses a tissue into my palm. "I have that chess set now. Frank tried to teach me on it too, but I wasn't any better a student than Maggie."

The smile that spreads over Madeline's face touches my heart with its sad beauty. "Maggie would have liked that."

She's quiet for a moment before she adds, "In all of my life I never again saw sparks like I did with Frank and Maggie, but I'm seeing them now. Treasure each other."

Two days later, after a call to Broderick, we are standing in front of Maggie's grave as a priest offers a prayer. When it's time for me to relinquish Frank's remains for good, I have trouble letting go. I send Frank my own silent prayer.

Thank you for always being there for me, for being my family. I miss you so much and I love you. If only there was a sign to let me know that this is what you want. I hope wherever you are, dearest Frank, that you are happy and that Maggie is at your side.

With great difficulty I hand the urn over to the caretaker and as soon as Frank is placed with Maggie, it starts to snow. My face tilts back to see the gray clouds as my heart sighs. It's my sign. Frank always loved the snow.

"Are you okay?" Logan asks with a soft tone.

I nod in reply and step into his arms to rest my head on his chest. I am and I think that Frank is now too.

CHAPTER FIFTEEN

"Frank left me a house in Upper Nyack and I would like to turn it into a sort of dormitory for students from abroad studying at the colleges and universities in New York. There will be a staff, den mothers responsible for providing a homelike environment, and therapists to help these teenagers with the transition. I haven't a clue where to start, but I am hoping that you will help me through it," I say to Logan's brothers.

After seeing Frank in his final resting place with Maggie, I am more determined to give them both this legacy. Dante and Broderick were kind enough to join me in the lighthouse to plan. To Frank, I believe that house was a reminder of what he had and lost. And though in life he never married Maggie and they were never legally bound, I want to bring their legacy together now. I told Madeline about my hopes for Dupree House. She gave me a few pictures of Frank and Maggie that I will frame and have on the walls in the Nyack house as a tribute to them.

"Absolutely, we'll help. There are thousands of steps from here to opening the doors. Dante and I can help you through the legal and business ends," says Broderick.

"I would like that, but I imagine it's all very detailed. I'd hate to make it even longer for you since you're donating your time for this."

"Okay, we'll take it as we go. Creating the job descriptions for the staff, the den mothers, and therapists you mentioned, that's a good place to start. But before we do anything, you need a sit-down with the Board of Directors for the governing board of higher education for the state of New York."

My confusion must be easy to see, so Broderick explains. "You're looking to set up a dormitory that will house students, paying students, for the universities and colleges this board represents. You want Dupree House listed as a housing option, but off campus. That goes against most of the established rules regarding matriculating freshman. You need to pitch your idea, explain what Dupree House can offer these students coming here from abroad. You need to sell them on the idea. If they like it, you'll qualify for funding through the state, which will help with the ongoing cost to keep Dupree House running long-term."

"I was so excited with the idea, I didn't think it all through."

"It's a great idea, Saffron, but without their approval, Dupree House will never get off the ground. That doesn't mean we can't try another tack, but affiliation to the universities and colleges will be out."

"Let's use me," Logan says from his spot across the room.

"What do you mean?" I ask.

"David Cambre, he's an example of the kind of student you're trying to help with Dupree House. I'll come with you and publicly support your idea, share with them my own experiences and how I could have benefited from a place such as Dupree House."

"But you hate all the press David gets."

"Yeah, but this is a chance to use David's celebrity for something good. Hell knows, I've dealt with the downside of it. Now we can capitalize on the good side of it."

"You would do that?"

"For you, absolutely, but it's more than that. Frank was a good man, and this idea of yours, it's just plain good."

"Thank you." After a moment I turn to Broderick and Dante. "All of you, seriously, thank you."

"Our pleasure," Broderick says and adds, "besides, Logan would have kicked our asses if we said no."

———

I'm in town food shopping, taking a break from the job descriptions I've been working on all morning. Dante called earlier and got us a meeting with the Board of Directors, so I need to start thinking about my pitch, but first I need food. We've been away long enough that I'm going to have to feed Reaper dust bunnies.

I see Chastity farther down the street and am tempted to duck into a store because the Seaweed Festival is coming. Though I have been blackballed, there is still the chance she'll find something, most likely unpleasant, for me to do. The way she's walking, unlike her normally brisk no-nonsense walk, finally penetrates. She's almost dragging her feet. Picking up my pace, I come up next to her only to see her flushed face and damp cheeks.

"Chastity, are you okay?"

I've surprised her, as evidenced by the snapping up of her head. At first it doesn't seem she recognizes who I am. "Saffron. What? Do you need something?"

"Are you okay?"

"I'm fine. I've just got a ton of things to do for the festival."

"It's seaweed, Chastity. There can't be that much."

She doesn't immediately bite my head off, her usual response when I disparage the festivals. Instead her shoulders sag. "You're right. I don't know why I am doing this."

"Seaweed?"

"All of it."

I'm momentarily lacking in words, since I can't believe Chastity, the biggest proponent of the festivals, is questioning why we have them. "Are you serious?"

"Yes!" Now she bites off my head.

"The festivals are a lot of fun." For some people.

"Are they? With the way people bitch about me behind my back, I wonder why I bother."

Oops. I hope it isn't me she heard dishing, though I haven't bitched about her in a few days.

"Did you know I was married once?"

Wait. What? "No."

"Married right out of high school. Never knew why he picked me, but I saw our lives together: we'd live grandly and be so utterly in love. We didn't live grandly and we weren't utterly in love but we were a team. Twenty years into our marriage, he left and never came back. No explanation, no warning. Just gone. I hadn't gone to college. I'd dedicated my life to him, and suddenly the reason I got up every morning, the reason I took care of the house and gardens, the reason I learned how to cook and balance a checkbook, was gone. I woke one morning, a woman in my forties with half of my life over and what did I have to show for it?"

"So you got involved with the festivals."

"At first it was a distraction, keeping me from thinking about what a failure my life was, but later it gave me purpose. Keeping them going means I didn't fail again."

"Your husband failed, not you, Chastity. And I understand what motivates you, but I think you're selling yourself a bit short. You are a valuable resource to our community, but you push people away. You dictate like a general."

Insecurity lingers just beneath bravado. "I don't want to fail again. That's why I'm so hard."

"Ever heard the expression you attract more flies with honey? Don't order. Ask. Engage them and I think you'll find people will respond to it. They'll talk to you instead of about you."

"Have you talked about me behind my back?"

"Repeatedly."

She stares at me a minute before breaking out into laughter. "At least you're honest."

After my Dr. Phil moment with Chastity, I finish my shopping and am waiting to cross the street with my bags. All those years thinking she had a partner only to find out she really didn't—it's sad. In the next second, car brakes squeal just as I'm about to cross the street. A strong hand pulls me back, and a familiar voice says, "Are you okay, Saffron?"

A car zooms off down our small street.

It's George. "Yeah, I guess I just lost my balance."

"Good thing I was here. That was awfully close. Here, let me help you with your bags."

He takes a few and walks with me to my car. My hands are shaking, so it takes me a few tries to get the key in the lock. George deposits my bags and looks me over. "You okay to drive?"

"I am and thank you."

"Drive safe." He starts off down the street, and my thoughts turn to what nearly happened. I probably wouldn't have been killed, but I would have definitely gotten a few broken bones. It isn't that, though, that's bothering me. It's the fact that I didn't lose my balance. It felt like someone pushed me.

<hr />

It's been two weeks, but now I'm sitting in the office where the Board of Directors meets, officially waiting to pitch Dupree House. Broderick is here as my legal counsel, which is fortuitous. Logan waits at the back of the room, while Broderick and I touch on a few last points.

I'm nervous, but Dante has put together a fantastic packet of information citing other states with similar housing options and the success of their programs. He has stats on the acceptance rates of overseas students and the actual numbers who attend our universities. There are even a few e-mails from parents of foreign teens accepted into our schools, but who declined because the biggest obstacle for their children was the separation and distance from everything they knew. If there had been the option of housing like Dupree House for their children, they would have been more inclined.

I don't know the specifics of how he's acquired all this information, but I do know it was very good advice from Logan to recruit Broderick and Dante. The way they are able to work the system is amazing to watch.

"How are you doing?" Broderick asks once we finish our strategy session.

"Nervous, but I'm ready."

"Between your pitch, Dante's research, and Logan, I think we've got a really good chance. Remember, push it as a pilot. If it's successful, it can be the first of many. Dante's research supports the effectiveness of a program like this."

Logan takes the seat to my left, reaching for my hand.

"You're going to be fine. It's a wonderful idea, Saffron, just let the idea sell them."

"Thank you for doing this. I mean it, it's above and beyond."

"Nonsense."

At that moment, the door opens and in files our audience. "You got this, Saffron," Logan whispers. I hope I do.

An hour later, Logan lifts me into his arms and spins me around on the steps outside the building. "You did it."

"We did it. We've got to call Dante," I say. Dupree House is officially a go.

"Already on it," Broderick says, his phone in his hand.

Logan drops me back on my feet. "So it begins."

———

That night we have a party on the beach behind my house. The gang is all there.

"This is so exciting. What a wonderful way to honor Frank," Gwen says as we sit around a fire.

"There's so much to do from this point to getting the doors open, but it's going to happen."

Logan and his brothers cooked dinner, chicken and burgers on the grill. "I couldn't have done it without them." *Them* are currently finishing preparing the rest of the food.

"It's fitting that you've got them helping. Frank was family. Logan, I suspect, will be family, and his brothers are his family, so it's a family thing," Gwen says.

"What do you mean Logan will be family?" Sure, I see us tying the knot but I get the sense there's more to Gwen's statement, like she knows something.

"It's no secret the man adores you. You don't think it's leading to a ring on your finger and a big white wedding?"

"I do, eventually. Why? Do you know something?"

"No," she answers awfully quickly.

"Speaking of family, I spoke to my mom. She told me I was shooting too high, wasn't good enough for Logan."

"Well, she's stupid." Gwen's sporting her mean face.

Chills move through me. The idea of marrying Logan is intoxicating.

"You have our approval," Josh says. "He's a good guy. He loves you, that's clear. He's tight with his brothers, which says something. Plus, he's just so fucking nice to look at."

This earns him a look from Derek, to which he replies, "And you aren't thinking the same thing."

"I am, but silently, no need to voice the obvious."

Josh chuckles. "Wedding dress shopping in Bar Harbor after he pops the question."

"Seriously, do you guys know something I don't?" Where is all of this coming from?

"Maybe, but I'll think it silently since there's no need to voice the obvious," Josh says.

The distinct sound of motorcycles comes from the front of the house. We invited Dirk and his friends, since they were going to be in the area.

A few minutes later, Josh says, "Who the hell is that?"

"You weren't kidding this town is small. I think if I sneezed I would have driven right through it," Dirk says in way of greeting.

"Likely. You hungry?" I ask.

"Yeah."

"Beers are in the cooler and we're grilling. Let me introduce you to the gang."

Later, after everyone has left, Logan and I walk along the beach. It's late and I'm tired, but it was such a great day that I don't want to see it come to an end. "It was great seeing Dirk. I'm so glad he took us up on our offer."

"Me too."

There's a thoughtfulness to Logan, as if he's distracted. I'm about to ask what's on his mind when he says, "Do you know what made me want to be an artist?"

"No."

"Our house in Scotland is in Glen Isla, that's on the eastern edge of Scotland, about eighty or so miles from Glasgow. The Grampian Mountains are the backdrop and the glens are cradled between the steep slopes, a lush green that seems to go on forever. I was five, sitting in my yard playing and I saw a horse in the distance. It was wild. We have them in Scotland, but the sight of that white horse seeming to just appear, I thought it was magic. One only I could see. I drew it on construction paper with crayons, that horse in that glen. My mom framed it. It still hangs in our living room.

"When I got older, I understood what it was about that horse that pulled at me so. The feeling I felt at watching it running through that glen, wild and free, it's how I feel when I create. Alive, not just living, but drunk on life. Through the years, and perhaps as I became a professional artist, I lost that feeling. I didn't realize I had lost it, or even missed it, until I walked into Tucker's and saw you, beautiful, wild and alive."

I stop walking. Overwhelmed, happy, drunk with love for him, I can do nothing more than stand there and soak in those feelings.

"Saffron?"

"That is, hands down, the sweetest compliment I have ever received."

"Maybe now you understand exactly how much you mean to me. I heard you talking to your friends about your mom. She's completely wrong. Don't ever doubt what I feel for you, it's as vast and as lasting as that bay."

"I have doubted it, but I won't again."

"Good. Now I want to make love to you, here or inside doesn't matter to me, so I'll let you choose. You've got to the count of ten."

I move, but not toward the house. "Why not love me here and inside?"

His arms wrap tight around me, drawing me into his warm embrace. "I like how your mind works."

———

The day of the Seaweed Festival has arrived. I'm on my way into town for the parade because nothing says seaweed like a parade. While I understand Chastity better after our talk, part of me still doesn't even want to go. Yet, considering that Logan has really gotten into this festival, I can't not show up. The man is making a kelp cake, for Christ's sake.

He was up and out of the house before I even awoke: leaving me a note stating he had some last-minute festival things to do. What those things are, I have no idea, unless he's dredging the ocean for more seaweed.

Reaching the heart of town, I see people lining the street. What if we are some alien experiment to see how far the human imagination can be pushed before it's suspended? I think with this festival, my imagination is about at its limit.

Reaper trots along next to me, oblivious to the fact that the town is gathering to celebrate the wonders and allure of seaweed, though he's clearly smelling the nasty stuff, since his nose hasn't stopped twitching. I can't help but sniff the air myself for the traces of the airborne narcotic that is clearly being pumped into our town's air supply.

Reaching the bakery, I see Josh and Gwen waiting for me—Josh has my coffee and Gwen is holding Reaper's doggie bagel. Bless them.

"Thank you," I say as I take that first most welcome sip.

"I have to say, I am more than a little surprised by the turnout," Gwen says, but I'm looking around her for Mitch.

"Couldn't get Mitch jazzed about the weed of the sea?"

She throws me a look and grins. "He's joining us later at the ball."

"Another ball? Are you kidding me?"

"No," Josh offers.

"Are we dressing up?"

Josh looks completely affronted. "Of course we are dressing up."

"Well, I have nothing to wear," I say.

"You do," Josh offers cryptically.

Immediately I'm suspicious. "Meaning?"

"It's taken care of; you're going and you're going to like it. Your man has been working very hard to make this a successful festival, so the least you can do is show up and look pretty."

I have the strongest urge to stick my tongue out at him, but I refrain and turn my head toward the parade that has started.

The Harrington marching band, all seven members, is followed by the cheerleading squad. The car that appears after them makes the coffee I just sipped go down the wrong pipe. As I try to pull air into my lungs, Josh whacks my back with far more enthusiasm than the situation requires. When I'm able to breathe again, I ask, "Am I the only one having this nightmare?"

"No," Gwen says with genuine surprise in her voice. "What is she wearing?"

It is only when the car gets closer that we can see what Shalee is wearing.

"Oh my God, she's wrapped in seaweed. What the hell is she thinking? I didn't think there was enough seaweed in the world to cover those." Josh gestures to his chest with his hand.

"They're barely covered," Gwen says.

"Where's Logan?" I ask.

"He and George must be putting the last-minute touches on the cake."

I suppose that's possible, since the man is an artist and takes pride in his work, even if that work is a kelp cake.

"I can't watch this anymore," I say.

"Yeah, let's go to Tommy's," Josh offers.

Alcohol, brilliant. Necessary. "Yes, let's do that."

———————

As I sit in the booth with Gwen and Josh, I can't help but think of Shalee. The vision of her dressed like that in a tub of soy sauce pops into my head, but I immediately dismiss it and have another sip of wine. The parade seems to have ended as people start filing into Tucker's for lunch. Reaper is in Tommy's office on his doggie bed: one of his most favorite places to sleep. When the door opens again, Broderick and Dante enter and we call them over to join us.

"Did you see the parade?" Broderick asks. I know he means *Did you get a load of Shalee?*

Lifting my glass, I eye him over the rim. "I'm trying really hard to pretend that I didn't, but the image seems to be burned onto my retina." I take a sip before I place the glass down. "Who does that? Voluntarily wraps themselves in seaweed?"

"There are spas where you'd have to pay to have that done," Josh says.

"Whatever," I say. "Where's Derek?"

"He's resting up for the ball. You know him, he's a dancing fool."

"Why didn't I know anything about this ball? Everyone seems to know but me."

"Logan didn't tell you?" Josh asks.

"Nope."

They all seem to exchange glances but say nothing.

"Outside of the surprise of Shalee, I think the day has been quite a lot of fun. I'm looking forward to the ball," Dante says right before Sarah places his beer on the table.

"Me too," Gwen says. "Hopefully we three will have a better showing than the last one."

My reply is immediate. "I rather liked the last ball, quite a lot actually."

Reaper is right on my heels when I head for the closet to dress for this event, but when I open the door, I let out a startled gasp. Hanging in plain sight is a Hervé Léger peacock-colored bandage dress with thin shoulder straps and a deep V neckline. The dress is made of nylon and spandex, so when I get it on, it is going to hug every inch of me. It's gorgeous, sexy, and more daring than anything I've ever worn. A note pinned to the hanger in Logan's handwriting reads: *Wear me.*

I start to pull it from the closet, but glance down as I do. Christian Louboutin crystal-covered peep-toe pumps with the signature red sole? My eyes practically pop out of my head. Another note resting against them says: *Wear us too.* I grin like a fool as I pull my treasures from the closet.

Once my hair is dried and pulled into a twist after my shower, I take my time applying my makeup: darkening my lashes, using kohl and dark blue around my eyes, tinting my cheeks and lips.

The gown is such that you can't wear anything under it, something I have never done before, but as I slip it on, it feels like a second skin. It comes to rest at midthigh and the back is open to below my shoulder blades. Slipping on the pumps, I walk to my jewelry box for a pair of earrings, but a black leather box is resting on top. My breath stills in my lungs when I open it. The most beautiful pair of diamond chandelier earrings that I have ever seen is nestled in the black satin. Pear, marquise, and brilliant-cut diamonds are arranged in a staggering pattern, over seven carats, if I had to guess, and they're real. Of that I am certain.

My hands shake slightly as I lift each one and slip them into my ears—they sparkle every time I move my head. I think I'm in shock. They're too much, and I should insist that Logan return them, but I don't want him to. I step in front of the mirror and can't believe it's me looking back. Never in my life have I ever felt as sexy as I feel right now wearing this incredible ensemble.

No wonder Logan has been MIA for days—the man has been very busy. He's spoiling me and I love it. Why all of this for the Seaweed Festival? I can't say, but I'm having too much fun to care. I'm pulled from my reflection by the sound of someone at my front door. Opening it, I find Broderick and Dante, who can't hide their surprise at the clingy bandage dress.

"Nice," Broderick says. "We're here to take you to the ball. Logan's meeting us there."

I grab my wrap. "I'm ready."

———•———

Traffic, a first for our little town, is clogging our way. The closer we get to our destination, I see the news vans and reporters.

"What's going on?" I ask.

"I guess the Seaweed Festival has attracted interest," Broderick offers.

Why? My airborne narcotic theory is looking better and better. We park and walk up the steps, but we're delayed as our pictures are taken. I have to say that I feel a little bit like I'm on the red carpet. When we get inside, we see far more people than I was expecting. Everyone looks so beautiful. As soon as we're spotted, attention turns to us. It's odd, but before I can ponder it, more of my friends emerge from the crowd. The men, like Broderick and Dante, are wearing tuxes and Gwen is wearing a gown, the color the barest of pinks, a Carmen Marc Valvo couture, I believe, and against her skin tone it looks ethereal.

"You look stunning, Gwen."

"Thank you. And you, you look"—she wipes at a tear rolling down her cheek—"happy, Saffron, really, truly happy. You deserve this."

I want to ask, deserve what? But Josh speaks up. "Shall we?" He gestures toward the doors leading into the ball and takes my wrap from me.

"Where's Logan?" I ask.

"He's already inside." Broderick holds out his arm. "Ready?"

I'm clearly not on the same page as everyone else and then the doors open on a room looking like something out of a magazine. The ceiling is draped in pale-gold fabric with white twinkling lights that give the effect of being both whimsical and elegant.

"I thought this was the Seaweed Festival. Where's the kelp?" My brain is clearly not working on all cylinders, stunned by the beauty before me.

"No kelp, Saffron," says Josh.

He can say that again. The walls are also covered in pale gold. Scattered throughout the large space are six-foot-tall, free-standing, four-arm silver candlesticks holding gold candles, and nestled within their arms rest arrangements of flowers: pink and white sweet peas, white and purple hydrangeas, dark-pink peonies and yellow roses accented with lycopodium. Large circular tables with delicate gold chairs, artistically arranged around the large space, are covered in pale-gold cloth, fine bone china, crystal stemware, silver cutlery, and centered in each is the same floral arrangement, just on a smaller scale.

Logan, dressed completely in black, walks across the floor in that elegant way of his. "You look exquisite."

Tingles work along my skin, not just at the compliment, but at the expression on his face that reads loud and clear: *mine*. As magnificent as it all is, I'm completely confused. "I don't understand. What is all of this?"

He doesn't answer my question, but asks, "Did you see the cake?"

On the opposite side of the room on a table draped in gold is, in fact, a cake, though that word seems weak given what I see. It's six-tiered, pearly white, with flowers cascading down the side, edible versions of the flowers in the arrangements. "It's beautiful. Is that the kelp cake? You and George made that?" They had missed their calling.

He laughs as the band starts to play "One Thing" from Gabe Dixon. He draws me out onto the dance floor.

His lips brush over my jaw before he whispers, "Do you like your surprise?"

I pull slightly back. "I'm still not getting it."

A smile curves his lips, but he says nothing and only holds me closer. I rest my head against his chest and realize we are the only ones dancing. Not only aren't people dancing, but everyone is standing around the dance floor watching us while camera flashes spark around the room. When the song comes to an end, Logan takes a step back from me and gets down on one knee. My heart slams into my ribs. He reaches for my hand.

"From the very first moment I saw you, I knew that you were the one for me. I love you, Saffron Dupree. I want a lifetime with you, getting nailed in the face by funnel cakes, watching movies in our pj's, avoiding the Fletcher car when we're walking down the sidewalk. I want to get drunk on your laugh and lose my breath when I look into your eyes. Marry me."

The tears that had collected in the corners of my eyes are now running down my face: happy tears, ecstatic tears. I'm shaking my head yes, trying to push the words out, but he doesn't need them. He stands, takes my hand, and slides on his ring: an oval diamond that's at least four carats, framed by baguettes and nestled in a platinum band. Flashes go off around the room, but he doesn't seem to notice as he looks deeply into my eyes. He lowers his head and presses his lips to mine, a mere brushing of lips, and then he cradles my face in his palms and takes the kiss deeper.

———•———

As dinner is being served, I'm still in mild shock. Logan proposed—I guess my friends did know something I didn't. I'm deliriously happy. My insides are all tingly like bubbles in champagne; the fact that I haven't splintered apart into sparkly wonder is amazing. What I don't get, though, is why all the cameras. I lean a bit closer to Logan and whisper, "This is all incredible, but why the fanfare?"

There's love looking back at me. "For better or for worse, David Cambre is a part of who I am and if I want to share all of myself with you, then a part of that is sharing you with David's world, which is why I invited the press. Besides, I want everyone to know that I'm in love"—he traces the line of my jaw—"and that my heart is no longer my own."

We share a moment as I let those words settle over me. "So, is it safe to say there is no seaweed ball?"

He chuckles and rests his hand on the back of my chair so his fingers can brush along the nape of my neck.

"We tried to think of the most absurd thing. Josh came up with seaweed."

Josh is laughing behind his hand.

"I'm actually relieved, because I was seriously beginning to think our town was under some kind of mass hallucination. Wait, so what was up with the kelp cake?"

"I needed to distract you while the party planner walked through town. It's also why I suggested visiting the house Frank left you. I needed you away."

My eyes widen a moment before narrowing. "You're sneaky. Chastity was in on it then."

"Oh yeah, liked the idea of tricking you far more than the situation warranted," Logan replies.

"And Shalee?"

I can tell from his blank look that he has no idea what I'm talking about. "Shalee wrapped herself in seaweed for the parade. Really, Logan, you missed her? She was sexy sushi right there on Main Street."

His eyes roam over me in a very slow and blatant perusal, before his gaze returns to mine and it's sex, pure and simple, in that hot stare. "I didn't miss anything."

"Oh dear God," I moan and reach for my water glass. Pity I can't just pour it right on my head.

Josh provides the insight on Shalee. "She heard about the camera crews, so she tried to get her fifteen minutes of fame."

"And so she thinks of a seaweed wrap? Well, I hope that worked out for her," I say.

"Actually, it didn't, because she got an allergic reaction. I'd never seen full-body hives before," Derek adds.

I shudder. I can't really help it.

———

Logan hasn't stopped kissing and touching me, and when he isn't near me his eyes just soak up the sight of me. I'm engaged. I don't think I've fully grasped that concept yet. What I have grasped is that Logan went to a lot of effort to make this night perfect. Even with all the reporters and cameras, it's still just Harrington and everyone I'd want to celebrate with.

We cut the cake, which, thankfully, is decadent chocolate, not kelp, have a champagne toast, and then Logan whisks me from the hall while the party is still going on.

"Where are we going?" I ask as we practically run down the steps of Town Hall only to find a limo parked and waiting with a chauffeur holding the door open for us. Once we're inside, Logan's mouth is on mine as his hands roam and claim every part of me he touches. He draws me back with him as he settles against the seat, his hands on the hem of my skirt, lifting it as he settles me on his lap so that my legs are straddling him.

"Have you ever done it in a limo?" he whispers, and he sounds just like a teenager before his lips burn a trail down my throat.

"No."

"Me neither." And then those eyes find mine. "But I really, really want to."

"Oh God, me too."

His eyes turn even darker before his mouth claims mine. I pull my mouth from his and press a kiss to his ear. "I'm not wearing anything under this."

Instantly, I feel him grow hard under me. I reach for the button of his trousers. His hands move up my legs to my hips. He lifts my dress so that my ass is bare. His hands moving over my skin make lust burn right down to my toes. I wrap my hand around his erection and pull him free and take a moment to fondle the length of him, loving the way he feels so hard and silky smooth. Guiding the head right where we both want it, I sink down hard, my body stretching to take him. He tugs my dress down to free my breasts and I respond my pressing myself into him as his tongue flicks my nipple. My hips take on the age-old dance and I slide up and down along his hard length. His thumb moves between my legs and when I come, I bury my face in his neck to stifle my moan. His hands tighten on me seconds before he comes, a growl rumbling low in his throat. When I lift my head, he looks positively sinful and sounds it too. "Definitely need to do that again."

Putzing around the house the next day, I can't seem to stop staring at my ring. I spoke to Logan's parents earlier; they're catching a flight next week. I'm really looking forward to meeting them in person, because the folks I spoke with over the phone were delightful. I'm also sad that Frank isn't here to walk me down the aisle, but I plan on asking Tommy, since he's been like a brother to me in every sense of the word. I give a passing thought to sharing the news with my parents, but the last conversation with my mom is still fresh in my mind, so I'm not feeling particularly chatty.

In the living room, my eyes fall on the chess set. Frank's last link to Maggie. I couldn't imagine losing Logan, watching him die and then being forced to live a full life without him. It's a testament to Frank's strength that he was able to do so.

A knock at the door has me changing directions. Broderick and Dante are on my front step. I don't even get a hello out before Broderick grabs me into a hug. "Welcome to the family."

"Don't hog, Broderick," Dante teases before he pulls me into a hug as well. "Now you are officially our little sister. Our brother is a rock head, but he's a good guy and he loves you."

So this is what it feels like to have a real family. Broderick says, "He'll make you happy. There's baggage with Logan, as you know, the celebrity part of his world can be a serious drag, but you do learn to deal."

"I've had a small taste of it and I know I'm going to have to get thicker skin, but it isn't going to make me walk away from him. Is that what you're worried about?" The worry I sense coming from Broderick is surprising.

"Logan has to deal with this nonsense, it's part of his gig, but you'll be forced to deal with it too. It can be overwhelming and, depending on how much the press sinks into the story, infuriating. But it does all eventually even out."

"I'll weather the storm, Broderick."

"And we'll be here to help you."

I won't ask, since Broderick is clearly concerned, but just how bad is it going to get?

"How are the job descriptions going?" Dante changes the subject.

"I just finished them before we went to New York, was going to drop by later, but I'll get them now."

"Yeah, that'd be good."

As I retrieve the papers, Dante is still talking. "We're going to need to make the house handicap accessible, which means getting a contractor to detail what needs to be done."

"I didn't think of that." I place the pages in front of Dante. "Okay, I need to look at furnishing the house too, how many beds in a room, etc."

"Not to mention bathrooms. The house has . . . three? We may need to add another in the basement. I have a list of contractors. We can get some references," Broderick suggests.

For the next hour or so we talk about Dupree House.

Broderick and Dante have just left when there's another knock at the door. Thinking they forgot something, I open the door saying, "Did you . . ." But my words die on my tongue at the sight of Darla. Surprise isn't a strong enough word to express my feelings about seeing Darla in Maine. What the hell is she doing here? She doesn't wait to be invited in. She breezes into my house like an old Hollywood starlet. She's still wearing Logan's ring. Is that why she's here?

"What are you doing here, Darla? How the hell did you get here?"

"Plane." That's spoken as if it's obvious, which I guess it kind of is. "You don't heed advice very well, do you?"

These are her words of greeting. I don't think I would have started in with that.

"Meaning?"

"I warned you to stay out of it."

It takes me a minute to understand what she's implying and, when I do, my mouth drops open. "Are you saying you're the person who sent me the threats?"

"Well, of course, who else?"

Right, who else? I suppose it's comforting to know that there isn't a line forming around my house or, more to the point, that the master-mind behind the threats isn't a criminal genius.

"I see you're still wearing his ring," I say.

"I'm engaged to him. Of course I'm wearing his ring."

"You really aren't, though. You haven't been for quite some time, and I'd think this would have sunk in by now. It isn't really a hard concept to grasp."

"What?"

"He's suing you. He has done everything he can to make it clear that you are over. Why won't you move on?"

"No, I won't move on."

I stand there and wait for more: the declaration of her undying love, her inability to live without him, or any reason at all that would make a grown woman continue to chase after a man who doesn't want her, and has made that clear via legal counsel. But I get nothing except another no, delivered much in the way Callie delivers her no when she doesn't want to go to bed.

Leaning up against the wall, I find I'm actually enjoying myself. "So what exactly is the plan here? You want him and he isn't interested, but you won't take no for an answer. What's next?"

An expression remarkably like that of a belligerent child crosses over her face. "I sent you the package."

I widen my eyes at that before I clarify, "The bird's head?"

"Yes."

"So your plan is to kill the competition?" Stepping from the wall, I glance out the window and, as suspected, there is a big-ass limo parked right in front of my house. I turn back to Darla.

"Okay, so you travel here, via plane, using your own name, I'm guessing."

"Well, yeah."

"Rent that"—I point to the limo—"under your name and park that huge white attention-getter right in front of my house, with a potential witness in the driver, so you can come in here and kill me? Did you think this through at all or are you just winging it?"

She clenches her hands into fists and stomps her foot before she half-screams and half-whines. "He's mine."

Honestly, it's like dealing with a spoiled child. Using my best mother voice, I snap, "Enough!"

Her rant instantly stops and her crestfallen expression still looks like that of a bewildered child.

"Are you aware that the sheriff has your little package and that a report has been filed? If I wanted to, I could press charges and have you sent to jail since you used the postal service, which automatically makes it a federal offense."

Her face immediately pales.

"Exactly. This isn't a game. You walk into my home and threaten me. Are you aware that as an intruder in my home you could get shot and the law would be on my side?"

I can tell from her deer-in-the-headlights expression that, no, she had not thought of that. "This is the real world, and not the pampered one you live in, so unless you're prepared to carry out your threats, I suggest you go home, have a good cry, and then move on." I step a bit closer. "I'll give you this one meltdown, but if you come at me again I will sic the law on you. And by coming here today in such a very visible way, you're helping to establish a pattern of aggressive behavior. You aren't making it very difficult for the cops to build a case against you."

And as if on cue, my front door opens and in walks Logan and Sheriff Dwight. Logan looks stupendously pissed.

"I warned you, Darla."

"It's okay. Darla was just leaving, weren't you?"

But her eyes are on my hand stretched out to pause the men, and the ring she didn't see earlier. When she lifts her head to Logan, her eyes are filled with tears. "You really have moved on."

Some of the harshness eases from his tone. "Yes."

Her expression is like watching a curtain lift to reveal the wizard as reality sinks in. She walks to Logan and yanks off her ring.

"Keep it," he says.

"No."

He holds out his hand and she drops it into his palm. "I won't bother you again."

And then she's gone, her exit a far cry from her dramatic entrance.

"Are you folks good?" Sheriff Dwight asks.

"How did you know she was here?" With timing like that maybe Logan *is* the wizard.

"I've got eyes on her. My PI told me she was catching a flight into Bar Harbor. Overestimated a bit on how long it was going to take her to get here."

———

The following morning I wake, but Logan's side of the bed is empty, and his sheets cold. Climbing from bed and pulling on the robe that Logan left draped over a chair for me, I go in search of him. I find him in his studio, but he isn't sitting behind an easel. Instead he is looking outside. I take a moment to enjoy the view, his broad, tense shoulders and muscled back tapering to his narrow waist.

"Logan."

He turns to me and the smile that spreads over his face makes my heart flip over in my chest. "I like you in my robe. Did you sleep well?"

"Yes." There's a flicker of something in his eyes in response. "Logan, what's wrong?"

He stops just in front of me and starts to gently rub his hands up and down my arms. There is something brewing in his expression, but before I can ask him what's troubling him, he says something that causes my heart to stop beating for a moment.

"I think I made a mistake."

My face pales. I feel the blood draining from it. I take a step away from him.

"Saffron, what's wrong?"

I can't bear to ask but I have to. "Mistake? Would that mistake be getting engaged to me?"

He wraps me into his arms. "I hate your parents, because their neglect makes you question what you know is true," he says with anger. "No, it wasn't a mistake getting engaged to you. I would marry you in front of all the world and be the happiest man alive. No, the mistake I made was inviting the press."

I pull back to look at him. "Why?"

He gestures toward the window and I look out to see reporters camped out on the beach below.

"Oh." I turn from the window to see him studying me.

"When I invited the press, I didn't think about the downside of it, namely the ones in it not for the story but for sensationalism. Some of them can be quite cruel, and I opened the door. That was a mistake."

Walking back to him, I wrap my arms around his waist. "How bad can it be?"

"You have no idea."

CHAPTER SIXTEEN

On one hand, Logan and I have grown closer every day since the engagement party, but the side effects of being with a celebrity are beginning to take their toll. Logan was right in that I had no idea of the impact of the press on our lives.

Now that people know David is in Harrington, there have been more visitors, mostly women, hoping to catch a glimpse of him. Yes, Logan is hot and sexy, but I just don't get it. If I knew that Brad Pitt was going to be in Manhattan, as much as I love him, I wouldn't be running off to see him, hoping to catch his eye in the middle of a crowd. Get a fucking life, or get laid, or something. But not only do these women travel to Harrington, they have, on a few occasions, followed *me* home. I don't understand this mentality. I realize that Logan is a celebrity, but he is still a person and should be treated as such. The other day at the bakery, I was actually confronted by a stranger who felt it necessary to tell me that I wasn't good enough for him and should do the decent thing and set him free. She offered these words of advice while devouring an entire coffee cake, right there in the store. I'll never eat another coffee cake as long as I live.

I haven't shared any of this with Logan, because what's the point? It will only piss him off and make him feel responsible, but I have to admit I really don't like it. Broderick's warning plays in my head, but so does his assurance that it all eventually evens out. That's what I'm doing, waiting for the light at the end of the tunnel.

Mr. and Mrs. MacGowan arrive today and so everyone is coming to my house for dinner. I have spent the past two days cleaning, everything from dusting to washing windows and wiping down baseboards. I'm making Italian dishes, since Logan's parents are partial. The lasagna is in the oven, the meatballs are simmering, and the antipasto and tiramisu are chilling. I have a fire log in the fireplace, candles artistically placed around the living and dining rooms, and the table set with my nicer dishes.

As the doorbell sounds, I give everything one last look before I reach for the door and pull it open. Cold paint splashes all over me and then I hear the sound of someone running away, but I don't miss the "bitch" called in retreat. I wipe at my eyes with my dress, and when I'm finally able to open them, I see the blue paint all over my foyer. Reaper is there, having come to greet our guests, so when he shakes, paint goes flying everywhere, before he trots away, leaving blue pawprints in his retreat.

Logan and his family will be pulling up any minute, but there's not a damn thing I can do before they get here, so instead of attempting to clean it up, I walk out the back door and head for the beach. It's cold, but I'm so angry that my temper is keeping me warm. Minutes later I hear the car, followed shortly by the commotion inside. I hear my name being called, but I don't answer because I'm so angry I can't speak.

"Saffron," Logan calls from the back door. Seconds later, he's right at my side. He turns me to him. "What the hell happened?"

Tears are in my eyes but I don't let them fall. "Apparently, I'm a bitch."

"Fucking Darla. She'll pay for this. Jesus, you're freezing." He takes off his jacket and wraps it around my shoulders before lifting me into his arms and carrying me back inside.

I rest my head on his chest. I'm feeling demoralized and pissed because the situation is completely out of my control. How do you deal with people who not only think about throwing paint at someone, but actually follow through? I mean, sure, I've thought about dragging the occasional person out of their car when I get cut off at a stoplight, but I don't. When faced with someone who does act on their baser instincts, you're helpless to do anything about it. My voice is hoarse from simmering anger. "I'm sorry."

"You have nothing to be sorry for." Rage drips from his words.

"Not really the first impression I was hoping for. My house is a mess." Wrapping my arms around him, I bury my face in the crook of his neck.

"I'm sorry, baby, I am so sorry," he whispers.

"It wasn't you who threw the paint at me."

"No, but it was because of me."

My head snaps up in response and I grab his chin, forcing his gaze on me. "It was no more your fault than it was mine. Don't."

He doesn't answer, but I can see something burning in those eyes. I don't like what I see, but before I can press him on what he's thinking, we're stepping into the house where Broderick, Dante, and Mr. and Mrs. MacGowan are standing. I gently push on Logan for him to let me down and unconsciously I arrange my skirt, which is pointless since most of it is covered in paint.

"Hello. I hope your trip was pleasant. I'm Saffron and . . ." My house is a disaster, it all is just too much for me to deal with. "I'm really sorry about this." I turn to Logan. "Mitch will be able to get you into The Harbor." I simply can't deal any longer and add quickly, "If you'll excuse me. Reaper, come."

I don't wait for a response as Reaper and I disappear down the hall to my bedroom. I listen for the sound of the front door closing, signaling my guests are gone, before I make my way to the bathroom and step fully clothed into the shower. Reaper jumps in after me—he loves taking a shower. Peeling off the wet dress, I shower the paint away before washing down Reaper. Climbing out, I dry off and then dry Reaper, who shakes, sending water droplets flying around the bathroom. Not all of the paint has come out of my hair, but I'll deal with that later.

After reaching for a bag under the sink, I squeeze out my dress and drop it, my panties, and shoes into it. In my state, the idea of taking my damn shoes off so I didn't track more paint around my house escaped me. Reaper settles on my bed to groom himself further. I pull on some sweatpants and a T-shirt before pulling my hair back, and then I tackle the bathroom until it sparkles.

Wiping up the paint I tracked into my room, I move to the living room, but I'm confused when I hear the voices as soon as I open my door. Reaching the foyer my feet just stop at the sight. Logan, Dante, and their mom are all on their hands and knees, cleaning the paint from my floor.

"What are you doing?"

It's Logan who answers me, and he sounds almost jubilant considering the circumstances. "What does it look like? We're cleaning this up."

"No, you're getting paint all over your pretty clothes." I hurry over to Mrs. MacGowan. "Please, I can do this."

Beautiful hazel eyes lift to mine with understanding and sympathy. "I raised three boys, so I'm used to this."

I kneel down next to her. "Yes, but you're dressed in Armani."

She grins and holds out her hand to me. "Briana. Nice to meet you, Saffron."

I smile, seeing so much of Logan in her. "It's nice to meet *you*."

"You might want to check on the lasagna. It smells delicious."

"Oh, right."

Jumping up, I start for the kitchen only to stop because Logan's father is already pulling the lasagna from the oven. He turns in my direction and I almost gasp because I'm looking at an older version of

Logan: every feature is the same. Even their bodies are built the same. I feel my legs go weak when a smile cracks over his face.

"Scary, isn't it?"

It takes me a minute to comprehend what he's saying. "It's uncanny."

He reaches for my hand. "Rory. Very nice to meet you, Saffron."

I can't help watching as he brushes his lips over my knuckles and I'm not embarrassed to admit that I experience my second ever crush, and for my own fiancé's father, at that.

The doorbell sounds, but I can't for the life of me think who would be paying me a visit. I'm somewhat reluctant to leave Rory, but I force myself from the room with a hurried "Excuse me."

My heart is literally beating faster than before, but then, is that really a surprise with how much the father is like the son?

Reaching the living room, I see Tommy and Gwen carrying hangers of clothes. Even though they smile, I can see the understanding in their expressions. And then my eyes take in my foyer and to my surprise, it's sparkling; there is not a speck of paint anywhere.

"Could I use your bathroom to freshen up?" Briana asks.

"I can't believe you got this done so quickly. There's a bathroom in the guest room. I'll show you."

Gwen hands me Briana's clothes, before I walk her down the hall to the guest room. I place the clothes on the bed. "Thank you," I say.

"It's what families do, and you are now a part of our family."

I'm smiling as I pull the door closed.

———

Dinner turns out to be lovely. The food and wine are delicious and the company is first rate. Throughout dinner, Briana and Rory entertain me with stories about Logan and his brothers, hysterical stories that make me laugh and the guys blush.

When they are preparing to leave, Briana takes me aside. "It takes a bit of getting used to, Logan's celebrity status. Knowing how much time and effort you put into this evening makes what happened even more infuriating, but he is worth it. I've never seen my son so happy. There's baggage with Logan, but you'll never find a better man."

My hands find hers. "I love your son and I realize I'll have some adjusting to do, but if Logan's the prize, I'll do it."

A smile spreads over her face. "That's what I was hoping you'd say." She presses a kiss to my cheek. "When you start planning the wedding, I'd be delighted to help."

"I would love your help."

Her entire face lights up at that.

I walk Briana to her husband, who immediately brings me close for a bear hug. "Dinner was delicious. We'll see you tomorrow, yes?" he asks as he takes a step back and again I'm struck with how much Logan looks like him. "Yes."

He brushes his lips over my cheek and my heart flutters.

"You better watch out, Logan, looks like you've got some competition," Broderick teases.

After saying good-bye to Broderick and Dante, the door closes and silence falls. Logan remains looking at the door before he turns and I see the look I saw earlier. "I'll go clean up the kitchen."

He starts away from me. "Logan?"

He threads his fingers through his hair, his temper simmering just under the surface.

"You went to so much trouble for tonight and then some asshole throws paint at you. I mean, what the fuck? You don't deserve to be pulled into the bullshit of my life and to have your quiet life invaded. I did this, I opened the fucking door and they just walked right on in and there's nothing I can do to protect you from it."

"Tonight was trying, but it's a part of you and I love you so if I have to deal with the occasional crazy fan, so be it."

"If it was Darla tonight, I'll deal with her. If it wasn't, from my experience, it's only going to get worse." He frames my face with his hands.

"What I wouldn't give to be just an average guy who didn't have to watch the papers every day to make sure the media isn't feasting on the woman he loves." He wraps his arms around me. "If I could be that man, if there was something I could do to become anonymous again, I would. I'd do it for you."

Trying to lighten the mood, I reply, "Well, you're tolerable too, I suppose."

He looks devilish as he tosses me over his shoulder. "I'll show you tolerable, brat."

———

After the paint incident, things seem to settle down. The town starts taking a more active notice of those visiting Harrington. Sheriff Dwight assigns a squad car to drive down my street a few times a day.

The MacGowans are heading back to Scotland but are planning a longer trip closer to the wedding. Briana and I have exchanged e-mail addresses and phone numbers, so the distance won't affect us working together on the wedding plans.

After Logan and his parents leave for the airport, I head to Tucker's for work. When I arrive I see Gwen and Josh waiting for me at the bar.

"I want to know all about your visit, but first, you okay?" Gwen asks.

"Honestly, I don't know. I'd been adequately warned about what to expect being linked to David, but I wasn't expecting something so invasive. I can't get my head around the idea that people can act so unhinged all because of a pretty face. It's disturbing."

"I've never heard of anything so ridiculous. I heard the sheriff was asking at the local hardware store about any purchases of blue paint recently. What kind of person does that?" Gwen asks.

"Someone who isn't completely stable," I say.

"And Logan?"

"He thinks it's Darla. He's catching a flight to New York to deal with her."

"You don't look like you agree that it was her," Josh guesses accurately.

"I don't. When she came to the house . . . actually, more when she realized that Logan truly had moved on, she got it. So no, I don't think it was her."

"Maybe the sheriff will have luck, but in the meantime we'll just have to be extra cautious. Now spill about his parents," Josh says.

"They're wonderful. After a disastrous beginning, we all sat around like longtime friends talking about everything and anything. They're sweet and smart and they put me at ease, made me forget how the evening started, and I know they did it on purpose. Briana is going to help with the wedding plans, was so excited to be included."

"And your parents?" Gwen asks.

"Debated about calling them, but I did. I left a message. I haven't heard back from them, but I'm not really expecting to."

"They won't offer to pay for it?"

"Doubtful. Logan wants to pay for it, has insisted, even though I offered to help with the money that Frank left me. He wants me to keep that for Dupree House."

"Like I said, we totally approve of Logan. Let's talk dresses. Any idea what you're looking for?"

A dreamy look passes over my expression at Gwen's question. "No, I don't know. I guess we need to go shopping so I can try some on and get ideas."

"Sounds like a trip to Bar Harbor," Josh and Gwen chime in together.

"We'll have to schedule something, and soon. And with the Swordfish Festival coming up in a few months, I'm thinking that Logan and I should get married on that day. Call me crazy, but it's when my relationship with Logan changed."

"And forevermore swordfish will be synonymous with your love. How romantic."

I clock Josh in the head. "You're an idiot."

The door to the bar opens, and in walks Shalee. Apparently, her sea-weed allergy finally healed, because her skin is once again smooth alabaster. As soon as she sees me, she starts over before settling herself on a stool. "You're engaged to David Cambre. How the hell did you pull that off?"

"Excuse me?"

"Look, you're pretty and all, but David Cambre? You aren't in his league. You're a poor bartender. Do you have any idea what the people in David's social circles are saying about the engagement? They're counting the months, I assure you. You're an embarrassment to him."

"Shalee, that's enough." I've never heard Gwen so angry before. Her anger almost rivals my own.

Shalee stands to go, but she levels me with a rather sincere look. "I'm not trying to be mean, but his world and your world just don't mesh. Have you even considered the impact on his art an engagement to you will have? Part of the allure of David Cambre is his availability—the dream just out of reach. You've seen the women coming here to get a glimpse of him, for the idea that he'd point to them in a crowd and make all of their dreams come true. Marrying you will make him lose that, and his art will suffer. And as much as he may love you, he loves his art and sharing it with the world. He could one day grow resentful that marriage to you took that away from him."

A coldness settles over me as Shalee takes her leave. As much of a bitch as she can be, she made some remarkably insightful comments. When I look over at Gwen and Josh, I know that they are thinking the same thing.

As we're dress hunting in Bar Harbor, Shalee's comment from the other day is still rattling around in my head. I don't necessarily agree with it, but I don't disagree with it either. I could dwell on how Logan and I come from two different worlds but I won't, because all that matters is that we love each other.

Moving on to more pleasant thoughts, I say, "There are two bridal boutiques I want to visit. We have appointments at one and four."

"So you still thinking the Swordfish Festival for the date?" Gwen asks.

I chuckle, recalling the conversation Logan and I had earlier that morning on the subject of setting the date. Now was the date he preferred.

"I'm waiting to hear back from the pastor to find out what his availability is. I'd like to have the ceremony at the lighthouse, right on the bay this spring, so I'm still thinking the Swordfish Festival."

"Spring gives us a few months. We should be able to swing that," Josh says.

"Mitch can coordinate with his team to cater the food."

"Would he do that?" I wanted to approach Mitch about that, but I felt bad suggesting he work during a day he should be relaxing and celebrating.

"Absolutely."

"I can't believe I'm planning my wedding. It's one of those things you think about from the time you're a little girl, but now it's reality. I almost want the day to be here already, but I want to plan it too."

"It'll be here before you know it, but first things first. We need a dress."

The first boutique was a bust. The dresses were all too fairy princess for my taste. As soon as we entered the second shop, I see my gown: a strapless lace sheath. Simple and yet elegant.

"That's it."

"Oh, that is it," Gwen says dreamily.

Half an hour later I'm standing in front of a three-way mirror and, oh, the dress is even more perfect. It's only a sample. The actual gown will be custom made for me.

"Wait until Logan sees you in that," Gwen says what I'm thinking.

"This is the one."

The bridal consultant beams. "Then let's get your measurements."

After placing a deposit for my wedding gown, we head to a restaurant. "Are you going to do a veil?" Gwen asks as she reaches for her cosmo.

"I don't think so, but I do want my hair up."

"I can do that," Josh says. "Maybe we can tuck a few flowers into it."

"Perfect."

"Isn't that your neighbor, Saffron? That Elise chick?"

Gwen's question yanks me from the happy wedding bubble I'm in, and I turn in the direction that she's staring. "Yeah, that's her. I wonder what she's doing here?"

"Well, she's not buying those clothes in Harrington." Josh reaches for his water glass. "And I'd bet money she doesn't take her car to Jake's garage, fine German engineering and all."

"Saffron." Elise is forgotten with the arrival of Dean. I had called him to tell him we'd be in town and would love to hook up for dinner. "Hey. Long time no see. You remember Gwen and Josh?"

"Yeah, how are you?"

"Good, glad you could join us," Josh says. "What are you drinking?" He flags down our waiter.

"Jameson, neat. So what brings you to Bar Harbor?"

"Wedding dress shopping. I got engaged."

Genuine joy washes over Dean's face. "To Logan?"

"Yes."

"Congratulations."

"Thank you. What about you? How have you been?"

"I'm good, keeping busy with work. Well, it isn't just work keeping me busy. I met someone recently—Katherine."

"And?" It's all the encouraging Dean needs to talk about the new lady in his life.

Returning home, I'm greeted by Logan, who is relaxing on my sofa with Reaper. After kicking off my shoes, I settle at his side, his arm wrapping around my shoulders and tucking me more closely to him.

"How did it go?"

"A success."

"I suppose asking you to describe it would be fruitless."

"Yup. I called Dean and invited him to dinner. I was happy he could join us."

"Lawyer Dean?" His body has tensed ever so slightly in response to that news.

"Yes, he's seeing someone. He sounds quite smitten."

"Really? So he no longer has eyes on my woman?"

"Your woman?"

"Yeah. My. Woman."

Shifting, I straddle his lap. "So very caveman of you, Logan. I like it. What do you think about getting married on the day of the Swordfish Festival?"

"Seriously?"

"Well, it is when your feelings for me deepened."

He laughs, such a great sound. "True. You don't mind that we will be eternally linked to the swordfish?"

"I've a whole new outlook, remember?"

He smiles, as if recalling the fond memory. "Okay, then let's do it."

"Really?"

"Yeah, but you're going to have to include Chastity in the planning."

"Right." And then I remember the day she opened up to me, and, under her harsh exterior, that she's just looking to fit in. "I can do that."

His hands drift up my back to tangle in my hair just before he pulls my mouth down to his. Lips mold, tongues battle, and the need to get closer builds until Logan is ripping my shirt up over my head. He yanks my bra down and closes his mouth over my breast. Linking my hands behind his head, I hold his mouth there as my hips start to move, rubbing against the hard length of him, seeking to ease the ache that his tongue is stirring.

He flips us and in the same motion, peels my jeans and panties off. Our gazes are locked as he undresses in front of me until he is standing there brilliantly naked and aroused. Kneeling on the sofa, he spreads my legs wider, running his hands to my thighs, and kisses me right on the nub that's throbbing.

"Oh God, yes." His tongue moves over my aching flesh, pushing into me, deep and hard. My hips move, seeking deeper penetration. He works me until I'm about to come, and then he moves up my body, shifts his hips, and drives into me. My body spasms, the orgasm washing over me in magnificent waves. He doesn't stop, his thrusts moving harder and faster until he tenses, his muscles flexing from the fierceness of his orgasm.

He drops onto me. I take his weight, his heart beating hard and fast, his breathing as labored as my own.

"We scared the shit out of Reaper," I say in his ear. My baby isn't used to Mommy having sex on the sofa.

He laughs, the sound flowing over me, and to my surprise I feel him growing hard. His head lifts and he says, "The more he sees us, the more comfortable he'll get."

He shifts and almost completely leaves me before he sinks back in, really slowly. I moan.

"This for Reaper's benefit?" I ask.

In response he bites my nipple. The slight pain in combination with what he's doing between my legs has another moan escaping.

"Yep. I'm a real animal lover."

The first negative story about the engagement of David Cambre to his sex kitten is printed only a few days after I find my wedding gown. I'm standing in the grocery store reading a magazine article that details how I lured David into marriage through inventive and kinky sex play. As I'm reading, Tommy comes up next to me.

"I heard the Fletcher sisters talking. They want to ask you what kind of sex play gets such effective results."

I'm embarrassed, but I can't help but laugh, because it's completely ridiculous. I know everyone in Harrington knows it's completely ridiculous, but how does the press come up with this shit?

"There isn't one shred of fact in this entire article. Did you know that, prior to being a bartender at a nearly topless bar, which I still haven't figured out what that means, I was Brad Pitt's paramour? How the hell did they learn I like Brad?"

"Who knows," Tommy says, but he reaches for my hand. Concern clouds his expression. "Are you okay?"

"Yeah, I'm okay."

"Everyone important knows it's bullshit."

I squeeze Tommy's hand before I put the magazine back. "I know."

That night Logan lies in bed, but he's brooding and I can only guess it's because of the article. He confirms this when he says, "I'm sorry about the article in that ridiculous rag. My lawyers are demanding a retraction."

"You're going to have to grow a thicker skin, because we're news and the stories written about us are not going to be flattering. No one understands why you're marrying someone so completely beneath you."

He sits up at that, the anger in his expression startling. "You don't believe that, do you?"

"I believe that Logan MacGowan and Saffron Dupree are perfectly matched."

"But?"

"I think that David Cambre is way out of my league."

"But I'm both."

"I know, and so we're going to have to get used to stories like the one in that rag mag because no one will ever understand why David Cambre would settle for a bartender from a little poor fishing town."

He whispers, "Bartending is what you do, who you are is the most loving, sweet, fun, and adventurous woman I've ever known. You make me laugh, you make me love . . ." But quickly, he turns serious. "Have you noticed anyone lurking around your house?"

I'm not sure where that came from and why he looks so determined all of a sudden. "No, why do you ask?"

"It may be nothing, but I have the sense that someone's been snooping around the lighthouse. The reporters are gone because I kicked them off my property, but I still feel as if someone is watching us. Darla didn't dump the paint on you, as it turns out, so I'm uneasy. I'm probably being paranoid, but I would really like for you to be very careful and make sure you bring Reaper with you when you go out on the beach. If there's someone around, he'll sense it."

"Okay."

I'm uneasy now too, but I promise to make an effort to be more alert.

———

I was okay with the first article, my introduction into the celebrity realm, but it seems the other tabloids have decided to have fun at my expense. Each story printed is more unbelievable than the next.

Again I'm in the market reading about myself in the tabloids. There's one story that claims I am a high-priced prostitute and the picture that accompanies this is one of Logan and me at The Pierre coming home from the gallery show. I wasn't even aware we had our picture taken and for these assholes to take such a beautiful memory and twist it into something sleazy really pisses me off. And if this isn't bad enough, further into that same story is another picture of me, at least they claim it's me, and I'm kneeling in front of some man I've never seen before. Hateful. Just because I tend bar at a fishermen's watering hole doesn't make me a slut. As much as I know I'm being foolish to allow it to hurt me, it does all the same.

As I drive home from the market, I try to pull myself together. I really don't want Logan to see how much this is hurting me. As soon as I pull up to my house, I walk around to the back toward the beach. I know it's all bullshit and that these people don't know me, but it's hard not to take it personally.

Logan, having heard my car, seeks me out and without a conscious thought, I blurt out, "I know it shouldn't upset me, but it really does."

I can feel the anger radiating off him, but when he speaks his voice is soft. "I am so sorry. I had no idea they would be so cruel."

"How could you have known?"

"I should have guessed. The thought that you're being ripped apart and your character being defamed only because you are with me . . . I want to rip their fucking throats out. I want to buy their magazines and shut them down."

"You can't fight all of them."

"Fucking David, I am seriously growing to hate him."

"But he's you."

"He is what that world created and he is kept going by that world."

"Regardless, he's a part of you and that means he will be a part of us and everyone will believe that they have a say in our lives."

He steps away from me, and when he looks back I can see the fury turning his eyes almost black. "I don't want that kind of life for you. I want anonymity again, and if there's a way to make it happen I will. Do you understand what I'm saying?"

"Not really."

"Just promise that you will listen with your heart as well as your ears."

"What are you up to?" I ask, but I'm not sure I want to hear the answer.

"Just reaching for the dream. And in case there's any doubt in that pretty head of yours, you are the dream. Remember that."

"Okay."

He takes my hand as we start back to the house. "I would like to have an alarm system installed in your house. Are you okay with that?"

"Should I be concerned?"

"I'll do the worrying, you just be careful."

"You aren't telling me everything."

He reaches for my other hand. "I'm not, because I think you have quite enough to deal with, but if I feel you need to know in order to keep you safe, I'll tell you. Deal?"

"Deal." I see the tension fading from him as well as the anger. We start down the beach again and then he says, "So I had a dream about you. You were naked and there was caramel sauce." I look up to see his lascivious grin. "Tell me, love, that you bought caramel sauce."

How he can switch moods so quickly I don't know, but my body is suddenly throbbing. "I did."

He releases my hand as a mischievous grin curves his lips. "I'll give you to the count of three."

Three days after our adventure with caramel sauce, the stories are still going strong, but I'm trying to separate myself from the woman depicted. It isn't me they're writing about. To the press I'm a person of interest only because I'm connected to David. Eventually, the media will move on.

However, when the hate mail starts arriving, Logan takes that very seriously. He's got the sheriff tracking the mail and he's added additional locks to my house. I know there's more to what's fueling him than just the mail, but I find I don't really want to know the details. There's already so much going on.

Outside of turning my house into a fortress, I've noticed that he spends a great deal of time planning. It's the only word I can think to describe his actions. And there are times when I'll be reading and he'll be at his desk working and I'll look up to see him watching me with such sadness in his expression that it breaks my heart. I've tried to talk to him about it, but he always turns the conversation to making love. Almost all the time now, he's carrying me off to the bedroom and sometimes we don't even make it that far. It's wonderful, but there's a desperation about him—as if he's trying to get his fill in because there's a time limit.

Thinking of him makes me miss him, so I walk to the lighthouse, but when I arrive I hear something shatter. I find Logan standing in the midst of his ruined studio: fragments of sculptures, broken canvases, and the pile of wood I can only assume was his easel. His chest rising and falling from exertion and his hands are clenched into fists.

"Logan."

He doesn't seem to know I'm there until I walk closer and repeat, "Logan. Logan, what are you doing?"

"Some mistakes you never stop paying for," he whispers before he slowly turns around to face me. "You should run as far from me as possible."

"I can't."

"It's just as well, because I'll never let you go."

And then he's kissing me. When his mouth leaves mine, he lifts me into his arms and starts from the room. "I'll always come for you. Even when it seems impossible, I will find a way to come for you."

"Logan?"

"Just remember that. In this world, all I want is you."

Though our lovemaking is beautiful, I can't help having the sense that the other shoe is about to drop.

———

Driving home from a wedding session with Gwen, my thoughts are on the florist I need to call tomorrow. We spent the night discussing flowers. Logan was invited because he has taken a very active role in planning, but his expression when he learned what we had planned for the night was comical.

The roads are not very well lit at this hour, so I'm going under the speed limit. It's been two weeks since Logan had a meltdown in his studio. I've repeatedly asked him what caused it, but he politely dismisses the question, usually turning the subject to something else. Rain starts when I'm about halfway home, making the roads pretty slick. Reaching the top of a rather steep section of the road, I apply my brakes to slow my descent, but nothing happens. I don't immediately appreciate the trouble I'm in. My foot still slams down on a pedal that's not responding, my speed picking up at an alarming rate. The road bends at the end of the decline, and I try to downshift, but the car is really moving. I can't make the turn. Even as I'm pulling the wheel to the left, I know I'm not going to make it.

My headlights illuminate the guardrail seconds before the sound of crushing metal fills the silence. My head jerks forward and back so hard, pain immediately erupts in my skull and shoots down my spine. The car comes to a shaking stop, but it takes me a bit longer to react since shock has set in. My purse had been next to me, but it isn't now. I'm about to reach for it, but flashes of all those shows where you're not supposed to move someone with a neck injury keep me from doing so. Especially with the pain radiating from my back. I don't want to cause more damage. Panic sets in. Logan will be waiting for me; when I don't arrive he'll come looking, but until then I'm stuck and alone in the dark.

Unconsciousness threatens, but I force myself to stay awake.

My car is totaled; I don't need to see it to know. It's my own fault. Buying such an old car, it was bound to malfunction, even though I did have Jake look it over. Wear and tear is natural, especially on older cars like this.

I can only imagine Logan's reaction. At this point I don't really care how he reacts just as long as he's here at my side. It's only about a twenty-minute ride to Gwen's. How much time has passed? The thought just leaves my head when I see headlights appear over the horizon, another set coming up from behind me. Logan barely puts the car in park before he's flying to get to me. He thinks I'm dead. The sight of him illuminated by my headlights will haunt me for a long time to come.

"Saffron." With a second of profound relief, he turns deadly serious. Pulling his phone from his pocket he calls for an ambulance.

"Does it hurt anywhere, baby?"

"My head and back."

His grip on my hand is nearly painful. Gwen and Mitch appear next to Logan. They must have been in the other car.

"Oh my God, what happened?" Gwen's crying, Mitch looks rattled, but my focus is completely on Logan because the expression on his face scares me. If I had to put a word on it, I'd say resolved. But resolved about what?

Hearing the sounds of the sirens and knowing that Logan's with me, I succumb to the darkness that's been threatening.

Two days later, I'm home. I have a neck brace due to whiplash and some bumps and bruises, but other than that I came through my ordeal intact. My friends take turns staying with me, making me meals, walking Reaper, and keeping me company. And though it isn't necessary, I am glad for the company because they help to keep my mind off Logan.

He has not left my side since the accident and, as wonderful as he's been, something is still off. He's distant, the best I can express it, like he's an observer. In the nine months since we've been together and the six before that when we circled each other in silence, there was never a barrier.

Asking him about it, about his change, gets me nowhere, even though I'm only looking for confirmation, since I already suspect what's going on in his head. Sheriff Dwight arrives to talk to me and that's when I get my confirmation.

"Saffron. How are you feeling?"

"Achy but, considering how much worse it could have been, I'm great."

"About that. Need to ask you some questions."

"Okay."

"Have you noticed anyone paying you specific attention? I realize with your engagement and who Logan is, you've had more attention on you than you'd like, but does anyone stand out specifically?"

"Not since Darla."

"Have you seen anyone poking around your place, your car?"

"What's this about?"

Rubbing his hand over the back of his neck, he takes a minute to reply. "Your brake lines were cut."

I could not have heard that correctly. "I'm sorry, could you say that again?"

"Got a call from Jake after we had your car towed there. It's standard procedure to have the car examined after an accident. It wasn't mechanical failure. Your lines were intentionally cut."

"Does Logan know?"

"Yeah, I intended to wait until I could tell you, but the man can be very insistent when he wants to be."

Fear slices through me. Knowing Logan as I do, he'll feel responsible and he'll take steps to ensure I'm not put at risk—and thinking about what those steps will be terrifies me.

"So have you seen anyone poking around?"

"No, I haven't. Since no one has attempted to kill me before, I'm guessing you and Logan are both under the impression this threat on me stems from my association with him."

"Most logical answer."

Damn.

I'm home for a week when the proverbial other shoe drops. I'm in the living room with Reaper going over the report from the contractor for Dupree House when Logan appears in the threshold. He makes no attempt to step farther in the room—distancing himself from me, both physically and mentally. If I'm being completely honest, in my heart and my head I know what's coming, have been fearing it for some time.

"I can't marry you."

Even knowing those words were coming, I'm still eviscerated. A welcoming numbness spreads over me—I'm guessing it's my body's way of protecting me from the trauma his words have inflicted. And though I know argument is futile, I try anyway.

"Don't do this."

"I can't marry you." Stronger this time, more force behind his words, more determined.

"Why?"

And then the floodgates open and I am no longer looking at emptiness, but rage and fear so savage it's frightening. "Someone fucking cut your brake lines. You could have died and when I approached your car I thought you were dead." He comes at me, a more primal Logan. "My beautiful, wild and alive Saffron, dead because some sick fuck has a hard-on for me. No, I will not marry you, I will not live in a world where you don't. I love you, I love you enough to leave you be."

"And then what? I get to live safe but alone?"

"I need to know who came at you, I need to protect you. When the threat is gone, I'll be back and I hope that when I do, I'm not too late."

"Too late? Like I'd move on? You're the fucking air I need to breathe. Are you speaking your own feelings out loud?"

He's on me, my papers torn from my hand as he yanks me from the sofa and crushes me to him. His kiss is violent and so full of need and desperation. Feeling the same, I rip his shirt up over his head, my mouth on him, licking, tasting, before I sink my teeth into his shoulder, marking him. Grabbing my thighs, he lifts me, my legs coming around his waist, his mouth closing over my breast through my shirt. But it's not enough, we need skin to skin. Moving to my room, he drops me to my feet and removes my clothes as I frantically remove his and then we're tumbling on the bed, all legs and arms, mouth tasting and touching every part of each other we can reach. My legs spread and he drives into me. The pace we set is almost brutal, my fingers raking down his back, his teeth marking my neck and shoulders until my orgasm nearly splits me apart. He's relentless, pounding into me, but when he comes he scoops me up, cradling me against his body, the gesture beautiful, almost reverent, and unmistakably a good-bye. I burst into tears. He holds me until I fall asleep. When I wake in the morning, he's gone.

CHAPTER SEVENTEEN

For the two days Logan's been gone, I've done nothing but sit on the beach looking toward the horizon. He left me. I know why he left, understand what motivated him, and can honestly say if the roles had been reversed, I'd have done the same. In my head, I get it, but in my heart, he left me. With all the pain churning through me, I should at least have the right to hate him. But I can't, because he didn't leave me, he just left me to keep me safe.

"You're not sitting out here for another day. If Logan saw this, he would not be happy, particularly since the only reason he left was to keep you alive. This isn't living." Tommy sinks down next to me on the sand.

"Yes, but maybe if I wallow long enough, he'll drop the chivalrous bullshit and come home to me."

Tommy takes my hand, shifting my focus to him. "He thought you were dead. Seeing your car mangled, he thought you were dead. How the hell did you think he was going to react? Saffron, you could have died in that accident."

A shiver works through me as it does every time I think about what-if. "You're right. My head totally gets it. But he's gone, Tommy. I have a wedding dress being made I don't even know if I'll ever wear. The man I want to marry, the man who wants to marry me, is off trying to find out who tried to kill me. What the fuck? I think, under the circumstances, I can have a few days to be pissed and sad and angry and lonely."

"A few days and then you're getting your ass back into your life," Tommy says with tenderness. "Logan will be back and you'll be married during the Swordfish Festival, which I think you're completely insane for even thinking. Your life will go on. Give him this. He feels responsible. He needs to do this."

Resting my head on his shoulder, my gaze turns back to the horizon. "How did you get so smart? Did you, like, eat smart people's brains?"

"Well, if I did, you'd certainly be safe from me."

My laugh feels really good. "Love you, Tommy."

"Back at you."

As the days turn into weeks, the female population thins. David is gone and so are the groupies and unwanted cameras. Not that they don't take a few parting shots, seeming to enjoy the juicy tidbit of our broken engagement. The common thread is that David was slumming but has finally come back to his senses. I sit in my pretty little living room with my dog at my side. I don't deserve such cruelty from people who don't know me at all.

A moving van drove past a few days ago; Elise apparently really had been here only for the story and she didn't even say good-bye.

Hearing my phone, I go into the kitchen to grab it. I'm more than a little disappointed to hear my mom. This is the first time she's called since I left them the message about my engagement.

"Saffron, is it true you are no longer engaged to David Cambre?"

Way to stick the knife in. "Yes."

"What did you do?"

"Excuse me?"

"Well, you must have done something to make him go. Why can't you be more accommodating? Why do you have to be so hardheaded? You've been like that since you were a small child. Always had to go your own way, never listened, never followed, always charging ahead without thought to consequence."

"Why is it that every time we talk, you're finding fault? Why don't you ever call to say, 'Hey, Saffron, how are you doing?' or, 'Saffron, so sorry to hear about your breakup. Are you okay?' You only ever find fault with me. Why can't you just offer love and support without censure?"

"I wasn't aware you felt that way about my parenting."

"You don't see it?"

"No, I hear an ungrateful girl who's whining because she wasn't kissed more on the head. Sometimes I wonder if babies weren't switched at the hospital, because I just simply don't get you. Being your mother has not been easy, Saffron. You should be thankful for what it was we did give you."

"What exactly? Love? No. Support? No. Understanding? No. I got all of that from Frank. Hell, Dad can't even get on the damn phone for the ten minutes you allot me a month. If being my parent is such a burden, I can make that very easy for you. Lose my number, because I intend to lose yours. I've spent my life seeking your approval, hoping for just one pat on the head, but I know I will never get that from you and frankly I'm just tired of the whole pretense."

"If that's how you feel, fine."

"Oh, and in my opinion, any bitch in heat can have a kid. Being a mother is an entirely different scenario. You were never my mother." I don't wait for a reply and hang up.

"Saffron."

At the sound of Logan's voice on the phone, my heart takes off into a gallop. "Logan."

"Can you talk?"

"Yes." I turn the heat off on the stove where I had been boiling water for pasta and settle on the stool by the bar. "How are you?" I ask.

"Miserable, and you?"

He sounds like I feel. I chuckle. "The same. I wasn't expecting to hear from you."

"Just because I can't be with you, can't fucking marry you . . ." I hear the inhale, his attempt to calm down. "I needed to hear your voice."

"I'm glad you called, *ecstatic* is probably a better word."

He chuckles. Well, that's better than him being pissed. "I'm sorry I left the way I did, sneaking off in the middle of the night. If I'd waited until morning, I would have lost my resolve and I really do believe you're safer with me away. Speaking of which, has there been any more trouble?"

"Not the kind you're worrying about, but somehow I think you already know that."

"True, the sheriff is on speed dial. What other kind of trouble is there?"

"I had a falling-out with my mom. I told her to lose my number."

His concern comes through the line and wraps around me. "Are you okay? As sad as it is to say, I think that outcome has been in the making for a long time."

"You're right. It's just taken me this long to finally reach my limit. In the long run, it's for the best. I'll never measure up and now I won't be setting myself up for the inevitable hit."

"They don't deserve you. How they can see anything but the incredible woman you are is totally fucking beyond me."

"You're swearing an awful lot," I tease.

"Pent-up frustration does that to me."

It's my turn to chuckle because he sounds so disgruntled, a sound I am not used to hearing from him. "How are you? What's happening with your investigation?"

He's silent for a moment and, when he does answer, I don't get the sense it's a full answer. "I'm making progress—something from my past, but I'm dealing with it."

"Will you tell me about it?"

"Do you remember we talked about crazy fans on our way to Salem? Well, I'm pretty sure that's what we're dealing with. I've got investigators confirming a few things for me."

"And then?"

"I'm going to confront her."

"Is that smart? Seems to me if she's unstable enough to cut my brake lines, then there's very little she won't do."

"I have to try, Saffron."

"You know who this is. She's more than just a fan. Is she the one who broke in to your house?"

Silence meets my observation for a few beats. "You really do know me so well. Yeah, I do know her, but it isn't the woman who broke in to the house."

"Who?"

"I'd rather not say until I know for sure. If I'm wrong, then I'm defaming someone's character and that makes me no better than the assholes who have taken shots at us."

"Fair."

"If I am correct, though, my decision to leave was right, because this person has a history of mental illness, so there's no telling what she'll do. Reasoning with her may not work, so I'm hoping her family can convince her that she needs to seek help but how long that will take, who the fuck knows. I want to be with you, but I suspect the moment I set foot in Harrington, or you come here, it'll set her off. Maybe even crazier than before because she's thinking she's broken us up."

I want to know who this person is and at the same time I really don't. Fear traces my spine at his words. "We're safer apart for now, but she isn't going to keep us that way."

He doesn't miss a beat. "Agreed."

The weeks turn into months and before long the Swordfish Festival heralds my wedding day. I stand in my room staring at my wedding gown. It's beautiful, perfect, and I'm not wearing it.

"You'll get to wear it. It's just a matter of when. Besides, if you had worn it today, it would have picked up the smell of the swordfish." I know Josh is trying to help, but I don't think there's enough banter in the world to make me smile today.

Gwen walks into my room with Chastity. Her presence momentarily pulls me from my funk.

"Chin up, Saffron. This is a minor setback, nothing more. I mean, hell, with the time and expense Logan put in to ask you to marry him, the boy loves you. He'll be back and until then it's festival time."

"I'm blackballed, remember."

"I'm going to lift that considering the circumstances."

"Great, that's a real pick-me-up."

She turns serious, and it's the look of genuine concern that snaps my mouth shut from any further sarcasm. "Getting out among your friends, this day in particular, is exactly what you need. It may not be the day you had planned, but life does go on. Find happiness in the day despite your disappointment. And to help with that, I've officially included the food fight as part of the activities."

"Really?" Josh is as surprised by that as me. "Why?"

"Because people flooded me with e-mails saying they wanted it in." She cocks her hip. "So, you think you can get yourself motivated to come fling cakes at your neighbors?"

I can't believe I'm smiling.

———

That night I'm in bed when the phone rings and, seeing it's Logan, I answer on the first ring.

"How was the Swordfish Festival?" There's humor in his voice.

"Chastity nailed me with five cakes."

"Payback."

"And that's why I let her." Didn't really want to ask, but I did want to know. "How's it going with the woman?"

"I really don't want to talk about that tonight. We should have been married today and this would have been our wedding night." Silence, then he says, "I miss you—seeing your smile, hearing your laugh—and I ache for you. Are you in bed?"

My entire body clenches. "Yeah."

"I want to try something. If this makes you uncomfortable, just say."

I have a feeling I know what he wants to try and already I'm aching.

"Touch yourself, wet your finger and rub it over your nipple."

The ache moves to between my legs.

"Are you touching yourself?"

I lick my finger and brush it over my nipple. "Yes."

"Twist it, pull, and move your other hand down your body, slowly. Imagine it's my hands on you, running over your ribs and stomach, slipping under your panties. Touch yourself right on the nub that's aching. Are you touching yourself?"

My moan is involuntary. "Yes."

"That's my mouth sucking on your nipple and it's my fingers moving through that wet heat between your legs. Tilt your hips and push your finger inside, slowly, and imagine it's me."

Yanking my panties off, I spread my legs wider and push my finger deep. "I want to touch you. Wrap your hand around your . . ." the word gets stuck in my throat.

"Say it, wrap my hand around what?"

"It's crude."

"Say it."

"Cock, wrap your hand around your cock and imagine it's my mouth, taking you deep, sucking hard. Are you stroking yourself?"

His pleasurable moan is answer enough. "Push another finger into that sweet, wet heat, and pull them out slowly until your body clenches for me, begging me to bury myself deep inside you. Push them back in. That's me in you, feeling you tightening around me. You're wet, so fucking wet."

"I am wet and aching for you. You're swelling in my mouth. I know you're getting close, I can feel you getting harder and thicker, can taste the saltiness leaking from the tip."

"Fuck, yeah. I'm going to come. Make yourself come, Saffron. I want to hear you come while my seed pumps out of me."

My hips rock around my own hand; it feels so good and the nub aches as I squeeze and rub. Oh God. My back arches off the bed. My entire being is locked on his voice and my hand between my legs.

"I'm coming, Saffron. It's your body milking me. Come with me."

"Oh God, I am."

And I do, my body spasms around my fingers just as Logan releases a loud, sexy moan over the line.

Tingles linger, my breath labors, and, instead of feeling embarrassed by what we just did, I love it. Loved knowing he touched himself, made himself come while thinking about me.

"That was . . . holy shit, that was fun," I gasp, nearly breathless, but, holy shit, that really was fun.

"You sure? It wasn't too much?"

"Hell no."

"Good. This time when you come, I want to hear you scream."

—————

The contractor finished up the work on the house in just under a month. My original plan was to hire an interior designer to furnish the empty house until I realized I already have the perfect person for the job: Josh. He has wonderful taste and he's family. I'd much rather he decorate Frank's home than someone who doesn't know the story behind the house.

The plan is to take a week measuring rooms, windows, and the like before we start shopping. When the furniture is delivered, Josh and I, and probably the rest of the gang, if I know them, will spend a weekend setting it all up. It's exciting how close we are to the finish line.

Broderick and Dante made the trip with us, eager to see the progress on the house, but they left earlier—traveling on to Manhattan to take care of some other business.

I'm in the basement with Josh checking out the work the contractor and his crew had done—the new bathroom, the soon-to-be media room, and the elevator.

"This house is amazing. We are going to have a hell of a good time decorating it," Josh says, his arm draping over my shoulders.

"I was thinking we could bring the gang for a weekend and put it all together once we've got everything purchased."

"Excellent idea."

"So where do you want to start?" I ask.

"Down here is good. Let me get my things."

———

At the end of the week, I'm feeling really great about the progress we're making. The board forwarded several potential candidates for fall matriculation. We have two months before classes start, but I'd like to have the kids move in a week prior. We're getting close but I think we're going to make it.

I owe much of this to Broderick and Dante, who have tirelessly handled all the legal matters. I'll need to do something for them as a thank-you.

Josh and I have decided to call it an early night because we're both so exhausted. Who knew shopping online could be so tiring? Reaching my room at the hotel, all I can think about is dropping on the bed and sleeping for two, maybe three, days. I slip my key card into the slot and the door opens on Logan. I'm convinced I'm daydreaming, so I stare, soaking up the sight of him. But it's not a dream—Logan pulls me into the room and slams the door shut with his foot. He crushes me against his hard body and fuses his mouth to mine. My hands frantically try to get past the clothes to flesh as we move together toward the bed, trying to disrobe each other without breaking our kiss.

When he steps back to discard my blouse, his intake of breath makes my toes curl. "God, you're beautiful."

And then we fall onto the bed and our clothes are being tossed here and there. When we're finally skin to skin, we don't waste time as Logan moves between my legs and pushes into me in one hard motion. My hips move up, my legs spread wider, and I just close my eyes and enjoy the feeling of being connected to him again. Logan lifts my hips higher and starts to move with deep thrusts in and out. The exquisite movement pushes me over the edge, my body pulsing with my release, seconds before Logan tenses as his orgasm burns through him. He gives me a minute to catch my breath and then he flips me onto my stomach, lifts my hips, and sinks into me again. His mouth is near my ear when he whispers, "I want to hear you scream this time."

Déjà vu washes over me at the words from our phone sex. This time it's so much better.

I wake to the feel of Logan brushing his fingers over my bare back.

"If I'm dreaming, please don't wake me."

"Not dreaming."

Lifting my head, I ask, "Why did you come?"

"Having you so close, I couldn't stay away."

"Let's stay here for two, maybe three years."

"I'd like that. Broderick stopped by to see me. Dupree House is really coming together."

Sitting up, I wrap the sheet around my breasts. Logan doesn't like this, pulling the sheet from my hand so it settles around my waist. "It's been too long. Please don't cover yourself."

It's not so much his words, but his tone is full of longing, and something darker I can't pinpoint.

"Tell me about the house?" he asks.

I want to ask him what he's thinking, but somehow I know he won't share. "The contractor's finished, so the house is now handicap accessible and the basement is finished. We should be ready to open in a month. The students are scheduled to arrive in seven weeks."

"You've done an amazing job. Frank would be so proud."

Those words choke me up a bit. "Thanks."

Wrapping my arms around him, my gaze locks on his. "I miss you."

"I'm coming home."

"Wait. It's done?"

"Yes. She's being institutionalized."

"Who is it?"

"I can't say. It's part of the agreement I made. She's mentally ill, but on her meds, she's a productive member of society. She needs a chance, once she gets back on track, to have a real shot at a life. I have taken steps though to ensure you're safe."

This person has put us through so much, and yet he can show that kind of compassion. "You're a good man."

"When I come home, I want to marry you in front of everyone, and soon. I'll tolerate hours, even days, but no longer."

"I have my dress and I'll bribe the pastor with a lifetime supply of Mitch's lasagna."

"Good. I never want to be more than the distance of Harrington from you."

"I can get behind that plan."

And then he kisses me as he moves his body in the cradle of mine. "My wife."

"My husband."

"I've lived with you and I've lived without you. Never going to live without you again."

"Thank God, 'cause these months have sucked."

"Agreed. Now kiss me and mean it, woman."

———·———

Logan left earlier, after a weekend of laughing, talking, and loving; he had a pressing meeting that he unfortunately couldn't miss. Josh had been so surprised to see him when he knocked the morning after our reunion he almost dropped the coffee he was carrying. And then he immediately pulled the door closed and left us alone for the weekend. I felt bad since we purposely chose a flight home on Monday so we could take in some sights in Manhattan over the weekend. Josh didn't mind at all. He actually insisted we not leave the room. Logan is going to juggle some things so he can pack up and come home. He promised to call later so we can discuss timing for the wedding. Ten minutes after he arrives home is his preference.

Our flight isn't for another few hours, so Josh and I head to Dupree House to do one more walk-through. Josh drops me off and takes the rental car to get us coffee because the hotel stuff just isn't cutting it for him.

Standing on the front stoop, pride washes over me. The carrier bus Broderick arranged, the one that will drive the students to the various colleges in and around the city, is parked in the driveway I had extended to the side of the house. With the trees and bushes, the bus won't stand out when it's parked there.

Keying into the house, the smell of freshly cut wood greets me. Some of the molding needed to be replaced. The fireplaces have been cleaned and inspected. I replaced all the appliances in the kitchen and put a new washer and dryer in the mudroom.

Each of the four bedrooms will have bunk beds, two students per room. The other two rooms will be for the den mothers, the women who'll be staying to cook meals, help with homework, etc. The responses to the job were impressive, especially with a job that requires so much of someone.

I do a quick walk-through before I head for the front door, and that's when I smell the smoke. Running through the house, I see nothing until I look out back to the small shed I had built to store the grill, sports equipment, and bikes. Without another thought, I run out back to the shed. Yanking the door open, I just stare at the fire burning in the middle of the concrete floor. What the hell? And then I'm pushed, hard, in the back, just as a laugh sends a chill down my body. I throw my weight against the now-closed door, but it's solid oak—I asked for only the best. There's nothing with which to put out the fire, so I stomp on it. The flame licks up my legs, yet I manage to beat it down to a smolder, but the now-smoldering fire clouds the space with that deadly smoke. Hunching down, hoping for clean air, my lungs burn with each inhale.

My purse is in the living room and my cell is in my purse. There are no windows, only the door that won't budge. Josh went in search of coffee in an area he is unfamiliar with so he could be awhile and at the rate the smoke is filling the shed, there is a very real possibility of me asphyxiating.

I can't believe this is it, that just when my life seems perfect, it ends so horribly, so tragically. Thinking about Logan and what this will do to him gives me a surge of strength. Rolling to my back, I slam my feet into the door over and over again. My chest is on fire, my legs are burning, and the damn door is too solid. I don't want to die, so I don't stop slamming my feet into it.

"Saffron!" Josh's hysterical call is the sweetest sound I have ever heard.

"In the shed . . ." Uncontrollable coughing keeps me from finishing.

In the next second, the door is nearly ripped from its hinges and I'm being yanked into the cool, sweet air.

"What the hell happened?" Josh is on his knees at my side, his phone in his hand dialing 911 at the same time. "What the fuck happened?"

"Someone started a fire in the shed and locked me in there."

Immediately he looks around. "Did you see who did it?"

"No, I only heard her laugh." But I know exactly who did this. Logan and I thought it was over, but it's definitely not over. His fear of her escalating if she knew we were still together proves rather intuitive.

"You could have died."

"I think that was the plan."

———

Logan charges into my room at the hospital like a raging bull. Fear, anguish, and fury pulse off him. He yanks me into his arms, almost dislodging all the tubes and monitors I'm hooked up to, holding me tightly against his chest, his heart pounding so hard.

"Are you okay?"

And then he releases me and looks me over, running his hands over me to make sure I'm really here and okay. *Menacing* is the word to describe the expression that floods his face at the sight of my bandaged legs. Moving his gaze up to mine, he kisses me, a deep, desperate kiss, before he pulls away.

"I'll be right back."

He steps out of my room and I hear bits and pieces of his conversation with Josh.

"Too fucking close . . . second degree . . . definitely intentional . . . a two-by-four jammed against the door."

Stepping back into my room Logan displays a look deadlier than any I've ever seen before. He settles next to my bed and takes my hand. When he does finally speak, I don't recognize his voice with the emotion choking him.

"She almost killed you. She tried to fucking kill you."

"Who, who is she?"

He stands up so fast, his hands fisting. "She won't stop. She won't ever fucking stop. If Josh hadn't arrived at the moment he did, if he had gotten stuck at just one light . . . fucking Christ. This shit is done. She isn't going to get another shot at you. No fucking way."

"Logan, you're scaring me. What the hell are you going to do?"

"Whatever the fuck I have to do to make sure you're safe."

He's across the room and his mouth is on mine in a heartbeat. Warm hands on my cheeks, tongues warring, but it isn't just a kiss—it's a pledge, a vow. His eyes turn almost black when he pulls from me, his fingertips pressing into my neck. "Love you. I'll see you soon."

"Logan, what are you going to do?"

He starts from the room and I try to pull the damn cords off me so I can stop him. At the door, he turns to me, and I see the tears in his eyes. "Mine, only you, always you." He kisses his two fingers and then he's gone.

"Logan! Josh, damn it, stop him." I finally manage to free myself. Nurses come running in, but I push past them and stumble out of my room, but the corridor is empty. Limping down the hall, I don't even know I'm crying until I can't see.

"Saffron, what's wrong?" Josh runs after me. "Why are you out of bed?"

"Where's Logan? We have to find him."

Josh grabs my arms. "Calm down, Saffron. You're going to hyperventilate."

"He's going to do something stupid." My body starts to shake uncontrollably. Logan being Logan, there isn't a damn thing I can do to stop him.

CHAPTER EIGHTEEN

I've been home for a week with no word from Logan. His brothers, after a frantic call from me at the hospital, went to New York to track him down. So far, they've been unable to find him. It's like a cloud hanging over me—I just know something really bad is going to happen. My fear is that Logan will retaliate against the woman targeting us, acting out of emotion, and make matters even worse. And Logan in jail for life is definitely worse.

My friends, trying to take my mind off of it and convinced that Logan is just cooling off, are encouraging me to continue on with our plans for the wedding. We're setting up picnic tables right off my back patio for the reception, but I'm just not into it. I'm angry that Logan left the way he did, angry that he didn't tell me what he was up to, angry that I'm angry.

A movement at the back door announces Broderick and Dante. Finally, they found him. I hope Logan is with them, because I am seriously considering shoving my size seven up his ass.

"Saffron. I don't even know how to say this," Broderick starts, but chokes up as tears fill his eyes.

"Broderick, what is it?" I turn to Dante. "What?"

"It's Logan. He was on his way here. He decided to drive through the night. The police say it looks like he lost control of his car and it veered off the road and"—Dante can barely get the last words from his lips—"his car went over the cliff."

I can't feel my body and my heart doesn't seem to be pumping hard enough to get blood to my brain, because I am not making any sense of Dante's words. "What are you saying?"

Dante's voice barely breaks a whisper. "Saffron, Logan's dead."

Gasps come from behind me, but I barely register them because shock has shut down my brain.

That night all the news channels are running the banner of the death of David Cambre, dead at the age of thirty-six—a genius taken before his time.

Sitting on my sofa, I'm silently fuming because of all the idiotic ways Logan could have handled this, he choses to fake his own death. When I see him again, we will be having words. Why he didn't just tell me what he was up to, I can't say, but talk about drastic . . . I should have guessed. He said he'd do anything, said it often, which should have clued me in that he was planning something harebrained. I stand.

"Saffron, honey, where are you going?" Gwen hasn't left my side, none of my friends have.

"He isn't dead. He planned this."

Tommy steps in front of me and takes my hands. "Saffron, Logan's gone."

"I'm telling you, he planned this. He isn't dead. He'll wish he was when I get my hands on him."

I don't miss the looks I'm getting, the ones that fear I'm slipping from reality, that I'm so consumed with grief that I've lost touch. No point in arguing. They'll see when Logan returns.

"Saffron, you have to face this," Tommy says gently.

My face gets right up into his. "I promise you, he is not dead. He's coming back to me." I say no more on the subject and head outside with my dog to wait for Logan to come home to me.

The next night Logan's parents arrive. I desperately want to tell them my theory because I can't bear watching their grief. Logan will hear about this too, what he put his family through. I don't miss the looks, why I'm not more broken up over the news of Logan's death. I won't mourn him, I've already had to do that with someone I loved. I'm not about to fake it for the one person I love most in this world.

The Coast Guard dredges the ocean for a week looking for Logan's body. They aren't going to find it. I'm sitting in my living room when there is a knock at the door. A few minutes later, Sheriff Dwight enters the room with two people I don't recognize, but they're wearing state police uniforms.

"Evening." Sheriff Dwight is running his hand nervously over the rim of his hat. "These gentlemen have news on . . . David's accident."

The tension in the room goes way up, everyone staring in wide-eyed fear at our visitors. The one man, the older of the two, starts to talk, his words slowly penetrating my dubious mind.

"The findings suggest that Mr. Cambre's car lost control on Route 1 just outside of Portsmouth. We believe his car rolled over the cliff, his side taking the brunt of the hit." Hesitation slows his voice; what he has to say next is not going to be good. "Based on the severe damage to the car and"—he takes a breath—"the amount of blood soaked into the seat, we think he was killed instantly or very shortly after. The tech team thinks a seat belt malfunction is the reason why we've been unable to locate . . ." He doesn't finish the thought; he doesn't have to. Logan's body. "We're officially reclassifying our efforts from a search-and-rescue to a retrieval. I am so very sorry for your loss."

At first I think I'm in one of those wicked nightmares that seems so real but isn't. This belief is dashed with a glance around the room to the devastated expressions staring at the police in horror. It's slow to penetrate, like a dam breaking, the water a dribble at first until the crack widens and it gushes. Logan is dead, my Logan, my beautiful Logan, is dead. Shaking, I try to stand, but my legs crumple beneath me and I fall to the floor. Amount of blood. A sob chokes up my throat. Logan's blood. Soaked into the seat. Dead. It can't be. The thought of him in that car, rolling, crashing over a cliff, bleeding to death alone and in the dark. Did he call out to me? While he was dying, did he call for me? I didn't tell him I loved him—the last time I saw him, I didn't tell him I loved him. Oh my God, how could I have not told him I loved him? My Logan, his beautiful body lost at sea, lost to me. A stabbing pain rips through me. My heart splits and the pain is so excruciating I can't breathe. A tortured sound echoes in my ears and I realize the sound of agony is coming from me. Logan *is* dead. He's not coming back for me, he will never come back for me. And in that moment I want to die too, want to follow him and escape the long life I'll be forced to live without him.

——————

Logan's memorial is being held at St. Patrick's Cathedral on Fifth Avenue. I don't remember dressing, don't remembering sitting in the car or being on the plane. The cathedral is packed, standing room only, and as we walk down the long nave toward the altar, I notice the photos of Logan set up on easels. His beautiful face captured for all time in that sexy, mischievous grin of his. In that moment it really hits me that I will never see him again. I will never touch that face or hear his voice. I will never catch him looking at me with love or feel his body against mine. And there isn't even a body to bury, a place for me to go to mourn and remember him.

I reach for Broderick's arm as my tears fall so fast I can't see. When he looks at me, I see my own pain reflected. I reach for his hand and hold it tightly in my own. Dante is there, taking my other hand, as we walk to our pew.

Before the actual memorial, one person after another steps up to offer something about David, his skill, his art, but no one is talking about the man. Only the artist. As broken as Logan's death has left me, this is the only chance I will have to honor him, Logan, the man. I stand.

"Are you up to this?" Broderick whispers.

My only response is a slight nod of my head.

As soon as I step up to the altar, the church falls completely silent.

"You speak of the artist, and his talent is without question, but he was so much more than an artist. He was funny, but able to laugh at himself. He wasn't a great singer, though if you asked him he'd say he was Michael Bublé. He could bake a hell of a kelp cake and could grill a mean steak. He rode a motorcycle like it was a part of his body and could move you around a dance floor as if your feet were no longer touching the floor. He completely missed the entire point of the *Alien vs. Predator* movie, and he could keep a secret better than anyone I've ever known. He was generous, donating millions and millions of dollars to organizations dedicated to the protection and welfare of children.

"He left behind a wonderful family—a family that will have to learn to pick up the pieces from his loss and somehow move on. And as for me, he was the best part of me. He was my lover, my best friend, my heart, and my soul, but now he's gone. And I am so sorry for you that you will miss his talent, but I will miss the man. In a few years when there's another to take over for David Cambre, you may think of him in passing, but his family and I will still be missing every single second that passes when he isn't with us. You had him in life, but in death he belongs to his family and me because we're the ones who have to bury our son, our brother, our soul mate, and find some way to survive—to live knowing that that wonderful human being no longer does." I look over at his picture, my heart turning to ash in my chest. "I will love you always and I will miss you every day for the rest of my life."

I walk from the altar, but instead of going back to my seat I just keep walking right out onto Fifth Avenue.

———

The day after Logan's funeral, I refuse to get out of bed. I don't want food or visitors. Lying there, I stare at his picture, tracing his face to memorize it. One day when I close my eyes, his face won't as easily come into focus. There'll come a day when I can't hear his voice in my head or remember his scent or the sound of his laugh. I can't bear the thought. Nearly frantic, I run to the closet and push hangers around until I find a sweater of Logan's. His scent is still on it. Holding it to my face, I inhale deeply. Pulling it from the hanger, I carry it back to the bed with me, cradling it close and wishing with all of my heart that it were Logan.

Three days after Logan's funeral I'm standing on my back patio, staring at the picnic tables that should have been filled with our friends a week ago as we celebrated our wedding and now only serve to remind me of what I lost. I hate those tables. Grabbing the bench of the one closest to me, I try to drag it to the water, but it gets caught on the table leg. All the sorrow, fury, anger, and frustration bubbles out of me and I start kicking the bench, out of control with my grief. Strong arms wrap around me and I think it's Logan. Turning into the figure, I see Broderick. Pushing away from him, I run back to my room.

Five days after Logan's funeral I wake from a dream that feels so real, I climb from bed and run out of my room looking for him. He's probably in the kitchen or out back. He'll laugh at how worked up I am over a nightmare. He'll draw me into his arms and kiss me and then he'll take my mind from it by carrying me to our room and making love to me. Calling his name, I search the house but I find only his family and my friends, all of them watching me with sympathy and worry.

A week after Logan's funeral, the police release Logan's personal effects to me, but I can't look at any of it. I hide the box in my closet.

Two weeks after Logan's funeral, I force myself to go to Tucker's, force myself to start interacting with the land of the living. It's an adjustment, because I don't want to talk. I want to lose myself in my head because it is the only place where Logan is still alive and with me. I go through the motions at work, but I am not healing, and this causes my friends to force an intervention.

I'm standing in front of the bar when Tommy locks the door, then joins Logan's family, who have trickled in without my noticing. They all look very grave.

"What?" I say.

"We need to talk," Tommy offers quietly.

"About?"

Briana says, "You aren't getting better. You aren't moving past your grief and you have to. As hard as it is, you have to move on. Logan would not want you mourning him this way—existing, but not living. He will always be a part of you, but you need to let him go."

"Have you let him go?" I ask softly, though I want to scream it.

"I'm trying to, but the difference between us, Saffron, is I am finding joy in life again. They are small things but they're there all the same. You haven't moved past the initial phase of grief."

My grief boils up and out of me and when I look back at the others, tears fill my eyes and run down my cheeks.

"How? Tell me how I move past the gaping hole in my chest that the loss of Logan has created? How do I find joy and happiness in life when I'm dead inside? I'm sorry that I'm not healing fast enough for you, but I don't think I will ever recover from the loss of Logan. I don't want to move on, I don't want to forget. I want him back, I want him here, I want him to walk through that door and I want this reality to all be some horrible nightmare."

I don't even realize the impact my words are having on the others until I see their tears, their pain and grief, which are as profound as my own. I sink to my knees. "I miss him so much I can't breathe at times."

Briana kneels down in front of me and wraps me in her arms. "Small breaths, Saffron. Take small breaths. He loved you, but he's gone and you are still here. Don't die with him. He wouldn't want that."

"I know."

"Miss him, love him—no one is asking you to forget him, but you can't hold on to the grief of losing him. Find your joy. Logan would want that for you."

———·———

Each day I try to heed Briana's words by finding something that makes me smile and every day I'm surprised when I actually do: when a smile touches my lips. And then one day, a week after my intervention, I have the moment when I know everything is going to be okay. I'm walking down Main Street and when I pass Logan's statue, instead of it bringing me sadness, I think of him on that day when I nailed him with the funnel cake. The memory is so clear and, instead of bringing me pain, it makes me laugh. I stand in the middle of the street laughing until tears fall and I know that I will always miss him and love him, but I realize that because of those memories and that love that I can live without him. He's gone, but he's still a part of me and always will be.

———·———

It takes me nearly a month after his death to work up the courage to go through Logan's things. I was surprised to see that many of his possessions were still packed from his move to Harrington, even though he had been living here for almost two years.

I sit in his bedroom on the floor and go through box after box. Most of the boxes are art supplies, and touching them makes me feel closer to him because only his hands touched these. Another box is full of clothes he never unpacked, but seeing the labels—Dolce & Gabbana, Armani, Burberry—it's not really a wonder why he didn't unpack them. In another box I find what looks like a man's jewelry box, but I can tell the box is handmade and, from the look of it, done by a child. Logan? I run my finger over the carvings and think of a younger Logan with those green eyes intent on the box before him. I open the lid—all of the treasures he's holding in this box are about me. I lift the black-and-white sketch of me standing on the beach with Reaper looking out at the water. There are the ticket stubs to *The Fault in Our Stars* that I dragged him to see and the shell I gave him, an imperfect shell, but the color swirled throughout it reminded me of his eyes.

Pulling out a little notebook, I notice pages of high tide schedules, current and riptide markings, depth readings, and water temperatures. I go through page after page but nothing is detailed, it's just disjointed notes. I take a moment to run my fingers over his handwriting before I place it back in the box.

The next day, there's a knock at my door and, when I open it, a huge vase of flowers is sitting on my stoop: the same arrangement as those at our engagement party. A numbness fills me as I stare at the flowers, afraid to blink for fear that they'll disappear, that they really aren't there. My hands shake as I retrieve them and see the card addressed to Saffron MacGowan. Reaching for it, I nearly drop the flowers when I read the three words.

Love you, brat.

Receiving flowers from Logan when he's gone is almost too much. Why? How? Today isn't anything special, so why the flowers? When did he arrange to have these delivered? I notice the number of the florist on the card—a florist located in Bar Harbor—so I walk to the kitchen for the phone.

"Monique's Floral. How can I help you?"

"I just received a beautiful bouquet from you and I was wondering if you could tell me when the order was called in."

"Sure, can I get your name?"

"Saffron MacGowan."

"One minute. Here it is. It's an ongoing order, once a week, with the first delivery for today. It was paid in full in cash and the transaction date was July third."

"Are you sure?"

"Yes."

"Thank you." I hang up, but my hands are shaking violently now. Logan's accident was on July 9. The significance of the transaction date is not lost on me.

The fire at Dupree House was July 3, the day Logan freaked out at the hospital, told me I was the only one, and left me. He arranged to have flowers delivered to me every week, starting on the one-month anniversary of his death. He *did* plan this, he planned to fake his death and then took measures to assure me that he was okay after the fact. Anger burns through me. He didn't fake his death, though, he actually caused it. *He* took himself away from me and the blinding fury that thought stirs has me hurling the flowers across the room.

The grand opening of Dupree House has finally arrived. The day before, my friends and partners and I did one last walk-through. Thankfully the fire was in the shed and not the house.

Dante uncorks a bottle of champagne and fills glasses, handing them around. Raising my glass, I take a minute. This moment is bittersweet. My tribute to Frank and Maggie is everything I hoped it would be, and yet I'm not filled with the joy and excitement the day deserves, because Logan's absence hangs heavily over all of us.

"It's been almost a year since I had the idea for Dupree House. We wouldn't be standing here had it not been for all of you. Broderick and Dante, to your tireless work in getting all the legal and logistical pieces in place. I truly would not have known where to begin. Josh, for turning this house into a home. And to Logan"—my words nearly get stuck in my throat—"whose encouragement was the catalyst to get the entire ball rolling. Thank you. Frank . . . he would have really loved this."

The tightening in my throat prevents me from taking a sip. Placing my glass down, I reach for the package I had sent special delivery. Ripping open the box and pushing aside the bubble wrap reveals a bronze plaque, two feet by two feet, that reads:

DUPREE HOUSE

IN LOVING MEMORY OF

FRANK AND MAGGIE DUPREE.

SEPARATED IN LIFE

BUT TOGETHER

FOREVER IN THE EVER AFTER.

———

Eight students will be first to make Dupree House their home. The following morning is move-in day. A little ceremony is given by both the township of Upper Nyack as well as the state of New York. Many of the members of the Board of Directors who approved the idea are in attendance. When the ribbon is cut, I watch with tears as the students eagerly move up the steps and into the house.

Life goes on, forges ahead despite whether we are willing to move on with it. Logan is gone. As much as I want him back, ache for the time when he was with me, I have to let him go. And so with a heavy heart, at the tribute to the man I thought of as a father, I say good-bye to the man I will always think of as my husband.

CHAPTER NINETEEN

Josh and Gwen and I are sitting around my living room watching Reaper chase his tail. He's now a full-size shepherd and still he chases his tail like a puppy.

Gwen is regaling us with stories about Callie's dance recital when I suddenly sit up, feel nauseated, and just barely make it to the bathroom before I hurl.

My friends are right there, holding my hair and rubbing my back as I empty my stomach.

"What did you eat today?" Josh asks.

I wipe at my mouth. "Nothing that would cause this."

"I'm not aware of a stomach bug going around," Gwen says.

"What's the date?" My question is more a knee-jerk reaction because, with everything going on, I didn't even realize I hadn't gotten my period in a while.

"October third."

"What?" Josh demands.

"I'm late."

"What?" Josh asks, but Gwen knows.

"How late?"

"Late, really late."

This is met with complete silence and then Josh jumps to his feet. "I'll get a pregnancy test. I'll be back in a jiffy," he calls from over his shoulder.

A half hour later the three of us are standing in my bathroom looking at two different tests, both of which are positive. Just a few weeks ago I came to terms with the loss of Logan, but he isn't completely lost, he left a piece of himself with me. For the first time since he died, I'm looking forward to the future. "I'm having Logan's baby."

I make an appointment at the clinic for the next morning and, when the pregnancy is confirmed, I call Logan's family and invite them over. Gwen, Tommy, and Josh insist on being there too, so once everyone is settled I just blurt it out. "I'm pregnant."

There is complete silence. Boy, do I understand that reaction. Suddenly Rory jumps from the sofa and hugs me hard. "Oh my God."

"You're going to be a granddad."

Broderick is almost impatient for his turn and, when he pulls me close, he whispers, "I'm going to be an uncle."

It makes my heart hurt to know that Logan will never know his son or daughter. This is a time to celebrate, though, so I force the sad thoughts from my head.

Dante hugs me so tightly before he quickly steps back and looks guilty, as if he somehow crushed his nephew or niece.

Briana steps up to me, her hazel eyes swimming in tears. "He isn't lost to us."

Broderick comes jogging up beside me as I walk Reaper on the beach. I haven't seen him since learning I was pregnant.

"Hey, what are you doing here?" I ask as I lean in for Broderick's kiss.

"I wanted to see you. How are you, how's my niece or nephew?"

"We're good. How are you? I haven't seen you in a few days."

"I've been really busy." He grows quiet and looks down at his feet as we walk along.

"Broderick?" The sadness in his eyes prompts me to ask, "What?"

"I've been settling Logan's estate."

"Oh. Is everything okay?"

"Yeah, he was incredibly organized and everything is completely in order. Do you realize that you are Logan's sole heir?"

I stop walking. "What?"

"He left it all to you, everything."

"No."

"Yes. He even stipulated in the will that when you refuse your inheritance I am to tell you to stop being a brat."

That is such a Logan thing to say. "I miss him so much."

"Me too." Broderick takes my hand as we start walking again and then he asks, "Are you curious?"

"What? About how much money he left me? I can't even begin to imagine."

And then he tells me a number that has my eyes rolling into the back of my head. I don't even think I can count that high. His penthouse is worth seventy-five million dollars and apparently that is only one of his properties.

"I can't think about it right now. Some of that will be put aside for the little one, but it's so large a sum that I can't even begin to imagine what to do with it. As a family we'll have to discuss it, but I'm just not there yet."

"I understand."

He reaches into his pocket and pulls out a sealed letter and hands it to me. "This was also among his papers."

I look down at my name and run my fingers over his handwriting. I wipe at the tears threatening and look at Broderick. "Thank you."

Broderick stays for dinner before we go to Tucker's to play some pool with Tommy and Dante. Later, when I'm in my bed, I pull Logan's letter from my drawer and, after a few deep breaths, I open the seal and start to read.

Hey, beautiful. This isn't an easy letter to write knowing that if you ever read it I'll be gone. I suppose that my death is a far better scenario than you leaving me. Sorry that I am not there with you and sorry that our happily ever after didn't come to be. I am changing my will, dearest Saffron, and am leaving you everything. I know you don't want it, but it's the sum total of my life's work and there isn't anyone else I want to have it but you, and hopefully our children.

I realize as I'm working on this that if there ever comes a time when we are parted there are things I need for you to know.

1. I love you. I love everything about you. I love your smile, your heart, your love for all things. I love that you can sit and watch a movie once and then adopt the dialogue to use in your everyday speech. (Yes, I am very much aware that most of what you say comes from movies). You have the rare gift of making everyone around you feel better for having known you. You are the finest person I have ever known.

2. I respect you. I respect that you follow your heart even if the road is difficult; even if the path is painful, you listen to your heart and you follow it. That is a strength of self that not many possess.

3. I want you to move on. If I am gone, grieve me, mourn me, and then live your life. You have so much love to give, so I'll understand if you give your heart to another, as long as it isn't Brad Pitt, because then I will have to haunt you.

4. Lastly, I agree with you. Predators are infinitely cooler than Aliens.

P.S. Promise me you will keep your mind open because sometimes things are not what they seem, sometimes the illusion is so real it feels true. Let your heart guide you and look into the crowd because if there was ever a man to defy death to be with the one he loves, I would be that man.

Yours always and forever,
Logan

———

Sitting outside thinking about Logan's letter to me, I notice the small box on my stoop. There's no postage or return address. Carrying it to the kitchen, I open it to see a small wooden figure—a swordfish. It's beautiful and the detail is so fine: unmistakably carved by Logan's hand. Where did it come from? Hope, like a small pinpoint of light, shimmers to life inside me. Is it possible that Logan left this? Is he really alive? Letting that hope grow, I hold the figure to my heart, knowing somehow that Logan's hands were the last to touch it. The shrill ring of the phone ruins the moment; I'm irritated already, but when I see who's calling, I'm pissed. But there's a healthy dose of confusion too.

"Darla? What the hell do you want?" I bark.

She stutters and I feel bad so I add, "You got me at a bad time."

"I'm sorry to just call, but . . . I can't believe he's gone." Silence falls over the line and then sniffling ensues. "I didn't want to call sooner, since

I know I'm the last person you want to hear from. I can't even begin to imagine how you're dealing with all of this."

"It's been unimaginably hard," I say.

"He loved you. It was so obvious. He was really in love with you. I'm sorry he's gone. I wanted to apologize for the calls and sending you that package. It was stupid, cruel, and in light of everything, so . . . thank you for not pressing charges and for being so incredibly cool with it."

"Considering the enticement was David, I get what motivated you. I don't agree with it and would never do the same myself, but I do get it."

"When Elise mentioned the idea, I knew it was stupid, but I wanted him so badly I didn't really think very clearly about what happened after I made the threats."

"Wait, Elise Grant, she's the one who gave you the idea?"

"Yeah. I thought it was creepy, but she said it would make you leave him and when he realized no one else would stick he'd come back to me, but I suspect now she wasn't talking about me at all. She's the one who gave me the bird's head."

Elise. Jesus, why the hell didn't I see that? And then rage fills me. Fucking Elise.

"I'm having a case of déjà vu," Darla says, pulling me from my dark thoughts.

"Why?" I ask.

"Because right before David died he came to see me and we discussed just this."

As soon as I hang up, I grab the closest thing to me and hurl it at the wall. She moved right after Logan left. Why the hell didn't I make the connection? But I wasn't the only one. Logan would have never left me if the one stalking him were so close. And when I think about it, he never had any reaction at all to Elise when we'd see her in town. He didn't know her, outside of being Darla's friend, and yet she was the one stalking him, the one he intended to confront. How is that possible? Rage so primal I've never felt the likes of it before burns through me. That bitch killed my man, maybe not with her own hands, but her craziness led to Logan acting recklessly, which led to his death. As far as I'm concerned, she fucking killed him. If I ever see her, I'll be arrested for murder because choking the living shit out of her is now top on my list of to-dos.

Sheriff Dwight visits a few days later and, though I'm still steaming about Elise, the reality is I have a baby on the way and he or she needs a mother. Killing Elise, however enjoyable that sounds, will take me from the last piece of Logan I have.

I'm outside sweeping leaves from my front step when I see his police cruiser pull up and stop in front of my house. I call a greeting to him when he starts up my front path.

"Hello, Sheriff, how are you?"

"I'm good. How are you holding up?"

"I'm okay. Can I get you some coffee?"

"That would be great if it's not too much trouble."

"Not at all. I like people drinking coffee in front of me, so I can smell it, since I'm not drinking the leaded stuff these days."

"Congratulations." And then I watch as his eyes turn sad. "I'm really sorry that Logan won't be here to see the little one."

"Me too. Come inside and let's make that coffee."

He follows me and settles at the kitchen island while I start to grind some beans.

"Have you had any other problems? Threatening mail or phone calls?"

"No." I turn to look at him. "Not since Logan—" I can't finish the sentence, so I grab the carafe and fill it with water.

He seems to understand what I didn't say and we're silent for a moment. "The reason I'm here . . . Logan contacted me before he died. Told me he knew the one responsible for the attacks on you. Said he was dealing with it, but he wanted me to be on the lookout, just in case. Anyway, after he died I started keeping tabs on this individual, wanting to make sure I knew her location. I didn't want her to surprise us with a visit. Saffron, she's dead. I've been waiting for confirmation before I came to see you and I received it just the other day."

Relief mingles with anger because I really wanted to see her one last time, not to kill her, but to get my closure by seeing her hauled off to jail. "Was it Elise?"

"Yeah, how'd you know?"

I need to sit down. Grabbing a stool, I drop myself onto it. "I got a phone call that pretty much put it all into focus. She's dead?"

"Yeah. Apparently after hearing the news of David's death, she drove her car into a tree."

"Oh my God."

"Her next of kin, her aunt and uncle, called me earlier. They wanted to contact you directly but thought it better to filter their request through me."

"What do they want?"

"They want to talk with you."

"Talk to me? What the hell could they possibly have to say that I'd want to hear?"

"I don't know, something about Logan. You want me to tell them you're not interested?"

"No. It might be interesting to hear them out."

"Their name is Martinelli and they live in Marlton, New Jersey. I'll write down their number and address for you. Do you want me to come with you?"

"I think someone in Logan's family should come with me."

"Okay. You need anything, you let me know."

"I will, thanks. Coffee's done."

———

The following day I walk to the lighthouse. As soon as Broderick opens the door, he knows something is off. "What happened?"

I tell him about my phone call from Darla and my visit with Sheriff Dwight and am surprised at his response. He curses like a sailor and hurls the closest object clear across the room. I completely understand that reaction.

"The Martinellis are the assholes Logan stayed with when he was younger."

My stomach tightens at that news. "Well, they want to talk with me about him. Will you come with me?"

"You sure as hell aren't going alone."

"There's something else." I hesitate a moment before I say, "I think Logan attempted to fake his own death."

I see the same emotions I myself have been battling: shock, hope, and anger. "What makes you say that?"

"Before he died, Logan kept making cryptic comments to me about doing anything to ensure I was safe and that nothing would keep him from me. And then I went through his things and he had a journal with markings: water temperatures, depth readings, current and tide schedules. At the time I didn't think anything of it, but then flowers arrived for me a month after his death, flowers sent by him. They were arranged a week before his death, the day of the fire, to start on the month anniversary of his death."

Broderick rakes a hand through his hair. "Jesus."

"And then there's this. Arrived on my front porch, no postage." I pull the satin pouch from my purse, open it, and remove the small wooden swordfish figure before handing it to Broderick.

He studies it for a while before his eyes find mine and his voice has a touch of wonder in it.

"Logan made this."

"That's what I think too."

"No, I know he made it."

"How?"

He turns it over and on the bottom is a small little crescent moon shape. "That's on everything he makes. He paints it into his paintings and carves it into his sculptures."

Hope, that little pinpoint, bursts big and bright. "I want to hear what the Martinellis have to say."

"Okay. Let's call Dante, fill him in, and then give those bastards a call."

——————

If the Martinellis once lived the glamorous life, they no longer do. Their house is a rancher in a not very nice area. The yard is mostly weeds, the black paint on the shutters and front door needs a good sanding and repainting. The cars in the driveway are at least ten years old and it's crazy to think it's because of Logan that they now live like this. I don't blame him for what he did. They deserve far worse in my opinion.

We walk up the front path and Broderick knocks on the door. The woman who answers doesn't look at all like I expected. Her blond hair is mostly gray and her blue eyes look very tired. She's dressed in black pants and a pale-pink sweater, probably purchased from Target or Kohl's, which is a far cry from what she probably wore once upon a time. She recognizes Broderick immediately, but what surprises me is she seems to know who I am too.

"We didn't think you'd come."

Patricia holds the door wider. Harold Martinelli looks as tired as his wife. His brown hair is mostly gone and what's left is liberally laced with gray. His tall figure is carrying extra weight in the middle and when he starts over to us, I notice he has a slight limp. When my eyes meet his brown ones I see resignation in them.

He shows us into a living room that is tastefully done. The furnishings are attractive, but not of good quality, and though the walls feature works from the greats, they aren't originals. Harold gestures toward the sofa and, once we settle in, he takes the chair opposite us.

"We're so sorry for your loss. Logan was a good man."

"Why did you call us here?" I don't want their sympathy.

"Elisabet was our niece. We knew she was unstable but we didn't realize how unstable she had become until after her death."

"Elisabet?" I ask.

"Her name was Elisabet. We were unaware that she had shortened it to Elise, but considering her byline on the paper was 'E. Grant' and Grant wasn't even her real last name, we can't say it was a surprise. Writers use different names for anonymity all the time, and with some of the stuff she wrote, we understand why she wanted to be anonymous."

"Is it true she drove her car into a tree?" Broderick asks.

"Yes. Distraught over David's death."

"Did Logan know her?" I ask.

"Yes, for a time before she went away for a little mental health vacation. When we moved here after she was released, she came to stay with us until she got back on her feet. Her parents, my sister, died in a car crash not long before Logan came to stay with us. She didn't take their deaths well, so we placed her elsewhere to help her adjust."

"Logan was with you for almost six years. How long did she live with you before she went away?" Broderick asks.

"A year."

"Her fixation with him started when she was just a kid?" A knot forms in my stomach at the thought.

"Clearly she had issues even before her parents died for her to react as strongly as she did to their deaths. But the doctors think her obsession with Logan stemmed from that trauma and the timing of him coming into her life."

"Logan didn't seem to recognize Elise when she was staying in Harrington," I say.

"She was twelve when she was sent away, and she used to be blond. It's not surprising he didn't recognize her."

"It was a ridiculously long mental health vacation," Broderick says.

"Like I said, she wasn't well to begin with and the doctors felt she needed it."

"When did you realize she was fixated on Logan?" Broderick asks.

"I knew something wasn't right when she learned of his engagement to Darla and she started acting oddly: angry and aggressive. Raging one minute, crying the next. Her interest went from infatuation to obsession. With her unstable to begin with, it was a disaster waiting to happen. We didn't realize—until Logan came to see us—that Elise had actually befriended Darla, sought her out."

"What are you saying?"

"I was the one to call Logan to tell him about her and to warn him. She was growing more and more unstable, but she refused to go in for treatment. I feared what she would do to him and you."

"But you warned him about Elisabet, not Elise. And you didn't tell him anything that could have clarified that Elisabet was Elise?" I was outraged because this could have all been avoided if we had known who Elise really was.

"We didn't know about her relationship with Darla, and we didn't even know Elise was in Harrington. When we spoke, she told us that she was in the city. My heads-up to Logan was really just that: a heads-up. I had no idea she was actually acting out against you."

"When was this?" Broderick asks.

"Probably about six or so months before he died. But he came here, shortly before he died, thinking a face-to-face meeting would have more impact than the countless phone calls he had made. The look on his face when he realized who Elise was . . . I've never seen anyone look so terrifying. And even so, with everything she had done, he still tried to reason with her. He had even convinced her to go back to the hospital. I really thought he had gotten through to her, but then . . ."

"She tried to kill me." It was probably after that phone call from Harold when I found Logan trashing his studio. *Some mistakes you never stop paying for.* That was what he had said. His time with these people was definitely a mistake. And once he learned his stalker's true identity, he called Sheriff Dwight so he'd keep his eyes out for Elise. It really was all he wanted, to keep me safe, even if that meant we had to be apart. In that moment the ache in my heart from missing him steals my breath.

"We know what we allowed to go on with him when he was younger was inexcusable, and, when he bought our gallery out from under us, we understood that too. Later, he offered us that life back. He said he realized he had been too quick to judge and though we had turned blind eyes to what our friends were doing all those years ago, it wasn't for him to take away our livelihood. The fact that he came here and tried to help Elise, knowing that she was unstable and could possibly bring harm to himself and you, after everything we had done to him, well, he turned into a very fine man."

I'm missing him so much that my temper flares. "Save it for someone who gives a shit. You pimped him out. He came to you, and instead of sheltering him from the harshness of the world, you fucking threw him right into it. You're having guilt now. You should. But he's gone and it's because he was trying to protect me from Elise, another left in your charge whom you failed. If you're looking for absolution from me, you aren't going to get it."

Broderick covers my hand. I didn't realize I had balled it into a fist.

"You're right. We didn't ask you here to seek your forgiveness, we wanted to apologize and we wanted to give you some insight into what Logan was dealing with. He wasn't wrong to be worried about Elise."

"Meaning?"

Patricia, who was sitting quietly, spoke up for the first time. "We didn't discover this until after she died. Please come with me." Patricia walks us down a hall to the room at the end. When she opens the door, I see a little girl's room in varying shades of pink. The white lace canopy bed sits in the middle of the room, a dressing table with a pink gingham skirt to the left of the bed and a white dresser to the right. It's odd that it looks as it does—Elise was my age, but even more strange, she wasn't a kid when she moved into this house. There's a large double-door closet and an adjoining bathroom.

Patricia leads us into the bathroom to a linen closet, and when she opens the door I gasp—inside the closet are pictures taped all over the walls. They are of only two subjects: Logan and me. There are heart shapes around Logan's face and big, fat, red Xs over mine.

"She was so far gone that when she heard about David's death, she drove her car into a tree going sixty."

"Her toxicology report was clean?" Broderick asks.

"Too clean; she wasn't taking her meds," Patricia replies.

"Meds for what?" I ask.

"Her manic personality and, based on the report, she'd been off them awhile. Apparently, the drugs she was on would have stayed in her system weeks after her last dose."

Seems to me there was more going on with Elise than manic depression, because despite the fact that the closet is creepy as hell, it's disturbing in its childishness, as is her room. I ask, "So if she had been on her meds, would the outcome for her have been different?"

Harold answers, "She probably wouldn't have been so out of control. She had a tough time of it, but she was a good kid, and it makes me angry to think that we didn't see her spiraling out of control until it was too late."

When we reach the door we turn to say good-bye, but Patricia speaks first. "A few weeks ago we were informed that a substantial sum of money was deposited into our bank account with only one stipulation, that we use some of the money to educate people on mental illness: the signs to look for and how to seek help."

"Whom did the money come from?" I ask.

"It was anonymous."

A look passes between Broderick and me, the meaning of it very clear, though no words are spoken. Logan. Somehow I'm able to bank my rising excitement. "Where is Elise buried?"

"St. Mary's Cemetery," Harold supplies.

We say our good-byes and start for the car, but Broderick touches my arm. "I'll be right back."

A second later he's back up the steps talking to the Martinellis. A few minutes later he comes back to me, takes my hand, and helps me into the car.

Once we are on the road, I say, "I'd like to visit her grave."

He looks at me funny, but puts the cemetery into the GPS and before long we're pulling through the black iron gates. We stop at the caretaker's office for directions to her grave and when we reach it, the earth looks freshly tilled. This makes me think of Logan in such a place, but I push that macabre thought out of my head. I reach into my purse and pull out the figure of the swordfish.

"What are you doing?" Broderick asks.

"She was mentally ill, and, yes, I'm pissed and angry, but she loved him. I think she should have something of him."

"But he made that for you and, if my brother is truly gone, it's probably the last thing he ever made. Are you sure you want to part with it?"

I smile as I touch my belly. "I have the last thing he ever made right here. Maybe wherever Elise is now, it will give her a bit of closure having this small piece of him all to herself."

Broderick's expression softens. "You are a better person than I. Would you like me to dig a hole?"

"We can do it together."

We hunch down as Broderick pulls out his penknife. Looking at the swordfish, my eyes burn with tears. Kissing it, I settle it into the hole. Broderick covers it up and pats it down. He stands and reaches for my hand to help me up.

As we walk back to the car I ask, "Do you think Logan is alive?"

He doesn't reply, but I know he's heard my question. The silence stretches out and then he says, "I do." He stops walking and I do the same. "When I was settling his estate I noticed a rather substantial withdrawal from one of his personal accounts. I thought it was theft and asked Dante to investigate."

"But?"

"I went back to the Martinellis to find out how much money was deposited in their account."

"And?"

A smile spreads over his face. "What was deposited in the Martinellis' account and what was withdrawn from Logan's account are the exact same sums, right down to the penny."

It takes a minute for my brain to catch up to my ears and, when I realize the implication of what Broderick is saying, I start to cry. "Oh my God."

"I think he's out there and I think you should do as he asked. Look in the crowd for him because I think one of these days you're going to see him coming home to you."

<hr/>

Three weeks after our trip to New Jersey, Dean pays me a visit.

"Hey, stranger. What brings you to Harrington?"

He hugs me, takes a moment to process the small swell of my stomach. "You look wonderful."

"I feel wonderful. Come in. I just baked some cookies."

We head into the kitchen and settle at the counter as I plate up the sugar cookies I can't seem to eat enough of. The fact that my baby bump is small is a wonder, with the way I'm eating.

Dean slips something across the counter to me and it takes a minute for me to register that it's a wedding invitation. My head snaps up. "You and Katherine are tying the knot?"

"In January, and we both really want you to be there."

"I wouldn't miss it. When did this happen?"

"A few months ago. I realize we haven't been together all that long but we just knew and didn't want to wait."

Even now, a pain stabs through me. I know what he's too polite to say. Logan and I had waited. "I will definitely be there."

He looks uncomfortable, which is odd since he's here to share the news of his upcoming wedding. "What's on your mind, Dean?"

"There's another reason I'm here. Logan came to me right after he called off your engagement and asked me some rather pointed questions."

"About?"

"He wanted to separate his assets obtained as David Cambre from his estate in the Logan MacGowan name. He also wanted a few legal documents drawn up, including having a fund set aside in the event of his death. Any costs incurred at the time of his death or after could be paid out of this fund."

"Why did he come to you?"

"I asked him that very same question and he said he wanted it handled through a third party to establish impartiality."

"What he asked you to do, would it fall in line with the idea of him trying to fake his death?"

Dean pales and I know that's exactly what he thinks. "Yes, that's why I thought you should know."

"He's been leaving clues, at least I like to believe that he is."

The cloud that followed him in instantly clears. "Seriously?"

"Yeah. And now with this, I know he planned it, but he was injured based on the amount of blood the police found soaked into the seat of his car. Whatever his plan, it didn't play out like he intended. Did he die or is he healing from a serious injury? I don't know, but I'd like to think it's the latter."

His expression loses some of its spark. "You could be setting yourself up for disappointment."

"I could be and if I am, I'll move past it. I'll have this little one to help with it. But for now, I'm going to indulge myself and wish with all of my heart that Logan is alive."

Dean whispers, "Then I'll wish for that too."

———

Broderick is pacing in my living room, Dante's head is in his hands and his parents have tears streaming down their faces.

"I hesitated sharing this, but to deny you the hope that I'm feeling seems wrong. We may lose him all over again but if there's a chance, however small, that he was successful, I had to tell you what Dean shared with me."

"Why would he do that, fake his own death?" Briana whispers.

"He feared Elise and he wasn't wrong to be afraid."

"She killed herself, how terribly sad." Rory moves to stand behind his wife, resting his hands on her shoulders.

"He wanted me safe, wanted us free from her and, sadly, his death caused hers. In the end, he achieved what he set out to do."

"And it may have cost him his life, based on the findings of the police." Briana stands, her face turning red with the anger that's rapidly replacing grief.

"Maybe. Maybe not."

"If he is alive, why hasn't he contacted us?" Dante asks the question I'm sure everyone is thinking.

"He was injured, enough that it's believed he died. Maybe he is unable to."

"How long do we wait? How long do we hold on to the hope that he's alive and coming home?"

"I don't know, Dante. I imagine it'll be different for each of us. Personally, living in a world where there's a chance he's coming back is a much easier world for me to live in than one where he's gone. For the chance to see his face, hear his voice, to touch him, I'll happily wait forever."

CHAPTER TWENTY

We're all at my house, on the beach, celebrating Callie's birthday. I can't believe she's four. It seems like only yesterday I watched as she came into the world. My hand moves to my baby, to the life growing inside me. At night, I lie in bed and tell our baby stories about his or her daddy; it's just as much for me as it is for the baby. I ache for Logan. Not just my body but my soul, an emptiness that not even our child can fill. I had feared that I would forget his smile or his scent, that his memory would fade over time. It hasn't; closing my eyes, I can see him so vividly, his small smile that is so rare a treat, his quiet intensity he has when he's watching me, his laugh and the way it rumbles up his throat. It's days like these that I miss Logan the most, the small gatherings we have with just family and close friends.

Ever since our trip to New Jersey, a lightness fills my heart. Logan's out there. Believing that makes me eager to face each new day. One of these days I will see him in the crowd. I've been writing a pregnancy journal for Logan, documenting every day since that day in October staring at two tests confirming that Logan was still with me. Not stimulating reads—most entries are nothing more than details of raging heartburn or extreme exhaustion where I can only climb from bed long enough to walk and feed Reaper—but for Logan it will be a bestseller.

And it's while I'm thinking about Logan that our baby really kicks for the first time, and not the squishy sensations I've been feeling for a while. Love tightens my throat, my hand moving to the hard little lump. Closing my eyes, I reach out to Logan wherever he is. "Please come home to us."

"You okay?" Josh asks, moving across the sand to drag me back to the festivities, no doubt.

"The baby just kicked."

Josh yells, "We got baby kicking action over here."

Immediately I'm surrounded. Hands press up against my stomach. Rory and Briana's eyes grow wide with wonder when their grandchild kicks again.

Gwen steps up next to me and takes my hand. "Wait until they start pounding on your bladder, not as much fun then."

"No, I don't suppose that is fun."

"What do you think that is, a leg, a hand?" Rory asks in awe.

"I don't know, but it's damn strong." And it is, now that the baby has stretched, it seems it wants to continue to stretch, spinning around in there, nailing me in a circular pattern.

A laugh bubbles up my throat. Standing here with my best friends and family, feeling Logan's baby moving inside me, I need for them to know.

"I need to tell you guys something." And I just launch right in. They listen without interrupting and when I'm done, I notice that their eyes all seem overly bright.

Gwen speaks up first. "Do you really think he's alive?"

Briana and my gazes meet—the same feeling of hope and excitement is burning through her. My focus shifts back to Gwen. "I know I shouldn't, because if he isn't really out there, I'll lose him all over again, but I really do."

Tommy's voice sounds harsh, but I know he's trying to rein in the swell of hope. "What's he waiting for?"

"I second that," Broderick says, but it's not anger that feeds him either, it's love.

"I don't know. Maybe just making sure all talk of David Cambre has faded before he reappears."

"I can't believe that about Elise. You didn't like her. From the very beginning, you didn't like her," Josh says.

"No, but I didn't realize she was sick. Maybe if she had gotten help, it never would have spiraled so far out of control."

"If she had learned that you were pregnant . . ." Josh doesn't finish that statement, but it does cause a chill to go through me, because I imagine if Elise had learned about that, it would have been the last straw. She wouldn't have tried to kill me—she would have made sure she killed me.

Gwen pulls me from that creepy thought when she says, "I think it's romantic, the flowers, the figure, the letter. Don't get me wrong, if he is alive I'm going to smack him hard when I see him, but I can't deny it's very romantic too."

"Get in line for the smacking," Dante says.

I couldn't agree more, he has a solid whack coming and then I'll kiss him until we're both breathless.

"How long do you suppose he'll wait? It's been six months already," Gwen says.

"I don't know, but I hope it's before the baby comes. I have to believe he knows and that he's watching. He's planned it all out so carefully," I say.

Pain slices across Tommy's face. "You were right; when we first learned of his death, you said he wasn't dead. We didn't believe you. I'm sorry, Saffron."

"Don't. You were worried about me, worried I wasn't coping, and under normal circumstances your concern would have been justified. Our situation is so not normal."

He wraps his arm around my shoulders. "I really hope he is out there and that you get your happily ever after."

"Hear, hear," agrees Rory.

"You still up for walking me down the aisle?" I ask Tommy.

"Absolutely."

"We'll need to get you a new dress."

Josh's comment is so not what I'm expecting that I look at him like he's on fire. "Why?"

"Well, because by the time you get married, it's very likely you'll be the size of a barn. Taking out a dress one size, maybe two, is doable, but to cover all that"—he gestures with his hands—"no one is that good a seamstress." I smack him at the same time Gwen does.

"Oh dear." Briana looks like she wants to smack Josh too.

"Hey." He almost sounds affronted as he looks to Tommy and the other guys. "Aren't you going to help me?"

"Hell no. You walked right into that one," Tommy says, and at the same time the guys all take a few steps away from Josh, even Derek.

"Nice friends you are," Josh mutters.

His eyes glaring at his love, Derek winks, so clearly he isn't feeling repentant. And then he says, "Not going to work. I ain't stepping into that, not with a pregnant woman. Too many hormones."

"Two," Gwen says.

"Two what?" Josh asks.

"Two pregnant women."

My gaze flies to Gwen, taking in her flat stomach. "You're pregnant?"

"Yes. I wasn't sure if I should say anything since it's your first, but I thought since we're all sharing."

"Oh my God. How far along?"

"Two months."

"We can do this together. Gain weight, eat chocolate, cry for no reason whatsoever."

"Don't forget the non-stop peeing, back pains, and heartburn."

"Yay!"

She grins at me. "Spoken like a first-timer."

Briana hugs Gwen, a true mom hug. Gwen has awesome parents, but I love that Logan's family and my friends have grown as close as they have. But then, under the circumstances, I suppose it was inevitable.

"Congratulations, Mitch," I say.

His smile is pure perfection. "I was having trouble keeping it to myself. You aren't upset, are you?"

"Not at all."

"I told her that." He looks at Gwen and, though he's teasing her, I can see the love. "I told you."

"You did."

He kisses her hard on the mouth before he hands her the glass of juice.

"Look at them," Broderick says. The entire group turns in the direction of the kids. Michael and Callie are imitating Reaper, all three of them chasing their tails, well, imaginary tails for the kids.

"They get that from Mitch's side of the family," Gwen teases, which earns her another hard kiss from her loving husband.

"Hey, I want to play," Josh calls to the kids as he and Derek hurry over to them.

"He isn't really going to spin himself in circles, is he?" Rory asks me, but he's still looking at Josh.

"Probably," Gwen, Tommy, and I say together.

"Maybe I should go find a bucket," Briana says, but she's already started off toward the house.

"There's one in the garage," I call after her to be helpful.

Broderick lingers with Tommy, Gwen, and me. He says, "We should have known. You're glowing, more so than usual."

Broderick's right. "Why didn't I see it?" I ask.

"You've had a bit on your mind lately," Gwen replies.

Two months later it is once again the Swordfish Festival, my mental and emotional two-year anniversary of Logan and me becoming us.

Everyone is meeting in front of the bakery. I'm escorting Logan's family so, when I enter the living room, I catch the tail end of Rory's question.

"I'm still a little confused by the swordfish funnel cake. What exactly is that?"

"A weapon," I say. And then I add, "Don't eat one, believe me, you don't want to eat one."

I can tell he wants to know why, but at that moment Broderick looks at his watch. "We should get moving or we'll miss the parade."

Right, the parade. Every festival now has a parade. After the Seaweed Festival, Chastity was smitten with them. I start for the door, Reaper at my side, as we all head to what is now my favorite festival.

———

As we sit along the parade route I can't help but think of the new festival this year, the one that kicked off the year of activity: the Quahog Festival. It was the first time I watched a parade since the Seaweed Festival: the bogus festival Logan planned so he could ask me to marry him. I miss him every day and every day I still search the crowd for him.

We've staked out a position just outside the bakery, where I sit drinking my decaf coffee with Reaper at my side. Josh joins me.

"Are you ready for the parade? I heard the Fletcher twins are in it. They actually requested to participate."

"That's odd. I wonder what they're up to," he says.

Before I can reply, Gwen, Mitch, and the kids arrive. Callie immediately climbs up onto my lap.

"Hello, Miss Callie. Are you ready for the parade to start?"

"Yeah." She flashes me her dimples.

Mitch's voice comes from just behind me. "How are you doing?"

"Hey, Mitch. I'm good."

"And the little one?"

"Kicking."

"Thatta boy."

Tommy is the last to arrive, coming from a bakery, with a big pink box that he opens for Michael and Callie first. Gwen and I being pregnant get third and fourth choice: it's a chocolate-covered cream donut for me. Yum.

The sound of the band makes its way down the street, followed by another sound: the unique sound that only the Fletcher car can make. Josh and I throw each other a look before we turn our attentions to the Fletchers' car, which is slowly making its way down the street.

The convertible top is down and the seventy-three-year-old twins are sitting on the back like prom queens. As they approach, I lean up a bit to try to understand what they're wearing. Josh figures it out first and immediately covers Callie's eyes. Gwen, seeing his gesture, covers Michael's eyes before she even understands why. But in the next few moments a silence falls on Main Street, because the Fletcher twins are going for their very own kind of sexy.

Their outfits are very reminiscent of Princess Leia's slave-girl costume from *Return of the Jedi*. Their bras are made from clamshells and hang rather low. So much of their torsos are showing that the sight is a bit scary, and though their skirts are long and flowing, the side slits show off their skinny, withered legs.

Josh pleads, "Blind me, dear God, stab me in the eye."

People are talking—or really, there's whimpering, laughing, and gasping coming from the crowd, but even through all of this I hear that familiar deep baritone that always had a way of cutting through the other sounds around me. "If there's a butter knife handy, you can take care of that for him, Saffron."

My head jerks in the direction of the voice, but there's no one there. I look up and down the street for a tall, black-haired man, but Logan is nowhere to be seen.

Broderick must have seen my odd behavior, because he leans over and asks, "Are you okay?"

I answer without thought. "Yeah."

But as I turn back in my seat I can't help but wonder if I'm starting to hear voices in my head. Am I going to be one of those people who walks down the street talking to the voices only I can hear? A grin touches my lips at the thought, because I wouldn't mind that at all as long as the voice I am talking to is Logan's.

Once the parade is over, the other activities will start, including the food fight. Josh helps me up and we start over to George's stand and, as it was last year, there's a line for swordfish funnel cakes.

"So you don't eat it?" Rory is clearly mystified by this entire day and I can't blame him. Seeing it through his eyes, I'm surprised he hasn't called for the paddy wagon.

"It was meant to be eaten but . . . swordfish funnel cake. Enough said," I answer.

A noticeable shudder goes through him. "Agreed."

"Saffron," George calls. "You don't need to wait in line. Come on up here, I've got your stash."

I'm a bit of a celebrity on this day. Maybe I could get Chastity to agree to a coronation ceremony with a crown and everything.

Seeing her working her way through the crowd, I call, "Chastity, what are the chances I can be queen for the day?"

I know she heard me. She looks right at me, but instead of answering, she rolls her eyes.

"I'm guessing that's a no?"

"You're ridiculous," Josh says, which earns him my mad face.

"Like you wouldn't want to wear a crown."

"I'll just take yours. You're too fat now to catch me."

"Josh!" Gwen's trying for outraged but giggles instead.

George hands me a few cakes before passing the bucket to Tommy.

"These are heavier this year," I say, since I'm already envisioning nailing Josh after that fat comment.

"Yep, we should get some serious distance."

"When are you opening the factory? An assembly line for the mighty swordfish?"

"It's not far from that, had to use the kitchen in Town Hall in addition to my own to make all these. Got help from some of the local kids as well. Have you seen the number of people here?"

I hadn't really noticed, but it's true, the crowd is unusually large.

"You stumbled onto a success, Saffron. Who doesn't love a good food fight?"

"With no cleanup," I add.

"Even better."

What a picture we must make. Main Street is packed—everyone holding funnel cakes—as Chastity stands on a small podium. All eyes are on the clock tower of Town Hall. As soon as the large arm strikes noon, insanity erupts. Cakes are just flying everywhere. I'm pregnant so no one is targeting me, but that doesn't keep me from nailing my friends. Got some good hits in too. I'm just reaching for another cake, since I've got a clear shot of Broderick's back, when I get nailed in the side of the face.

"What the . . ." My hand tightens on the cake, since I'm loaded and ready. Changing my target from Broderick, I scan the crowd for my attacker. He's standing about thirty feet from me. Dressed in faded jeans and flannel, he has longer hair. His face is completely covered in whiskers, but it's the brilliant green eyes soaking up the sight of me that has the cake slipping from my numb fingers. He starts toward me, his long stride eating the distance between us. I can't move, my body refuses to respond, as I watch Logan moving through the crowd, coming for me. He stops so close our bodies are almost touching, our eyes locked.

Every emotion I've felt since his death explodes in me and my reaction *is* raw and honest: I slap him hard across the face, and then

I throw myself into his arms and bury my face in his neck to breathe him in. His arms feel like steel bands when they close around me and hold me close. "I'm sorry I put you through that."

My mouth covers his; desperate, I suck his tongue into my mouth, needing him closer. My tears blend with his, the saltiness flavoring the kiss. His lips move, brushing over my cheeks, my eyes, my nose, before he buries his face in my neck. I can't believe I'm feeling his body again, tasting him, seeing him. It all proves too much for me when my tears turn to sobs as the reality of what is happening hits me.

"Please don't cry," he whispers as he pulls me even closer, but I can't stop the torrent of tears. "I love you so goddamn much, Saffron."

I can't speak yet, so I tighten my hold on him. He rubs my back, soothingly, as he whispers to me how much he loves me, how much he missed me, how much he wants to make love to me, and soon my sobs start to subside because he is really here. I look into the eyes that have haunted my dreams just as he asks, "Can you forgive me?"

"You're alive. I can forgive you anything."

He holds me to him again and, after a very long time, he steps back, and I see that I'm not the only one crying. His eyes stay on mine, but his hand is on my stomach. "I do believe you have to marry me now," he says with wonder and love.

And just like that he makes me laugh, but not for long, since I'm still so overwhelmed. "You came back to me on our anniversary."

"I fell in love with you during the first Swordfish Festival, so it only seemed right that I return to you during this one." He cradles my head and kisses me before pulling his mouth from mine. "Did you figure it out?"

"Yes. Everyone close knows."

His lips brush against my ear. "I have some explaining to do, possibly groveling, all of which I am prepared to do for you and my family, but after that I need to make love to you or I'm going to go mad."

"I really, really want that too."

He reaches for my hand. "Then let the groveling begin."

————•————

Much later that night Logan and I lie cuddled together, sated and exhausted, but even now his touch is making me want him again. My fingers brush over his new scar, one that goes from just under his left arm to his thigh. It's a big, ugly scar—a wound that nearly gutted him. Sitting up, I press my lips to it, little kisses over every inch. I turn my attention to his face to see him watching me with an endearing little smile curving his lips.

I say, "Explain yourself."

"After I called off the engagement, I wanted to kill David. When I realized who was behind the attacks, I visited the Martinellis shortly before I visited you in New York, and when I saw that their niece was Elise, I swear I almost killed her on the spot. She had been right here under our noses the whole fucking time and I didn't know. Worse, I left you with her still here."

He's working himself up into a fit. Straddling him, I massage his shoulders, hoping to calm him. "It's over, Logan."

His hands come to rest on my hips, the anger fading. "It was after that visit I began to seriously contemplate the mechanics of killing David, because she was so unstable. Depending on her to follow through on what we discussed was too much of a leap of faith for me to take."

"And then there was the fire," I say.

"Yes, proving that I was right, that she was never going to stop. She followed me that weekend, and waited for a chance to get to you. Someone capable of that is capable of anything. I had already contacted Dean to set my affairs in order, and I hired a person I had worked with before and trusted to keep my secret to assist me with the logistics of my plan. I thought I'd spend the months after moving around with Dirk's crew, but then the accident didn't go completely as I planned. The cold water slowed the bleeding, but I took months to heal and then the Swordfish Festival was looming and it seemed the perfect time to come back to you."

He sat up, his gaze searching mine. "I didn't tell you because it needed to be real. Your mourning had to be real for people to believe that David was really, truly dead." He touches my cheek as his eyes fill with tears. "I saw the airing of my funeral; I saw you standing up there being so brave and telling half of Manhattan to go fuck themselves. I fell in love with you all over again. When I found out you were pregnant, I sent the swordfish because I needed you to know I was coming home. The idea that you believed you'd be raising our baby alone . . . I couldn't stand it."

"David's dead, so what will you do about your art?"

"I wanted to shift my focus to painting anyway, so I will do so under the name Dupree, if that is okay with you."

"I think Frank would like that quite a lot, actually. You know that Elise is dead?"

"Yes."

"The figure of the swordfish, I gave it to her. I buried it at her grave. I thought she should have a piece of you."

"And there is that passion I love so much about you."

His hands move to my stomach.

"I can't say I condone what you did, In fact, what you did was insane."

His expression turns somber, but there's conviction behind his words. "Desperate times call for desperate measures."

Like icy fingers, fear tingles down my spine thinking about how close he came to dying. He's home, he's alive, so I force those thoughts out of my head.

Knowing that now we can get lost in the woodwork, that you can just be Logan, I am thrilled with the results of your efforts. That being said, any future insane ideas you get, please talk to me first. Even minutes away from you is simply too long and we have this one to think of now."

"Agreed." He leans over and presses a kiss on my belly and gets a kick in the face. His laugh is music to my ears. He pushes me back on the bed and there is nothing but love looking at me. "I have eight months of separation to make up to you."

I grin as I pull my hands through his hair. "And I am going to let you."

———•———

Logan and I got married, right on the beach, with only our family and friends present. I couldn't wear my dress, as Josh had predicted, but I didn't want to part with it either, so it's wrapped and stored in my closet. Maybe one day, someone will get to wear it. Instead I wore a tent, well, not really a tent, but pretty close. Tommy walked me down the aisle, Gwen was my matron of honor, and Broderick was Logan's best man. In the end I didn't want all the pomp and circumstance, I just wanted his ring on my finger and mine on his. We did write our own vows; they're framed and on the wall and every day I read them, remembering that beautiful day.

I, Logan, take you, Saffron, to be my lawfully wedded wife. To have and to hold, to drizzle caramel sauce on, to walk along the beach and to chase after Reaper with, to hold you when you cry, and to have your back when you attack your friends with pantry items. I'll protect, love, and cherish you and only you for as long as I live.

I, Saffron, take you, Logan, to be my lawfully wedded husband. To have and to hold, to cuddle with in our pj's and veg out, to skinny-dip with in the bay, to drive your car, to soothe you when you're angry, and to tease you because I can. To love you and only for as long as I live.

———•———

Logan painted a mural in the nursery—one that features our favorite aquatic animal, the swordfish. As a wedding gift, I gave Logan the painting I had done of Harrington Bay and his reaction to it was as if I had given him some rare, priceless treasure. He has it displayed proudly in the living room with one of those museum lights hanging over it. When I saw him standing in front of it once, I asked him why he loved it so and he said because I painted it. When he looks at it, he thinks of me.

About a month after Logan returned to me, he presented me with a gift; it was another swordfish like the one I left with Elise, but this one came as one of the pieces of a chess set and each piece was specific to us. The board is made from white oak and rosewood and the figures include a VW bug, Reaper, a limo, an Alien, a Predator, a yeti, a butter knife, and a lobster trap. I love it and have it sitting next to Frank's and, unlike Frank, Logan succeeded in teaching me the game. Just thinking about some of his teaching methods makes me blush.

I'm a few days past my due date as Logan and I sit at said chess set. I'm uncomfortable and really ready for this baby to come. Reaper is vacationing with Gwen and family and, since the kids want a dog, I'm thinking a new puppy is in their future. I look at Logan as I think about the weeks since he's returned. He's shaved again. He didn't need to keep the facial hair since one of the benefits of a small town is that we know how to keep a secret, especially for one of our own. Once the town realized he was alive and home, the citizens all banded together to keep the secret safe, and as a community we're all closer because of it.

Josh and Derek tied the knot in a private ceremony and are now talking about adoption. Tommy started dating Sarah from the bar. I am apparently not that observant to pick up on the sexual tension in my workplace. Gwen knows she's having a girl and she and Mitch decided on the name Sabrina Michelle. Rory and Briana will be returning to Scotland after the baby is born and Dante to New York, but Broderick has moved to the lighthouse permanently. He has no desire to be more than walking distance from his nephew. We grew very close, he and I, and it's nice having a big brother, of sorts, who's always watching my back.

Dupree House is a success, so much so that the board is thinking about opening several more in the surrounding areas. I want to believe that Frank and Maggie are smiling down at us about that.

We set up the third bedroom as a studio for Logan, but he hasn't spent much time in there since we're still wanting to see each other every second of every day. Maybe in a few months, years, we'll be able to handle not being in the same room.

I realize that while I'm reflecting, Logan is looking right at me and smiling that smile.

"What are you thinking about?" he asks.

"How very much I love you."

"That, my dearest Saffron, is something I understand completely. How are you feeling?"

"Huge."

"You look beautiful."

"I look like Jabba the Hutt."

He rolls his eyes at me as he starts around the table to help me out of my chair. "You're gorgeous," he says as he places his hands on my stomach. "And this makes you even more so. In fact, I think I would like to see you this way three or four more times."

I'm incredulous and hot all at once. "Let me have this one first."

"If I must." He lowers his head and kisses me and that's when I feel the water running down my legs. I jerk away.

"What's wrong?"

"My water just broke."

"What?" He just stands there with a slightly terrified look on his face.

"Logan?"

His voice is barely over a whisper. "Don't leave me, please don't leave me."

It takes me a minute to realize what he means and, when I do, I frame his face with my hands.

"Never, Logan. It's only childbirth; people do it all the time. Besides, I've only just gotten you back. I'm afraid you're stuck with me and that is a very long, long life sentence."

He turns his head and presses a kiss in my palm before those eyes find mine again. "I'm going to hold you to that, wife."

"Count on it, husband."

And then he smiles that smile again. "I better get you to the clinic, brat." He wraps his strong arm around me and leads me to the door where he reaches for the bag that has been packed for weeks. He settles me into the car, pulling on my seat belt and latching it, before kneeling down next to me and pressing his lips to mine.

"I want you to know that as much as I am going to love this child and any other children we create together, you will always be the holder of my heart and the keeper of my soul."

And with those beautiful words I start crying again. He closes the door and slides across the hood to climb behind the wheel. As we start down the street, his hand reaches over to wrap around mine and he squeezes it as a smile spreads over his face. I smile back and then the contractions start.

EPILOGUE

Tucker's is packed as I stand behind the bar and build a Guinness. Broderick is watching Hunter tonight and is actually having his first solo sleepover with him: something Broderick has been pestering us for since Hunter was born. It has been six months since Hunter Frank MacGowan was born. To say he is the spitting image of his father and grandfather is not an exaggeration. Fatherhood for Logan has been a truly wonderful sight to behold, to see such a strong man brought to his knees by a little bundle. For me, I have the family I always wished for and the reality is so much better than I ever imagined.

There are times when I'll be doing something simple like cooking dinner or washing laundry and I stop to offer thanks for the wonderful life I have: for the man, the child, the family, and the friends. Even more humbling to me is Logan. As close as he is with Hunter, there's something more when he looks at me, some connection that seems to transcend everything. When he looks at me, his heart is in his eyes and his love for me is so pure and absolute. I understand how he feels, since it's the same for me.

The door to Tucker's opens and in walks the man in question. He's dressed in jeans and flannel and his hair is pulled back into a ponytail.

Unlike the first time he entered Tucker's, Logan's face is clean-shaven, so nothing hampers the view of his magnificent features. He walks toward the bar and takes his seat a moment before Tommy calls to me.

"Saffron, can you get him a Harp?"

"Sure thing."

I pop the top and walk on down the bar before placing the bottle before him. "You new around town?" I ask.

His eyes hold mine a moment before he replies, "Yeah."

I lean my hip against the counter. "What brings you to Harrington?"

"A woman."

I attempt to raise my eyebrow and fail miserably. I notice the humor in those green eyes staring rather intently at me before I say, "Chasing after a woman? Not many men would admit to that."

He lifts his beer and takes a pull. "I guess that would depend on the woman."

"Is she worth it?"

"Hell yes."

"Really?"

"Sexiest woman I've ever known." His gaze unwavering, he adds, "She's loving and generous too, even if she tends to be a brat at times but"—he leans farther over the bar toward me—"her meatloaf could be used in masonry work."

"Nice."

"She's insatiable. Can't seem to get enough of me day and night."

"You don't say."

He takes another pull from his beer. "Yep."

Someone calls an order to me and I start to head down the bar when his hand catches mine. When I look back, the love in those emerald eyes stills my breath. He yanks me closer as he stands.

"And I love her to distraction, want her every second of the day, and thank the stars that she's mine."

His hands come up to frame my face. "I love you, wife."

"I love you, husband."

And then right in front of everyone in Tucker's, Logan kisses me to the sounds of whistles and catcalls. I'm still feeling the effects of his kiss, so it takes me a minute before my brain catches up to realize that Logan has once again taken his seat. I start down the bar to fill a few orders, but when I return a bit later to Logan, he's just sitting there watching me in that silent way of his.

I lean against the bar. "Do you want anything else?"

"Just you."

That's it, I'm cooked. I take off my apron as I walk around the bar and reach for Logan's hand. "I'm going home, Tommy."

I don't wait for a response as I pull Logan from the bar, and when we're outside, he draws me to him. "That worked like a charm."

And then his mouth comes down on mine. It took us a long time to get here but he was so worth the wait.

ACKNOWLEDGMENTS

As always thank you to my husband and children for not only understanding when I put in eighteen-hour days for weeks at a time but letting me put in eighteen-hour days for weeks at a time. I love you.

For my sister, thanks for just being you: my best friend and sounding board.

Thank you, Thom and your team, for your tireless efforts with marketing my books.

Jessica, for being on point to answer any questions I've had during this wild ride of publishing.

Thanks to my copyeditor, Michelle, and proofreader for adding your expertise and rounding out the last of the rough edges.

Thank you to the design team and the incredible covers you create.

Maria, thanks for loving Saffron's voice and Logan's quiet intensity as much as I do.

To Krista, my editor. This is the fourth book we've worked on together and we have definitely hit our stride. I love how this book turned out, from the rough first draft to the final product, incredible. Thank you.

To all the bloggers who have helped with spreading the word about my books, most especially Kylie from Give Me Books, thank you.

To my ill-mannered cats, Salem and Saphira; our chases around the house, believe it or not, actually help with my creative process. Now please get off the piano.

Artemis, you really are the best dog ever.

Willow, rest in peace, little one.

ABOUT THE AUTHOR

L.A. Fiore is the author of several books including *Beautifully Damaged, Beautifully Forgotten,* and *Always and Forever.* She's also the social secretary for her two children, a tamer of ill-mannered cats, the companion to one awesome dog, and married to her best friend. She likes her wine red, her shrimp chilled, and her social gatherings small and intimate. She loves hearing from readers and can be reached through Facebook at: www.facebook.com/l.a.fiore.publishing.